The battering ram had caught in the remains of the wall, its bearers exposed. She plunged to the right side of it, her sword driving into one man's chest. She didn't bother wrenching it free. She kept running, spearing the next man. He screamed. She twisted sideways as the battering ram, no longer supported on the right side, crashed down.

With a crunch, the massive log shattered the still-screaming man's legs. Jendara's breath caught in her throat a second. That could have been her under that log. Her mind faltered, but her arm knew what to do. It was already pulling her sword free of the two skewered men.

But she wasn't ready for the shield that smashed into her face. She toppled backward, tripped over a snapped timber, and fell into the mud. Her nose throbbed with agony. She grabbed it and squeezed it back into alignment, ignoring the streaming blood. She could feel her face swelling as she pulled herself to her feet.

A Kalvaman pushed past her, knocking her aside with an elbow. The runners carried torches beneath their shields, protecting the flames with their bodies. They were headed straight for the meetinghouse.

Jendara swayed on her feet. Her head spun and she had to spit blood to keep from choking on it. Her sword fell from her aching fingers . . .

She lashed out with her toe and kicked up the hilt. She caught it in her left hand. Despite hours of practice using her left hand, the weapon didn't feel right. But nothing felt right. Her body resisted her every attempt to spur it forward.

"To me!" she mana

D0829124

The Pathfinder Tales Library

Skinwalkers

Wendy N. Wagner

Cover art by Michal Ivan.
Cover design by Emily Crowell.
Map by Crystal Frasier.

Paizo Publishing, LLC
7120 185th Ave NE, Ste 120
Redmond, WA 98052
paizo.com

ISBN 978-1-60125-616-4 (mass market paperback)
ISBN 978-1-60125-617-1 (ebook)

Publisher's Cataloging-In-Publication Data
(Prepared by The Donohue Group, Inc.)

Wagner, Wendy N., 1978-
  Skinwalkers / Wendy N. Wagner.

  pages : map ; cm. -- (Pathfinder tales)

  Set in the world of the role-playing game, Pathfinder.
  Issued also as an ebook.
  ISBN: 978-1-60125-616-4 (mass market pbk.)

  1. Vikings--Fiction. 2. Cannibalism--Fiction. 3. Mothers--Fiction. 4. Good and evil--Fiction. 5. Pathfinder (Game)--Fiction. 6. Fantasy fiction. 7. Adventure stories. I. Title. II. Series: Pathfinder tales library.

P3623.A3564 S55 2014
813/.6

First printing February 2014.

Printed in the United States of America.

For Fiona,
my Kran and fellow word-hunter.

Chapter One
Pig-Sticking

Jendara dropped to a knee, studying the crushed undergrowth. She pushed back a snapped bilberry branch and smiled at the splash of red the greenery had hidden. Vorrin's spear must have gone deep if the boar was still bleeding. It would be weak when she found it.

She got to her feet, picking through the brush in near silence. The narrow game trail opened up into a pocket meadow, warm with late summer sunshine. The air smelled of rich, sweet bilberries. In the distance, a bird called.

Jendara turned in a slow circle, listening hard. There should be more sounds than this. The rest of the hunters should have caught up by now, their footsteps thudding softly on the loam, their gear rustling. Small noises, but distinct ones. They must have lost her trail.

Her fingers tightened on her spear and she forced herself to relax. *An arm that's tight, throws not right*, her father always said. And also: *a closed hand holds nothing*.

He had a nugget of old-time wisdom for every occasion. Somehow they were always right.

Jendara cocked her head. Was that a sound? A small crunching, maybe, like a branch snapping behind her. The breeze shifted and blew a strand of her hair free of its braid. It tickled her cheek.

The crunching grew louder. The wind change had given the beast her scent. The boar should be running away from her, but something had spurred it back her way. Maybe the rest of the hunting party had circled around. They were going to miss out on all of the fun. Jendara's heart quickened, but her breathing stayed smooth and controlled.

Blood on the ferns at the edge of the clearing caught her eye. A big smear of dark red blood.

The boar burst out of the brush, leaping over its own bloodstain, its voice shrieking pure, hot rage. Jendara twisted aside, setting her spear as she moved. The boar hit with a horrible crunch.

The solid ash shaft snapped off in her hand, the base slamming into her right wrist. She knew she'd hit the boar's ribs, maybe cracked them, but had missed the heart. She drew her sword, but the blade slipped out of fingers numbed from the wrist blow. Good thing she had plenty of smaller weapons.

The boar growled, the sound rumbling up in its chest and rising into a screeching roar. Hate and anger powered the beast now. She eyed her sword, now out of reach, and bared her teeth at the boar. She freed her handaxe from her belt. She could throw left-handed just as well as she could right.

With a snort, the creature charged again, but Jendara had already launched the axe. There was a hollow thud as the axe buried itself in the boar's eye. The creature stumbled. Jendara snatched up her sword and rammed it through the boar's throat.

Blood burbled over her hands, hot and bright. The boar collapsed.

The sun beat on Jendara's neck as she lowered her eyes to the stricken creature. It would have been better if it had died in her first spear-thrust. She preferred a clean hunt. But she'd been alone, after all. The thing could have killed her.

She reached for her handaxe. The iron and ash wood in the weapon was older than her, an heirloom of her father's, the leather bindings replaced time and again over the years. Even over the smell of boar's blood and bilberries, she could smell the linseed oil she rubbed into the bindings to protect them from sweat and sun and rain. The axe was the most precious thing she owned. She'd lost count of the times it had saved her life.

She tugged on the handle, but the boar's skull held it fast. Another yank failed to loosen it. She hesitated, then braced her foot on the boar's cheek.

"I mean no disrespect," she murmured, and wrenched the axe free with a squelch.

She couldn't help remembering the first time she'd gripped the axe's handle, prying it free from the swollen, blackened hand it had pinned to the wall of her father's house. The hand had fallen free with a wet plop. It dropped into a clotted spray of blood beside the broken spade her father must have used to lop off his immobilized attacker's head, and Jendara had hugged the axe to herself as she vomited up her breakfast beside her father's corpse.

Jendara shook her head. This corpse was just the carcass of a boar. And her father had been dead for many long years, buried and well mourned. She wiped the axe's blade on a handful of ferns and slung it from her belt.

But the past clung to her like a hungry tick, even as she reached for her sword. The boar's slit throat looked so like much her father's, split wide as a second mouth while he hung from a stake.

Jendara closed her hands into fists, watching the tattooed skulls and crossbones of the pirate goddess stretch across her tendons. Her old life was truly behind her now. After that visit home, she'd buried herself in piracy to forget. Yet even the thrill of the hunt had lost its flavor after her husband, Ikran, died.

She squeezed her fist tight. The rest of her hunting party had better show up soon to help her dress this carcass.

Twigs crackled and weaponry jingled. Jendara unfurled her fists. Her friends *had* circled around. Perhaps they had flushed the boar ahead of them, and that was the reason for its strange, maddened charge at her.

"You know, most people save their swords for battle, Dara." A low chuckle accompanied the words. "Pig-sticking works better with a spear."

"Pig-sticking is usually done with dogs, too, Morul." She aimed a smile at the three men picking their way through the heavy underbrush. "How's the hound?"

"He'll live." Morul nudged the boar's body with his boot. The big, orange-bearded man shook his head. "No thanks to this beast. Dog got lucky."

Vorrin put his hand on Jendara's shoulder. "Are you all right? You look pale." His dark eyes studied her face.

She patted his hand. Vorrin was a good man, her best friend. But she couldn't tell him about the crunch and pop the axe had made when it pulled out of the boar's eye, how its dark flesh had reminded her so much of that dead hand out of her past. He'd known her a long time, but not even long friendship could make it easy to speak of the things that had been done to her family—things that she should have been there to fight against. She shook her head and hoped she looked nonchalant.

"Are you sure?" He squeezed her shoulder.

"I'm fine. Just thinking about hunting with my dad. And maybe feeling a bit winded. Look." She inclined her head. "That thing broke my spear."

"What a beast," Morul said. "It's pushing six feet long. Gonna be heavy." He knelt beside the big pig and pulled a coil of rope from his bag. He tied a slipknot and caught the boar's feet up in it, then tossed the end of the rope over the nearest tree limb.

His brother, Yul, helped him hoist the pig up off the ground, then tied the rope off. "He's got plenty of lard on him. A real good 'un." He folded his arms across his chest. "Ayuh, this would have been a good hunt for Kran. Seeing a beast like this fighting for his life would have taught him some respect for his dinner. He'd have been proud to see his mother beat it, too."

Jendara crossed her own arms. "No. Not a boar hunt. He's just a boy. He's not ready to hunt dangerous animals."

"I was hunting with my father once I passed my eighth winter. Morul was out there when he was only seven. A boy belongs at his father's side."

Jendara leaned forward. "Yul, you're a good friend, and I hold dear the way you've treated Kran, letting him stay with you these past few summers. You're the best foster father a boy could ask for. But you are *not* his father."

"Neither are you," the big man argued. "You don't know what it means to be a man of the islands. You smother him. He should be out here learning to be a man!"

"He's a child!" Jendara sliced her hand through the air.

"You treat him like a baby because of what's wrong with him."

"Stop," she warned.

"I'm telling you there's nothing wrong with Kran. Not being able to talk doesn't make him different from other boys." Yul's face flushed, his blond beard standing out like snow on red clay.

Vorrin stepped between the two. "Hey, stop it. We're all friends here. We all want what's best for Kran." He pushed them back from each other, his face turning from one to the other. "I do, too. I promised my brother I'd look out for his boy, and I meant it.

"Yul, we need to trust Jendara here. She has a right to worry about her son, and she knows him better than anyone. The lad grew up on a ship, not in the forest.

He's healthy and strong, but maybe another summer might be good for him to get some woodcraft under his belt."

He wagged his finger at Jendara as she was opening her mouth. "And Jendara, you need to trust Yul. He's more objective than we are. If he says Kran is ready to try hunting, he obviously believes in what the boy can do."

She hooked her thumbs on her sword belt and set her jaw. "Fine."

Yul checked the point of his spear with his thumb. "Fine."

"Now, shake hands. This is stupid."

Jendara and Yul rolled their eyes. Vorrin waved his hands as if to push them together, and Jendara had to suppress a grin. He looked so earnest, and so out of place among all these hulking Ulfen islanders. His dark hair, a few strands of silver catching the late morning sunshine, had pulled out of its binding and now swung around his face, a chartreuse bit of lichen caught in it. Yul and Morul both had wives to stitch their yellow braids tight with yarn, just like Jendara had sewn her own. She should have helped Vorrin, she realized. Perhaps he would have felt more like the other men that way.

The unexpected thought softened her. She took Yul's hand. "I'm sorry, Yul. Perhaps you're right. I'll talk about this with my son."

Surprise showed on Yul's face, but he replied with diplomacy, "Thank you for considering my words."

Diplomacy was a fine art on the Ironbound Archipelago. No one could value more highly the skills of negotiation, trade, and sharing. Life on the mainland had taught Jendara that most people believed Ulfen—and especially island folk—to be uncivilized raiders, fur-clad barbarians with nothing better than fine ships and good swords. And to be sure, raiding neighbors was a fine art cultivated in every island soul. Jendara had crewed a few raiding trips in her youth before her turn to true piracy. But no islander depended solely on raiding. Life was too hard on these cold scraps of rock to survive like that for long.

Yul, for example, was a farmer. He grew rye and turnips in the short summer, and lots of beautiful lingonberries that his wife turned into heady lingonberry wine. Morul oversaw the tannery, where the hides of sheep and cows and wild game were transformed into the kinds of supple leathers Jendara sold at a high price on the mainland. They were no mere barbarians, no matter how furiously they might fight in battle.

"Good. Now that you two aren't bickering, maybe we can get this boar butcher—" Vorrin broke off, nose crinkling. "What's that ghastly smell?"

Morul chuckled. "While you three were standing about gossiping, I got to work." He nodded at the skinned and gutted boar carcass swinging from the tree. "Now just to finish the hide and get back home."

Yul laughed. "Except your torch just went out." He reached into his bag and took out a bundle of pine twigs, dried herbs, and cattail fluff. "Here. Use this."

Morul caught it neatly and lit it with his flint striker. He stooped. He had spread the boar's hide out on the ground, and now he waved the smoking brand over the raw side of the hide. The pungent smell of herbs filled the clearing.

"What are you doing?" Vorrin asked.

"Old wives' tale," Jendara murmured.

"You leave an uncured hide around, a witch can work magic on it that'll make a man into an animal," Yul explained. "A skinwalker."

"What would the witch do with a . . . skinwalker?"

Yul shrugged. "If it was a mule, she'd probably train it for the plow. A bear, now, that would be something. Probably turn a bear on her enemies, kill them all."

Morul snorted. "You don't really believe all that stuff, do you, brother?" He tossed the bundle of twigs on the ground and kicked dirt over it.

"Old wives' tales," Jendara repeated, louder this time.

"Hey, I know a man down on Battlewall, and his cousin's grandmother actually saw a witch turn a man into a dog," Yul said.

"Must have been a big dog." Morul laughed and clapped Yul on the shoulder. "When you were a boy, you were always afraid Kalvamen would come and eat you, too."

Yul shook off his brother's hand. "Don't be an ass. Kalvamen are a story for children. Skinwalkers, now that's something that could really happen."

"Kalvamen are real enough," Jendara snapped. "Just because they don't sail often doesn't mean they won't ever."

Morul snorted and crossed to the tree where Yul had tied off the rope. "Sure. You and Yul, worrywarts both."

Jendara crossed her arms. "If you don't believe in skinwalkers, why did you smoke that hide?"

"Yeah," Yul added. "You always smudge your hides. Why?"

Morul struggled with the knot a second. "Yul, you tied this too tight. Sailor man, come untie this."

Vorrin smirked but went to help him. "I think you should answer Jendara's question."

The knot came loose, and Yul lowered the carcass on the hide. He began to wrap it into one neat bundle.

Morul lopped the limb off the tree. "Leyla says meat wrapped in a smoked hide isn't as gamy. I'm not going to argue with that."

He lashed Yul's bundle onto the tree limb and the two big islanders took each end of the limb.

"Leyla says it makes the meat less gamy," Yul repeated, eyebrows raised.

"Right." Morul studied the sky. "Clouds have all burned off. Going to be a warm walk back to the village."

"Then let's hurry," Vorrin said. He pushed aside the wall of brush with the tip of his spear. "I want to take a nap before our going-away feast."

Morul had some kind of humorous answer, but Jendara missed it. She let the men step out ahead of her. The dark mood she'd felt after killing the boar had settled over her again. She'd been feeling it more since she came back to the island—a burst of heaviness that made her heart hurt. It came at the most unlikely moments: while eating lingonberry pie, or swimming with Kran off the north end of the island, looking for the warm upwellings just as she and her sister Kalira had. Maybe coming back to the islands had been a bad decision. There were just too many reminders of her past.

"Dara?" Vorrin called. He must have come back for her.

She smiled at him. "I'm coming."

She picked her way over the still-steaming pile of boar guts and followed him into the forest. Somewhere in the sun-dappled trees, a bird gave a cry of alarm.

Chapter Two
The Quarry

The thwack of wood against wood jolted Jendara awake. She squeezed her eyes shut, but the sound reverberated throughout her whole head.

"I shouldn't have had so much of that lingonberry wine," she grumbled.

Wood cracked outside again. Jendara pushed back the furs and swung her feet over the side of her bed. She padded out into the hallway. Kran's door was open and his bed stood empty, his clothes missing from their hooks.

She sighed. He'd avoided her all day yesterday, and skipped the going-away feast. She shrugged on her sheepskin coat and trudged into the main room of the cottage.

"Kran?"

But he wasn't to be seen. His latest woodworking project sat on the plank table, the tools neatly in their case. A half-eaten slice of bread sat beside it. Jendara reached for her sword belt, hanging by the door, and buckled it on.

"Kran?" She opened the door. A swath of mist swallowed up the rest of the village. It cast a wintry pall over the summer morning, and Morul's house, just a few hundred feet away, was so shrouded in fog that it may well have been on the other side of the world. Fog was common here in the islands, but she never enjoyed the otherworldly cast it spread across the landscape, or the clamminess it left on everything.

With a sigh, she stepped out into the damp morning. Her toe squished on something wet and ropy on the doorstep, and she whipped her bare foot back.

It was the neck cord for Kran's slate. If the boy had taken it off, it was a sure sign he didn't want to talk.

Jendara's lips compressed. She didn't have the luxury of waiting around to settle this. In a few hours, the tide would change and she and the crew of the *Milady* would take their last trip to the mainland before winter's snow and ice hit. The thud resounded again, and she followed the sound to the back of the house.

She rounded the corner of the little cottage and saw Kran's shape, the woad-blue sweater and shaggy black hair. He stood just past the wood-chopping block, his attention on a stick of firewood balanced on top of a fence post. His pants, she realized, cleared the top of his boots by a good half an inch. He was going to be tall, like his father. Like her father. The boy was made up of the best of both sides of his family.

She didn't know where the muteness came from. When he'd been littler, she thought it was something she'd done wrong before he'd been born. Maybe she should have made offerings to other gods beside Besmara, dark loady of pirates. Maybe she should have stayed on land instead of climbing so much rigging. But she'd never found a real reason for Kran's inability to speak, and she had to admit that as he'd gotten older, it didn't seem to matter much to the boy.

Kran wound up his sling and lobbed a shot at the firewood. It hit dead center and launched the wood far out into the mist.

Jendara clapped.

Kran spun around. His face, for one instant bright with his own success, went dark. He spiked two fingers toward his eyes, then pointed out over the fence line. The gesture spoke for itself: *See?*

"I saw. You've got a nice release." She held out her hand. "Can I take a look at your shot?"

He reached in his coat pocket and held out a handful of wooden marbles. She rolled one between her fingers. It was smooth and heavier than it looked.

"You carved these?"

He nodded.

"Makes a world of difference, using shot that all weighs the same. Can really improve your aim." She tossed the marble in the air. "May I keep this? I need a good shooter if we play marbles on the ship."

He tapped his full belt pouch, suggesting he had plenty more.

"You still practice with rocks at all?"

He shrugged a shoulder.

"You should. What if you run out of shot while you're out hunting? Be sad to miss out on a really good snowshoe hare just because you forgot how to adjust for the weight of an off-balance stone."

At the word "hunting," his face crunched into a scowl. He reached for his chalk and board and made an exasperated sound when he realized he'd left it behind.

Jendara took a seat on an old driftwood log and patted the spot beside her. Kran didn't sit. "Look, I'm sorry I didn't take you hunting yesterday. I was afraid. Boars are trouble. I've heard of too many things going wrong on a boar hunt."

Kran was quick to tap his ear, then raise his eyebrow and point at his eye. He didn't know much of the sign language other mutes used, but he was good at finding his own ways to communicate.

"That's true: I've only ever heard stories, I haven't seen anything. But I know a man whose uncle—" She broke off, suddenly reminded of Yul's ridiculous story about the skinwalker. "Look, Morul's dog was almost killed yesterday. Hunting is dangerous."

Kran shook his pointer finger at her and then crossed his arms. He must have picked the gesture up from Yul over the last few summers spent ashore. She wondered, not for the first time, if perhaps she should have insisted the boy accompany her on trading journeys. He was the son of two sailors. He should practice his seamanship.

She reminded herself to focus on the problem at hand. Her son was angry. She had only a few hours before the tide turned and she set out on a two-month-long journey. She rubbed her head and wished it would stop aching.

She switched tactics. "You're going to be eleven in spring. That's pretty grown up." Really grown up. At age eleven, she'd gone with her father on her first raid, sailing to the mainland and stealing five sheep and a gallon of Chelish brandy. He'd let her drink it, too.

The boy kept his eyes on her face, his own expression guardedly neutral.

"If you can show me that you're ready for hunting big game, then I'll take you hunting with me. Maybe moose, down on Flintyreach. They're dangerous, but you haven't lived until you've made your own moose jerky."

He tapped his belt, beside his belt knife. She knew just what he meant.

"Yes, you'll get to take your own weapons. I'll even make you your own hunting spear. A good ash one, like my father made me."

Kran frowned and made a gesture with his hand like a half-closed fist, the thumb lifted. Jendara cocked her head, mimicking him. He repeated the gesture, raising the fist to eye level and giving it a little snap. She stopped in the middle of raising her own.

"No." She shook her head, even though it hurt. "My father didn't give me my belt axe. I took his when he died. To remember him."

Kran stepped over the scraps of wood and put his arms around her. She leaned her head against his. He normally considered himself too mature for babyish hugging.

He released her and beckoned toward the house. She got up off the log and paused a moment to brush wood chips off herself. Beyond her own small garden space, kept tended by Kran and Leyla, the fog was lifting. She could see all the way out to the harbor now, although the view was hazy. The *Milady*'s yellow-and-blue pennant already waved. She smiled a little. She'd bet a gold coin Glayn had raised it before the sun had even reached the horizon. The oldest member of the crew, the gnome loved the *Milady* as much as she did.

She scanned the path leading up to the village. A familiar figure was approaching, the ridiculous peacock feather in his felt cap bobbing along. Vorrin, of course. That must mean the *Milady* was ready to set sail.

Jendara waved at Vorrin. She was happy to see him, even if she wasn't ready to leave Kran just yet. But she knew a good way to buy a few more minutes with her boy. "Kran!" she called. "How would you like pancakes for breakfast?"

"Pancakes?" Vorrin asked. "You know I can't resist pancakes." He gave Kran a friendly punch in the shoulder.

The boy punched him back with a grin. Vorrin slung his arm around Kran's shoulder. "You sure you don't want to go with us? We're going to swing south a bit to meet Boruc—he's Morul and Yul's brother, and some kind of hermit-artist-genius. He lives in a mine."

"A quarry," Jendara corrected. She stooped to gather up Kran's slate and pass it to him. "I guess he lives in Averaka most of the year, but in the summer, the quarry reopens and he goes out to get first dibs on the best stone. Yul says all Boruc does is carve rock, drink mead, and chase wo—" She eyed her son. "Chase parties," she corrected herself. "He likes to have a lot of fun."

"Maybe we're glad you're not going," Vorrin said. "Boruc doesn't sound like a very good influence."

Kran rolled his eyes. *Boats are boring, and so are statues*, he wrote.

Jendara ruffled his hair. "I love you, Kran."

You, too, he wrote. *Pancakes???*

Vorrin laughed. "It's good to know the lad's mind is in the right place."

Flintyreach, one of the largest islands in the Ironbound Archipelago, lived up to its name. Off the *Milady*'s bow, the gray rock of the island's bones stretched down to the water, no softness of soil or grass to invite a sailor off her boat. A few stunted shrubs sprang up out of the cracks in the rock. But although these plants were small, Jendara felt certain she'd never seen any such a happy green. The people of the islands were like that: a hardscrabble lot, quick to fight, but quicker to reach for the mead. Every day was a celebration when you worked so hard to survive.

"I can't see why Yul's brother wants to live in a place like this," Vorrin said, leaning his elbows on the deck railing beside her.

She reached into her pouch for a bundle of leftover pancakes and passed him one. "Boruc's a stoneworker."

"He could go anywhere to find stone." Vorrin waved at the gray expanse. "There aren't even trees here."

Jendara pointed to the south, where greenery climbed up the steep flanks of Flintyreach's inner hills. "The beaches look harsh, but most of Flintyreach is forested. Unfortunately, the interior is also infested with trolls, giants, and ettins. The folk down in the villages organize hunting parties, but it's still dangerous. People stay close to the sea here. It's safer."

The *Milady* began to swing around, preparing for its approach to the docks. In a few minutes, the ship was tied up and the twelve-man crew ready to explore the little fishing village of Alstone—or at least, its tavern. Vorrin consulted with Tam, the big blond first mate who'd grown up on Flintyreach, and then met Jendara at the edge of town, where a little cart road ran off toward Alstone Quarry.

"Tam says he and the crew will pick up our other trade goods, so there's no rush to get back to town." He eyed the sun, about three fingers above the horizon. "But let's try to be back by nightfall."

Jendara nodded. Morul claimed there hadn't been any major problems with giants or trolls in this part of Flintyreach lately, but she didn't want to risk a run-in. Wild animals were bad enough, but giants . . . Jendara could definitely live without running into any of them.

As the cart road snaked away from the shoreline, the scrubby trees grew taller and the undergrowth thicker. Still, the place didn't feel anything like Sorind, the island she'd just left behind. The trees here had grayer bark and twisted limbs. They did little to soften the wind coming off the ocean.

Jendara glanced over at Vorrin. He had gone quiet, his teeth working the edge of his mustache like he did when he was worried. She watched him a minute longer.

"All right, what's bothering you?"

"Nothing. It's just getting awfully late in the season."

"It'll be fine," she said. "Sure, we've had a busy summer and it's kept us moving more than usual. Maybe we're a few weeks behind, but it's no big deal.

And you've been wanting more variety in our trade goods. Boruc's carvings might be just the moneymaker you've been looking for."

He sighed. "I understand the logic, but that doesn't make me any more comfortable. We playing it close this trip, Dara. You and I both know summer fades fast out here."

She gave him a particularly winsome smile, one that rarely failed to soften him. "This is our last stop before we leave for Varisia. We'll be fine."

"It's going to make for a hard trip back to Sorind, and you know it. That's why you've been so awkward with Kran. Because you're worried."

"I'm not worried, and I haven't been awkward." She paused, her eyes scanning the brush. "Did you hear something?"

Vorrin shook his head. "No. It's perfectly quiet."

"Now it is. But just now, I thought . . ." Jendara trailed off. She sniffed at the air, but smelled only smoke and the faint scent of roasted meat. "We must be getting close to the quarry."

"I hope Boruc's work is as good as Yul claims it is. Our shipment this fall is too ordinary. Too many furs and wines, not enough ivory. If we could get some walrus—"

Jendara cut him off with a wave of her hand. "Hush." She listened for a long moment, head cocked. "Don't you think it's too quiet?"

He didn't answer. There were no birds calling, no squirrels rustling the branches. Jendara broke into a run. Vorrin hurried after her.

The road tilted downhill. A few ruts showed where carts loaded with rock must have dug into the surface, and Jendara avoided them, glad it hadn't rained lately. The smell of smoke intensified, as did the heavy smell of roasted meat.

Vorrin grabbed her shoulder. "Wait."

"What?"

"It's a long time till dinner. Why would anyone be cooking right now?" He shook his head. "Something feels wrong."

"We should be careful." Jendara moved closer to the edge of the road, ready to dive into cover at any moment. She crept forward.

A crow exploded from the bush in front of her, its scream launching her backward. She fell onto her backside and pushed herself away. The crow rose up, cawing once, twice as it cleared the treetops.

Vorrin helped her to her feet. "You okay?"

She nodded.

They moved forward again. The cart road turned a sharp corner. Jendara and Vorrin stopped, staring down at the encampment at the edge of the quarry. Nothing moved.

"It's too quiet," Jendara murmured.

"Jendara," Vorrin whispered. He pointed.

Beside a cart, a man stood awkwardly, head hung low, arms behind him, legs too straight. It took her a minute to make sense of the strangeness of his pose, to see the stake running through him, lifting his feet inches off the ground. To see the black puddle beneath, clotted with flies.

A crow settled on his shoulder and nipped at his cheek.

"No!"

Even as she ran, she knew it was stupid, knew it couldn't change anything. But she couldn't just watch the bird eat his face. Her sword jumped into her hand.

"Jendara!"

The bird fluttered aloft, but the sword was already swinging, already biting into its neck. For a second, the crow hung in the air, eyes fixed on her face. Then its head soared out over the brink of the quarry. Its body fell to her feet.

"Damn it, Jenny!" Vorrin spun her around by the elbow.

"Don't call me *Jenny*." She shook him off and began pacing, too upset to hold still. "I've seen this before."

"We need to scout out the camp," Vorrin said, keeping his voice low. "We need to know if there are any survivors."

"Or worse, any attackers." She took a deep breath, regaining a little control. "You're right, we need to go through the whole place."

"Do a quick perimeter check. I'll head west, you go east. And don't take any chances." He reached out for her, brushed his fingers against her cheek. "I don't like this."

"Me neither," she whispered, but she was already turning away from him. She still couldn't hear any sounds save for her own footsteps crunching the gravel underfoot. That was bad.

She sank into her hunter's crouch and approached the nearest building, the largest around. The presence of a tin stovepipe suggested it might be the kitchen and mess hall for the quarry workers. Jendara pressed her ear to the wall and listened hard. Still quiet, save for a faint drip-drip-dripping. She wished she could look through the window, but the shutters were closed.

Jendara's fingers trembled as she reached for the doorknob.

She snapped open the door and almost staggered backward at the overpowering stench of blood and offal. The kitchen looked like a scene from a nightmare. Bloody handprints covered the counters. Flies buzzed over raw-looking heaps that she didn't want to name, and blood slicked the floor. Jendara swallowed hard and took a step inside.

"Is there anyone here?"

She didn't know why she called out, except in the faint hope that someone hiding might hear her and come out to explain that this was all a joke, this was all animal blood, those weren't human intestines curled around that sack of onions, there was nothing horrible in the big pot sitting on the stove. She kept her grip on her sword, but her knees wobbled a little as she picked her way across the room. She had to look. Had to know. She peered over the lip of the pot.

It was empty.

Jendara sagged. She had expected . . . she shook her head. Silly perhaps. Whatever happened here, it must have happened fast, and whoever did it hadn't stopped to cook. They weren't that civilized. She knew they weren't that civilized.

After all, she'd seen this before.

She shook her head and pushed forward.

A door opened up into the dining hall, and she stepped out into the space. The dripping was louder here. With only a few windows, the big room was almost too dark to see into, but she saw enough. Something squelched under her boot as she crossed to the nearest table and righted a bottle of milk. The puddle on the table kept dripping, a soft slow pattering onto the tin mug lying on its side on the floor.

The door burst open. Sunlight poured in, lighting up a long sweep of blood leading outside. Vorrin stopped in the doorframe. He took in the empty room. "I see you forgot we were just circling the perimeter. Any survivors in here?"

Any survivors. Such a flat way to say the worst. She shook her head. "It's empty. Just blood and parts."

The dripping stopped.

"This must have just happened," she realized. "A lot of this blood is still wet. And the milk bottle couldn't have been knocked over more than a few minutes ago."

"We must have scared someone away. A looter, maybe. From what I saw, I think most of this was done longer ago. Maybe this morning."

"Most of what?" Her voice sounded faint even to her own ears. An attack at dawn. That was what happened on Crow's Nest, her father's island. Her sister's island. She thought of the man tied to the stake and felt sure it was no coincidence. She stiffened her shoulders. "Show me."

They stayed silent as Vorrin led her around the side of the nearest building, passing by a clothesline with a few limp garments hanging in the still air. An open door showed a basket of dirty shirts and a washtub. Ordinary items in an ordinary washhouse.

They rounded the corner. A heap of bodies lay ahead, a raw mound of broken and bloody dead.

"Gods," she breathed. "That has to be eighteen or twenty men."

Vorrin circled around the pile. "Some of these bodies don't look . . . whole."

"What?"

He waved her over. Jendara knelt to look at a body on the bottom of the stack. She was glad she couldn't see his face; only his feet and legs stuck out—or more aptly, his mutilated legs and *foot*. Jendara's stomach twisted. "Is it just me, or do his legs look like the meat's been cut off in strips?"

"I don't want to think about it." He pointed to the remains of a small campfire. "Someone definitely built a fire here, like they stayed a few hours."

Jendara stooped to hold her hand above the ashes. She nudged a flat rock in the center. "Still warm, and if I had to guess, I'd say those were grease stains on this stone."

Vorrin blanched. "I don't want to think about it," he repeated. He pressed his fist to his mouth, skin pale.

Jendara felt her own gorge rise, but swallowed hard. "We should check out the rest of the camp."

She moved to the next building, a woodshed. Jendara freed her sword to circle it. Behind her, Vorrin moved quietly, only the occasional crunch of gravel giving away his movement. There was no blood in the woodshed.

Jendara steeled herself to walk past the mound of dead again, but Vorrin caught her eye. He tapped his ear and nodded toward the gaping pit of the quarry.

She listened. She heard nothing at first, but then caught a small sound: a scrape of leather against stone. "Do you think it's our milk spiller?" she whispered.

He nodded. They crept toward the cart road. As they passed behind the washhouse, Jendara felt a momentary gratitude that its bulk hid the grisly mound, a feeling which passed all too quickly was the tiny sound of a foot crushing gravel caught her ear. There really was someone down there. She wondered how deep the quarry went and tightened her grip on her sword.

The cart road led to the rim of the quarry—a deep stony bowl cut out of the hillside. It stretched a good quarter of a mile across. Jendara peered over the edge. The narrow track continued down into the rocks, following the curve of the walls. For the first hundred yards or so, mounds of yellow sandstone lay piled up on the shoulders of the road. Trees and brush obscured the turn beyond. Jendara leaned out farther. The bottom of the quarry looked empty, the flat expanse of sea-green stone like a placid lake.

Jendara turned back to Vorrin. "Whoever went down there, they haven't reached the bottom yet."

He glanced over the edge. "I don't like that descent. It's too easy to rig an ambush on a road like this."

Jendara laid her hand on his arm. "*If* the person we're chasing is dangerous. This could be a survivor, scared out of their mind after what they saw back there. Or it could be a witness, some woodsman who just walked into a nightmare. No matter who they are, I want to talk to them."

"Let me go down."

"No. I'm a local, they're more likely to trust me." Jendara pointed to the far side of the quarry. "I think you'd better follow the top of this cliff around to the far side. The ground's rough, but I think that looks like a footpath leading out of the quarry, don't you?"

Vorrin squinted a moment. "I see it. Good plan." He gave her a sharp look. "You'll be careful, right? You're not running down there with your sword half-out just because of what you saw back there?"

Jendara began walking down the steep path without sparing him a backward look. "I know I'm doing, Vorrin. Just watch the trail."

As she went, she studied the path ahead for clues. There was no way to make out tracks on gravel this heavily traveled, but blood would stand out. No way to kill that many people without getting bloody. And it was hard not to leave tiny signs of passage that a good set of eyes might pick up: with every step, a person shed spoor like hairs and threads and fragments of the foods they ate.

She paused to listen for other footsteps. The quarry was silent. Jendara took a few steps forward, focusing on the sound of the gravel beneath her boots. She knew how to step lightly, but the tiny stones made a certain amount of noise no matter what. She paused again. *There.* That might have been the rustle of a foot passing over pea gravel.

She resisted the urge to run toward the sound. It would be all too easy to think of those bodies piled up by the wash house and let hot rage whip her into a run, but she pushed the anger aside. If she ran toward a survivor, it would only further terrify the poor man or woman. And if it was a killer, well, it would still be just as easy to die by falling to the bottom of this pit as it would be to get jumped by a slavering cannibal.

Cannibalism. Just the thought of it sickened her. The only cannibals she'd ever heard of were the Kalvamen, those reclusive island dwellers far to the north. Few risked the trip to Kalva to see the massive barbarians with their milk-white eyes and sickening eating habits, and no Kalvamen had raided the islands in generations. Morul and Yul weren't the only ones who thought the Kalvamen were nothing to fear. If asked, most islanders would agree that the people of Kalva were too deranged and inbred to manage a sea crossing.

Maybe they should be more afraid, Jendara thought. After she'd returned home that day to find her father dead and her sister missing, she had taken to her ship and scouted the island of Kalva from the sea. It was true she had seen no sign of ships large enough to travel the ferocious seas between Kalva and the Ironbound Archipelago, but it was also true that plenty of islanders had sailed remarkable distances in small raiding vessels. She had never discounted the Kalvamen just for lack of seafaring ability.

She tripped on a stone jutting out of the worn path, and at the last second caught herself on a massive boulder. She clung to it a moment, trying to catch her breath. She needed to pay better attention if she didn't want to kill herself.

A few feet beyond her, someone had cleared away the piles of fallen rock and brush, and she could clearly see the bottom of the quarry. The current work zone stood out from the rest of the rock floor, with racks of gear and tools stacked around a square perimeter. Piles of rock sat waiting to be loaded onto carts. Jendara knew little about stones or masonry, but thought the green stuff might be soapstone. It was always in high demand, being easy to work.

The hairs on the back of her neck prickled. All those piles provided easy cover for an ambush.

She picked her way forward and kept low to the ground as she came out into the flat stone-working area. A massive chunk of green rock sat beside the edge of the path. There was no way to see behind it.

Jendara brought out her handaxe. She pressed her back to the stone and reminded herself that whoever was down here might not be a white-eyed cannibal killer.

"I don't want to hurt you," she called out. "I just want to talk."

No reply.

She threw herself around the side of the stone with her axe ready. She saw no one.

The jolt of unused adrenaline made her legs go to jelly. She ignored it, kept her axe at the ready, and began to walk the perimeter of the quarry. She'd expected the worst. It felt strange not to face a monster when she was ready for one.

She stopped. She'd reached the side of the quarry bottom almost directly below its entrance, and a dark blot lay on the ground. The crow's head she'd lopped off at the top of the quarry. An ant crawled over the still-glossy bead of its yellow eye.

She had to avert her gaze. Beheading the crow had been a bad idea. She'd been raised to uphold the old clan traditions, and the crow had been her clan's totem. Life at sea had been one way to escape the bird's constant presence on dry land—the only time she had to look at them was when the ship docked, or when she saw someone wearing one of those crow-shaped traveler's pendants. She tried not to look at those necklaces for too long. She'd bought one once for Kalira, her sister. The younger girl had adored it.

Jendara had circled most of the way around now, and still hadn't seen anyone. Where was the person who'd gone down into the quarry?

Above her, something scraped. Jendara looked up and swore. She'd missed the entrance to the little footpath, and now her prey was escaping up it.

"Vorrin!" She had to warn him.

But a roar answered her shout: the rumble of something huge rolling down the hill. Vorrin might not be in danger, but she was.

She somersaulted over the soapstone block, pressing her face against its rough surface. Dust filled the air. She couldn't see. Or breathe. The soapstone shuddered as something massive hit it and stone shards rained down on her. Jendara hissed as one pierced her sleeve and drove into her forearm.

Coughing, she managed to get to her feet. Chunks of rock lay all around the soapstone block. If she hadn't moved behind it, she would have been crushed.

She scanned the trail above. Dust obscured all details. She was going to have to climb it blind.

Jamming her axe back into her belt, she scrambled forward. The ground was steep, the yellow sandstone of the main cliff walls unstable. She kept sliding backward in the stuff. Jendara grabbed for a handhold and dug her fingers into a gnarled root. The dust was clearing.

Something dark moved up ahead.

Jendara reached for the next handhold. Until she got her feet under her, she didn't dare try to attack the thing. She had a good arm, but on a nearly vertical path, the odds of her hitting him with her handaxe were small. She pulled herself up over a knoll of solid stone and caught her breath.

There he was. A man—a tall man in a long, shaggy cloak—hurried up the trail. He pulled himself up the steep hillside, snatching at the branches of the overhanging trees like rungs on a ladder.

"Hey!" she shouted, and reached for her belt axe. She'd never really believed she was chasing was an innocent bystander, but the man's grace and mass made his guilt a near certainty in her mind. No islander would have just stood by to watch his friends be ripped apart and eaten, not unless he was sick or crippled.

He leaped forward and disappeared between a pair of bushes. A rock as big as Jendara's head rolled out of the brush, bouncing and tumbling straight toward her.

"Damn it!" She threw herself aside and skidded on the path. She caught herself on a tree and raced up the hill.

Up above, Vorrin gave a sudden shout of surprise. Jendara hurried, but by the time she reached the top, Vorrin was just picking himself up, pinching a bloody nose and swearing.

"It got away," he growled. "I turned away for a second—I thought I heard something behind me—and it jumped me. Looked like a bear."

Jendara shook her head. "A bear? I was following a man. A big man, but a man."

Vorrin shrugged. "It happened fast, and there was a lot of dust in the air. Could have been a man, I guess. But it looked furry. And it had claws." He held out his hand. A gash ran down the back of it.

Jendara looked out into the forest. Some kind of trail continued into the forest, but here the trees were thick and the bracken dense. If anything wanted to disappear out here, it would. And back at Alstone Village, the crew of the *Milady* were waiting.

"Let's get out of here," she said. "Someone should know about this."

Chapter Three
Funerals

Jendara rubbed her forearm. She'd barely noticed the cut she'd gotten back at the quarry, but it had started stinging as they hurried back to the fishing village. Probably just her sweat working down into the wound, but she'd still like someone to take a look at it. Maybe she hadn't dug out all of the stone before she'd tied it up with her handkerchief.

"So just what do you think attacked those workers?" Vorrin looked pale, a smear of blood drying across his cheek from his bloody nose.

"Something terrible. We've got to get a hunting party out to the quarry so we can track down the killers."

"You think there are more of those things?" Vorrin looked almost hopeful. He didn't appreciate being attacked from behind.

"I do. That man, or bear, or whatever it was—it was strong, and it was fast. But it wasn't strong and fast enough to slaughter an entire encampment of quarry workers."

Vorrin walked in silence a moment. The first of the village's cottages appeared. A little boy waved at them. A dog barked. The normalcy was comforting.

"What are we going to tell Yoric and Morul?" he asked.

"I don't know." She couldn't imagine telling either man that his brother had been murdered and possibly eaten.

A seagull fluttered down, squawking to itself. Jendara remembered the crow at the quarry and shuddered. "We can't just leave all those bodies out there," she said. Vorrin just nodded. Perhaps he was thinking the same thing.

Jendara led them to the closest building guaranteed to have people in it at this hour: the tavern. The barkeep frowned at them. "You're with the *Milady*, aren't you? You look like hell."

"Something terrible has happened," Vorrin said, and began to tell the man what they had found.

Two wagons stood at the edge of the forest, their drivers waiting patiently for the five big men to finish checking their weapons. Jendara approved of the assortment of arms: spears, bows, swords, handaxes. She just hoped that it would prove unnecessary.

"It was probably a troll," the leader, a man named Wilfric, said. He'd said it before, back at the pub. "You probably frightened it away. But at least we'll be prepared."

"I've never seen trolls butcher anything like this," Jendara said. "Or cook anything. Have you even considered something more human?" She hesitated.

No one was going to appreciate what she said next. "Like the men from Kalva. They do this sort of thing."

He smiled kindly. "The Kalvamen haven't left their island in at least a hundred years."

"Doesn't mean they can't," Jendara growled.

"Don't forget that we're fishermen." The smile shrank a little. "We're out on the sea every day. If any Kalvaman wanted to set foot on this island, they'd have to take a boat, right? And if there were any strange boats around, we'd have noticed. I think it was a troll."

One of his companions climbed into the back of the wagon. "A troll's bad enough, anyway. Let's not borrow trouble."

Wilfric waved at the wagon's driver, who stirred up the stout mule in its trace. The wagon began to roll.

"Keep your eyes open," Vorrin warned.

Wilfric nodded. "Will do." He moved to the front of the wagon, taking the mule's halter.

Jendara watched them go. "I should have gone with them."

"Hey, we've got business of our own to attend." Vorrin jabbed his thumb back at the docks. "If we hurry, we can make it to Sorind to break the bad news about Boruc and catch the tide for Varisia tomorrow morning."

The crew was just loading the last of the cargo onto the *Milady*. It was indeed feasible to make it back to Sorind before midnight. But the thought of telling Yul and Morul what she'd seen out there made Jendara wish she could stall.

She sighed. Waiting wasn't going to making it any easier. "You're right."

They headed down to the main dock, a long pier stretching out into waters deep enough for a big ship like the *Milady*. Shorter piers bristled the shoreline, filled with smaller fishing boats and raiding vessels that could moor a lot closer to shore. Jendara watched a medium-sized fishing craft ease itself up to a lower dock attached to the pier. A red-headed boy stood in the prow and waved at her. She felt a sudden pang of loneliness for Kran.

Vorrin paused to watch the boat tie up. "Nice looking little vessel."

Jendara smiled. His infatuation with watercraft amused her. "You should have been a shipbuilder."

"And you're a barbarian who wouldn't know a clipper from a yacht." His eyes twinkled as he said it. He knew her well enough to know her heart had room for only two kinds of watercraft: Ulfen longships and the *Milady*.

She linked her arm in his. After the horror they'd seen, it was good to be next to the sea on a sunny day with her very best friend. He pulled her closer to his side.

"Jendara, I—" he broke off. "Your arm's bleeding."

"It got cut back in the quarry." She frowned and pointed. "Now that's an accident just waiting to happen. That guy's trying to carry way too much."

Vorrin looked back at the boat. The boy waited at the bottom of the just-dropped gangplank, calling back up at a knot of people. A heavily laden man staggered on the steep planks. The top crate of fish slid a little.

"Hey!" Jendara raced back up the pier, leaping down to the lower dock.

The boy turned his head, seeing at the last second the man behind him. He stiffened, not sure where to go. The wobbling crate tumbled free.

Jendara launched herself at the boy, somersaulting down the dock with him in her arms. They tumbled and rolled. Jendara crashed into a mooring cleat and lay there gasping.

The crate smashed just inches from where the boy had been standing.

"By the gods! Lady, are you all right?" The big man put down the last crate and jogged to Jendara's side.

She lifted her head and then let it thud back on the dock. "Wind . . . knocked out."

The boy scrambled to his feet. "I'm sorry, lady. I think I crushed you."

They offered her their hands and hauled her to her feet. She rubbed her gut, which felt tender. Up close, the boy looked older than Kran, maybe thirteen or so. He was short, but compact, and he was already grinning. She had a feeling he rarely stopped.

The man laughed. His round belly jiggled. "That's our Rowri, crushing his rescuer." He bowed a little. "I must thank you for rescuing my young friend. I am Boruc Sanderrson, at your service."

Jendara stepped back, her mouth falling open a bit. "Boruc? Sanderrson? But—"

"We thought you were dead!" Vorrin exclaimed, appearing behind Jendara. He had taken the long route around the docks.

"Dead?" Boruc's ginger eyebrows shot up. "Where'd you get that idea?"

47

Jendara looked at Vorrin, uncomfortable. Vorrin spread his hands weakly. "We were just at the quarry. Every worker was killed in a horrible attack."

"What?" Boruc turned pale.

"Did something happen?" A woman with Rowri's coppery hair and black eyes jumped down from the boat. Freckles covered every inch of her face. She pulled Rowri closer to her. "You all right?" she murmured, just loud enough for Jendara to hear.

The boy nodded and wriggled away. A man with his arm in a sling and an elder with the tattooed cheeks of a wisewoman made their way down the gangplank to join the group. Vorrin repeated the story of what he and Jendara had found.

The man shook his head. "This sounds bad. We haven't had any real trouble on Flintyreach in years. Folks down in Averaka have organized patrols to keep things quiet around here."

The redheaded woman narrowed her eyes. "This kind of attack doesn't sound like anything I've ever heard of."

"It's been more than thirteen years, but I saw something like it once," Jendara said. "My family— my father and sister—were killed in an attack like this. Back at the quarry, we saw a man impaled and mutilated. The things that killed my father did that. And the bodies were . . . savaged in a similar way."

"Eaten," the redheaded woman said flatly.

"Yes," Vorrin said. "Right now a group of men are headed back to the quarry to collect the bodies. Or what's left of them."

"Most of the quarry workers have families in the village." Above his thick beard, Boruc's face paled.

"Husbands and wives helping on boats or working in the smokehouse. Children, too."

The woman shot her boy a quick glance. "Those poor souls. Thank the ancestors no one ever built family quarters out there."

The man with the sling stepped forward, clapping Boruc's shoulder. "Lucky thing I wrenched my shoulder yesterday. If you'd gone back to the quarry instead of fishing with us, you'd be dead now."

Boruc rubbed his beard. "You're right, Sven. I owe you my life."

"Just as Rowri owes the lady his." The old woman hadn't said a word yet, but now she stepped close to Jendara and studied her closely. Her blue eyes, the same color as the tattooed spirals on her cheeks, gleamed beneath her fringe of steel-hued hair. "What's your name, stranger?"

Jendara resisted the urge to take a step back. The old woman barely reached Jendara's shoulder, but her fierce gaze was disconcerting. "Jendara. Lately of Sorind."

She put out her hand, but the woman ignored it. She scanned Jendara up and down, studying her clothes and braid.

"Mud-brown hair," she mused. "And a familiar face. If I'm not mistaken, I knew your father. Erik. A good man. Homesteaded out on Crow's Nest."

The old woman's rudeness made Jendara bristle, but she forced herself to remain civil. "That was my father," she agreed.

"You're much like him," the old woman said. "In face and in action. That's a compliment."

Jendara hesitated. She still didn't like the woman's attitude, but it was clear she meant no slight. "Thank you."

The freckled woman stepped forward. "The past is the past, no matter how much Gerda likes to speak of it." She shot the older woman a disapproving look, then smiled at Jendara. "I am glad that you're here, no matter who your father was. I am Fambra, and this is my husband, Sven. Gerda is his mother."

Jendara shook the offered and equally freckled hand. Fambra had a strong grip, her palms as callused as Jendara's own.

Sven spoke up. "You saved my son back there. We owe you supper at least."

"Well . . ." Jendara looked at Vorrin, who cast a look at the *Milady*, then sighed and nodded. "Yes. Yes, please."

Boruc looked down at the broken crate and its scattered contents. "I hope you like fish."

Jendara put down her mug of mead and pushed back Fambra's white curtain, peering outside. "The wagons have returned from the quarry," she said. "It looks like they've brought the bodies back. At least their families can have a decent funeral."

Fambra put down the potato she was peeling. "Our clan takes funerals very seriously." She wiped her hands on her apron and moved beside Jendara. She closed her eyes for a moment, clearly upset.

The recovery team had thought to cover the bodies with canvas, but no amount of fabric could really hide that horror. The men accompanying the wagons looked haggard and pained. Sven opened the door and raised his hand in a solemn wave as they passed by.

Boruc made a low, choked sound.

"It's all right, man," Vorrin murmured.

Jendara turned to see the big man clench shut his eyes and shake his head furiously. She crossed to him and put her hand on his shoulder. She knew just what passed through his head.

"It's never all right," she said. "It might never really be all right. The pain hurts less, but you'll still feel it sometimes."

Vorrin frowned at her. She put down her mug. "I'm going to go help them unload."

"Then you can give me a hand preparing the bodies." Gerda reached for a shawl on the hook by the door and wrapped it around her shoulders. "It looks like to be a lot of work."

"I'll come, too," Fambra said. "Rowri, you finish making dinner."

"I will," Boruc said. "I can't go out there—I may as well make myself useful."

"I'll help you, Boruc," Vorrin added, quickly. He caught Jendara's eye and held it.

She turned away. Maybe Vorrin was right. Maybe her words weren't the kind of comfort Boruc needed. But she couldn't see the point of lying to him. Not when he knew that he was alive and his friends were dead and only luck had saved him. She followed the other women out the cottage door.

Of all the cottages, only Fambra's had a crushed shell walkway leading out to the main wagon road, and only Fambra's sported real curtains in the window. The rest of the buildings had an unloved look, the shutters hung haphazardly, the gardens crowding the walls themselves. Jendara looked around herself, shaking her head.

"Don't judge it too hard," Gerda said, looking back over her shoulder at Jendara. "We're only here during the summer. The rest of the year, we're in town."

"Averaka?" Jendara raised an eyebrow.

Fambra nodded. "The harbor stays open all winter; never really ices up. Not a lot of good fishing, but plenty of crab and shellfish."

"How are the neighbors?" Jendara asked.

"Lots of half-orcs, but they're good folk. Just because they've got a little orc blood don't make them any worse neighbors." Fambra laughed. "In fact, we've got a couple of half-orcs in our clan. You'll see some in the village."

"Your clan." Jendara studied the houses. She realized now that all the front doors were painted the same shades of blue-gray and striking green, some with clan banners waving above the lintels. When had she stopped noticing such things? She tried to remember her own clan banner. It leaped into her mind's eye, surprisingly clear after all these years: red and black and yellow running in stripes behind a crow's profile. She wondered what had happened to that banner. She hadn't kept it.

"Clan Dagfridrung of Flintyreach." Gerda's voice swelled with pride. "We go back over two hundred years, farming and fishing on this island."

"Aye, it's a good life," Fambra agreed. "I'm glad to be a part of it."

They had slowed as they approached the wagon, sitting now in front of the meetinghouse. Jendara's feet seemed to weigh more with each approaching step. Wilfric and his men stood in a knot on the hall's brightly painted steps, faces gray and drawn. Their hands and faces were clean, but most of their clothing was streaked with blood or worse.

"It was just as bad as you said it was," Wilfric said. "Never seen anything like it."

"Were no clean battle," a man mumbled.

"No," Jendara agreed.

"How many?" Fambra asked.

"Nineteen," Wilfric answered. "Your cousin Abjorn among them. And my nephew."

Gerda touched her heart as if it hurt her. "That's almost a quarter of our clan."

"Aye."

She straightened herself. "This is a sign. I warned them that our clan has always been a clan of the sea and shore. What were we doing, digging in the earth? This is our punishment for turning our back on our ancestors."

Jendara put her hands on her hips. "How can you think that? This was a random attack. No one could have predicted it."

Gerda raised an eyebrow. "You think so?" She turned back to the men. "Have the rest of the village bring wood and rushes. We'll prepare for the ceremony here, in front of the meetinghouse."

Fambra leaned closer to whisper in Jendara's ear. "Gerda is very old-fashioned. She lives for the past and the old ways. But she's a good healer, and the people in this village trust her."

Jendara set her jaw. She wasn't going to argue with anyone about their religious beliefs. Not here, not now. "What do we need to do to prepare the bodies?"

The work proved just as long and horrible as Jendara had feared. As other members of the clan brought wood and rushes, preparing the ground for the cremation ceremony, Fambra and Jendara laid out the bodies. Gerda anointed the dead men and women's brows with scented oils and washed their hands and faces with seawater. As the sun sank lower in the sky, families appeared to wrap the bodies of their lost loved ones and sing their souls onto their final paths. Some of the souls would move on to their eternal reward, but many would stay on this plane as the ancestor spirits that guided the wisewomen and their male counterparts.

Or so the wisewomen and shamans claimed. Jendara had her own doubts about the powers of the ancestors.

Fambra knelt beside the last of the bodies. "Look at this," she murmured, pointing at the dead man's torso. The attackers had stripped off his shirt, and his remaining skin looked pallid in the twilight. Jendara stooped beside her.

"Here." Fambra pointed to an incision just below the man's collarbone. "This looks like a knife wound. The edges of the flesh are perfectly smooth." Her voice sounded clipped and utterly unemotional. Jendara could understand. She'd kept her own mind focused on the work at hand, cleaning the gore from each body in just the methodical way she would scrub the deck of the *Milady*. Whenever she thought of the mutilated figure as an actual man, rage and sorrow threatened to overwhelm her.

"Yes," Jendara agreed. "They started the cut there and removed a neat square of flesh."

"Nearly square," Fambra agreed. "I'd say they simply followed the line of the man's muscle."

Jendara's eyes narrowed. "Like butchering a deer?"

"Exactly. You just follow the outlines of the muscles and the body breaks itself up into parts." Fambra pointed to another cut, a long slash running down the man's ribs on the other side of the body. "But this doesn't look like a cut. It's more of a slash, and whatever did it was much wider than a knife."

"It almost looks like the marks a bear claw leaves," Jendara mused.

"Exactly. And here on the neck, the flesh looks *chewed*." Fambra's face twisted. "What kind of creature uses both a knife and its teeth? This makes no sense."

"Geirr? My Geirr!"

A half-orc woman flung herself down beside the body, tears running down her green-skinned cheeks. Fambra got to her feet, as did Jendara. They watched the woman kiss the dead man's forehead and lips.

"That man's the father of Rowri's best friend," Fambra murmured. For the first time, tears appeared in her eyes. "Whoever did this . . . they deserve to die."

Jendara stared at the rows of dead men and women, their bodies shrouded in white linen that gleamed in the last rays of daylight. The smell of spices and pine boughs overpowered the stink of death, but nothing could hide the pain of the families gathered around their dead.

"Death is too good for those monsters," she growled.

Her hands balled into fists, and she felt the old familiar heat rise in her tattoos, the marks of the bloodthirsty pirate goddess.

Death would be too good—but it would be a pretty good start.

Chapter Four
Invitation to a Hunt

The last hint of sunset's lavender melted into the sea, and the stars brightened in the black velvet of night. Not a cloud moved in the firmament; not a breath of wind stirred the air.

"Going to be cold tonight," Jendara mused to no one in particular, and Vorrin put his arm around her shoulders. They stood on the edge of the crowd with the crew of the *Milady*. Most of the sailors hailed from Varisia, Cheliax, or farther, but none would stay on the ship during a funeral like this. The dead commanded respect.

Jendara turned back to the funeral site. Torches burned in a rough circle around the massed dead and the people who had come to morn them. Gerda stepped onto a log so everyone could see her.

"My people," she began. Her voice rang out over the silenced community. A child sniffled, but went quiet. "We gather today to send our brothers and sisters into the hands of our ancestors."

Jendara's fingers curled into her palms, the nails nipping at the skin. She hadn't gone to her father's funeral. She supposed that some time after she'd alerted friends on Flintyreach about the attack, they had sent out a wisewoman, or possibly even a priest of the stag god, Erastil, to perform some kind of ceremony for the dead. Jendara had burned the remains she'd found and buried her father's body in a stone cairn. That had been funeral enough for her.

Gerda continued speaking, but Jendara only heard the vague rise and fall of her voice. She thought back to the altar her father had built on Crow's Nest. He had believed so strongly in the power of the ancestors. It would pain him to know she had lost her own faith in them.

What *did* she believe in anymore? Did she still believe in the pirate goddess whose totems she'd inked on the backs of her hands? She was there, that goddess. She had looked down on many battles and reveled in the blood and fear. But outside of those darker moments of piracy, did Besmara care?

Jendara squeezed shut her eyes. Had Erastil *cared* when her father had whispered his prayers to the hunter god? Had the spirits of her father's ancestors bestirred themselves from their shrines when he'd begged for them?

Yes, Jendara realized, opening her eyes and glaring at the now singing wisewoman, she believed in gods and spirits. She believed they couldn't bother to concern themselves with what happened to ordinary people.

The crowd sighed. Gerda stepped off her makeshift podium and pulled a torch free of its stand. She raised it high above her head, then swept it down to the edge of the pine boughs spread beneath the bodies. The oils she'd applied earlier caught immediately, the flames racing out over the funeral mound.

"Your ancestors call you home," Gerda intoned, reaching into her belt pouch. She tossed a handful of dust onto the flames. With a crackle, blues and greens shimmered in the flames.

A cheap trick—Jendara had seen enough fireworks to know mineral salts when she saw them—but effective. The mood of the crowd changed, grew less dark and more reflective. A few people sighed. A woman began to sing.

A man approached Gerda, and Jendara recognized the lanky build of the barkeep. The old woman embraced him, and then he turned and made his way through the group, touching hands and kissing cheeks before breaking free.

Jendara squeezed Vorrin's hand and nodded toward the bartender. They followed after him, and the crew hurried to catch up. These were the moments of a funeral where a stranger felt the least welcome, the moments where the grieving came together to comfort each other. For a stranger, the best comfort came from a cask of ale. Especially a stranger like Jendara, whose insides still churned. What did a funeral help any of those dead men? Where had their clan spirits been when they'd been tortured and eaten? She ordered an ale and wished the tavern had something stronger.

Jendara hadn't quite finished her second tankard when the mourners began drifting into the tavern. They crept inside in quiet little knots of twos and threes, mostly men, and they nodded politely at her when they entered. But they didn't sit too close and they didn't speak.

Wilfric and two of the men who'd brought back the bodies pushed open the door and came to the bar. Wilfric took a seat beside Jendara. He ordered mead and tossed back the mug entire.

He wiped his mouth on his sleeve. "Tomorrow we go hunting," he announced. "Whatever did this is still out there."

Jendara nodded. She would be glad to sleep on the *Milady* tonight, that was certain.

"Will you join us?"

She hesitated.

Vorrin opened his mouth to speak, but Wilfric raised his hand. "From the stories your crew was tossing around, you're both fine warriors. And we'll need every hunter we can get."

Jendara squeezed her tankard tighter. "Do you still think it's a troll?"

"It's the best guess."

She wondered if she should remind them about the man she'd seen—the man that had looked like a bear to Vorrin. Maybe it really had been a looter, plain and simple, with no connection to the crime. That's what Wilfric had thought when she'd told him about it. She gulped her ale.

"A smart troll, maybe," one of the other men said. "Something we ain't seen before."

Vorrin tugged Jendara closer to him. "We need to get moving. The *Milady*'s loaded up. We should catch the morning tide."

He was the captain, in charge of transport. She was the business brain. She should be listening to him. But every time she blinked, she saw that man on the stake. "I just . . . want to find out what did this. I need to."

His brown eyes held hers as if he could look beneath their blue depths and read what was written on her mind. He frowned. "Are you sure?"

"Vorrin." She paused, searching for the right words and failing. She took a final swig of ale. "Look, we can catch the afternoon tide. It wouldn't hurt the crew to sleep in."

He sighed. "Fine. We'll go hunting."

Wilfric clapped Jendara on the back. "Good! Ale for everyone. I need to get drunk after what I've seen today."

Jendara made her way down the *Milady*'s gangplank before the sun nosed over the horizon. A few clouds sculled across the sky, but the breeze didn't reach the land and the air was already mild. The sea was flat as polished steel. She felt a moment's twinge, looking out at it. They should be on the water right now, looking for wind and headed for the mainland.

"We'd just have to row, anyway."

She spun around. Vorrin smiled down at her from the ship's deck.

"Were you reading my mind?" she asked.

He shook his head. "Just your face." He strode down the plank, his gear jingling. He brushed her chin with his fingers. "After all these years looking at it, I ought to be getting good at that."

She gave him a quick, fierce hug. "You're a good friend. I'm lucky to have you."

"Jendara! Vorrin!"

They turned toward the shore. Rowri waved at them, a bundle in the crook of his arm. The pair hurried up the dock to meet him.

"My mom sent you some breakfast." He thrust the bundle at them. "And some sandwiches for later. She'd come, but my dad's real eager to see if that big run of herring is still out there." He crinkled his nose. "I'll probably get stuck pickling all of it, but I guess it's good money."

Jendara laughed. "Tell your mom thanks, all right? And good luck out there."

The boy started walking backward, and added: "Oh, we'll need it. We're a man down, what with Dad's arm still hurt and Boruc going hunting. See ya!" He turned around and raced toward the shorter dock, where Jendara could just make out Fambra carrying a cask toward their fishing boat. She waved and hoped Fambra saw it.

They walked toward the meetinghouse. Men were already beginning to gather on its broad stairs, sitting and talking and readying their gear. Jendara saw many carrying hunting spears with heavy iron tips that looked more serious than the ones she'd seen on Sorind. This was Flintyreach, after all—it wasn't entirely unusual to see giants come down out of the hills. She'd almost forgotten how much safer a tiny island could be.

Wilfric got to his feet. "Jendara. How are you with a spear? I've got a spare."

"I'm all right—but I've got nothing on Vorrin. Man's amazing with a spear."

"Then you should take arrows. You can use my bow." Wilfric passed Jendara a quiver of arrows and a bow, then cocked his head and studied Vorrin as if seeing him for the first time. "He's got reach," the man agreed. He hoisted the big spears. "You want to carry this?"

Vorrin reached for it. "We're hunting trolls. Damn right, I want this thing." He tested its balance. "That's a fine weapon."

"New forged tip, ash shaft. Wood's almost as hard as iron, but with just enough flexibility when pressed." Wilfric looked around the group. More men and a few women had joined. "All right," Wilfric called. "Let's start at the quarry and see if we can pick up any tracks."

"Wait."

The meeting hall doors creaked open and Gerda slipped out between them, bearing a horn cup in one hand. She raised the other.

"This is no ordinary hunting trip. You go in pursuit of the creature or creatures that felled some of our clan's best men and women."

A murmur of agreement passed through the crowd. Jendara looked around the group of hunters and realized every face looked angry, hard. The village was set on punishing the creatures that took their men, that much was clear. She wished she felt the same fire in her belly. After all, one of those creatures had almost killed her. But all she felt this morning was a mounting fear that filled her guts like cold water. She couldn't understand it.

Gerda moved forward, extending the blue-and-green-painted horn cup. Steam rose up from it. Jendara could smell the concoction now, the pungent herbal tang of heated balsam liquor. Spirit wine, the wisewomen called it.

"I offer the blessing of our clan spirits. Receive it and go with strength."

Wilfric stepped up first. He sank to his knees and the wisewoman dabbed warm liquor onto his lips. It left a black stripe that sank into his skin. He bowed his head a long second before rising again.

"For the clan," he intoned. Gerda kissed his forehead and sent him down the stairs.

The other hunters stepped up to accept the spirit wine. Afterward, they stood quietly, without the chatter that characterized an ordinary hunting expedition. The black stains on their lips looked like a strange dark slot—a button hole, a catlike pupil. Jendara averted her eyes and studied the clouds bunched overhead.

"Strangers," Gerda called.

Jendara dropped her gaze to the old woman's face. Gerda smiled.

"Our clan spirits would wish you luck in this hunt, as well. Please step up."

Vorrin stepped forward. "I'm honored."

The old woman dabbed his lips and kissed his brow. When he turned back to Jendara, he was doing his best to hide a grimace. Balsam liquor, even heavily spiced and sweetened for these moments, was an acquired taste.

"Jendara." Gerda beckoned to her.

Jendara raised her hands, showing the jolly rogers tattooed on the back. "I can't. Once I was bound to Besmara—and she's a jealous goddess."

Gerda's lips pursed in disapproval. "These are your ancestors. Their presence at your side does not diminish your love for any god."

Jendara shook her head. "Not my ancestors, Wise One."

Gerda frowned. "Your hunt will not go well for you, Jendara. Not if you have turned your back on the ancestors. All the clans were once one clan. All the ancestors are here for your protection. Are you really too proud to let them help?"

Jendara folded her arms across her chest and met the woman's glare.

"It's time," Wilfric called. "Daylight's burning."

Gerda spun about and reentered the meeting hall. The reverent silence left with her. People chattered as they collected their gear. Arrows clacked in their quivers and a dog barked. The first of the hunters moved onto the road.

Vorrin and Jendara waited at the edge of the group and fell into place beside Boruc. They were silent as they strode along the cart road. Just yesterday, Jendara had walked toward the quarry in the pleasant expectation of good trade and a new friend. Now she was prepared for the worst.

She glanced across at Vorrin. The spear in his hand looked solid and lethal. She thought of the creature she'd seen at the bottom of the quarry and wished she'd taken a spear instead of arrows.

Jendara knelt at the edge of the quarry, studying the scuffed gravel on the cart road. She couldn't tell her own prints from any of the dozens that had been laid down in the ordinary course of the quarry's work. She also hadn't seen any print that stood out as trollish.

"Lots of foot traffic on this path," Wilfric mused. He brushed at a blade of grass bent over the edge of the road. "Doesn't give us much to work with." He got to his feet, studying the ground in both directions. "How big did you say the thing that attacked you was?" he asked Vorrin.

Vorrin shrugged. "About my size, I guess. I didn't see much—there was a lot of dust. By the time I got to my feet, it was gone."

"Suppose it could be a juvenile troll," Wilfric said, rubbing his beard.

"It was about the size of a man," Jendara interjected. She got to her feet. "I saw it climbing up the hill, and I thought it was a tall man wearing a fur cloak. That's too small, even for a juvenile."

"Maybe it's a very small kind of troll," Wilfric said. "Trolls on Flintyreach have always run smaller than average, anyway. With pressure from all the patrols, the bigger ones might be dying out."

"I suppose." Jendara bit her tongue. Wilfric had his mind made up. There was no point arguing with him.

A man ran up. "Wilfric! We've a trace. Black hair, coarse like a troll's, caught on a branch just past the dining hall."

"That's our spoor," Wilfric said. "Let's go."

"Wait a second," Vorrin said. "When that thing cut out of here, it was definitely headed south. I told you that already."

Wilfric raised an eyebrow. "Maybe it doubled back. Wouldn't be that unusual. But if you're sure, we'd better split up." He caught the eye of a few other men. "Nol, Rak, you go with our friends here. See what's on the south side of things. Take pitch in case you find that troll—you know fire's the only thing that takes them out."

"I'll go, too," Boruc said.

"I would have thought you'd want to be in the action." Wilfric's words gave away his opinion of the second party's mission.

Boruc frowned. "I owe Jendara. I'll stick with her."

"Suit yourself." Wilfric put his fingers in his mouth and whistled sharply. "Let's move out!" He looked over his shoulder at Vorrin and Jendara. "Be safe."

"You too," Vorrin called, but Wilfric was already clapping his tracker on the shoulder and jogging west.

The two men he'd ordered to accompany Jendara's group looked at her. Nol's seamed face creased around a smile, friendly enough to make up for his companion. Rak, only a little taller than his hunting spear and sporting the barest wisps of a mustache, glowered.

"Why'd you ignore that spoor, lady?" he grumbled. "We're never going to see any action going south."

Vorrin narrowed his eyes. "We're going south, and that's final. Your headman told you what to do. Now let's get moving. You lead."

The group trudged southward. There was no southbound road, and the trail Rak set them on looked unused and choked with bracken. They'd gone a few hundred yards when Nol raised his knobbed hand. He said nothing, but pointed out a crushed fern.

Someone had come here before them.

She squatted down beside the old man and touched the broken ends of the plant. Wilted but not desiccated, the fern could only have been crushed a few hours earlier, maybe a day.

Nol gestured at the earth beneath the fern. "Something scraped this moss, here." He duck-walked ahead another two feet. "And here," he said, pointing out a crushed bit of lichen on a stone.

Jendara stretched her arms from one point to another, getting a sense of the distance. "About an average step for a man."

"Ayuh," Nol agreed. He stood up and took the lead. Rak looked interested despite himself.

Vorrin let Jendara catch up with him. "That old man's got sharp eyes."

"We're lucky," she agreed. "I might have missed that."

"It gives me hope," Boruc said. He rubbed his thumb over the head of his axe. "Maybe I'll get to use this."

"Be ready, friend." Jendara resisted the urge to touch her own handaxe. It would be ready when it was time. No point loosening it in her belt.

The old man led them about a mile along the track before he stopped. Jendara moved up beside him at the head of their line. The trees had thinned as they walked, and she recognized the sound of surf somewhere nearby.

"What's wrong?" she asked.

He looked at the sky a moment, then studied the ground ahead. "Tide's started to go out."

A cryptic answer. She waited for him to explain.

"Up yonder's Skinscour Causeway." He jabbed his finger in the direction of the ocean's soft rumbling. "Good sea urchins out there."

Jendara mulled over that information. The sea urchins might explain the path, she realized. It was probably a shortcut to a popular gathering site. And a causeway . . . she remembered what he'd said about the tide.

"How long before the causeway's above the water?"

He gave her a surprised look. "You been out there?"

"Just put two and two together. Will we have a long wait?"

Nol studied the sky again. "'Bout another hour."

"Okay." She turned to the others. "We'll make our way to the shore, break for a meal. There's a good chance this thing's gone over a causeway up ahead."

Jendara hunkered down on a rock and found Fambra's sandwiches in her belt pouch. She bit into the coarse brown bread and grunted at the sharp bite of homemade mustard and smoked herring, the leftovers of a dish from last night's late supper. The ale after the funeral had helped Jendara's mood, but not nearly as much as a meal with good people like Fambra and Sven.

The others pulled up fallen tree limbs or took seats on the ground, saving the biggest and smoothest rock for the old man. He sat down beside Jendara with a pleased sigh.

"Feels good to settle the old bones after a morning like this. Hell of a hunt we're on."

Jendara nodded, her mouth crammed full of sandwich.

"Reminds me of a bear hunt I went on 'bout thirty years ago. I was a real hotshot tracker back then. Used to travel all over, offering my services for big game, man hunts, what have you."

Jendara put down her sandwich, studying the man. After his performance on the trail, she readily believed his claim—even expected he might be understating his experience. His gear suggested some large paychecks in the past. The tooling on his belt could have only been done by a master leatherworker.

He saw her eyeing him, but continued without concern. "One hunt, down on Battlewall, a bear was wreaking some real havoc. Tearing things up. Attacking people. It even found its way into the city of Halgrim and ate a real famous raider. Not a good man, but well known. So the city guard put together a hunting party."

Nol paused to take a pinch of shredded dried fish from his belt pouch and chew it thoughtfully. Vorrin, sitting at Jendara's feet, squeezed her ankle. Rak leaned back on his hands, trying to look disinterested. His eyes, riveted to the old man's face, gave him away. Jendara tried not to smirk. She knew far too many boys like Rak, dead certain they knew everything and half-pissing themselves with the fear someone would find out just how little their brains really held.

"Lots of people joined the party, all good hunters. Me, to track. My sister Gerda—you might have met her back at the village—as a healer and archer. A lot of big men with reputations for toughness. One you know, Jendara. Your father."

Jendara stiffened in her seat.

Nol kept talking. "You all should have seen that man. Tall as they come, shoulders as broad as any two men's. And this big white beard, shiny like snow. He claimed he had to keep it covered when he went night fishing or the fish would jump out and bite his face!"

Everyone laughed except Jendara. A memory of her father leaped into her head, his funny brown mustache and white beard pressed against her cheek, his hand on her shoulder as she sighted on an elk. She'd been so eager her hands had shaken. But when he told her to let the arrow fly, it had flown true.

She came back to the present with a lump in her throat.

"Anyway, we spent three days wandering that island, sniffing at bear scat and rooting in the mud for tracks. We were just about to give up when the bear charged out of the woods and attacked us in our own camp! It lifted up a full-grown man and tossed him into the trees like it was throwing out an apple core."

Jendara looked around the clearing. Rak's mouth had fallen open. Everyone's eyes were on the old man.

"I wasn't sure whether to piss myself or run away, but your dad just jumped to his feet and *roared*. Roared like he was a big ol' bear himself! And the bear stopped in its tracks! Stopped cold. Gave us the chance to grab our gear and fight back. My sister wound up taking it down with an arrow through the eye, but we would have all died if it weren't for Erik White Beard and his roar."

Everyone laughed. Vorrin looked up at Jendara. "Did you know that story?"

"I'm not sure. Dad had lots of stories." She stuffed the last of her sandwich in her mouth to stop further questions.

Vorrin frowned. "I don't think you've told me any."

She shrugged.

"That's a crying shame," Nol said. "Erik was a good man. Everyone on the islands knew him. He could have been a king if he wanted to. But he was busy helping people and doing what he liked. Couldn't have done that in Halgrim, I s'pose."

Jendara smiled at the old man. "You think the tide's changed yet?"

He looked at the sky. "Reckon it might be low enough. Let's go see."

No one seemed to mind the change of topic, but Jendara didn't meet Vorrin's eyes as she got to her feet and gathered up her gear. She had never told him much about her family, and she wasn't going to start today.

Chapter Five
Skinscour Causeway

The air hung dead and heavy over the narrow spit of land connecting the main island of Flintyreach to the forested mound ahead. Jendara missed the wind. She scowled up at the gray sky and wished for sun, a breeze, even drizzle: anything besides that thick humidity and gloom. She looked back at the causeway.

"The tide's still going out," she said.

"Ayuh," Nol agreed. "Them rocks be slippery right about now."

A wave flopped over the neck of the causeway, leaving behind a layer of white foam that fizzed in the open air. Slick stuff, Jendara knew. They were going to have to wait a little longer.

"How long do you think it will take before it's safe?" Vorrin asked, with his usual talent for reading her mind—or her face, as he insisted.

Boruc suddenly pointed. "Is that smoke?"

Jendara squinted into the distance. A fine trickle of white rose up from the little forest across the causeway.

She might have missed it against the background clouds, but it stood out now like a bright ribbon. "Do you think there are any sea urchin collectors camped out there?"

Rak snorted. "You saw the entire village last night. Ain't none of us on that spit."

"Do trolls build campfires?" Vorrin asked.

"They fear fire," Boruc said. "It'd be a pretty rare troll to want a bonfire."

"All right." Jendara checked her gear. Wilfric's bow had a heavy draw; it was clearly meant for a larger archer than even a tall woman like herself. But she could make it work. She'd always been a good shot. "Everyone ready? Rak, you've got the pitch in case we find a troll?"

He rolled his eyes at her. "Course."

"All right. Let's move out slowly. Whoever's down there isn't going anyplace. The waves have the causeway pretty well cut off. We'll get in place, and when the rocks look safe enough, we'll cross."

They picked their way down the urchin gatherers' trail. The elements had scoured away the soil, leaving only the bare rocky bones of the island in steep descent to the causeway. Jendara picked her steps carefully. A slip here could send her tumbling into the ever-hungry ocean.

They reached the causeway. The waves leaped up the sides of the narrow finger of land, but they no longer lapped over the top. Nol waved Jendara behind him and took the first step.

"It's not too bad," he called back over his shoulder. "Just take it real slow."

Jendara nodded, although he had already turned back to watching the path, and took her first step onto the causeway. Her boot slid, just a little. Her heart leaped into her throat. It was one thing to be on a boat in the open sea—if she'd fallen overboard off the *Milady*, she could tread water until someone threw her a line. But out here, there were no lines. No swimming. The waves would smash her against the shore before she could even call for help.

She took a deep breath and kept her eyes on her feet. It wasn't a long walk. She'd be fine as long as she took it slowly. Nice and slowly.

It only felt like a few steps before she was at Nol's side and waiting for the others. Vorrin skidded a little and Jendara had to look away. She shrugged her shoulders up and down a few times, trying to work the nervous stiffness out of the muscles.

Vorrin cleared his throat. "You okay?"

She gave him an impetuous hug. "I've seen people who fell in places like this."

"Hurt pretty bad?"

She rubbed the back of her now-sore neck. "They didn't come out alive."

He looked back at the rocks he'd just crossed. "Glad I didn't think too much about that while I was out there."

"You made it look easy," Boruc complained. "I thought I'd fall in half a dozen times."

Vorrin laughed. "What can I say? I grew up on a boat. I just imagined it was a gangplank standing between me and dry ground—and a tavern," he added with a wink.

Vorrin's stab at humor worked. Everyone smiled, and even Jendara felt herself relax.

Nol looked at the sky. "The tide should be at its lowest in about two hours. I'd like to be finished with this island before then."

Everyone agreed, loudly, and the group set out. Jendara stooped to study a branch of a nearby tree, recognizing the blue-gray needles of a spruce.

"Jendara."

She looked up to see Nol squatting beside a clump of tiny herbs. She recognized the fronds of yarrow among the greens, but drew a blank on the others. The indentation at the edge of the plant group, however, was more than familiar.

"That looks about the same size as the footprints we saw back on the trail," she said.

He nodded. "Pretty sure whatever came down that trail is here now."

Jendara scanned the skies, but now that they had entered the forest, the faint line of smoke had disappeared. "Too many trees to see anything."

"Can't be far ahead. I'd say if we cut left, we'll run into it."

Jendara unslung her bow. "Ready weapons."

The forest thickened around the hunting party, the dense spruce boughs forcing them to stoop. The sun's light, already filtered by the thick gray clouds, waned as the trees knotted more closely together. The air clung to Jendara's skin, clammy and heavy with the scent of the sea. No birds sang. No creatures rustled in the ferns.

"I don't like this," Vorrin breathed.

"Me, neither."

Nol hesitated. "Do you smell that?"

Jendara sniffed. "Smoke."

"And wet ashes. Our quarry's moving." Nol rushed forward, knocking back branches with the tip of his spear. The group hurried to catch up with the old man.

He burst out into a scooped hollow of earth, just catching himself on a knotted bunch of roots. The immense tangle massed around the snapped body of a very tall spruce tree. Its limbs stuck out everywhere. "A windfall," he gasped. He grabbed his knees for a minute to steady himself and catch his breath.

Jendara examined the root ball of the fallen tree. The roots had spread themselves over an area wider than she was tall, and now they towered above her, pried up out of the ground and revealed for all to see. The tree must have fallen in the spring storm season, for nothing yet grew in the soil clinging to its massive root system. The earth still looked raw in the dug-out hollow the roots had torn out of the ground.

Nearest the tree, the earth looked smoother, compacted in one neat oval that stood out to Jendara's trained eye. She nodded at Nol. "Think it slept here?"

He touched the soil, crumbling a bit between his fingers. "I'd stake money on it."

"Here's our campfire," Vorrin said, his voice grim. He nudged something with the tip of his spear. "Dara, you'd better take a look at this."

She slipped between Rak and Boruc to the little campfire. Situated between two massive limbs of the spruce, the fire had been larger than she'd expected, the ground scraped clean to keep the fire in line. The kind of fire a seasoned outdoorsman might make.

"No troll built this," she murmured. She picked up an abandoned stick of firewood and noticed a few strands of coarse dark hair caught in the splintered end. "But this looks like the hair they saw back at the quarry."

"Hmmn." Vorrin pointed at the clump he'd nudged out of the ashes. "What do you think about that?"

Jendara leaned closer. She smelled something now: a whiff of scorched meat. Boruc squatted beside her, watching closely as she reached for a stick and scraped off some of the ashes.

"Shit!" Boruc threw himself backward. "Is that a foot?"

Jendara shoved it away. The grisly thing flopped over. The breeze stirred, blowing away a wisp of ash.

"It wasn't burned," Vorrin mused. "But it was mostly buried in the ashes."

Nol squatted beside Jendara to better look at the thing. "Like someone was trying to hide it?"

"I got to piss," Rak blurted, stumbling into the woods. He didn't make it far before the sounds of retching began.

Jendara used her stick to turn the foot around to study the thing's stump. "It was removed with a blade," she said. "The bone looks sheared through."

"The fat pad at the base of the heel's been removed," Nol noted. "Bitten clean off."

Jendara got to her feet. "Whatever we're following, it's been eating human flesh." She dug a hollow in the fire pit and pushed the foot into it. "We can pile rocks over it. At least keep the animals from digging it up."

They began building a cairn, stacking the rocks quickly. No one spoke.

"You guys!" Rak crashed back into the clearing, nearly falling over a tree limb. "You guys! I saw something." He paused to catch his breath.

"What is it?" Vorrin got to his feet.

"Something big. And furry. I couldn't really see it. It took off too fast." Rak shook his head. "I don't think it was a troll."

"Let's move out," Jendara said. "Good thing you saw it, Rak."

The boy grabbed up the pot of pitch and hurried to catch up with her. "It started moving, and pretty fast. Headed for the end of the island."

They moved quickly, unhampered by the need to look for footprints or clues. They had a real sighting of the creature. The thing that had killed the quarry workers was just ahead.

But was it really the thing that had killed them, or just some kind of scavenger? Maybe it *was* a troll, a pathetic troll reduced to scavenging. That could happen to an orphaned young creature. Hell, even a bear could have wandered into the quarry, drawn to the smell of the dead.

Jendara thought about the boulder, tumbling down the hill toward her. That hadn't been the work of a bear. Neither had that fire pit back there. Something humanoid had been out here in the woods.

The crash of waves on rocks was clearly audible here, and in a second, the group broke through the edge of the spruce forest. Jendara's eyes smarted at the sudden burst of sunlight. Then her heart sped. On the rocks ahead, someone raced toward the end of the peninsula, his long legs pumping and fur cloak trailing behind him. Definitely human.

"That's him!" Rak shrieked.

Jendara reached for her quiver. She didn't want to kill the man, just slow him down. They needed to know what he'd seen back at that quarry.

"Hey, you!" Vorrin bellowed. "Stop!"

The man dropped to his knees and then leaped up, suddenly looking thicker, hairier. Jendara blinked. Had her eyes been dazzled by the light? The man-thing hit the end of the island and skidded for a second on the damp rocks. Its shape stood out, as bulky as a six-foot-tall black bear.

Jendara slid to a stop on the lichen covered rocks, nocked her arrow, softened her breathing, and let fly.

The arrow flew true, slicing through the air and striking just between the bear-man's shoulder blades. The beast gave a pained growl, and then its body toppled forward, hitting the edge of the rocks and tumbling down the edge of the island.

"Catch it!" Jendara shouted, breaking into a run, but it was already too late. Vorrin and Boruc stopped at the edge of the cliff, peering down into the sea. When Jendara stopped herself beside them, she could see the surf pounding down below. The ocean had swallowed up the beast.

"That was the bear that jumped me back at the quarry," Vorrin said. "It was the right size, for sure."

"Bear?" Nol shook his head. "Look." He pointed to the ground, where a worn leather moccasin had caught between two rocks.

"No bear made that campfire," Boruc reminded them. "That had to have been a man. And he didn't want us to catch him."

"So it was a man wearing a bearskin cloak," Jendara said. "Or . . ." She broke off, thinking. "He was so strong and built so strangely. I mean, I really thought he was a bear or some kind of monster. Could it be some new kind of troll we've never seen?"

No one had an answer. The sea roiled below. Nothing, man or beast, bobbed in the rough water.

"If it was a man, what was he thinking?" Vorrin mused. "He ran over here like he thought he had a way out."

"He waited out there in the woods a long time," Nol reminded them. "Almost as if he was waiting for something in particular."

"Why would he do that?" Boruc asked.

"The tide change, maybe," Jendara mused.

Nol stroked his beard. No one said anything, but they all followed his gaze out to the deep water between the islands.

"He could have been waiting for a boat," he said, very softly. "A boat on a schedule."

Jendara stared at the horizon. She didn't see any boats, but that didn't mean they weren't out there. A fog bank was already moving in across the sea.

"Let's get back to the village," she said.

Chapter Six
Sea Snakes

The group made its way through the spruce forest in silence. It was impossible to make sense of the man she'd shot back on those rocks. Was it a man? It had run like a man. It had made a campfire. Yet it had certainly sounded like a bear when it fell, and it *looked* like a bear at the moment she sighted it. Jendara tried to remember what its ears had looked like. Did it have the small rounded ears of a bear? Her memory refused to show her anything except its black silhouette.

They followed the path down to the narrow bottleneck of the causeway. The waves pattered around the base of the rocky finger of land, lower than they had been. The tide neared its lowest ebb.

"Maybe it was some kind of gorilla," Vorrin suggested.

"Gorilla?" Rak scoffed. "What's that?"

"A creature from Garund," Vorrin said. "I saw one once in a market down in Katapesh. They're kind of like men. More like men than a bear or a troll."

"Do they use fire, though?" Nol asked.

"I don't know," Vorrin said. "I only saw the one, and it was in a cage."

"What about a skinwalker?" Jendara asked, thinking of Yul's stories.

This time Rak laughed outright. "Now you're just messing with me. I'll buy that maybe there's something called a gorilla down in Garund, but nobody out of diapers still believes in skinwalkers."

"Watch yourself, boy," Vorrin growled.

"Gorilla, bear, troll—all I know is that Jendara hit it, and I'm wore out." Boruc laid down his spear to rub the back of his neck. "Any chance of a rest break?"

The spear rolled sideways. Boruc lunged for it, but the tip plunged into a crack between the rocks. Boruc swore.

Nol laughed. "Maybe you should go out hunting more often. Grab your spear, Boruc. Let's hurry home so we can drink."

Boruc tugged on the end of the spear. "Thing's stuck."

Rak sighed. "Can we just get moving?"

Boruc pulled harder. "Must be wedged in the rocks." He got onto his belly, peering down into the depths. "This gap goes an awful long way down."

"Give it a twist," Jendara suggested. "Probably just that flange on the iron point, catching on something. Turn it, it'll come out."

He grunted. "Can't twist it." He gasped. "Something's yanking on it!"

Jendara stepped closer. "What?"

There was a splintering sound, and the end of Boruc's spear flew up out of the crack.

"Run!" Jendara shouted, but she was too late.

The green head of a massive snake popped up out of the ground, its mouth closing on Boruc's arm. Jendara grabbed the back of his tunic and yanked, but he lurched forward, his arm disappearing down the crevice in the rocks.

"Help!" Jendara bellowed. Her feet slid on the still-damp rocks.

Vorrin grabbed her wrist. Boruc screamed and pushed himself up off the ground, the muscles in his neck bulging hugely. Vorrin managed to get his other arm around Jendara's waist, pulling back on her as she pulled on Boruc's tunic.

The snake exploded out of the hole in the ground, its scales shimmering blue and green—sea colors. It reared back to strike at Boruc's face.

Jendara felt his tunic slip out of her grip.

The man ducked under the snake's attack but kept falling forward, no longer anchored by Jendara and Vorrin. He hit the edge of the causeway and tumbled down the cliff side.

"Boruc!" Vorrin launched himself across the rocks, thrusting his spear down into the rocks at the last second. It held. Vorrin swung out over the edge of the rocks.

The sea snake struck at Jendara, but her sword was ready. She slashed at the creature, but the blade slid off it scales and only turned its head. She doubled-up her grip. As the snake twisted back around at her, her steel scored a long gash down its side. It spat with pain.

Jendara risked a glance behind her. She didn't have much room, and the snake moved fast. She guessed it was twice as long as she was tall, its girth almost the same as hers. Big and dangerous.

It twisted left, and she parried its move, her blade not quite touching its side. With a hiss, it struck out at her again, this time shooting in low, aiming for her legs.

She was ready for it. Her sword bit through the scales just behind its head, severing its spinal cord. She danced to her right, just missing the spray of hot blood. A rock rolled beneath her boot, but she leaped over it, coming down beside Vorrin's spear.

"Vorrin!"

"I'm all right," he called, his voice thin.

He'd kept his hold on the spear, and his other hand gripped Boruc's scraped and bloodied hand. The two looked up at her, each pressed firmly to the rock wall. The ash shaft groaned beneath their weight.

"A little help, maybe?" Vorrin asked.

She threw herself to her belly and stuck out a hand, digging her free hand into a crack in the rocky ground. The spear's shaft crackled ominously. With a grunt, Boruc scrabbled up the rocky wall a few inches more. He loosened his grip on Vorrin to grab her wrist. For a moment, he didn't move. Then he gritted his teeth and found another toehold. His whole face went white.

"You okay?" Jendara asked.

"Think I broke my leg." His fingers dug into her wrist as he grabbed for the stones at the top of the causeway.

She sagged a little when he released her and swung himself up onto the walkway. She reached out to Vorrin. His fingers closed on hers just as the spear, with one final protest, snapped in half.

Vorrin scrambled up the rocks and lay back on the ground, panting. Jendara rubbed her wrist surreptitiously against her shoulder. Boruc was not a small man. She'd have bruises for sure. Vorrin had been holding up Boruc's weight a lot longer than she had. His arms must ache.

"Big creature for an island snake," Nol noted.

She felt a moment's anger that the older man hadn't helped her with the snake or Boruc's rescue. Her lips tightened.

He looked up at her from where he knelt beside the beheaded sea snake. "You move awful fast," he said.

She remembered then that he was older than her father and felt the anger subside. She was fast. And not everyone's skills lay in fighting. She shook out her sore wrist and joined Nol beside the creature.

"A shame we had to kill it," he said. "It's a beauty. And our clan symbol."

Jendara groaned inwardly. She had a feeling a certain clan wisewoman wouldn't like the fact they'd killed such a creature.

Jendara plopped herself onto the stairs leading up to the Alstone Village meeting hall and let her head fall back. The trip from causeway to village had taken four hours. They had to build a travois to drag Boruc through the forest, and it had been rough going. Everyone had taken turns, but she'd tried not to let Nol work too hard. He looked pale as he sank down beside her.

"I'm getting too old for this," he muttered, rubbing his shoulder. "I thought we'd never make it past the quarry."

Jendara thought of the steep rocks and zigzagging track they'd managed, and made a face. They'd given up dragging at that point and flat out carried the man. He'd tried to walk, but when Jendara saw the blood seeping through his pants, she'd forced him to stop. It was a bad, bad break.

Gerda emerged from the meeting hall. "I see you managed to seriously injure Boruc."

Rak jumped to his feet. "We were attacked by a sea snake!" His eyes shone a little in the late afternoon sunlight. "And Jendara killed it, but Boruc got knocked over a cliff. He would have died if Vorrin hadn't caught him."

Vorrin smiled fondly at the young man. Jendara covered her own grin. Maybe this hunting trip had been good for him.

Gerda raised an eyebrow. "A sea snake?"

But Jendara didn't have a chance to answer. Wilfric waved at her and strode toward the hall. "Any luck?" He extended a basket that smelled wonderfully of bread.

Jendara grabbed a piece and bit off a hunk. "Some. We ran into someone out there. We tried to catch him, but he fell over a cliff before we could interrogate him."

Wilfric frowned. "A man?"

"Well . . ."

"It looked kind of like a bear!" Rak interjected. Wilfric raised an eyebrow and the boy flushed. "It looked like a man, too. Kind of."

Jendara shrugged. "I don't know exactly what it was. It looked something like a man and something like a bear. We found some of its hair next to a campfire, so that suggests it was manlike."

"And you killed it?" Wilfric asked, disappointment sounding in his voice.

Rak grinned. "She did! She shot it with an arrow, and the arrow went all the way through its chest. It would have died for sure if it hadn't toppled over the cliff."

Wilfric combed his fingers through his beard thoughtfully. "Werebear, you think?"

Gerda shook her head. "Not likely. They're very moral creatures. After all, their shape is a blessing from the ancestors."

"What if it was rabid?" Rak asked.

Gerda frowned. "That's always possible, I suppose. But unlikely. What happened at that quarry was pure evil."

"Evil, and now washed out to sea," Jendara said. "I guess we'll never really know what happened, or what the creature was."

"But it sounds like it's probably dead," Wilfric mused. "That's good. I have to congratulate you on your hunt, Jendara. We didn't find a single sign beyond that spoor. I should have listened to you."

Jendara smiled. "Thank you, Wilfric. But you're the expert on creatures on your own island. You did what you thought was right."

She put out her hand, but Gerda pushed it aside, scowling around her at the tired hunters. "Shooting a strange creature is all well and good, but you mentioned a sea snake. An attacking sea snake."

"Yes," Nol said. "A good sized male, very territorial—"

She cut him off. "A *sea snake*. Don't you see? The totem of our clan. And this morning, I offered you all the blessing of the clan spirits." She shook her finger at Jendara. "But you wouldn't take it, no, no. Not you. Our clan spirits' blessing wasn't good enough for you."

"What are you talking about, Gerda?" Nol snapped. Jendara remembered that Gerda was his sister.

"I'm talking about the anger of the clan spirits. I'm talking about vengeance." The old woman spat on the ground. "You brought this upon yourself. You should be the one in there with your leg in plaster."

Jendara felt the blood pound in her ears. She dug her fingernails into the tough woolen fabric of her pants and bit off the retort at the tip of her tongue.

Rak snorted. "You think that snake was sent from the clan spirits? How does that even make sense? Jendara shot and killed the creature that ate a third of our clan! The spirits ought to throw her a party!"

Wilfric cleared his throat. "I don't know about the spirits, but I do believe a party is in order. Tonight, my wife and I will feast you all. There's plenty of last summer's loganberry brandy, too."

Jendara forced herself to laugh. "I can't say no to brandy."

Wilfric put his hand on Gerda's shoulder. "Gerda. I have a few questions for you about my still. I know you're an expert, so if you could take a look at it." He led her away.

Jendara rubbed her eyes. Every inch of her sagged with tiredness, and she only felt more exhausted after the confrontation with Gerda. That superstitious old biddy. That kind of attitude made Jendara want to vomit.

Rak rubbed his chin. "Do you think Wilfric would still be throwing this party if he knew what happened to that spear he lent Vorrin?"

Nol laughed. "Let's not tell him."

Chapter Seven
Blackbirds

Jendara tapped on the front door of Fambra's house and slipped inside without waiting for an answer. The fisher and her family had already made their way to Wilfric's party; it was their unwilling guest Jendara hoped to see.

She was in luck. Boruc blinked up at her from a makeshift bed beside the fireplace, his eyes droopy from the painkilling concoction Gerda had given him.

"Hey," she said. "How you feeling?"

He pushed himself up on his elbows. "Well, I don't hurt half as much as I did. As a healer, Gerda sure knows her stuff."

Jendara pushed a mound of pillows and furs under him so he could sit more upright and he sagged back, clearly exhausted. He managed a smile. "Thanks."

"Do you need anything? Food? Water? Gerda already warned us you can't have any of Wilfric's brandy. I guess the combination of herbs she gave you doesn't really agree with liquor."

"Figures." He closed his eyes for a moment. "That stuff makes it hard to stay awake."

"I'll just let you get back to sleep."

"Wait a minute." He coughed, and Jendara hurried to the cask of water on the kitchen counter to get him a dipperful. He nodded his thanks.

"Jendara, I need to ask you a big favor."

She studied the dipper. "What's that?"

"I can't go back to the quarry, not after what happened. No way I could sleep in that house again. And with my leg like this, I can't do much. I was thinking maybe I could go back to my family's place. Over on Sorind."

She sat down on the hearth beside his bed. "Why exactly did you leave Sorind?"

He twisted his face. "Lots of reasons. One part's the business—no stone better in all the islands than Flintyreach stone. But mostly because, well, you know how Yul and Morul are. I'm not sure Sorind was big enough for all three of us."

"I think I understand." She nodded, more to herself than to Boruc. She'd had a nearly famous father that half the people of the islands still remembered. Of course she could understand needing to get out of the shadow of two larger-than-life big brothers to find his own place in the world.

She brought her attention back to the big ginger-haired man. "So you're asking if we can take you back to Sorind when we leave tomorrow?"

He nodded. "I could pay with my carvings. They're still back at my house at the quarry, but they're all yours."

Jendara felt her heart pound. "I just have to go get them."

"Right. And if you wouldn't mind bringing back some of my other gear. When I get back to Sorind, I'm still going to need to earn my keep."

"Of course." She smiled at him. "You can count on me."

She hurried out of the house, suddenly very eager for morning to come. With all the hunters traveling through the quarry yesterday, she wasn't likely to find any untrampled evidence—but that didn't mean she didn't want to look. Wilfric and the rest of his clan might be content with the comfort of a dead possible-werebear. She wanted the truth.

Sleep was a long time in coming. The next morning, Jendara found herself groggy and bleary-eyed as she headed up the cart road to the quarry for the third time. She urged Wilfric's mule forward. It tossed its head and took a balky step forward, then hesitated. She couldn't blame it for being spooked. They'd left Alstone Village before the sun had even appeared on the horizon, and now, in the still-dark, misty woods, Jendara felt cut off from the world. Every shadow hovering in the corner of her eye made her reach for her handaxe. She reminded herself that she had wanted to come alone. It would help her focus on the task at hand.

"It's okay, critter," she called out. "Let's get this done." She flicked the reins and it plodded onward.

They were nearly there now. She recognized a lingonberry bush she'd crushed during their struggle with Boruc's travois. Just a few more yards before the path curved and she could see the quarry.

The mule made a soft, distressed sound and stopped in its tracks. Jendara cursed to herself. She should have expected this. After all, if she could see the quarry, the mule would certainly be able to smell it. Even two days later, the place must stink of spilled blood.

She jumped down from the wagon and studied the track. Bunches of smaller ferns flanked the dirt road, clamoring for the extra sun afforded by the clear space. She uprooted one and brushed the dirt off its root. The sweet scent of licorice rose up.

"Hey, buddy." She held the root in front of the mule's nose, piercing the root with her thumbnail to release more of the powerful smell. With any luck, the aroma would overpower any other scent. "Come on." With her free hand, she took hold of the mule's harness and led it forward. It shuffled along, stretching its neck toward the aromatic fern.

They rounded the last corner and the quarry workers' quarters appeared below them. Jendara had missed the cottage on the western side of the work area on her last visit, but she saw it now, and led the mule toward its wattle fence. It looked as snug and sweet as her own cottage, built into the side of the hill to minimize the winter winds. A kitchen garden bloomed in the front, bees already bumbling over the borage and mint flowers. Boruc's house was a fine house.

She felt a moment's sadness for him. He had made a good place for himself here on the island. It was too bad the massacre had driven him away from it.

There was only one room inside the cottage, and Boruc had given her good instructions. It took less than twenty minutes to pack up and load all of Boruc's gear and to find the crates he'd already loaded for sale on the mainland. She slid the crates into the wagon and wondered what today might be like if her trip to Flintyreach had gone as planned. She'd be well on her way to Varisia by now. She wouldn't have met Fambra or Nol, and she would never have heard Gerda's grating voice.

And she wouldn't have seen nineteen dead men and women, half-eaten by some kind of monster.

She scratched the mule behind the ears. It grumbled a little, stretching its neck to reach Boruc's rose bushes. It seemed calm enough, but then, the wind was blowing in its face. It couldn't smell the bunkhouse or mess hall behind it.

But Jendara knew what was back there. Wilfric's men had collected the dead, but they hadn't stayed long enough at the quarry to do any real cleaning. All the blood and bits still lay there, waiting for the beetles and flies to finish tidying up.

She gave the mule one last pat. All the mess was still there—and so were the clues she needed. She strode toward the closest building, the mess hall where she'd seen the overturned milk bottle and realized someone, or something, had just left the building. She paused. The door stood open, a long thin mouth into blackness.

Anything could be in there.

The door creaked on its hinges, stirred by the wind.

She hurried back to Boruc's house and snatched a lantern off the mantel. She wasn't going to find anything in the dark.

Back outside the mess hall door, she fumbled for her flint striker and lit the lantern. The comforting smell of cheap whale oil filled her nose. She let herself hope the strong-smelling stuff might help cover the stink of three day-old offal. She raised the lantern and stepped inside.

The lantern didn't light all the mess hall, but its wobbling golden glow pushed the darkness back into the corners. The sound of flies buzzing in the kitchen was very loud. Jendara turned in a slow circle, trying to imagine what had happened in this space. An overturned bench at the farthest table suggested panic, an attempt to flee. But there was very little blood here. Just the trail that led out the door.

She peered into the kitchen. So much blood. Something terrible had happened here, great violence done quickly to several people. She waved curious flies away from her face, but they covered every surface. A rat ran over the toe of her boot. There were simply too many vermin to get a clear picture of what had occurred here. With a shudder, she backed out of the kitchen. She'd only go back in there if she had to.

Once she was outdoors again, she studied the area. Gray dawn didn't provide many details.

She tried to remember what the scene had looked like when she and Vorrin had first arrived. She closed her eyes. There'd been the man just beside the cart road, front and center when viewed from above. She tried to let her inner vision pass over him without recollecting the details of the stake plunged into his gut, emerging from his open mouth. She couldn't.

Impaled, just like her father. Impaling wasn't an ordinary method for murder. It didn't just kill a man; it left him behind as a message. What were these murderers trying to say when they left this man hanging on a skewer?

Her feet crunched on gravel, searching for the hole where the post had been planed. Wilfric's men must have taken down the stake, but a bloody stain marked the spot. She squatted beside it, moving the lantern over the ground. A meaty, rotten smell rose up from the ground.

She turned her head and waited for her stomach to settle. It was all too easy when envisioning that poor man to make his face her father's. Her father had been the only man in their tiny village left mostly intact. A spear had run him through and he'd dangled six inches off the ground, his weight tearing open his abdomen. But he'd gone out fighting. She had his axe to remind her of that.

Jendara brought her attention back to the bloody spot. When she had found her father, he'd been dead several days. The vultures and coyotes and bugs had gotten a good start on their work, and it was hard to make out the details of the scene. It had rained once, washing away tracks. She hadn't had a chance of catching the devils that wiped out her clan.

But it hadn't rained here. And while at least a dozen people had gone over the area yesterday, they hadn't gotten too close to the actual death sites. No one had walked here except the men who'd taken down the body. The imprint of the stake was deep and clear, the blood thick and unstirred. She knew she was being too hopeful, but she couldn't persuade herself that this particular spot was unimportant.

Something glinted at the bottom of the stake hole.

Jendara pulled her belt knife free and pushed it down inside the hole, catching a black strand on its tip. She lifted it carefully, holding her breath.

In the light of the lantern, the black strand revealed itself as a long string of braided leather, the kind used for necklaces. A bit of black soapstone hung from it. She touched the edges. Sharp, recently broken.

She dug the tip of her knife around the stake hole, feeling it scratch against something stony. She wished she could reach inside, but the opening was too small for her fingers. She twisted and turned the knife, feeling something balance on its blade. She eased it up.

It was the rest of the soapstone charm. The ground must have been soft when the stake was dug in it. The charm had stayed surprisingly intact, except for the break at the bored hole where the cord had run through. Even without holding it in the lantern's light, she would have known that shape: a crow, with its wings outstretched. The traveler's good luck charm.

She turned it over and gasped. A tiny pair of fiery orange eyes winked up at her. She brought the lantern closer, wondering at the play of the light on the miniature orange jewels. Fire opals.

Her heart skipped over itself. Her first trip out to sea, she'd visited a market where an old woman sold charms worked with beautiful jewels. Jendara had bought her sister Kalira one of the soapstone crows, one with fire opals for eyes, and the girl had loved it.

Jendara's fingers closed tightly over the figurine.

Someone had been here, on Flintyreach, wearing this soapstone crow. Someone, possibly the impaled man, struggling with his attackers, had broken the cord and the necklace had fallen to ground, only to be smashed by the butt end of the impaling stake. Then the necklace's broken bits had been pushed down into the ground, protected by the rain-softened soil.

She sat back on her heels and hugged her knees to her chest, puzzling over the clues. The killers here at Alstone Quarry had killed and eaten their victims and had even impaled one—just like the attackers who'd destroyed her village and impaled her father. But here at Alstone Quarry, no one seemed to be missing. When Jendara had gone through her own village, there had been many bodies unaccounted for in Crow's Nest, including her sister's. Otherwise, the attacks were painfully similar. Was it a coincidence, finding this necklace here? Here, where the victims has been mutilated in just the same fashion as those of Crow's Nest?

Jendara tried to throttle a faint feeling of hope, but it kept fluttering inside her chest. Maybe she would finally be able to revenge her family's destruction.

Jendara gave up driving and walked beside the mule the last half mile of the journey home. She needed to move, to get out of her head and into her body. There was just too much filling her memory, too much horror in the past. Walking beside the mule, which kept biting at her arm, kept her mind occupied.

After what felt like hours, they passed out of the spruce forest. Jendara stood still a moment, enjoying the wind whipping off the ocean. The salt spray smelled clean, the air fresh. A few fishing boats bobbed in the harbor, heading out toward deeper water.

"Jendara!"

Jendara started. She hadn't even noticed Fambra standing at the tree line, a bucket in hand. Jendara gave a half-hearted wave. "What are you doing up so early?" she asked.

Fambra raised her bucket. "Collecting spruce pitch. Handy for sealing birch buckets and oilcloth jackets." She closed the distance. "Sven's shoulder is feeling better, so he and Rowri took the boat out this morning by themselves for an early crabbing run. They ought to be back any minute. And you?"

Jendara nodded back at the wagon. "Getting some of Boruc's things. He's coming with us to Sorind, you know. To be with his family."

"I'll miss him." The freckled woman studied Jendara's face closely. "Was it hard? I don't know if I could have gone. Those people . . . well, what was done to them was an abomination."

"Yes." Jendara felt a sudden burning in her palm and realized she'd been squeezing the soapstone crow so tightly its wings were biting into her flesh. She shook out her hand, frowning at the red welts across her calluses.

Fambra held out her hand. "What's that you've found?"

Jendara closed her hand quickly, then relented and held the pendant out to Fambra. "Something I found at the quarry."

Fambra turned it over. "It looks like a traveler's pendant, but these gems are really amazing."

Jendara nodded.

Fambra looked more closely. "And it's not new. If you look at the back side, it's clearly darker, as if it's picked up oils from its wearer's skin. Soapstone's fairly absorbent, but that still takes years of constant wearing."

Jendara stroked the mule's nose, wondering if she ought to tell Fambra just what the necklace meant to her. She bit her lip.

Fambra watched her, curious. "I know we don't know each other very well," she said, "but I'm a good listener." She held out the necklace.

Jendara took it and held it up to the sun for a second. "I don't mind telling you. This necklace—I gave my sister a necklace like this. Same gems and everything. But my sister disappeared almost fifteen years ago."

Fambra put down her bucket. "And you think it's the same necklace?"

"How could it not be? Fambra, my sister disappeared when our village was wiped out by people—or things— that cooked and ate at least four of their victims. And my father was impaled, just like one of the men up at the quarry."

"That doesn't sound like coincidence." Fambra's eyebrows drew themselves together as she mulled over Jendara's story. "Did you ever figure out what happened to your family?"

"I suspected the Kalvamen immediately. After all, they're known cannibals. It's not common for them to leave their island, but it happened in stories."

Fambra picked up her bucket and waved for Jendara to follow her. "So what did you do?"

"I was working on the *Milady* at that point. Not yet married, but close to the captain. We sailed for Kalva and even made an expedition into one of their villages. I never saw signs of my sister, but the Kalvamen drove us off the island. I wish I could have at least found her killer."

"You're *sure* it was humans, and not a creature?" Fambra reached for the mule's reins and tied them off at her own garden fence.

"I found a man's hand." Jendara's face twisted, remembering the hand her father's axe had pinned to the wall. "An ordinary man's hand, but I can't believe ordinary men could become so savage. No, the men of Kalva are my best guess."

Fambra made a quizzical face. "No one's even seen a Kalvaman in generations. Did you see any ships? Can't pillage without ships."

Jendara jammed the crow necklace back in her belt pouch. "No. But they could have hidden them. The island's riddled with caves."

Fambra raised her palm high. "Just asking." She opened the garden gate and held it for Jendara. "What about the creature you shot out on the causeway? That didn't sound like a Kalvaman."

Jendara shook her head. "I don't know. I thought it was a man when it was running, but then it looked like a bear. Vorrin said it was." She sighed. "I can't ignore the evidence I've seen. We're not dealing with some stupid troll or an animal. I don't know what did this. But—" she broke off, glancing out to the open sea beyond Flintyreach's harbor. She lowered her voice. "But I do know one thing: I'm not sure that creature was dead when it hit the water. My shot was good, but it could have missed the heart."

One hand on her door's latch, Fambra stopped. "I don't like the sound of that."

"Me, neither. If I were you, I'd sleep with my belt knife under my pillow and all the shutters latched."

"I already do," Fambra said, with a wry smile.

Jendara waved goodbye to Fambra and Wilfric and the rest of the villagers who had come to see the *Milady* off. It was a surprisingly large group to say goodbye to a bunch of strangers. The thought made Jendara wave harder.

"Nice folks," Vorrin said.

Jendara looked over at him. He gave the group at the docks another casual wave before turning back to inspect the ship.

"Everything looks shipshape," he mused. "Even if we hit bad weather, we should be just fine."

Jendara watched the figures diminish to doll-size. "Are you expecting bad weather?" She hadn't noticed any clouds on the horizon, and the ocean looked flat.

"At the rate we're going? On our way home from the mainland, we're definitely going to see serious weather. Real, nasty, wintry weather."

She turned to face him. "It's not that bad, is it?" She grinned, keeping her voice light.

Vorrin gave an exasperated sigh. "Look, while you and my brother were out enjoying a pirate's life, I was doing this. Running cargo and travelers around all the west coast. So yes, I think I know what the weather will be like off the coast of Varisia at the end of autumn."

She had never heard him speak so coldly of Ikran. Her eyes narrowed. "It wasn't just fun and games, Vorrin. We risked our lives every day."

"You risked your lives attacking ships like this one," he snapped. "Now you're trying to make yourself feel better by leading a decent life. That doesn't mean you have to go out of your way to solve everybody else's problems."

She took a step backward, her hand balling into an automatic fist. "What's that supposed to mean?"

Vorrin winced. "I didn't mean to say it like that. It's just . . . ever since we came to these islands, you've been really focused on helping other people. Like when you first met Yul and fought those goblins. You didn't have to get involved in that."

"They took Kran," she spat.

"You still stayed to fight after we got him back, but okay—bad example. But back there at the quarry? You didn't have to go on that hunt. Look at Boruc. His leg is going to take months to heal. That could have happened to you or me. Don't you care about *us*?"

"We can handle ourselves." She spun on her heel and began to march across the deck. "Or at least I can."

Jendara slumped onto the deck rail, glaring at the sea. She rubbed the back of her hand, feeling the black ink of her tattoo standing out from her skin. It always responded to her anger. When she'd been a pirate, praying to Besmara before every battle, she'd reveled in the sensation of the jolly roger rising, flaring like her bad temper. But now . . . ever since Kran had been born . . .

She stopped rubbing the tattoo and gripped the deck rail. It had gotten easier to control her anger, but that didn't mean it wasn't still work.

A hand touched her shoulder. She glanced up at Vorrin, rage and shame filling her in equal measure.

"I'm sorry," he said.

And just like that, the rage was gone. "I'm sorry too," she blurted.

"Look," he said, "I grew up on the wharves of Kintargo. It wasn't exactly a tight community. You people have got something special here on these islands, something I don't quite understand. But I can see it's worth fighting for."

"Thanks," she said, and looked back at the sea. They were almost out of the harbor now. Any minute Vorrin would order the crew to raise sails for full speed, and they'd be winging their way to Sorind. But if they swung around just a bit to the west, they could make Crow's Nest this afternoon.

She opened her belt pouch and pulled out the crow pendant. "I know I've been really focused on this quarry business. And yes, it's because what happened reminds me so much of what happened to my family. If you could have seen the village . . ." She trailed off. After seeing the massacre at the quarry, she had no doubt Vorrin could imagine what the pillaged village had looked like.

"I'm sorry," he said again.

"It's not your fault." She held up the pendant. "There's more." She pointed out the unusual fire opal eyes and explained about the pendant she'd purchased for Kalira.

Vorrin raised his eyebrows. "You think whoever committed the murders at the quarry are the same people who killed your father and sister?"

"Yes. The way the bodies showed signs of being eaten, the impalement of a single victim, and now this necklace—I don't have any doubts that it's the same group of people. Or creatures," she added, remembering the strange hairy thing she had shot on the causeway. There were plenty of creatures in the world capable of organizing brutal attacks on small settlements.

"When you put it like that, I see your point. But . . . you're working to put your past behind you, Dara. You cut all your old pirate ties, except for a few of the old crew members like Tam and Glayn. You don't even worship Besmara anymore. You've got an all-new life. Chasing these . . . *things* down isn't going to bring your family back."

Jendara's hand fell to the axe in her belt. It felt heavy today, its weight digging into her hip. She squeezed its handle.

"I killed Ikran's killer for revenge," she said. "I tried to track down my family's murderer for the same reason, but I failed. You're right that I'm trying to put that part of me aside. I don't want to feel that raging fiend inside my veins, the one who so gladly made offerings to Besmara and rejoiced in violence. This isn't about revenge anymore." She caught Vorrin's eyes and held them. "This is about stopping these things before they hurt anyone else."

Vorrin stared. Finally, he gave a curt nod. "All right. That makes sense."

"Now if only we knew how to find them."

They both fell silent as the cabin boy hurried by with the ship's spyglass clutched close to his chest. It was kept safely stowed belowdecks while the *Milady* was in harbor, but the navigator would need it to make it safely to Sorind. Jendara glanced up at the helm. Tam stood at the wheel. Like Jendara, he'd grown up in the Ironbound Archipelago. He knew the area so well he didn't need any calculations or reckoning to find his way around.

Jendara's eyes widened. Navigation was all about connecting two points. Maybe she could navigate her way through this mystery. "What if there's a connection between the two islands that we're just not seeing? If we can figure out that connection, maybe we can figure out what's motivating the killers and figure out what they'll do next."

"It's worth a shot," he agreed.

"Then we need to go to Crow's Nest. If there are any clues, we'll find them there."

The sails crackled as they caught wind, and the sea ahead sparkled in the late morning sunshine. Jendara felt the surge of excitement that always hit her when her ship got the wind in its teeth. She could never get bored of the taste of sea salt at high speed.

As quickly as the surge of hope had come, a dark cloud moved over the sun, sending the deck of the *Milady* into gloom. Jendara scowled up at it. Then her mouth fell open.

It was no cloud. Crows filled the sky—dozens, maybe hundreds. They moved across the sun like a cloud pushed by gale winds, bunched so close together their black wings blotted out the light.

"An ill tiding," Tam murmured, reaching for the lines of the main mast, ready to reef in the sails. Ready for a storm, even if it was just a storm of birds.

"Tam! Don't touch those sails," Vorrin growled. "It's just a bunch of migrating crows. They're heading someplace cozy for the winter, that's all."

Tam leaned over to reach Jendara's ear. He was a tall man, even for an islander. "Doesn't the captain know birds fly *south* for the winter?"

Jendara didn't answer. She watched the birds pass across the sun, headed north.

The same direction as the *Milady*.

Chapter Eight
Homecoming

Milady approached the island of Crow's Nest from the southeast. Jendara pointed out the massive rocks lying off the coast. "On a spring tide," she explained to Vorrin, "you can actually see them. On an ordinary day? They're waiting just below the surface."

They gave the rocks a wide berth, circling around the north shore of the island and finally dropping anchor a few yards off a deep, sandy cove. Old pilings still stood nearby, their tops given over to bird nests and their sides stained and battered. Jendara nodded at them.

"My father put in a pier, but it must have washed away. It was hard work, getting those pilings put in. He brought in a crew of half-orc divers from Flintyreach." She spoke rapidly, eyes roving every surface, absorbing the changes and alterations of the space.

Vorrin and Tam lowered the dinghy, and Tam held it steady for Jendara and Vorrin to clamber inside. Vorrin grabbed an oar and shoved off from the ship.

"How'd the island get the name 'Crow's Nest'?" he asked.

"My sister." Jendara pointed at the rocky knoll above the shore. A grove of skeletal spruce sprang up from what looked like bare rock, their trunks streaked and stained with bird guano. A cormorant circled over the grove and landed on a branch, adding its own white streak to the tree. "A migrating cormorant colony lies over in the summer, building nests and raising a general ruckus." She let out a little laugh. "When we first came over to the island—about a year after my mother died—Kalira was still pretty little, and she was just learning to talk. She called every bird a crow. She started calling the rock a crow's nest, and I guess it just stuck, what with the crow being our clan totem."

"That's a sweet story," Vorrin said.

"My father certainly thought so. He told it often enough."

Vorrin jumped out to help tug the boat up onto the shore. "What was your father like?"

She tied the towline to a stunted spruce struggling to grow at the edge of the sandy cove. "He was a great hunter. A raider who used diplomacy and trade to get more than he could have ever taken in a pitched battle. An amazing sailor."

"Okay," Vorrin said, "but what was he *like*?"

Jendara looked up from her mooring knot to see Vorrin studying her. She could feel the color rising in her cheeks. She took a deep breath and let the air out slowly.

"Look, he's not an easy person to talk about. He was a good leader, good enough that he could have been a king, and a lot of people thought he should have tried. But then my mother died, and he changed. He just wanted to settle down—raise goats and catch fish." She brushed back a strand of hair that had escaped her braid. "Everybody thought I should have turned out just like him."

Vorrin swatted her shoulder. "Well, you are a pretty good hunter. Not as good as me, but you know, who is?"

She rolled her eyes but smiled anyway. "So, here's the path. It's going to go about a quarter of a mile before we hit the village."

They climbed in silence. The first sign of habitation was a wooden fence whose beams sagged in the middle. A few posts had toppled over. Wind and sun had bleached the old wood silver.

Jendara patted a remaining fence post. "The goat meadow. We're getting close."

The path cut through the meadow, which had once been a pleasant field. Now its grasses were mostly overgrown with bracken and berries. A few spruce seedlings straggled up from the earth.

She tried to see the field as it had been when she was a girl. She'd spent most of her time snaring rabbits while she kept an eye on the goats. There were plenty of small animals on the island. No big ones. Her father took her to Flintyreach or the mainland to hunt bears and wolves.

The first house sat just beside the field. Once, there had a barn for goats and chickens, but there was no sign of the smaller building. Through the open framework of the dead house, the chimney and fireplace stood, still solid.

"This is where I found the first body," she said quietly. "A torso. It had been a man, but they'd taken the limbs and head. There was a heap of polished bones on the other side of the village; probably some of them belonged to him. I have no idea who he was. He must have come to the island after I left."

She picked up a fallen stick of wood and pushed at a mound of bracken a few feet beyond the first house. "I think this was my cousin Malva's hut. Looks like the ferns really took over here." She stood up straight. "I never found her body, although I think her skull was in the bone pile. She had a gold tooth. Pretty unusual around here."

Jendara pointed out the broken remains of the village meeting hall and the scattered fragments of other houses in the former village, most it heavily shrouded in bracken and brush. She had a story about each of the inhabitants and what condition their bodies had been in when she'd found them. Vorrin listened, but he seemed to have left his voice in the field outside the village.

The last of the village's buildings, a stone-and-timber structure, had maintained its shape. Two of the walls sagged, but the doorway stood square and true. It was an old-fashioned house, dug deep into the ground, and the earth had supported the structure even after the wind had torn away the thatched roof. Only a few plants had made their way through the gaps between the rough planks of the floor.

Jendara rested her palm against one of the heavy cedar beams. "Father always said he built this house to last."

"This—" Vorrin cleared his throat, tried again. "This was your house?"

Jendara nodded. "For eight years." She stared up at the lintel. "I came back from my second sea journey ready to brag about what I'd seen and done. I had the pirate goddess's tattoos and a belt pouch full of gold. But instead, I came up that path to find my father staked through the gut in front of his own house."

"That's horrible."

She ran her thumb over the handaxe at her belt, the axe that had pinned that swollen, rotting hand to this very house. "The devils paid for the blood they took," she said. "Father went out fighting."

Vorrin turned in a circle, staring at the little ring of houses. Jendara followed his gaze. Six houses, most falling down or rotted away. The old village site had a lonely, abandoned feeling about it.

"Everything's so overgrown," Vorrin said. "I don't see how we're going to find any clues."

Jendara sighed and walked a few yards beyond her father's ruined house. Here, where the woods had already swallowed up the last edge of the village, a weather-beaten shrine still stood, its roof supports sagging over the big stone shelf where once villagers had left offerings to their gods and ancestors. Jendara picked up a broken soapstone figurine.

"A crow, of course." She offered the totem to Vorrin, then picked up another chunk of stone. "Here's its head."

He took it from her and pressed the head piece to the body.

"My father put out milk and bread every day for the clan spirits. He sang ancestor songs at every holiday and lit candles on full moons. He believed in the honor of the Eirkillsing clan and attributed our successes to our ancestors' guidance."

She picked up a nubbled green stone and turned it in her fingers a moment before recognizing it for a copper coin. She flipped it on her thumbnail and it clanked against the stone.

"All those years venerating the ancestors, and did they even bother to give him a warning? They couldn't have said, 'Hey! There's a party of deranged cannibals coming your way! Grab your sword!'"

She brought her fist down on the shrine, hard enough to make the tarnished coin jump. "He didn't even have his sword! That's the worst thing."

She closed her eyes and rubbed them with her fists. "I broke the clan totem. I ripped up our clan flag. And I'd do it again."

She opened her eyes and looked at Vorrin. He set the soapstone figure back down on the shrine without a word.

Jendara shook her head. "I don't know why I wanted to come back here. There's nothing." She reached into her belt pouch and removed the crow pendant, then tossed it into the ferns. "Let's get back to the *Milady*."

Vorrin let her go first. She heard his boots crunch on the ferns behind her and knew he was retrieving the crow pendant. She didn't tell him not to.

The sea breeze blew through the abandoned village, stirring branches on trees that when she'd been a girl hadn't been tall enough to even cast a shadow over the village green. The tiny town had been bright, filled with sunlight and the booming laughter of her father's people. Everyone on Crow's Nest had laughed like him.

Now, beneath the heavy trees, it seemed impossible to imagine anyone ever laughing in this broken place. Time lay heavy over the ruins. The salt smell of the sea clung to everything.

But it wasn't silent. Somewhere in the distance, something roared. A low, booming roar, the sound of a bear or troll. The kind of creature that hadn't set foot on Crow's Nest as long as she'd lived.

"Did you hear that?" she called over her shoulder.

"And I don't want to see what made it," he said. "Let's get out of here."

They raced back the way they'd come: across the goat field and down the winding, spruce-lined trail. Jendara peered over the edge of the trail. Far below, waves sparkled on the soft brown sands of the cove, and the *Milady* bobbed by the stumpy ruins of the old pier. Everything looked peaceful and serene.

The roar sounded again, shaking the air.

"It's closer," Vorrin warned. He grabbed Jendara's hand and tugged her forward.

A faint whistle sounded overhead. Instinct made Jendara leap toward the inside of the trail, pushing Vorrin into the hillside. Fragments of bark and branches exploded everywhere as a tree smashed down on the path ahead of them, wedged in a steep V against the rocks.

"You okay?"

Vorrin rubbed his side. They scrambled under the fallen tree in silence. White cormorant dung crusted patches of the tree's trunk. Jendara paused a moment in the shelter of its outspread limbs. Its lower quarter swung over the side of the cliff, attached only by an unbroken strip of thick bark. Jendara's mouth went dry at the sight of its thick, earth-covered roots.

"That didn't just fall," she whispered. "Something uprooted it!"

The roar resounded again, and this time she tracked the sound. She stared up at the cormorant knoll. It stuck out against the sky like a raised thumb, its flanks sheer basalt. "I think it's up there."

"Then let's hurry before it comes down," Vorrin growled. They began running again.

Above them, something crashed through the rock and scree. Jendara risked a glance upward and felt her boot slip on exposed rock. She snatched at Vorrin's sleeve, but too late. Her other foot came down on only bracken, and she tumbled over the edge of the path.

She hit hard and lay stunned. She'd landed on the next switchback, her head inches from a hunk of stone the size of a big dog. The perfume of crushed ferns filled the air. With a groan, she rolled to her knees. She wasn't hurt, but she'd had the wind knocked out of her.

Another tree smashed onto the path, just feet beyond her. Thicker than the last one, its limbs filled the path like a wall.

"Dara?" Vorrin's voice sounded thin and sharp on the far side.

"I'm okay!" she called. She hoped she sounded less terrified. She was just lucky this tree hadn't exploded into bits like the last one.

A horrible roar made the ferns around her tremble. She jumped to her feet. Something bounded down the side of the hill, following the swathe of broken plants she'd left behind. Something huge and green and leathery.

A troll.

It swung a broken tree limb at her head. She rolled beneath the wild blow, but a twig scoured her cheek. She swore and swiped away blood as she sized up her opponent.

The hair on her neck stood on end. She'd helped hunt trolls years ago, but she'd forgotten just how big they really were. This one must be young, standing only about seven feet tall. Its gray, stringy body hair was streaked with guano.

Jendara drew her sword. Her best hope was to confuse it, throw off its sense of space and rush it over the edge of the path. She charged to its left.

"Jendara!"

The troll spun toward Vorrin's voice. Its nostrils flared, drawing in the man's scent. Then, in a surprise burst of speed, it charged toward the fallen tree. Jendara swung her sword and missed by a mile.

She leaped after the troll.

Vorrin swung himself over the top of the fallen tree trunk just as the troll reached it. He didn't even have time to shout before the troll's palm caught him in the chest and tossed him backward.

Jendara's eyes widened. For one second, the image of Vorrin, smashed against the rocks of the trail, hung in her mind. The thought was so perfectly real she could almost hear the crunch of his bones as they hit the stone.

Then her sword plunged into the troll's back and skewered it to the tree trunk. It shrieked in pain. Its arms flailed and legs kicked. Ignoring its death throes, Jendara grabbed handfuls of brittle moss off the tree. She just needed a dry stick of wood for a torch.

She stretched to reach for a dead branch above her head and the troll's fist grabbed the back of her shirt. She plummeted to the ground. Her blade made a damp suctioning sound as the troll twisted itself so its face turned her way. Blood trickled out of its tusked mouth, but anger still gleamed in its piggish eyes.

She thought of Vorrin again, and something shifted in Jendara, that hot bristling force she remembered from her pirating days. Her axe jumped into her hand and she slammed it into the beast's eyebrow, rupturing its eye. Her teeth flashed with pure joy as yellow ichor rolled steaming down its cheek.

With a roar, the troll pushed itself free. The tip of her sword stuck out from its belly and blood streamed down its legs. Jendara hurled her axe, but it ricocheted off the troll's collarbone. It lunged at her, claws just missing her face. She dropped to the ground and rolled into a thicket of ferns.

Fire. She needed fire. She snatched at a low-hanging branch and yanked it free.

The troll spun around, searching for her with its one good eye. She glanced around. The spruce tree beside her must have lost a major limb during the last storm season—a raw spot in its bark leaked strings of sticky pitch.

The troll roared. Its eye had already stopped dripping. Its nostrils flared as it searched for her scent. She only had a second.

It was between her and Vorrin now. The anger inside her flared. She had to keep it from him. She rolled her tree branch in the spruce pitch, then dove aside as the troll's claws slashed through the air, ripping out the brush around her. She could see her sword hilt still jutting out of the creature's back. The blade must have lodged itself in something hard, probably the spinal column. On any ordinary creature, it would have been a paralyzing blow, if not a fatal one. But the troll's flesh was already healing around the blade, writhing unnaturally back together.

She launched herself at the hilt, bringing all of her weight down on the cross-guard. Something inside the beast crunched.

The troll roared as its legs collapsed under it. Its face slammed into the ground. Jendara gripped the torch between her knees and dug in her pouch for her flint striker. The makeshift torch caught at the first spark, and she leaped forward onto the troll's shoulder blades, snarling and laughing. Her tattoos prickled on the backs of her hands. She pressed the torch into the troll's neck and ears.

It slapped weakly at her, claws piercing her layers of wool and leather. Its back bucked, hard, and she tumbled off it. The scratches burned. Were trolls' claws poisonous? She couldn't remember. Her brain had choked with blood rage. She kicked the troll in the temple. It rolled onto its side to kick back at her.

But she had forgotten any fear she ought to have felt, and lunged forward to stab the torch into its belly. The troll screamed, a piercing sound. Jendara snatched her knife from her belt.

It had hurt Vorrin. It had tried to kill her. It had to pay.

With one boot, she pinned down its neck, then plunged her knife into the troll's good eye, driving it deep and twisting the blade, digging through bone. She was laughing again. The blade rose and came down again, squelching as it stirred through something soft, deep within the troll's skull. Flames crackled as the torch's sticky pitch clung to matted hair.

"Jendara. Stop."

Vorrin grabbed her shoulders, dragging her away from the troll. She struggled and twisted, but he stuck to her like a burr. "Stop," he whispered.

He spun her around and pressed her face against his cheek. The backs of her hands went cold. She sagged against him, suddenly exhausted. "You're okay," she breathed.

"I'm fine," he said. "We're both fine." He stroked her back. "We're both fine."

She pulled away from him and moved to the troll's side. She began piling deadwood around it, wishing she didn't have to look at it to finish it off. The troll's body lay twisted on the ground. Its legs twitched, trying instinctively to push it away from the guttering torch. Days of living on the island's limited resources had taken a toll on the creature. Its ribs showed through its hairy green hide, what little of its skin wasn't obscured with guano or blood.

Its face was the worst. The meat of its left cheek hung off the bone. Both eyes were gory, accusing pits.

Jendara grabbed onto the nearest tree and vomited.

She had done this. Butchered this pathetic creature. Tortured and mutilated it. It was a hungry, desperate animal, starving on this tiny island.

The smell of smoke brought her back. Vorrin had finished what she'd started, and the small flames he rekindled were already licking at the deadwood. Her knife lay on the ground beside it, carefully wiped clean. He looked up at her. "Are you all right?"

"No." Her shoulders shook. "This was wrong."

Vorrin gave her a confused look. "It was a *troll*, Jendara. It would have killed us."

"So we killed it. But that didn't give me the right to do *this*." She gestured at the ruin of its face, then swiped at the snot and tears streaking her own. "This was sick."

"You were scared," he said, cautiously. The troll bucked and shuddered beneath its pyre.

"No," Jendara said again. "I wasn't scared, not then. I knew what I was doing, Vorrin. And I *liked* it. That's what really scares me."

She stumbled over to the troll and reached out for her belt knife. As she grasped it, she caught sight of the black skull and crossbones on the back of her hand. "I wish I'd never let you under my skin," she whispered.

The pair made their way down to the cove and their dinghy. Jendara could smell her own stink now, troll blood and sweat and bird dung. She wished it had been the sweet spruce smoke that clung to her, and not the funk of battle and shame.

She knelt beside the breaking waves and watched them sluice away the filth on her boots. Vorrin untied the dinghy while she scrubbed her hands with sand.

"Looks like the weather changed while we weren't looking. There's a serious fog bank moving in."

She drew herself wearily to her feet. "It matches my mood. We should never have come here."

Vorrin held the boat steady as she climbed inside. "It's awfully strange, finding a troll on an island this small. It looked pretty malnourished.

"I can't even make a guess how it got here," she admitted. "My head hurts from all of this. The murders at the quarry. Finding Kalira's crow pendant. Seeing this place again."

He offered her a handkerchief and she waved it away.

"It'll be good for me to get away from the islands," she said. "Getting away—that's what I did after Ikran died. I killed that slaver captain, then tried to hole up in Absalom. A nice big city to disappear into."

Vorrin knew as well as Jendara did that "kill" was not an adequate description of her treatment of the man who had murdered her husband. She tried not to remember that he'd been with them on that trip, trying to make trade connections in Katapesh. It pained her to think that he'd seen her at her most malicious, worse even than she'd been up there on the knoll.

She looked over at him, trying to read his expression. His dark eyes were serious. "That's when I told myself I was giving up piracy," she admitted. "When I came back to myself and saw what I'd done to that man. The rest of my own boarding party wouldn't even look at me."

He folded his handkerchief and put it in his pocket.

"I don't want to feel like that ever again," Jendara said, her voice stronger. "It's one thing to kill. It's another to enjoy it. I should be better than that."

"You are, Dara. And I know you're not—" Vorrin frowned. "Do you see that?"

She followed his gaze and saw the light winking off the *Milady*'s foremast. The ship stood outlined against the immense fog bank rolling toward it. "They're signaling us."

He jumped to his feet. "Let's get moving."

They ran down to the beach and launched the dinghy, Vorrin rowing hard toward his ship. Within seconds, land had vanished behind them, the encroaching fog bank obscuring even the skeletal spruce trees on the cormorants' knoll. Jendara strained her eyes toward the *Milady*, but the fog closed around the ship in heavy curtains. Their oar strokes resounded in the stillness of the fog bank.

"Ahoy!" Tam shouted as they approached, although he himself was invisible in the mist. A gaffing hook appeared from above, pulling the dinghy in tight to the *Milady*'s side. Vorrin scrambled up the rope ladder Tam had already lowered.

"What's wrong? Why'd you signal?"

The fog clung to Jendara as she grabbed the dinghy's mooring line and tossed it up. She reached for the rope ladder and shivered as a tendril of mist wrapped around her wrist, all cold and damp. She climbed fast.

At the top of the railing, Tam appeared. He offered Jendara his hand. Sailors already scrambled to pull the dinghy out of the water. Jendara looked back over her shoulder. There was no sign of the island she'd just left—only fog.

Tam gave her bloody gear a double take. "Well—" he began, but another voice cut him off.

"There's a vessel out there," Boruc said, voice tense. He nodded up at Vorrin from his perch on a barrel, his plastered leg hoisted on a crate. "Out in the fog."

"We tried to hail it," Tam said. "I couldn't make it out too clearly, but I think it was a longship. I saw just one sail, and by sounds of it, it carried a good-sized rowing crew."

"They must have hounds with them," Boruc said. "Glayn and I heard a ferocious lot of growling and barking."

"We signaled with lanterns, but they didn't respond," Tam continued. "I used the spyglass, trying to determine their course, but the fog's gotten too thick out there."

"And now the fog's hidden the island," Jendara mused. "If they're not familiar with the area, they're not going to know about the underwater rocks."

Vorrin shook his head. "I'm less concerned with them, and more concerned about us. Hounds on a longship? Ignoring a friendly hailing? I'm betting they're raiders. I think we should put some distance between us and them."

"We can't risk raising the sails," Tam said. "*Milady*'s a deep-water ship. Wouldn't take much to run her aground."

Out in the white dampness that had swallowed the world, something howled. Jendara felt goose bumps rise on her arms. She'd heard plenty of hunting hounds howl before, but she'd never heard ones that sounded this eerie.

"We could use the dinghy to try to catch up with that longship," she said. "A small crew under paddle power to warn them about those rocks—or to scout them out."

Vorrin's eyes flashed. "And if they're raiders? We just let that crew row out blind?"

Jendara sighed. "No, I'd go slow and quiet, so nothing bites me in the ass. If the *Milady* is stuck here in the fog, we're better off knowing what's out there."

Out in the water, something splashed. Vorrin jumped.

His face twisted. "All right. I don't like feeling there's something out there planning to harm my ship. Tam, I want this ship ready to sail at a moment's notice." He turned to Jendara. "You go find Alex. He's probably just waking up, since he stood night watch. But he's a good man with sharp eyes. You two take the dinghy out in the direction Tam saw the other boat."

His voice was pure captain at that moment. Jendara nodded and hurried to the hatch leading below.

"And Jendara?"

She turned to face him. "Yes?"

"Keep in mind that you're the cargo officer and business manager of this ship. Don't go getting heroic out there."

Jendara saluted. As she climbed belowdecks, she realized she wanted nothing more than to stumble into her own hammock. Hammocks, not heroics, she thought. That's what she wanted. But duty called.

"I don't think we'll find anything tonight, Dara," Alex said. The second mate rubbed his eyes and spread his hands. "I mean, look at it out here."

Glayn nodded. The green-haired gnome had been sailing with Jendara since the old days of piracy, and she was glad he'd insisted on coming with her. The little man had sharp eyes and sharper hearing.

"There's naught out there but devils and ghosts," Glayn said. "If there's ever been a more cursed patch of water, I ain't seen it."

Her skin crawled. She wished it was just a reaction to the clinging dampness against her skin, but she knew it came from his words. Cursed. Maybe this island really was.

A few feet away, something splashed. The fog had rendered the world beyond the dinghy invisible. Jendara was more worried about the rocks beneath the mist-shrouded water than she was any kind of attack.

"Hello?" Jendara called. "We're a scouting vessel from the trade ship *Milady*. Is anyone out there?"

A breeze stirred the mist, parting it in places. Jendara squinted. She thought she caught a glimmer of red, like the red-and-white-striped sails popular on older longships. "Call out if you can hear me," she shouted.

More splashing, but softer. Jendara was reminded of the sound oars made when wrapped in canvas. She'd used that technique on more than a few raids. She wished she'd brought her bow along for this little outing.

"Let's pick up our pace," she whispered to Glayn. "I don't think that boat wants to be caught, and I want to know why."

They rowed hard, but the fog didn't clear. Jendara leaned forward in the bow, eyes straining for signs of another craft.

Ahead, a shape loomed. She gave an angry blast on her whistle. "This is an expedition from the trade ship *Milady*. Identify yourself now!"

"Jendara? It's us!" Tam's voice sounded thin and forlorn and somehow nearby.

Jendara frowned. "Tam?"

Alex stopped rowing and let the current carry them forward. Off the starboard side of the bow, the soft yellow glow of a lantern appeared. "We must have gotten turned around out there," he muttered.

Glayn spat over the side of the boat. "Cursed waters."

They glided neatly up to the *Milady*'s side.

"Did you find anything?" Tam asked.

"Not really." Jendara answered. She peered back over her shoulder. Had she really seen those sails out there, just moments ago? She couldn't doubt the evidence of her eyes, but that meant a longship had slipped by only a few yards beyond the *Milady*'s prow. Had it been circling aimlessly in the fog like Jendara's dinghy? And why had no one answered her hails?

She shook her head. "If there's someone out there, they don't want to be found."

In a few moments, Tam had them back aboard their ship, and by the time all the gear was stowed away, a hint of sun had appeared behind the curtain of fog. But no one relaxed until the anchor was lifted and the *Milady* was moving quickly away from Crow's Nest.

Chapter Nine
Black Ship, Cold Water

The fishing vessels of Sorind appeared first, the usual congregation of smaller boats whose owners called a friendly halloo as the big ship slipped by. Jendara grinned. Her dark mood had fallen behind her, blown away by the wind and the simple joys of working in the rigging.

The *Milady* moored with the ease of a ship's crew that had worked together a long time. Jendara helped Tam wrestle the gangway into place and realized they'd been moving the balky thing together for more than five years—two and half covering this trade route, and those three lean years carrying cargo off of Varisia. He must have signed on just around the time Ikran died.

But he and Glayn were the only two of the crew that had been on the *Milady* in its pirating days. The gnome was already going over the skiff she'd used this morning, checking for any scraped paint or other quick repairs. Glayn shot her a smile as she crossed the deck, looking for Boruc.

He was sitting on his cask, admiring his plaster cast, now painted in gaudy shades. She had to laugh. "Did you get bored?"

"I thought a spot of color might add a bit of cheer." He reached for a pair of crutches someone must have found down below. "I have my reputation as an artist to maintain."

"You're not like other islanders that I've known, Boruc. You're . . ." She searched for the word.

"Eccentric?" he asked.

"Artistic," she said. "And lighthearted in a way that not a lot of men can pull off."

"I go my own way," he reminded her. "You should try it. Who cares what other people think as long as you're happy?"

The man hoisted himself onto his crutches and made his way toward the gangplank. Tam rushed forward to help him down to the pier.

She watched the pair stump their way along. Yes, if there was one thing Boruc did well, it was go his own way. In a family of farmers and fishers, he'd become a talented sculptor. She had no doubt his carvings would sell well on the mainland. There was a power and grace to his soapstone figures that was unusual in stonework. If Jendara was looking for an idol for her clan altar, she would want Boruc to carve it.

She felt a tiny twinge. Someone had carved the totems back on the altar at Crow's Nest, someone who had worked hard to capture the likeness of a crow. She'd snapped it in two without even the slightest thought of the craftsperson who'd made it. She'd been too absorbed into her own rage.

Vorrin waved from the end of the dock, and she pushed away her musings on the past. She had a new life to focus on.

Jendara picked up her pace, giving Vorrin's shoulder a comfortable bump when she reached his side. "Did you see Boruc's cast?"

He grinned. "A definite improvement. At least it adds color to the place."

"What did you do to my brother?" Morul called. The island leader stood in the village square, tapping his toe as he waited for Jendara and Vorrin.

"I had to rescue Jendara from a sea snake," Boruc said, eyes twinkling. "The others will all agree that my heroism was unparalleled."

Jendara laughed. "He was very brave." She paused, not sure how to explain everything that had happened during their trip to Flintyreach. An entire group of workers murdered, a bizarre monster tracked, Boruc's leg broken . . . it made for a long story.

Movement in front of the meeting hall caught her eye. Kran, collecting a spear from a target set up on a pile of straw bales. She nudged Vorrin, and the whole group turned their heads to watch the boy march back to the "firing line" he'd drawn in the dirt. Yul stood with the boy, making a few adjustments to Kran's stance. The man fell back and the boy raised the spear.

Jendara held her breath.

The spear soared in a controlled arc, thudding into the target and slicing through the straw behind it. Jendara beamed.

"Strong arm on that boy," Boruc said.

"And a good shot, too," Morul pointed out. "That was pretty close to center."

"Takes after his mother," Vorrin said, but his pride in the boy was obvious. Jendara wasn't sure she'd ever seen the man smile so wide.

Morul cleared his throat. "So what really happened out there? We weren't expecting to see the *Milady* back in harbor for a number of weeks, and we certainly weren't expecting Boruc to come with you."

The group explained what had happened back on the island, Morul listening quietly. When they finished, he scratched his yellow beard, eyes focused on some distant point as he thought.

"I don't like this," he said, finally. "I don't like the fact that you only found one creature and that it may or may not be dead. I wish you'd just found a pack of vicious trolls."

"I don't like it, either," Jendara agreed. She thought about the troll she'd faced on Crow's Nest. It had been vicious, dangerous, and terrifying, but she didn't believe a creature like that could pull off the kind of killing she'd seen back at the quarry. Trolls weren't entirely stupid, but they definitely lacked the control it took to kill a group of men and then leave their remains in a neat pile. "Trolls would be a lot less worrying, really."

"Hey!"

At the call, they spun toward the docks. Glayn waved at them, still holding his tarry caulking brush. Jendara and Vorrin hurried toward him.

"Something wrong?" Vorrin called.

The gnome bobbed his head. "A boat! A small one. It's floating in on the tide, but it's not under any kind of control. Tam's taking the skiff out to get it, but it's in ugly condition."

"How ugly?" Morul had caught up, and his voice was grim. Boruc stumped along behind him, straining to see beyond the *Milady*.

"Well, the sail looks good, but that's not the bad thing." Glayn looked from Vorrin to Jendara. "There's blood all over it. Might be folks left inside, but it was hard to tell with just my old spyglass. The boat's full of gear and debris."

Vorrin's mouth tightened. "Let's go help Tam salvage it."

Tam had moved quickly. The skiff was already trudging toward shore, the other craft strung behind it on a towrope. Jendara studied the bloodstained boat. A faering, she'd guess, the kind of small craft a family might use to visit their kin on another island, or to take their furs to market. It could run fast with just a few oarsmen or the small sail. Despite the bloodstains, the hull looked sound. What could have happened to it?

Jendara waited for Tam to toss out a mooring line while Vorrin hurried to grab a grappling hook. As the two boats eased toward the docks, he hooked the side of the abandoned boat and slowed its approach. He suddenly stiffened. "Did you hear something?"

Jendara listened. Waves slapped the sides of the dock and the boats. Sea gulls shrieked. But there was another, smaller sound, like the groan of an injured man.

"I think there's someone still on board." She jumped aboard. Wads of shredded and bloodstained canvas filled the bottom of the boat. A rank, musky scent hung over it all, the kind of stink she associated with animal lairs.

She pulled back the corner of the nearest scrap of canvas.

"No!"

A jagged length of wood shot out at her. She barely twisted aside in time to evade the spiky thing—a broken oar. She wrenched it away. Someone was babbling, shrieking, sobbing. Jendara tossed aside the canvas.

The man beneath slapped at her with one bloodied hand. His other cradled a long, gory slab or something to his chest. Jendara brushed off his blows.

"You're okay," she said, in the voice she saved for upset animals. "You're safe."

The man trembled. "Safe?" He pulled his grisly burden tighter to his chest, shifting it a little so that Jendara could make out the blond hair and light beard of a young man's cheek. The younger man was definitely dead.

She squatted down so she was at the survivor's level. An ugly gash ran from his eyebrow to his hairline. The eye beneath it had swollen half-shut.

"What happened to you?"

He shook his head wildly. "They came out of the dark, growling. Some kind of creatures. Couldn't see!"

"It's all right now," she said, quickly. She studied the corpse of the young man. The flesh had been ripped off the left side of his face, and his left arm was missing entirely. She could see the pale glint of an exposed rib between the red shreds remaining of his torso. The youth had probably been dead for several hours. Jendara was suddenly glad she hadn't had any breakfast.

"Can you stand up?" she asked, keeping her voice soft and friendly. "I think your head needs stitching."

He made a move to get up and fell back, hissing with pain. "Hurts to move."

Jendara glanced over her shoulder. She saw Morul and Yul hurrying down the docks, Glayn and Sorend's wisewoman, Chana, just behind them, and felt a surge of relief. There were no people she'd rather have at her side right now. The combination of a head injury and obvious terror could make this man hard to manage.

"We're going to take you to our wisewoman," she said. "She'll help you. But we can't carry two of you at one time, so you're going to have to lay your friend down."

He shrank away from her. "Byrni! No! I won't leave him!" His eyes rolled in their sockets.

"He'll be right behind you," she said. It was like talking to a child. She stretched out her hand to stroke his shoulder and he began shrieking insensibly.

Someone shouldered in beside her. "Now, now," Chana crooned. The dark-haired wisewoman's hand shot out, a tiny vial gripped in her fingers. In an instant, she had the vial between the injured man's lips. "You just need some sleep."

The man pulled away from her, but whatever was inside her vial had already slipped down his throat. "Sleep," he repeated. His open eye, a pale gray, blinked heavily. "Don't want to."

His head dropped forward. Chana felt at his throat. "The pulse is strong. He'll be fine once I get that cut stitched."

Glayn brought over a plank to lay the wounded man upon, and with Tam and Vorrin's help, they had the injured man out of his boat in a few moments. The four men eased the plank up onto their shoulders and began trekking up the hill, toward the meetinghouse. Jendara watched them go, thinking.

Creatures coming out of the dark. It sounded like something out of a story—the kind used to frighten children. But she had the half-ruined body of a young man lying in the bottom of the boat to illustrate this tale. She knelt beside the corpse to get a better sense of the wounds. Whatever had attacked the two sailors, it had been tremendously strong. The boy's left shoulder looked as if it had simply been sheared off.

Something caught her eye, and she bent lower. Where the post of the dead man's belt buckle met the frame, several long, coarse hairs had caught. They looked like bear fur.

Like the hair the trackers had found at Alstone Quarry.

The sound of footsteps made her look up. Kran was running down the pier toward her. She flipped a piece of canvas over the mutilated corpse and climbed out of the boat.

Kran stopped beside her, spreading his hands questioningly.

"I don't know what happened," she said. "I guess we just wait for the man to wake up and tell us."

He frowned at her, then offered her his hand. She took it, touched. His hand felt rough, callused. The hands of a hardworking boy.

She resisted the urge to pull him to her chest and ruffle his hair.

"It's too late to leave tonight." Vorrin sank into a chair with a sigh. He propped his boots up on Jendara's hearth.

Kran pumped a fist in victory. Vorrin shot him a sour look.

"Hey," Jendara said, clapping a hand on each one's shoulder. "It's a good thing. We can all have dinner together. It'll be a nice change of pace."

"And maybe I can convince Kran he wants to leave with us tomorrow morning," Vorrin said brightly. "What do you think, big guy?"

Kran reached for his slate. *Yul wants me to help him build a pole barn.*

"Would you rather build a pole barn or explore Magnimar with your favorite uncle? There could be pastries in it for you."

The boy grinned. *I like pastries.* He squeezed past Jendara into the kitchen. He took down a cutting board, and without being asked, began cutting onions. Jendara gave him a grateful look and went to sit beside Vorrin.

"Aren't you at all curious about the man in that boat? Don't you want to find out what happened out there?"

"Not enough to miss sailing in this weather." Vorrin reached for the poker and adjusted the logs in the grate.

"But . . . the creatures in the dark? The animal hair in the younger man's belt?"

He raised his eyebrows. "That man who survived had a concussion. He's just lucky his skull is in one piece. And those could have been dog hairs, Dara. Plenty of big dogs around."

Jendara blew out her cheeks, frustrated. "I don't believe in coincidences, Vorrin. Not finding those two so soon after that attack at the quarry."

"Fine." He dropped the poker on the hearth and got to his feet. "How about you go take a look at the guy's boat while Kran and I work on dinner? If you find anything strange, then you're right. And if all you find is a busted-up boat, then . . ." He shrugged. "Anything could have attacked that guy, Dara. Even another party of raiders. People with head injuries aren't exactly the most reliable witnesses."

She reached for her jacket. "You're right." She shrugged on her outer gear and grabbed her spare lantern. "But it bothers me."

"It's not our business," he called, but she was already closing the door on him.

A salty breeze blew down her jacket collar, surprisingly chilly after such a sunny day. She buttoned the top button and wondered if Vorrin was right. Maybe none of this was her business. What *was* her business was the journey to and from Varisia. After all, she'd spent all summer building up that cargo. If it didn't sell—well, it would be a long hungry winter with no money.

"I've got to get focused on this trip," she muttered, kicking a stone ahead of her. The words fell flat in the wind.

She frowned, thinking harder about the winter clawing its way south. In just six or seven short weeks, Sorind's first snowstorms would be battering its shores, the snow carried by wild winds no sane captain wanted to maneuver his ship through. Vorrin was right to be worried. No matter how intriguing this new mystery was, she had to admit that.

Jendara scowled at the injured man's boat. In the twilight, it didn't look nearly as battered or bloody. But standing alone beside it, surrounded by shadows, the boat's timbers creaking as they rubbed against the fenders of the dock, she understood just what had piqued her interest in this craft and its story. "You're connected somehow," she murmured. "You've got to be the connection between Crow's Nest and Alstone Quarry that I just can't see."

The injured man had been attacked by growling creatures. She'd shot a strange beast she would have sworn was a man. What had they both really seen?

Thinking hard, Jendara ran her hand over sailboat's prow. The wood was sleek and well maintained.

She scoured the outside of the boat first. If they'd been caught at sea by another boat, the attackers would have used grappling hooks to bring the two vessels together, then tie them tight. That left signs. She wished she'd looked over the boat while the sun was up. Her lantern wasn't half bright enough.

She stepped inside the cabin and took a moment to orient herself. The sailboat wasn't very big, maybe twenty feet long, the single mast pressed up close to the foredeck and a wooden slat in the stern for seating. A couple of crates were lashed underneath the seat. Despite the boat's small size, she'd seen plenty of this kind of boat used as raiding vessels—they were a nice size to stash in a cove someplace while the owner raided a sheep or smokehouse. Odds were good that the injured man and his dead friend had been on the same kind of expedition, just two idiots hungry for a little action before the winter freeze. She'd seen plenty of their kind.

Hell, she'd been their kind, only the professional model.

She nudged the bloody pile of canvas that she'd found the men hiding beneath. It was heavy stuff, and oiled on one side. They probably used it as a cover while they slept—there was just enough room in the bottom of the boat for two people to sleep awkwardly, head to foot. Jendara thought a moment, then crossed to the crates. Their lashings were nice and snug, and when she undid them, the supplies inside looked neatly sorted and carefully packed. There was a jug of schnapps, but it was nearly full.

Jendara plopped back onto the seat with a groan. Nothing. Not a damn thing. She'd been hoping for some kind of real clue, maybe a talon or a fang that she could identify, or a bloody bootprint. If she wanted to be really honest, she'd hoped she'd find something that directly linked this attack to Kalvamen. She'd been ridiculously optimistic. More than that: the oiled canvas suggested the men had been asleep. Even if the boat's owner woke up feeling fine, he wasn't going to have much of a story.

She climbed out of the boat, shaking her head. She was too eager to see monsters and cannibals to be objective anymore. It was time for her to get back to sea.

Jendara put her arm around Kran. It was good to have him with her on the deck of the *Milady*, close beside her and surrounded by crew members who had practically raised him. Sure, the time he spent on Sorind was good for him. She couldn't deny that he had gotten stronger and faster and that Yul had taught him a number of useful skills. But this was where he belonged. Where he was safe.

She looked back over her shoulder at the island, diminishing behind them with the power of a good wind. It had seemed safe, too, once. When she had first decided to build a house on the island and use it as her winter home, she had been certain there was no safer place in all the world. But now she had her doubts. Those men working at Alstone Quarry had probably felt they were pretty safe, too.

Kran wriggled out from under her arm, leaping over piles of rope and fishing nets to reach Glayn's side. The gnome patted the boy's shoulder—a stretch these days, Jendara realized with a pang—and sent him up in the rigging. Some mothers would have worried about letting their children clamber up and down a eighty-foot-tall mainmast, but Jendara didn't. Kran had been born on this ship. He could leap from spar to spar like a regular monkey.

Jendara gathered a pile of netting and stowed it in its place belowdecks. The crew did a lot of fishing when they traveled, but today was no day for it. They were moving too fast. Vorrin had the bit between his teeth and the wind agreed with him.

Kran slid down the ladder to land with a thud on the deck. He beckoned at her.

She hurried to join him. "What's wrong?"

He pointed back to the north. A small craft moved in the distance, headed back toward Sorind.

"It looks like a longship to me," Jendara mused.

Kran nodded. While he had been up in the rigging, he must have had a good view of the vessel, especially if he was carrying her spyglass.

"Did you get a look at the crew?"

He reached for his slate. *Too far away*, he wrote.

"Hmmn." Jendara held out her hand. "May I use the glass?"

He handed it to her. She brought the longship into focus. She couldn't quite recognize the figurehead. It was some kind of animal, its mouth opened in a twisted snarl.

She shook her head. "I don't see any crew."

Kran tapped her shoulder. *Maybe they have the boat cover pulled up?* he wrote.

Jendara looked again. "I think you're right." She looked around for her partner. "Vorrin! Come see this!"

He crossed the deck quickly. "What's wrong?"

She held out the spyglass. "Look at that boat. Kran noticed it, and that they've got the boat cover pulled up even though it's morning."

Vorrin took a look. "It's headed right for Sorind." He passed the spyglass back to Kran. "I don't like that." He shouted to the navigator and the *Milady* swung around in a quick change of course.

Kran pounded Jendara's shoulder.

She snapped her head back around and saw what he did: something spilling out of the approaching longship like a narrow black cloud. She gripped the deck railing, squinting at it. The cloud rose up, widening, swirling. It shrieked.

"Crows?" she wondered.

And then the wind from their beating wings pressed over them, a stinking carrion reek. Their cawing pierced Jendara's ears.

"Get down!" she shouted, pushing Kran down to the decking. Talons raked her scalp. Jendara swiped at the blood.

"I've never seen so many crows!" Vorrin shouted.

Kran smacked at a crow battering his head. Jendara snatched it from the air and dashed it against the railing. She drew her sword and struck down another.

"They're in the sails!" someone shrieked, and Jendara spun around to see. The black cloud had settled into the rigging, pecking at ropes, clawing at canvas.

Kran leaped to his feet, keeping his head ducked as he darted across the deck. Jendara hurried after him, swiping at the birds that dove at her head. Black feathers filled the air like rain. She put a burst of speed into her legs and reached the mast just behind Kran. She tried to catch his belt, but he was too fast.

"Damn it," she growled. She jumped into the ratlines and ran up them like a ladder. Kran swatted at a crow and it tumbled down the mast, its wing slapping Jendara's face and blinding her momentarily.

Another crow landed on the back of her neck. Its beak slashed at the unprotected skin above her collar. Jendara yelped. She hooked her sword arm into the ropes around her and grabbed at the thing with her free hand. The beak stabbed into the meat of her thumb.

She smashed the bird against the solid oak of the mast. Its bones crumpled with a gratifying crunch.

Kran struck out with a length of knotted rope. He whipped it into the cluster of birds pecking at the ropes around him, thick lines that ran up into the topsail. Jendara kept her eyes on the crows surrounding her boy even as she hurried up the lines toward him. They ignored Kran's attack, slicing at the rope even faster.

It was like they knew what they were doing, Jendara realized. Like they knew they could stop the ship if they could just disable its sails.

She twisted sideways, keeping an elbow wound into the ratlines. A group of fishing vessels floated off to her left, just out of hailing distance. She ignored them and scanned the waters beyond them, eyes sweeping the seas around Sorind. She stiffened. On the far side of island, something moved. A second longship, streaking toward the island from the northwest.

Then something struck the side of the *Milady*. Jendara brought her gaze down to the deck.

While they'd been distracted by the crows, the original longship had crept up on them. A grappling hook gripped the starboard railing.

"Boarding party!" she bellowed, and leaped for the nearest shroud line. She hooked her elbow around the heavy rope and slid down it at full speed. She could smell small fibers singeing off her coat. The deck rail flew up at her.

With a last-second twist, she swung out far over the side of the boat, getting a better look at the raiding ship below, something dark and hairy yanking on the end of the grappling line. She scrabbled to spin around and jump down to the deck.

Her boots skidded on slick wood for an ugly second, but she kept her mass low and came out where she wanted: by the railing where the grappling hook dug its iron fingers into the *Milady*'s oak. She sheathed her sword and reached for her handaxe.

"I've got your back!" Tam roared. She hadn't seen the big first mate approaching, but she was glad to see his massive figure appear beside her. "Watch out, Dara!"

The ears of a bear appeared at the edge of the railing. With a huge roar, the rest of it launched itself on board, its shoulder hitting Jendara in the cheek and snapping back her head. She tumbled backward, grabbing on to the beast in a mad attempt to control its snarling, biting muzzle. She twisted her arm up under its neck and jammed her elbow into its strangely hairless throat.

They hit the deck together, the bear's mass driving hard against her arm. It rolled away, growling. She hadn't hurt it much, but she'd given it reason to be wary. Jendara jumped to her feet, circling away from the deck railing.

"Tam, cut that grappling line!" she called, without taking her eyes off the creature. Its face was somehow malformed, the muzzle too flat, the fur patchy.

The bear reared up on its hind legs, its arms open and ready to slash her at any second. A fighter's stance.

Jendara's eyes narrowed. Bears didn't take stances. Bears attacked or they didn't—they didn't take the measure of their prey. This bear moved like a man, like that beast back on Flintyreach. She drew her axe.

Vorrin dropped out of the rigging behind the creature. The bear's head swiveled, but before it could turn, Vorrin thrust his sword deep into its spine. The creature's legs crumpled beneath it. With a grunt, Vorrin freed his sword. The bear toppled backward, but its forepaws slashed at the air. Vorrin brought his blade down in two crunching chops. Its head rolled a few feet, snout coming to rest against Jendara's boot.

Jendara kicked it away.

A thud shook the railing behind Vorrin, and he spun around. "They're trying a second grappling line!"

Jendara raced to the railing, handaxe ready. "Got it." She chopped at the rope, glad for the good edge of her axe. Below, a big bear stood at the bottom of the line, holding it steady for a smaller creature to clamber up.

"Shit." She chopped faster.

The smaller bear scrambled up a few feet. The rope pulled taut, and Jendara's work proved itself. With a twang, the rope split and the bear tumbled into the open sea.

Below, the big bear roared with fury. With a sudden screaming, the crows swooped down out of the rigging. The air around Jendara went black. Beaks gouged at her face. Claws dug into her scalp.

She dropped to her knees, pressing herself into the sheltering curve of the railing. The snap and dry flutter of feathers drowned out the world.

Something pounded against her, thumped her back. Bird bones crunched. The onslaught slowed, but Jendara kept her head covered, not yet willing to uncover her face. Blood trickled down her temples and from uncountable cuts around her scalp.

Kran's hand appeared, and Jendara grabbed on to it. Mounds of crow corpses lay on the ground around her. Glayn smashed one last bird down on the deck.

"Look." Vorrin pointed over the side.

Jendara wiped blood out of her eyes and peered down. The big bear snarled up at her, an arrow jutting from his shoulder. An arrow tip appeared in his chest, and he stumbled. Jendara found herself wondering at the strength it must have taken to shoot an arrow through a bear's chest.

The bear sank into the bottom of his ship, and oars splashed into the water. There must have been some kind of crew hiding beneath the boat cover after all. The longship lunged away from the *Milady*.

Another arrow shot across the deck of the retreating longship, and Jendara followed its path back to a fishing boat, where a woman with brilliant copper hair stood in the prow, longbow in hand.

"Fambra!" Jendara called, then winced. The cuts on her face stung too much to smile. But she was glad to see the other woman.

Jendara stopped waving. She had almost forgotten the longship she'd seen headed for Sorind. She darted to the mainmast and scrambled up the manlines. But she didn't need to make it even to the first spar to see the second longship moving away from the island as well, hurrying back northward.

Where was it going? If it was indeed a raider, why hadn't its crew sacked the port while the first ship distracted the fishing fleet? Had its crew turned back because it witnessed its sister ship's defeat?

She climbed down to the deck. This seemed like a bad time to leave Sorind.

Chapter Ten
A Plan

The fishing boats followed the *Milady* back to Sorind's harbor. Jendara tried to find Fambra's boat among them, but it was hard to focus with Vorrin dousing her crow-inflicted cuts and gashes with brandy. When he squeezed the deep gash on the end of her thumb, she hissed and jerked her hand away, nearly overturning the water cask she sat on.

"I'll just tie it up," she grumbled. He yanked back her hand and pinned it to his ribs with his elbow.

"It's deep," he warned her. "It might need stitches."

"It's my left thumb. I don't use it for anything."

He raised an eyebrow and then went back to examining the thumb. She gave up on escape and let her cheek rest against his side, her eyes closed. He felt warm and smelled faintly of the lavender she added to the laundry soap, but mostly of damp wool and fresh sweat. It was a nice smell, comfortable and familiar. She tried to remember what Ikran had smelled like and came up blank. She hadn't dealt much with laundry in those days; life aboard ship tended to wipe away such niceties.

Vorrin was jabbing at her thumb with the curved sailmaker's needle, but the pain felt distant. She let it wash over and through her, letting her mind circle around old memories. Watching Kran take his first steps on the *Milady*'s deck. Dancing with Vorrin while Glayn played the hurdy-gurdy. She smiled a little at that one.

She felt him lift her chin and opened her eyes to look up into his. They crinkled in a smile. "You were humming."

"Really?"

"That song Glayn plays so well on the hurdy-gurdy." His eyes were still smiling, still holding hers.

"It's a good song."

"It is." He leaned closer.

She winced and pulled away. "I think you're stabbing me."

The smile died. He sighed and reached for the brandy. "I just put three stitches in your thumb and all you did was hum. Let the needle poke your palm a bit, and suddenly you complain?"

She started to respond, then noticed Glayn and Kran approaching. She frowned. "What have they got?"

Vorrin stiffened. "The bear's head."

She'd forgotten about the dead creature, but of course the corpse couldn't be left in the middle of the deck. The head dangled awkwardly in Glayn's grip. Kran gave the thing a wide berth.

"You ought to take a look at this." Glayn held it out.

"Besmara's boots," Jendara swore. She stared at the thing. It had been a bear when it attacked her—she was sure of that. But this—this was no bear. The shaggy black fur wasn't attached to the twisted face beneath it; the head was merely shrouded in a bearskin hood. A man in a bear suit who looked and clawed and bit like a real bear." What is that thing?" Vorrin asked.

Its eyes stared out at her, their irises strangely milky, like a blind man's. There was no mistaking those blank orbs.

"It's a Kalvaman."

Jendara hurried down the gangplank and headed straight for Fambra. The woman pulled her into a close half-hug, pounding her shoulder with her fist. "I'm very glad to see you, Jendara," Fambra said. "Your worries seem to be coming true." She rubbed her eyes. "Damn, I'm exhausted. We sailed all night to get here."

Jendara led the woman up to the shore and sat down on an abandoned barrel. "What happened?"

"When you left Alstone yesterday, we set out for some of the northwestern fishing grounds. We met a few other Flintyreach fishing boats and spread out. After working for a few hours, we were just considering heading back when a group of raiding vessels appeared. They grappled one of the other boats. I tried to get to the boat, but the wolf-things on board—"

"Wolf things?" Jendara interrupted.

"They might have been dogs, I couldn't tell. There were men, too, and between the men and the wolves, the attackers had already pulled the three fishermen into their boat. Our boat gave chase, but we stopped when . . ." she trailed off.

Vorrin caught Jendara's eye. He had beaten her to the shore, and carried a mug. He pressed it into Fambra's hands. "Have some tea," he encouraged her.

She took a gulp and wiped her mouth with her fist. "I wish it were something stronger." She shook her head. "I'm going to have to drink myself to sleep for a week after that."

Jendara squeezed her shoulder. "You don't have to talk about it now."

"No, you need to know." Fambra took a deep breath. "The bastards had killed one of the fishermen. A guy I knew, young fellow from Orcmoot. They just stood him up in the prow of the boat and slit his throat, right in front of us. To show us.

"And one caught his blood in a mug and drank it."

She sagged, and hugged the hot tea close to her chest.

Vorrin pulled Jendara away. "She said there were wolves on board? And they attacked fishing boats?"

Jendara nodded. She thought of the bear-man Vorrin had decapitated. "The attackers we saw were men wearing bear hides that somehow looked and sounded like real bears."

"So maybe the ones Fambra saw were similar, but wearing wolf hides." He began to pace. "I've never heard of anything like it."

Jendara frowned. "I have. And so has everyone who lives on the islands. Remember our boar hunt?"

He stopped pacing. "What about it?"

Fambra looked up from her tea. Jendara nodded at her to included her in the conversation.

"Morul smudged the boar's hide with smoke so a witch couldn't use it to transform herself into an animal. I always thought it was a story. But what if it's not?"

He frowned.

"Skinwalkers," she mused. "We need to talk this over. Get everyone up to the meeting hall, as fast as you can. This is big trouble."

"More of my clan are coming," Fambra said, getting to her feet. "After what happened to our friend, we'll do whatever it takes to handle these monsters."

Jendara had no doubt of that.

Inside the meeting hall, lanterns filled the space with a soft golden glow. A low fire crackled in the central hearth, giving off the scent of good cedar. The afternoon should have felt peaceful, the hall cozy. Instead, the shifting and shuffling of close to a hundred nervous people made the space claustrophobic.

Jendara cleared her throat. "Is everyone here?"

Morul stepped up on the low podium beside her. "All the villagers are here, save for a few out in the farthest fishing grounds. I'm still waiting on the outer homesteads."

Jendara glanced around for Yul, but she couldn't see his corn-silk-colored braids. She would have liked to have him beside her. People always took the quiet man seriously.

Still, she had Morul, Sorind's richest man and chief. That counted for a lot. She raised her hands.

The crowd fell silent.

"Look," she began, "over the last several days, there have been a lot of strange things happening. Like that longship that attacked my ship yesterday, or the people who attacked my friend Fambra."

The crowd murmured a little. Jendara cleared her throat.

"I know many of you have heard rumors about what we experienced out on Flintyreach." The crowd gave small sounds of assent. Jendara knew more than a few crew members had gone drinking the night before, and they'd surely told tales at the tavern. It was time people knew the truth. "Well, it's worse than you might have thought it was."

She explained what happened at the quarry, the terrible violence. She asked Vorrin and Boruc to tell about the hunting expedition, letting them describe the creature she'd shot out on the causeway. She beckoned to Fambra.

"This woman has her own tale to share."

Fambra recounted the story of the wolf-things that had taken the fishermen. "That's not all," she said. "There were two other raiding ships. One harried us all night. We got away in the fog, but there's still a chance it caught our trail."

Mumbling in the audience turned to a dull roar punctuated by raised voices. People clamored to be heard.

Someone pounded the floor. Jendara turned around. She'd forgotten the injured man from the raiding boat, resting in the corner the wisewoman used as a kind of hospital.

"The same thing happened to me." He grabbed a shelf on the wall to pull himself to his feet. Vorrin hurried to help support him.

"I'm Hazan, from Battlewall. I've been saving up to build a homestead on one of the little islands up west of Dragon's Rib. Found a real nice spot, too." He winced and gritted his teeth. Beneath his loose linen tunic, Jendara could see layers of white bandaging—he'd probably broken a couple of ribs as well as cracking his head.

"My brother and I were headed north to make sure everything on my homestead site was ready for the winter."

The villagers went silent, their eyes riveted on the man.

"It was getting dark. It ain't safe to sail at night out there—too many rocks. So we were about to throw out an anchor and get some shuteye when Byrni saw something moving out in the fog. A lost longship, he thought. Good salvage." Hazan drew himself up to his full height. For an Ulfen man, he wasn't particularly tall, maybe even a little shorter than Vorrin. There was still blood streaking his dirty blond hair. "He steered us up to the longship."

"What happened?" Jendara asked.

"He went to tie us up to it, but then creatures jumped out of nowhere. I'd say they were bears, but they weren't like any bears I ever saw. Not that I could see much—mostly I just heard the growling." He stopped for a second, his breathing gone ragged. "One bit into Byrni's face. I tried to pull him back into my boat, but it knocked me down. I got back up, and something hit me in the head. Lights went off, and I fell. But before everything went black, I heard a bad scraping sound. I reckon we came up against a reef, and their longship must have taken damage. But I don't know nothing. I wasn't even myself until I woke up here in this meeting hall."

Lots of murmuring at that. Jendara shook her head. Those creatures had ripped off half of Byrni's torso.

"I was lucky," Hazan said. "The next man might not be."

The crowd riled up again, the voices climbing into pitches of fear and resentment. Jendara caught Morul's eye. This was getting ugly, but there was still one more piece the people needed to know.

"There's nothing for it," Morul whispered. "Tell them."

Jendara nodded, then stepped forward and spoke.

"I know who they are."

She kept her voice level, but the noise in the room suddenly dropped as people turned back to her, expectant.

"What do you mean?" someone demanded.

"The raiders," Jendara said. "They're skinwalkers. From Kalva."

The silence hung for a moment, like a drop of water falling through the air. Then it exploded.

"She's out of her mind!" a voice shouted. "Skinwalkers and Kalvamen!"

"People are dying, and she's telling us fairy tales!" yelled another.

"They're not fairy tales!" Jendara spat back, trying hard to keep her anger in check. "I've fought them—killed them! We cut off one of the bear-thing's heads and watched it turn back into a man's. A man with milk-white eyes."

"And where is it now?" A big, red-bearded man she recognized as a farmer named Helge pushed his way to the front. "Show us this magic head."

Damn. "We threw it overboard," Jendara said. "But my crew all saw—"

"Your crew aren't islanders," Helge shot back.

Jendara made a fist. "And what's that supposed to mean?"

Morul grabbed her shoulder. "Easy," he murmured, then louder, "Jendara's done more to protect this community than you have, Helge. She—"

"Idiots!"

The word cracked through the tumult like a whip. The crowd turned, stunned and silent, and parted down the middle.

Gerda stood in the back of the room, glowering and holding a walking stick like a scepter of office. She stalked forward toward the podium, the blue tattooed swirls standing out on her cheeks. Men twice her size looked down or shrank back as her disapproving gaze passed over them.

Gerda stopped in front of the podium and turned to address the crowd. "These raiders killed some of the best men and women in my clan, butchering them like animals. Jendara and her friends have fought and killed them to protect your island, yet you doubt her?"

Helge looked uncomfortable, but crossed his arms and bulled ahead. "Kalvamen and skinwalkers are just old stories."

"And you don't trust old stories?" Gerda spoke softly, but Jendara could have sworn the whorls on her cheeks began to glow in the firelight. The old woman turned to Jendara. "This skinwalker—describe his eyes again."

"Milk-white," Jendara said immediately. "All filmed-over like an old man with cataracts, but worse—across the whole eye."

"There it is, then." Gerda turned back to the gathered islanders. "You've all heard the stories. You know the signs. The Kalvamen have come south once more, and there's no time to waste arguing. The question now is what you're going to do about it." She stepped forward to join the assembly, then turned back to Jendara. "So what's your plan?"

Jendara hoped the surprise didn't show on her face as she squared her shoulders and looked out at the villagers. A few heartbeats ago, they'd been on the verge of shouting her down. Now they were all looking to her for salvation—even Helge.

No matter. It was time to think of all those town meetings she'd half-slept through when she was a wee sprog of a girl, all those times her father had crafted a way to feed the clan in a famine or cut off a mainlander raiding party before it reached their village.

A plan.

"What we really need is solid information about these monsters. We don't know where they come from or what they're doing on our islands, and we're running scared. My plan is to organize scouting parties—all volunteer, of course—and send them out into the northwestern fishing grounds to see if we can find those monsters. As my father would say, 'Who knows the land has the upper hand.' Well, we're going to take that upper hand."

Someone cheered. Jendara thought it might be Glayn. She risked a glance out at the faces in the crowd. They were still looking at her expectantly.

As they should. Sending out scouts was important, but until the scouts returned, these people were still facing an unknown danger that might or might not be planning an attack on their own island. She set her jaw. "In the meantime, return to your homes and prepare to defend them. Sharpen your swords. Keep your armor by your door. Tend your fields in pairs, and if you work in the village, post lookouts around the perimeter." She raised her voice. "Anyone interested in joining a scouting party, join us here at the speaking platform."

The crowd rumbled into motion and speech. Jendara knew it would take a while for the crowd to sort itself out.

She caught Vorrin's eye and gestured toward the back corner of the room. "Are you—"

"Organizing a scouting party? Of course. Tam and I can take the skiffs." He held up a hand before she could speak. "I know we've been working hard to get our trade goods to Varisia, but I'm starting to think people here are in immediate danger. Besides," he shrugged, "If we go late in the season, we may be able to make a better profit. Our goods will be unexpected. We'll have to stay on the mainland for the winter, but I have some connections. It won't be so bad."

Jendara's mouth opened and closed without sound. She hadn't expected any of this. "Stay in Varisia for the winter?"

"Or even Cheliax. Absorb some culture. It would be good for Kran, don't you think?"

She steered her mind back to the task at hand. "Kran. That's just it, Vorrin. You can't go on this scouting mission."

He shook his head. "What?"

"We were attacked in sight of Sorind. The island's clearly a target. I'm hoping to get the scouting parties in and out as fast as possible, but we can't leave Sorind undefended."

He folded his arms. "And you want me to stay here as a kind of nursemaid."

"Not nursemaid!" She was getting too loud. She needed to calm down. Jendara took a deep breath. "Look, this is as close to a home as we've got. I can't let anything happen to it."

He must have heard the strain in her voice, because he took her by the shoulders. "I know you won't." He pulled her closer. "And you're right. The Sorinders are strong, but most of them lack combat experience. They're not raiders or warriors."

She nodded. It was easier to relax, this close to Vorrin. Easier to think. She wondered why she hadn't noticed it before.

"That's why I should go on this scouting expedition," he said. "You should stay here with Kran and keep an eye on the village," he said.

Her hand crept to the handle of her belt axe. "I can't."

He glanced down and his lips thinned. "You're thinking about your father. About revenge."

"Not revenge, Vorrin. I just can't let what happened to my family happen to anyone here. That's why I have to go. If I can catch one of these bastards, maybe I can finally learn enough to stop them."

He dropped his hands from her shoulders and crossed his arms across his chest. "You've got to stop thinking about the past."

"Jendara," Morul called. "The volunteers are assembling."

She reached out. "Vorrin—"

But he just shook off her hand. "You've got a meeting. And I've got babysitting detail."

He pushed his way through the gathering volunteers without a backward glance. Jendara watched him go, her stomach twisting into knots.

There were far more volunteers than Jendara had expected, and it took some time to sort them into crews. Some had boats; most were experienced hunters. Some of the *Milady*'s crew wanted to go, now that they'd seen the creatures for themselves. Jendara was ready for a bottle of lingonberry wine by the time she got them sorted into appropriate parties.

She stopped them before they left the meeting hall to collect their gear. "Now remember: we're just scouting here. Try not to engage the enemy. We'll meet back here to determine what needs to be done, and if it looks too serious, we'll send a delegation down to Hagrim to get real help. White Estrid has the manpower to back us up."

She watched the volunteers file out of the building, sagging a little. It had been a long day.

A voice rumbled from the back corner of the room: "You forgot about your own scouting team." Hazan had propped himself up in the corner, watching the proceeds in silence.

She waved a hand as she turned to face him. "I'll be fine on my own. I'll get a ride on one of the fishing boats."

"There's another boat you could use," he said, getting to his feet. "Mine. It's in good shape, as long as you don't mind a shredded boat cover."

Jendara was tempted. His sailboat would move fast, and let her cover that much more ground. "You're just going to let me use your boat?"

"There's a price, of course." He crossed to the dying fire. In the flickering light, his face was impossible to read.

"Of course." Jendara felt wearier than ever. Some people would take advantage of any disaster to make a copper.

"You've got to take me."

"What?" Jendara shook her head, surprised. "What do you mean?"

"Look," he said, "those things killed my brother. I think I deserve a chance to help bring them down."

"You've got broken ribs and a concussion. Not exactly fighting form."

"I can still pilot a boat," he growled.

She felt a twinge of fellowship for the man. She could understand what he felt. But it also clearly pained him to stand upright.

"Please," he said. "I won't let you down. I . . . you've only seen me at my worst, but I'm a good sailor, and I can fight."

She crossed to his side and put out her hand. "All right. It's a deal. As long as you keep in mind that I'm the captain. I'm not going to let you do anything stupid."

He shook. "That'll be fine. I'm not in any kind of shape to do stupid things right now."

She had to grin at him. It sounded like something she would say.

She went home before she went to the docks to prepare Hazan's sailboat. She didn't know if she'd find Vorrin and Kran there or not, but it made sense as a starting point.

Kran looked up from a plate of cheese and bread when she came in. He gave a half-hearted wave.

"Hi," Jendara said lamely.

He reached for his chalk. *Do you have to go?*

She dropped down into the seat beside his. "I think so. There's . . ." She stopped. How could she tell her little boy about what she'd seen at the quarry? How could she explain monsters that tortured and ate their victims? She put her fingers over her eyes and rubbed the tired muscles. There were some things a mother just shouldn't have to do.

He kissed her cheek, quickly. Then his chalk squeaked on the slate. When she looked up, he had written: *I was in the meeting hall. I heard everything.*

She winced.

I'm sorry! he scrawled quickly.

Jendara felt stricken. "No, sweetie, I'm not upset with you. I'm just upset that you had to hear it like that."

Those things are monsters, he wrote. *I wish I could go fight them.*

"I'm glad you're not," she said, pulling him half-off his chair so she could give him a real, full hug. "These things—I couldn't take it if they got their hands on you. Because you're right, Kran. They are monsters."

A knock at the door cut off any reply he might have made. Jendara sighed. She didn't want to be interrupted right now, not for anything.

She threw open the door and stared at the old woman on her stoop. "Gerda."

The Alstone wisewoman slipped past her. "I brought you this," she said, waving a small ceramic crock. "Ointment, for those wounds."

"Thank you," Jendara said. She tried not to tense as Gerda strode into her house, like some sort of military commander on inspection. After all, the old woman had supported her during the meeting. "And thank you for saying what you did at the meetinghouse."

Gerda snorted. "Only a fool ignores the truth when it's right under her nose." She gave Jendara a pointed look, then put her hand on her hip and looked around the cottage. She made a disapproving sniff.

Jendara put her own hands on her hips. "I see. Well, the ointment is very generous, but I'm fine."

Gerda raised an eyebrow. "You're sure of that, are you?" She took a few steps closer to Jendara, peering at the claw marks on her face. "Those wounds look puffy to me. Like they're fighting an infection."

Jendara resisted the urge to touch the scratch marks. "They're fine. They were cleaned well."

"You know," Gerda said, leaning against the kitchen counter, "I've been talking to some of the other fisherfolk. Your crew, too. And you know what they've all mentioned?"

Jendara pressed her lips tight and didn't answer.

"Seeing crows on the attackers' boats. One, two, as many as a dozen. But no one else has been bothered by them. Funny, isn't that?"

"What are you implying?"

Gerda placed the crock on the counter. "I'm not implying anything. But these are all good people. People who are active in their communities. People who are loyal to their clans."

A muscle clenched in Jendara's jaw. She waved at the open door. "Thank you for the ointment, Gerda."

Gerda inclined her head. "You're very welcome." She gave the cottage a last evaluating look. "You know," she said, "I don't see a clan altar in here. Maybe you should change that." She smiled as she brushed past Jendara.

Jendara slammed the door behind the old woman and gave it a kick for good measure. She didn't believe clan spirits were any kind of protection against crows set on attacking a person.

She snatched up the ceramic crock, ready to toss it in the fireplace, then stopped.

Clan spirits might not be any kind of protection against crows set on attacking a person, but hers *was* the only ship the crows had attacked. Why was that? Why, of all the people who had seen them, had those crows decided to attack her?

She put the crock down on the table, next to the leather pouch she planned to fill with provisions. Absently, she cut off a slice of the bread Kran had set out. Fifteen years ago, she would have offered that piece to the ancestor spirits. A part of her wondered if she should listen to Gerda and put out an offering, but common sense stuffed the slice into her mouth. There was no point worrying about crows or spirits. She had a mission to lead.

Chapter Eleven
Chum

By late afternoon, the rest of the scouting vessels had split off from main flotilla, and Jendara was steering north, skirting the edges of the fishing grounds. This stretch of the seas on the outermost rim of the Ironbound Archipelago extended north and west of Flintyreach to flank the island of Dragon's Rib. The deceptively smooth waters lay over a collection of reefs and rocks that made the area a killing ground for big sailing vessels. Even Hazan's little sailboat had too deep a keel for the central waters. Most fishing boats simply anchored on the edge.

Out here, they should be safe, but to the west, a few tiny islands nosed up—and where there were islands, there were often offshore rocks. Jendara kept a close eye on the water. She shrugged off her sweater. With only a light breeze, the summer sun felt good on her skin. It was hard to believe winter was just weeks away. But that was life in the islands, she thought. Sunshine one day, snowstorm the next.

From the bow, Hazan coughed.

"You all right?" she asked. He hadn't complained all day, but it was hard to tell how he was feeling. He'd looked pale, so she had sent him forward to rest.

"Just fine. Keeping my eyes skinned. I don't like these waters." He spat overboard. "Sailed around here quite a bit while I was looking for my homestead site. There are a handful of islands out here. Just rocks, really. Mine's the biggest."

"How big?" She adjusted the rudder. There was something up ahead, maybe rocks, maybe debris. She didn't want to hit it.

"Big enough for a house, grass enough for a couple of goats. I don't need much. Mostly, I fish. In the summers, I go to Flintyreach with a crew and hunt trolls for bounty." He pointed ahead. "There's something on the water."

"I see it." She swung the vessel around so they'd ease up beside the debris. "You come back here and take the rudder."

She tugged the gaff hook out from under the seat and squeezed aside so Hazan could settle into place. She perched on the edge of the foredeck to sweep at the water, hooked a clump of something and pulled it closer. A bunch of rope. She frowned.

The tentacle snaked around her arm before she even saw it. She hissed as the suckers bit into her bare skin.

Forgetting everything she knew about squid, she tried to yank her arm free. The tentacle wriggled tighter. Blood streamed down her arm. The gaff hook slipped out of her fingers.

She twisted so her free hand could reach her sword. The thing tugged harder. Her boots scrabbled in the bottom of the boat for purchase. It was going to pull her overboard.

The sword caught in its scabbard.

"Hazan!"

"I'm coming!"

She gave up on the sword and clawed at her belt knife. Freed it. The tentacle wriggled higher up her arm, working up to her body. She couldn't let it pull her overboard. She drove the knife into the flesh of the tentacle.

Water exploded around her. The head of the squid shot up, its massive eyes angry black orbs. A pair of tentacles whirled over her head.

She stabbed the knife down again and sawed at the flesh. With a burst of pain, the tentacle popped free. Jendara flew backward, tumbling into the bottom of the boat.

At the bow, Hazan pummeled a tentacle with an oar. Jendara scrambled forward, ignoring the burning in her arm and the blood trickling down her wrist. She wasn't sure she could use her sword arm; the muscles felt crushed. She pawed at her sword, freeing it from the scabbard, then drew it left-handed.

Something snarled. She ignored it, swinging the blade around and chopping off the nearest tentacle. Hazan dropped to his knees to get out of her way. The backs of her hands lit up with the hot, cruel hunger of the pirate goddess.

The sword flashed in Jendara's hand, catching the sun. The light struck the squid in its big black eye, and the creature shook its head, making waves that rocked the ship. A big one, Jendara thought, and grinned. She dropped into a crouch, ready to plunge the sword into the beast's mantle.

The squid pulled back, shielding its face with one of its remaining tentacles. Clearly afraid of her.

The squid slipped beneath the water. The snarling died, and Jendara realized she was the one who'd been making the horrible sound.

She peered over the gunwale, watching the creature swim into the deeps. Blue stained the foam on the waves. The creature was bleeding badly. Any sharks in the area would flock to it. Her hands felt suddenly cool.

"By Erastil, you're bleeding like a stuck pig!" Hazan hurried back to the little storage locker and returned with a roll of bandages. "They've got teeth in their suckers, you know. It chewed some good holes in your arm."

The fading effects of adrenaline made her chatty. "We ate a lot of squid, growing up. Fishermen would hire my father to clear out the waters before the spring salmon runs. He had sucker scars up and down his arms, and a big patch across his chest."

Hazan tied off the bandage covering her forearm, and she winced. "That's tight."

"It needs to be. Spray off of the water makes the bandage wet, it loosens up."

"I never thought about that." She rubbed at the bandage. It looked neater than she would have tied it.

"Your father's not the only one who's made ends meet hunting squid." He sat back in the bottom of the boat, rubbing his injured side. "It's good money."

"It's hard earning a living when you don't have your own land, isn't it?"

He rubbed his arm absently. "Glad I finally got my own stake."

She frowned. "Did you hurt your arm?" She reached out for him.

He pulled the limb away. "Just an old scrape. Scab must be catching on the fabric of my shirt."

For the first time, she realized he was wearing a long-sleeved shirt, a heavy sheepskin jerkin over the top. In this sun, he must be cooking. But he didn't look uncomfortable. She wondered if he was running a fever. Chills were often the first sign of infection. "You feeling okay?"

He rolled his eyes. "Fine. Now, how about you finish pulling in that flotsam and see if it gives us any clues?"

"Sure."

She'd lost the gaff hook, but the flotsam had drifted up against the side of their boat. She grabbed a handful of the rope and hauled it in. A chunk of wood had tangled in its knots, and Jendara reached out for it.

Hazan grunted. "That look like the side of a boat to you?"

She poked at the white-painted wood, the broken curve of one side, and nodded. "If I had to guess, I'd say this was part of an oar port."

"Any of the other boats in our group running under oar power?"

Jendara thought a moment. "There's one other faering. Might have switched to oars out here around the rocks."

Hazan straightened up. "I see smoke."

Jendara snapped her head to follow his pointing finger. North and east of their current bearing, away from the little islands, black smoke stained the sky. She brought out her spyglass, hoping to make out the source. "Smoke's too thick to see through."

"Let's get going, then." He hurried back to his post at the tiller.

Jendara was already moving, adjusting the rigging for full speed. The light breeze filled the sails and the faering shot forward. Jendara couldn't help smiling at the sailboat's response. She was a fine little craft.

As they grew close, they had to slow. The smoke billowed toward them, graying out the sun. Jendara fumbled for her handkerchief and bound it around her face. Up ahead, the smoke looked even heavier and blacker.

The boat crept forward. The slap of the waves against its hull sounded very loud, but other sounds were muffled—just as they'd been in that fog off Crow's Nest. She squinted into the gloom.

Someplace up ahead, a crow called. Jendara's lips tightened at the sound.

"Movement off the port bow!"

Jendara turned in the direction Hazan called, but it was too late—something pale flashed and she recognized the figurehead of a longship all at the same time. And then the figurehead smashed into the side of Hazan's boat and Jendara flew through the air, hitting the water hard.

The handkerchief slid up, clinging to her nostrils and lips, blocking out air. She clawed at it, but the knot caught in her hair. She realized she was sinking.

She kicked hard and came back up into the air, darker than ever now. She spluttered for breath.

"Hazan!"

He didn't answer. Jendara felt the water dragging her back down.

There came the feeling of something twisting in her hair, and then the unsettling sensation of rising upward even as her scalp burned.

Something crashed on her head and the darkness became absolute.

She awakened to pain. Her head spun, even though her cheek ground against a flat slab of cold stone, and her sucker-torn arm burned as if someone had rubbed salt into the wounds. She remembered falling into the sea.

What had happened to Hazan? She tried to remember. A longship had appeared in the smoke and rammed Hazan's boat. She had fallen overboard.

Her head swirled and she heaved up her lunch, the mess catching in her bunched-up scarf and puddling under her cheek. She managed to turn her head a little to keep from inhaling the stuff.

A cold claw ran down her leg. "She's awake," someone murmured.

She wished she could see the rest of the man. The bear skin covering his hands and arms was thick and brown—grizzly hair. It was all too easy to envision some massive bear crouched over her, its claws poised to slice her open.

"Stop groping her. She needs to be alive for the ceremony," another voice whispered.

"I won't kill her."

"The ceremony's almost started. We don't want to keep the Crow Witch waiting." There was nervousness in the second man's voice.

Someone grabbed Jendara by the arms. Her damaged arm shrieked with pain, but she cut off her cry. Her vomit ran down her neck, stinging her skin. The man jerked her upright, sending her head into chaos. She heaved again, and her legs went out from under her.

Grunting, he dragged her by the wrists bound behind her, her tightly tied feet and ankles scraping on stones. She could hear other voices now, low chanting and drums. Another set of hands closed on her arms, and she rose up in the air. Rough wood scraped her skin, and then her weight settled on the bindings between her hands.

She couldn't stop the scream as her shoulders popped out of their sockets.

She sucked in air and choked on it. Coughing jarred her shoulders, made it worse. She was crying now, sobbing like she hadn't since she broke her arm at age seven. This was pain, real pain, and she couldn't steady her head long enough to get ahold of it.

Beside her, someone else moaned. Her heart sank. Was it Hazan?

She could still move her head, although she didn't want to. But she needed to know if she was on her own.

A man hung from his bound wrists beside her, but he wasn't Hazan. Only an arm's-length away, it was too easy to see the abuse the stranger taken. The ruddy firelight flickered on the flayed flesh of his face. Something huge and vicious had clawed at it, ripping off strips of skin and slicing through muscle and fat. Yellow goo clotted with blood shone where once there had been an eye.

Her stomach twisted again, from rage now instead of her concussion.

Her head still pounded and spun, but she could think around the pain in her skull and shoulders. She managed her first deep breath since she'd regained consciousness and took a good look around herself. While she'd been knocked out, the afternoon had passed by, and now only a faint lavender clung to the edge of the sky. She and her captors were gathered on a beach, facing a vast and empty sea. Not even rocks interrupted its stretch. No ships moved on that dark immensity.

The beach, however, was full of people. She tried to count and gave up, estimating sixty to a hundred people bunched together in front of her. There could have easily been more on the periphery of the gathering. Her night vision was ruined by the enormous bonfire burning a few yards away. She could feel its heat even where she hung.

She wriggled her feet. They were bound tight, but her legs had some movement. She bent her knees until her feet pressed against the stake, taking some of the weight off her aching arms. The pain receded further into the back of her mind. She couldn't feel her hands— they were so tightly bound they'd gone numb—but she knew her tattoos were heating up.

And then the drumming changed.

It had been soft, regular tapping that complemented the chanting. Now something had cued it to change, to roar, to crash. Jendara could feel the beat thudding inside her, deep within the very chambers of her heart.

The crowd parted for a woman. She stood in the gap they created, making no effort to move, simply holding the crowd's attention. Jendara couldn't look away from her.

The pale fabric of her gown clung to her form, sketching her lean shape like a chalk drawing on dark paper. The night receded around her. Her skin gleamed, as pale and polished as an alabaster lamp, and strands of nearly white hair twisted around her shoulders and waist. It made the contrast of her headdress more astonishing.

The black headdress glistened with an oily shimmer. It stretched wider than the woman's shoulders and dipped low over her eyes. Crow feathers and whole wings sprang up from an armature of wire and tiny bird bones that tapered down to grip the woman's head. Within the armature, something moved, and Jendara caught a glimpse of a gleaming eye. The imprisoned crow cawed softly, and the crowd cheered.

The woman stepped forward. People dropped to their knees as she passed. This had to be the witch her captor had mentioned.

She looked away from the eerie figure, studying the kneeling people. Most wore cloaks or robes of animal hides that still bore their heads and paws. Jendara saw bear hides and wolf hides, a coyote, even a woman wearing a wolverine headdress with a fur skirt—and nothing else. The air stank of meat and rancid flesh. Jendara could smell it even above her own sour vomit.

A man knelt before the Crow Witch, offering up a long knife. Its tapered blade winked in the firelight. The woman accepted it, then raised it to the sky. The last of the sunset had faded, but only a few stars broke the black expanse of night. Jendara had the sudden certainty that the witch was welcoming that blackness into the wicked knife. She braced her legs, ready to push herself free of the post she'd been hung upon. The odds of running into the forest and actually getting away were slim, but not half as slim as surviving that knife.

But instead the Crow Witch turned to the whimpering man. She stepped close to him and seized his jaw. Jendara stared in sick fascination. The woman had tipped her fingers with the white claws of a cougar. They dug into the man's skin. The man began to cry.

"You are weak," the priestess announced.

The claws sank deeper into his flesh.

"Your spirit is not the spirit of a survivor or a warrior. If you were one of us, we would have staked you in the woods to feed the animals."

The crowd roared with approval.

"Instead, you screamed and shrieked and begged. You whimpered and moaned, as not even our tiniest babe would whimper." The witch's teeth flashed in a grin. The firelight gleamed off her long canines.

Jendara shrank against the post holding her up. There was something hideous about that sick smile. Her stomach twisted.

"You have revealed your only power to be the strength of your tongue. And I will use that." The woman raised her voice so the crowd could hear her better. "The creature whose pelt we transform tonight is a creature whose cry stills the blood of its prey, and this prisoner's tongue will help strengthen the war cry of the warrior

I choose to bear this pelt." She dropped the prisoner's face, her claws leaving bloody trails on his jaw. "Bring the cauldron!"

Two men rushed forward, the first of the barbarians Jendara had seen without pelts. But their bared skin was not pale. The lumpy purple scars of old burns stood out across their shoulders; the tattooed outlines of wolves and bears ran down their arms. As they dropped the heavy iron cauldron at the witch's feet, Jendara saw the faces they raised in adoration. Geometric patterns and paw prints covered their cheeks, and black ink outlined eyes covered over in a milky-white film.

The Crow Witch twisted her fingers in the prisoner's hair and drew back his head. His larynx bobbed in the taut arc of his exposed throat.

The witch raised the wicked blade.

He didn't even have time to gasp.

Blood sprayed from his slit throat, his racing heartbeat pumping the stuff into the air. The crowd shrieked delightedly. The drums picked up speed and Jendara felt her own heartbeat quicken in response. The dying man's body must have responded the same way. The bloody fountain pulsed faster.

The witch clapped her hands. More tattooed assistants hurried to help bleed the victim, their own knives flashing as they carved off pieces of the dying man. If he'd had a voice, he would have screamed.

Jendara's head spun. The heat of the bonfire, the sickening roil of her own damaged skull, the sight of lumps of fatty meat tossed from hand to hand in the dancing firelight: it was abominable. Was this how it had been at Alstone Quarry?

Was this how it had been in her own village?

With a wrench, Jendara realized the witch had turned toward her. The madness of the scene had distracted her. She had wasted precious moments she could have used to free herself.

The crow headdress leaned closer. Jendara could hear the rustling movement of the bird trapped inside and smell the rancid flesh of the untreated wings mounted on the eerie thing. Up close, its many layers of bone and feather showed, the fresh wings and crow heads covering old ones that had rotted down to nubs. Jendara swallowed hard.

She pressed her feet against the wooden post and tried to shift her weight slowly, imperceptibly upward. If her timing was right, she could use her fall to crush the witch and even take her knife. She didn't trust her chances with the larger men.

"You look like a strong woman," the Crow Witch said. "You've shown fewer weakness than any of these soft islanders. I would see your face cleaned before I add your blood to my cauldron."

She snapped her fingers, and one of the tattooed men hurried forward with a cup of water. With a quick slice of his knife, he removed the filthy handkerchief she'd tied on a lifetime ago, back on the boat with Hazan, then scrubbed the crusting vomit from her face and neck.

He ran his hairy forearm across her face to dry it, then gave a curt nod. He stepped aside.

The Crow Witch took his spot.

"Let me look at you, woman." Her clawed hand reached for Jendara's chin, tipping it up to better look into her face.

The witch leaned in closer, struggling to see in the low light and the shadow cast by the black headdress. The odor of rotting flesh made it hard to breathe.

Jendara tensed her leg muscles, ready to leap.

The woman stumbled backward, the knife falling from her hand. Her mouth opened and closed, but for a moment, no sound came out.

Then, finally:

"Jendara?"

Chapter Twelve
Signs and Stories

Jendara trembled. The woman's blue eyes bored into hers. They looked horribly, horribly familiar.

"Jendara?" she repeated.

Jendara turned her face away. Inside her chest, her heart shattered.

When she had found the crow pendant, she had hoped to track down her sister's killers. The day she'd found her father's ruined body but not her sister's, she had been certain of the worst. If the kind of monster who would maim and kill and eat human flesh had carried Kalira away, then there was no way she could have survived the kinds of horrors they would have inflicted upon her on their own ground.

But she couldn't deny the truth of her own eyes. "Kalira?"

"Jenny!" Kalira threw her arms around Jendara, pressing her cheek against her sister's. The headdress smelled worse up close. Maggots wriggled in its depths.

The captive crow made a questioning sound. Kalira laughed. "Quentzal! Oh, Quentzal! At last, my sister, my Jendara!"

Behind her, the crowd had fallen silent, waiting for their leader to explain herself. Kalira pressed her hand to her lips, overcome. Her fingers were long and slim, just like Jendara's mother's had been.

Kalira raised her arms and spun to face her followers. "My people!" she called. "We have been given a blessing beyond my greatest expectations! My sister, lost all these years, has been found!"

The crowd cheered. The drummers, reassured by this announcement, returned to their beating. Kalira gave instructions to the men around her, sending the blood-filled cauldron into the night. They cut Jendara's bindings and lifted her down from the post.

Kalira clapped her hands. "Bring food and wine to my tent. I will need Brynorm and fresh bandages, as well. Come."

They carried Jendara as if she were a baby. She wanted to walk, but the burning and heaviness in her feet warned against the idea. She must have been bound quite a while before she regained consciousness; it might take some time for proper blood flow to return to her limbs. As they moved away from the beach, the cannibals' rude shelters appeared, lean-tos of hides and branches with the occasional small tent. The tents grew more frequent the farther they went from the bonfire. They passed the burnt framework of a house— Jendara could still smell the char. These people hadn't been on this island long.

Kalira stood outlined against the entryway of a well-made hide tent, braziers lighting the inside to daytime brightness. She held back the tent flap and waved Jendara's porter in. "Lay her on the bed."

He put her on a pile of furs. The inside of the tent smelled musty and faintly herbal, with none of the stink permeating the rest of the camp. Jendara sagged with relief. Perhaps her sister wasn't so far gone as she seemed.

Kalira dropped to her knees beside the bed. "Jendara," she breathed. She traced Jendara's cheek with her unclawed hand. "After you left us, I would sit on the beach and hold my crow necklace, waiting for you to come back. I was so lonely. And now we're finally together again!" A beatific smile lit up her face. It softened the thin, sharp planes of her face, and for a moment she looked once again like the sweet teenage girl Jendara remembered.

Jendara's heart sank. She'd never imagined that Kalira had felt abandoned when she left home. She'd never even thought about it. She blinked back sudden tears.

Kalira lifted off the headdress and set it aside. The crow hopped down to her shoulder. It cocked an eye toward Jendara.

Kalira rolled her head a little, stretching her neck. "The Black Crown is heavy," she admitted. "There's a great deal of wire in it, since I keep adding on to it." She ran her fingers through her wild white hair, massaging her scalp.

Someone scratched at the tent flap.

"Come," Kalira commanded.

A man entered. He stood head and shoulders above the other men Jendara had seen, and wore a bear skin swept over his shoulder like a cloak. He wore only leather trousers, but his torso was so heavily tattooed and scarred that it might as well have been clad.

His nostrils flared as he trained his whited-out eyes on Jendara. "This one has been a great deal of trouble."

Kalira laughed. "Of course, Brynorm. She's my sister." She waved the man to the pile of furs. "Her shoulders have dislocated. Set them."

The man scowled and crossed the tent. He squatted, studying Jendara's shoulders. After a moment, he slipped off his sandals, stepped onto the furs, and stooped to grab Jendara's arm at the elbow. He jammed his foot down on her ribcage and twisted her arm.

It was worse than the moment they'd hung her on the post. She growled at the pain, then gasped at the sudden feeling of freedom within the joint. It was fixed.

He repeated the process on the other side and sat down on the floor. "What are you going to do with her?"

Jendara couldn't even raise her head. Exhaustion had dumped itself over her. Her shoulders felt vaguely puffy and her head pounded. She could feel prickles of sweat itching in her armpits. It was very hot in Kalira's tent.

Kalira leaned over to smile down at Jendara. "It hurts, doesn't it? Don't worry, I have just the thing."

She disappeared from Jendara's field of vision, and Jendara stirred up the energy to turn her head. Kalira propped a drinking horn next to a small chest and took something gray out of a satchel sitting beside Brynorm. She crumbled it into the cup.

"Don't worry," she said, sweeping back to sit beside Jendara and hold the horn to Jendara's lips. "It's just a mushroom. It's very good for pain."

Jendara smelled wine and the darker funk of dried mushroom. She tried to recollect what kind of mushroom might be used as a painkiller and drew a blank. But the liquid pressed against her lips and she let herself sip. Kalira, no matter how changed, wouldn't kill her.

"What are you going to do with her?" Brynorm repeated.

Kalira fixed him a stern look. "She is my *sister*. She will join our tribe and help me lead our people to greatness."

The woman stood and began to pace. "Yes, Jendara will be the perfect person to oversee the sacking of Halgrim. She has our father's training, and his fierce disposition. She will have the islanders begging for our leadership."

"Sacking . . . Halgrim?" Jendara's lips felt twice their size, her tongue floppy. She blinked and watched reality ripple. Her head no longer hurt and her shoulders felt lovely, but she had the vague suspicion her mind had been lifted free of her body and its messages barely reached her limbs. She struggled to raise her hand and watched the thing flop back on the bed. "People on these islands won't let you just walk in and take over."

"Oh, but they will. You should have seen what it was like, down at that ridiculous quarry. Just the sight of my warriors filled those people with despair. No, when I get done with these islands, everyone will be happy I've come to lead them." Kalira laughed. Jendara had forgotten the silvery tinkling of her sister's merriment. "Dear Jenny, you must be so confused. Let me explain."

Someone scratched outside, and Brynorm opened the tent flap. A woman, clad in strips of fur, scuttled inside. She nearly tripped over a pile of dirty gear beside the wooden chest. Booty from captured prisoners, the functioning part of Jendara's mind realized. She squinted at it. Maybe her own sword belt was somewhere in there.

Jendara blinked as the pile shimmered, turned blue, then went normal again. She rubbed her eyes, hard. That mushroom was powerful.

The serving woman placed a tray and a small pitcher on the chest where Kalira had mixed the mushroom drink. For a moment the woman became two identical dirty figures, then shimmered and twisted back into a single nervous servant. Jendara squeezed her eyes shut for a second, then reopened them. The woman adjusted the bowls and plates on the tray and gave Kalira a deep bow before turning to exit. The black outline of a paw had been printed on her shoulder, the edges purple, ropy scar tissue.

"Brynorm, get the brands," Kalira murmured. The man arose and hurried away.

Jendara's stomach plummeted. "Brands?"

"There are few metalworkers on Kalva," Kalira began. She crossed to the tray the woman had left and examined the offerings a moment. "I'm lucky that Brynorm is a fine smith."

Jendara licked her lips, trying to force them into normal function. "How did you meet Brynorm?"

Kalira beamed. "He adopted me. He taught me to live like a Kalvaman." She waved a hand, indicating the tent and its contents. "I owe all of this to him."

She brought the tray to the bed. Jendara stared up at her, trying to read her expression.

"They've brought cod roe," Kalira said. "It's good food for a sick person." She scooped some onto her fingers and offered it to Jendara. The orange roe glistened in the light.

"I'm not hungry."

Kalira's eyes flashed. "It is our way to share food when we exchange stories," she said. "You must learn our ways now, Jenny."

Jendara opened her mouth wide. The eggs felt cool and damp on her tongue, pleasantly salty. But the heavy scent of rotting flesh clung to Kalira's hair and hands, and Jendara nearly gagged.

Kalira pressed the horn cup to Jendara's mouth and held it there a long time, her eyes growing distant. Wine covered Jendara's mouth, crawled up her lip, went up her nose. She wrenched her chin away, spluttering for air.

Wine ran out of the cup, soaking Jendara's shirt and the furs, but Kalira didn't notice.

"The Kalvamen came just before lunch," she murmured. "No one saw them coming. Our people fought well, but we weren't prepared for the fury of the Kalvamen. They laughed when we struck them. They cheered when their warriors died. And they swarmed over us, fighting as no islander has ever fought."

Her eyes focused on Jendara's face for a second. "Have you ever watched a woman scream as her lips are being chewed off? The sound . . ." She paused and took a deep drink of the wine. Jendara wondered if she dared speak, but Kalira continued.

"After they had eaten their fill, including Father's liver, spleen, and male member—I won't tell you the things they did to him, while he was still alive—they took the youngest of us and put us in their ships. We were both larder and playthings for the Kalvamen, and the three days and nights we rowed to their island were filled with screams." She touched her collarbone thoughtfully. "I prayed to the spirits that I would die. I prayed you would appear with your ship and save me. I prayed to every god and every ancestor every single second of that voyage, even as blood leaked from my ears and my nose and between my legs. I prayed and prayed."

Metal clattered behind Kalira. Jendara had not seen Brynorm return, but now she turned her head to watch him. He shifted his grip on a number of implements, including another brazier, which he put down to light. He propped a metal brand up on the wooden chest so that its insignia lay in the growing flames.

"What happened?" Jendara whispered. She didn't want to know. She didn't want to hear any more of the terrible things her sister had seen and felt and lived through. Hell couldn't have been any worse. But she had to know.

"Something answered." Kalira stroked the crow on her shoulder. "Quorna, Quentzal's grandmother. I don't know where she came from, but she flew down out of the sky and landed on my shoulder and gripped it hard." She tugged at the neckline of her dress so it revealed her collarbone. Three silver scars showed. They must have been large wounds on a young girl.

"Maybe our clan ancestors sent her, or maybe my heart felt the weight of the crow-shaped pendant you gave me. I'll never know. But what I do know is that Quorna wouldn't let anyone touch me. The Kalvamen left me alone after that."

Jendara glanced at the brazier and the brand. Its metal was still mercifully dark. But Brynorm had not been sitting still while Kalira told her story. After removing a metal bowl from the chest, he opened the satchel where Kalira had found the mushroom. Jendara bit her lip as he searched in the bag. She doubted anything that came out of there could be good.

She wriggled her toes and looked back at Kalira. "I'm glad you found a protector."

"I would have died without Quorna," Kalira agreed. "When she died, I saved her bones to make the black crown. It was a way to keep her spirit close to mine." She reached for the tray and lifted a long sliver of meat, dripping with some kind of sauce. With a wet rude noise, she slurped off the sauce.

Jendara recognized the knobbed shape of a man's forefinger and swallowed her gorge. She rolled her feet at the ankles, hoping no one noticed. She had to get out of here somehow.

Kalira wiped her mouth on her arm and put down her revolting meal. "Anyway, the Kalvamen dumped me in their slave hut. I was the only one left from Crow's Nest, but there were other prisoners in the hut, both from the islands and from other tribes on Kalva.

Brynorm was one of them. He watched me with Quorna and knew there was something special about me."

The man grunted and turned the brand so it would heat evenly. Jendara struggled to make out just what design had been worked in the metal. She closed her eyes. The tale Kalira was spinning sickened her. She wished it would end, but she feared what might happen afterward.

"He came for me in the night. Together, we killed our guards and set out across the island. We found a place for ourselves among a clan on the other side of the island. For many, many winters, they had been the weakest of all the Kalvamen. There were almost no women or children left, because they had been stolen away."

Jendara flexed her feet. Her legs had feeling again. Her head had stopped pounding and the effects of the mushroom were easing. If she got the chance, she could probably run. She'd jump to her feet right now if she could, but her need to know held her as tightly as the thick shroud lines held the *Milady*'s mast in place.

"With the help of Quorna and other birds I befriended, our new clan regained its strength. I meditated on what I learned from the creatures I met, and the powers inside me grew." Kalira's eyes gleamed as she spoke, fervor building in her voice. "I learned to speak and move like animals do. Eventually, I could take on their shapes. With my powers and Brynorm's strength, we wiped out his former clan, absorbing their women and children. The flesh of their men made our hearts hard as shields. We took their strength and turned it upon our neighbors."

She shook her head. "That was our mistake. Clans do not grow strong through simple raiding and eating. They must also know the art of diplomacy. Many clans came together to fight us. In one battle, we lost a third of our fighters.

"But eventually, we succeeded. With Brynorm's guidance and my powers, we unified several tribes on Kalva, and forced the rest to give us a wide berth. The clans were weakened after years of fighting, but I had a vision. I had been sent to the Kalvamen not just to lead them, but also to guide them to a better place. A place where there is always enough to eat and the spirits of the land are strong."

"The Ironbound Archipelago," Jendara whispered.

"The islands," Kalira agreed. "Few tribes on Kalva are boat-builders, and the ones that had come raiding south and taken me had paid the price, as other tribes had attacked while half their warriors were off raiding. Yet I knew that ships were the way to power. Just thinking of my old home filled me with hope, and it was then that Quorna and I had our other great idea. Had there not been witches on the islands in ancient days who had the power to change men to beasts? Who better than myself to bring back those magics?"

"Skinwalkers!"

Brynorm lifted the branding iron from the flames and spat on it. It sizzled for a second. The man grunted and lowered it back into the brazier.

"What's he doing?" Jendara wiggled her toes again and felt some of the tingling subside. She struggled to sit up and watched her vision dance with blue shimmers, just as it had when the serving girl had entered.

"Brynorm is helping you," Kalira said. She undid the top buttons on her gown, revealing the bones of her upper rib cage, and a blackened, lumpy image of a crow's wing. "See? We've all taken a brand."

Brynorm grunted, turning his neck so Jendara could see the clawed paw print seared into his flesh. He reached for the metal bowl she had seen earlier. While Kalira had talked, he had filled it with something black and tarry. It smelled powerfully of herbs and earth and faintly of rotting flesh.

"Don't worry, Jenny," Kalira assured her. "I mixed the solution myself. There are herbs to encourage healing. And just enough of my blood to let the crow spirit into your heart." Tears winked in her eyes. "I couldn't be happier. My sister! Becoming one of my people."

Brynorm grabbed Jendara by the wrist. Jendara tried to pull away, but his blacksmith's grip was incredibly strong.

"You'll be one of us," Kalira whispered. "You won't be able to hurt me. Never again . . ."

Brynorm's free hand snatched up the glowing brand and brought it down.

Jendara smelled her own scorched flesh and gagged.

He ripped off the branding iron and plunged her hand down in the bowl. For a moment, it felt cool and soothing, and then the damaged flesh prickled and crawled, as if something burrowed into it. The Kalvaman closed his eyes, smiling beatifically.

Jendara wrenched her hand free and pushed off the bed, knocking over the brazier as she somersaulted across the floor. She tumbled into the chest, feeling its corners scrape her ribs. Beside it, a scabbard spilling out of the pile of pillaged goods caught her eye. She snatched up the weapon and felt a surge of disbelief. It was hers, and still attached to her sword belt. No one had even bothered to remove her pouch or the axe lashed onto it. She raced out the tent flap.

She didn't hesitate: she ran to the right, toward the island's dark center. From the glimpse of the ocean that she'd gotten, she had to believe they'd taken her to the northernmost point of the island. She wanted to put some distance behind them while she made a real plan.

She crashed through the brush, hearing shouts behind her. She smelled smoke and realized the brazier she'd knocked over must have started a small fire. Good. Anything that slowed down Kalira was a blessing for Jendara.

Despite the lack of moonlight, the sullen glow of the Kalvamen's campfire provided enough light for Jendara to make her way through the brush. Instinct told her to watch her step, but fear pushed her faster. She leaped a fallen tree and came down hard on something that bleated anxiously and threw her off. She tumbled into the bracken, hitting her head on a tree root. She lay still a second, letting her head settle. The creature bleated again.

She sat up, rubbing her temple. "Just a goat." Her nose crinkled at the familiar smell. Whoever had owned the burnt house back by Kalira's tent had apparently started a homestead.

She got to her feet. She had to slow down if she wanted to be quiet. They were certain to have found her trail by now.

She picked her way a few more feet and stopped, head spinning, her body first very hot and then very cold. Her tongue felt too big for her mouth. She remembered the black goo Brynorm had burned into her hand. What kind of herbs had Kalira added to that sick potion? Shivering, she crept forward a few more feet.

Behind her, the goat shrieked.

Jendara leaped forward. She had almost forgotten she wasn't dealing with ordinary men or women, but beasts. Skinwalkers. Wolves and bears and animals with senses far superior to her own. A twinge of fear spiked her heart, lending her speed.

A crashing sounded in the bushes just feet away, and she pressed herself harder, pumping her legs faster. But something flew through the air, slashing her shoulder even as it passed over her head. She caught a glimpse of a long whippy tail and a cat's gleaming eyes—and then with a horrified shriek it disappeared.

Jendara skidded to a halt. The ground fell away in front of her, opening into a creek bed. She gasped for air, thankful for the cougar-skinwalker's warning cry.

A wolf howled in the distance.

She studied the shallow ravine. At the bottom, maybe ten or twelve feet down, a good-sized creek raced. She would have heard the creek's gurgling if she and the cougar-thing hadn't been making so much noise stupidly crashing through the undergrowth. She glanced over her shoulder. Nothing. But that wouldn't last long.

Jendara sank down onto her butt, feeling the top of the bank for handholds. She sighed, relieved. There were plenty of tree roots and a few sturdy rocks. She couldn't count on them continuing all the way down to the ground, but she didn't have much choice. She grabbed the largest of the roots and swung herself over the ravine's edge. Time passed strangely, possibly a side effect of the drug Kalira had given her. Each fumbling scrabble for a handhold felt like a lifetime.

But she could have only been climbing for a few seconds before the wolf appeared at the edge of the bank. It lowered its head and growled at her.

From the far side of the creek, a cougar snarled in reply. Jendara risked a glance over her shoulder. The sodden cougar shook itself and growled. She wondered how long it would take the beast to get back across the creek. It didn't seem to be injured. Unlike her.

Cursing under her breath, Jendara kicked her foot for the next hold. The wolf trotted a few yards farther along the top of the bank and then leaped down onto an outcrop of rock. Jendara couldn't believe she hadn't noticed that easy path.

She scrambled down another foot of bank. She didn't have time to look for the best path. She needed solid ground, right now.

The rock beneath her hand broke free and she tumbled down the slope.

The air went out of her as she landed. She hadn't fallen far, and she'd fallen well, without taking any knocks to her injured head. But the wolf was already leaping down to the creek side.

Jendara jumped to her feet and grabbed her handaxe. She didn't wait for the wolf to charge. She launched the axe at its misshapen head.

The axe cleft its shoulder instead. The skinwalker yelped in pain.

"Shit," Jendara hissed. She unsheathed her sword and ran forward. She couldn't afford to let this thing catch her.

Teeth flashed as the wolf plunged toward her. Her sword came down on a thickly furred shoulder instead of its throat, and now it was too close for another thrust. She kicked it in the ribs. It reared up on its hind legs, ready to slam into her shoulders and slash at her face.

The wolf-thing never saw the blade coming. Jendara's momentum sent the sword's blade right through its torso. The blade caught in the ribs on the far side, and she kicked the skinwalker aside. Its body fell limply to the rocks.

Something splashed behind her. The cougar must be crossing the creek.

Jendara dropped to her knees and yanked her axe from the wolf's shoulder blade. At the top of the bank, someone shouted. Still in the center of the creek, the cougar snarled.

Jendara turned and ran toward the big cat, axe ready.

She hadn't counted on the current. It yanked her legs, hard. Her feet went out from under her, and she could only struggle to keep her head above the water and her grip on her axe.

The creek rushed onward, out through the forest and toward the sea.

After a tumbling eternity, the icy current pushed her beyond the beach and into open water, and she made herself sink below the surface. She held her breath until her lungs screamed, then breached the surface to snatch a quick gasp of air. Waves pummeled her head and shoulders, pushing her in a new direction, up the coast of the island and past the still-massive bonfire. Her heart leaped at the sight of two small canoes pulled up and overturned on the beach.

She jammed her axe into her waistband and hoped it would stay in place as she swam hard for the boats. When she felt sand beneath her feet, she knelt in the waves and watched the beach for a long wary moment. Kalvamen and beasts kept racing into the woods on the other side of the creek, shouting to each other. The focused attention on that side of the island suggested that was where their real ships docked.

Her mouth twisted. Once she finally got a boat in the water, they could track her down all too quickly. Her only advantage was the cover of night.

Jendara crept forward. A woman sat on the sand, head down, totally relaxed. A spear rested across her lap next to a half-gnawed bone. The scent of roasted meat made Jendara's stomach growl. Then she remembered Kalira's dinner. With disgust, she wondered just what kind of meat this guard was eating.

The woman didn't stir. Moving in a crouch, Jendara crossed the open beach, her axe in her hand. The woman suddenly looked up.

"What?" she murmured, eyes blinking blearily.

The axe smashed down on her head. The woman jerked and spasmed. Jendara averted her eyes as the woman's heels dug in the sand, sending up a little cloud of dust.

Jendara wiped the axe off on the woman's leather vest. There was no honor in this killing; the guard had barely been awake. The half-chewed bone rolled onto the sand.

Dishonorable death or not, the world was not going to miss another Kalvaman. Jendara hurried toward the canoes. She righted one and began to push it toward the waves.

For a second, she thought about chopping a hole in the bottom of the second canoe to slow any followers, then discarded the thought. A hollow canoe would resound like a drum when she struck it. A better idea came to her.

She darted back to the spare canoe, rolled it onto its side and found its paddles. It would be easier to steal these than wreck the boat.

She dropped the paddles into her own vessel and pushed out into the water. Though the sky was moonless, no clouds obscured the stars. In moments, she was paddling away from the island, the canoe's nose angled south.

Chapter Thirteen
Followers

The sun's approach turned the whole sea gray. Gray sky, gray water, gray canoe. Jendara stretched her fingers and made herself pick up her canoe paddle again. It was just too cold to take a long break.

She scanned the horizon behind her. Not a single ship. The observation didn't give her any kind of comfort. Kalira wasn't going to simply give up on converting Jendara to her cause, just like the ugly brand on the back of Jendara's hand wasn't going to go away on its own.

Her eyes wandered down to her hand. Seawater hadn't helped it any. The scab on the burn was slimy and gray, the skin around it swollen. There was no way it would heal nicely. She wondered why Brynorm had branded her hand—her right hand—of all places. Was it just to serve as a constant, visible reminder of her sister and her sister's people? Or had he noticed the old tattoos in the shape of Besmara's sacred symbol and thought to close off that connection?

He needn't have worried. She hadn't made an offering to Besmara in years. Not since the day Ikran had died.

She brought her mind back to the sea around her. A few small islands dotted the eastern quadrant of visible waters. They had to mark the far edge of the fishing grounds. She hadn't really thought that they'd taken her all the way to Kalva—that trip would have taken days. Instead, she'd guessed the little island the raiders had set up camp on was one of the uninhabited rocks scattered across the northernmost tip of the Ironbound Archipelago. If that were the case, maybe she'd find one of her scouts soon.

And maybe she needed to pay more attention to her paddling. She sat up straighter. It was easy to become distracted by one's thoughts, but that was a sure way to get a body killed. Hadn't she already faced a giant squid in these waters? And of course there were always rocks to worry about, or simply the waves themselves. These waters could kill.

She looked back over her shoulder. Still no following ships. But plenty of seabirds moved through the skies. Kalira had shown a preference for crows, but given her ability to create all kinds of animal shapeshifters, Jendara worried any kind of bird might act as Kalira's eyes.

The wind stirred the salt-crusted collar of her shirt, and she shivered. What had the men called Kalira when they were taking Jendara to the ceremony? The Crow Witch? The name seemed a little too appropriate.

The canoe bumped against something beneath the waterline, and Jendara cursed. She probed the area with her paddle and flinched when she struck stone.

Rocks. Big ones. And right now she wasn't doing the best job watching out for them.

She braced the paddle against the stone, holding the canoe in place. She squeezed her eyes shut. They stung with exhaustion. She'd been up nearly twenty-four hours. Her shoulders ached from their dislocation and Brynorm's brutal repairs. Every inch of her skin felt scoured or scraped. If she had an anchor, she'd moor right here and take a much-needed nap.

The shriek of a crow made her eyes snap open.

The black bird lobbed itself at her face. She twisted beneath it and lashed out with her paddle. The bird whirled away.

"Damn you!" she shouted. "Damn you and all your people!"

The bird circled her and she swatted at it again. The canoe tipped and lurched.

"I'll never join you, Kalira! Do you hear me?"

The bird screamed and streaked away, whether reporting to Kalira or just scared of the woman with the paddle, it was no longer interested in Jendara.

Jendara sagged. She rubbed her damp arms for a moment to warm them up, then turned her eyes to the skies. There were no other birds headed her way.

She wriggled her feet. They still felt cold and wet from her swim. She reached down to adjust her boot and touched an icy puddle.

There was water trickling into the bottom of her canoe. She must have scraped the side more than she'd known, or bashed it a second time when she was trying to strike at that crow. Her stomach twisted. She needed to find help, and soon.

Jendara paddled faster. At least there was some sign of land ahead.

She'd stopped to bail several times, using her boot as a scoop. When the fishing vessel appeared, she resisted the urge to simply jump overboard and swim to it. She paddled toward it and cringed as her feet got wetter and wetter.

The boat adjusted its course toward her. A few yards away, a voice shouted: "Ahoy!"

"Ahoy," she called back. It didn't look like one of Kalira's raiding ships, but if it was, she'd deal with it.

"You a Sorinder?" someone called.

"I sure am!" she shouted, feeling a surge of hope.

"Jendara, is that you?" a woman bellowed, and Jendara recognized the voice.

Jendara grinned. "Aye-aye, Captain Fambra!"

They had her on board in moments. Jendara watched the canoe fall behind Fambra's boat and hoped it sank before any of Kalira's people discovered it.

"There's an island just a little south of here," Fambra said. "A bunch of our group headed there when night fell. We should reach it in about half an hour."

"Thank goodness. I have a lot to discuss with everyone."

Sven studied her, his eyes staying longest on her swollen hand. "I see you've not had an easy time of it."

Jendara sighed. "You've got that right."

"Gerda will give you the once-over once we've talked to the others," he reassured her. "You'll feel right as rain when she's done."

Jendara remembered Gerda's visit to the cottage back on Sorind. "I'd rather live with the pain," she mumbled, but Sven was already hurrying to check something in the boat's stern. Jendara sank into the bottom of the boat and closed her eyes. For now, it was safe to sleep.

Sven shook her awake all too soon. "Fambra's already gone ashore. She's waving to us, and looks upset."

Rubbing her eyes, Jendara followed Sven overboard. A mass of boats had tied themselves cleverly to the shore, smallest closest to land, and now Sven jumped from craft to craft until he reached an outcropping of island stone.

The sight of a familiar figurehead stopped Jendara in her tracks. That was Hazan's boat. How had he survived? And why hadn't he tried to help her?

Fambra ran toward them, her face hard. "You've got to see this! It's bad."

She looked so upset that Jendara followed immediately, despite instinct telling her to find Hazan first. Fambra led them over the little island's humped back. A few bunches of beach grass clung to the pockets of sand between the rocks, but other than that, nothing grew. The rocks were steeper on the east side of the island, with no beach to interrupt their descent into the ocean. The other searchers were gathered on these rocks, most sitting or crouching, some standing with their arms folded across their chests.

They were all looking at a body.

Jendara walked down to it. Someone had turned it over, and a waterlogged face stared up at the sky with black-hollowed eye sockets. Eyes never lasted long in the ocean.

"One of our clan," Fambra said. "Raik. A good man. There were two others on his boat."

Jendara remembered Raik. He'd come in the other faering, a new-looking model from the Battlewall boat yards. She remembered the smoke she and Hazan had seen, out in the water, and the bit of wood that might have been an oar port. It must have been from Raik's boat.

She brought her attention to his wounds. A jagged hollow glistened where his throat had once been. "Looks like something's ripped out his throat. A wolf'll do that if it gets a chance."

"A wolf at sea," someone murmured, fear heavy in their voice. "Like the ones that got those fishermen."

Jendara looked for the source of the voice. "Yes. Just like them." She broke off, catching a glimpse of Hazan huddled in the back of the group. She leaped to her feet and stalked over.

"You." She dug her fingers into his shirtfront and yanked him up close. "What the hell are you doing here?"

"Wait." Fambra laid her hand on Jendara's shoulder. "What's going on? Hazan said you two split up."

"He's a liar," Jendara spat. "I ought to kill him right now. Probably a spy for the Kalvamen!"

"No!" He shook his head, hard. "I'm a coward, yes, but no spy. I swear it!"

She gave him a rough shake. "I don't believe you."

"It was the squid!" His voice cracked.

Jendara scowled. "The squid?"

"Look at my arm." He raised his arm and the sleeve fell back. Puckered round sores showed all along his forearm. "It came out of nowhere. I think it smelled your blood when you fell overboard. Its tentacles burst out of the water. I was trying to grab you, and that's when it got my arm. I stabbed it with my belt knife and got loose."

She narrowed her eyes. "Convenient."

"It grabbed three of their men. People were screaming. I thought you were dead, Jendara. I went to the oars and rowed like crazy." He indicated his side. "It hurt like blazes. Don't row when you have three broken ribs."

She shoved him away and he fell back on his backside. "You thought I was dead. So why did you tell Fambra we split up?"

He pushed himself back up to his feet. "We're in the middle of nowhere, and there are monsters out there. They already killed my brother. Do you think I want to be alone if they come back? And do you think Fambra would let me stay if she knew I left you?"

Fambra cuffed him across the ear. "You coward."

He rubbed the side of his head, wincing. "I already said I was, didn't I? But I came out here to help you people. Maybe I should have just gone back to Battlewall, but I didn't. I want to fight these things, Jendara. I can't do it on my own. But if anybody can beat these things, it's you."

She didn't have an easy answer. If she could remember more of what happened out there, maybe she could be sure. He had certainly been attacked by a squid, which had to count for something. She pinched the bridge of her nose and wished Vorrin was here to talk over this kind of decision. But it was all on her.

"All right," she said, finally. "You can stay. If you're telling the truth, then we've got another fighter. If you're lying, at least I can keep an eye on you." She gave him a cold smile.

"I know you're just thinking about your people," he said. "But I want you to think about my brother and what he looked like when you found him. If that's not reason to be on your side, I don't know what is." He turned away, folding his arms across his belly.

Jendara scowled at his back for a moment, then turned back to the rest of the scouts. "Let's tend to Raik, and then I'll tell you what I've learned about our enemy."

The search party, somber now after sending their friend's body out to sea, gathered on the other side of the island. Someone found enough driftwood to make a fire, and food and drink were brought up from the boats. The sun came up as they breakfasted.

Jendara tried to eat, but her promised examination began while her mouth was full of porridge. Gerda prodded the back of Jendara's head. "This bump looks ugly."

"Ow." Jendara pushed away the probing finger.

"You'll feel better after I'm done."

Jendara winced and let the woman continue. Fambra caught Jendara's eye and sat down beside her.

"Tell us what you discovered."

Jendara began to explain about the Kalvamen and the rise of their new prisoner-turned-leader with her eerie powers, leaving out only the part about the witch being her sister. She wasn't ready to talk about that yet, and it didn't matter to their plans.

She looked around the group. There were nods, here and there, and revolted expressions. But no one looked doubtful or dubious anymore. Not when these people had seen their clan members killed, attacked by things that looked like wolves but moved like men.

"She can change them into animals," Sven mused.

"Skinwalkers," someone said. "Kalvamen. It's like we're living in the old tales."

"The worst of them." Fambra muttered, as she poured another mug of tea.

"So what do we do?" Tam asked. Jendara was glad to see his face among the others. "Can we just get together enough fighters and wipe them out?"

Jendara shook her head. "I don't know." She held out her hand. "They branded my hand and put some kind of black potion on the wound. I think it's part of some kind of ritual." She took a deep breath. "It sounded like they were trying to turn me into one of them. I don't know if they can do that, but I get the feeling Kalira's magic is pretty powerful."

"That means we'd better move, and quickly," Fambra said. "Witches are bad news."

"I agree." Jendara looked around her group. Hazan offered her a crooked smile. She refused to smile back. "Speed being our top concern, Hazan's faering is the fastest boat we've got. I say we take it and go see the king. She's the only one who's got the kind of manpower it'll take to knock out those Kalvamen before they cause any real harm."

"Our boat's fast, too," Fambra said. "And I've got family down in Battlewall. A cousin in the Iron Shields. He might be able to help us."

Jendara nodded. "An Iron Shield? If you can get the Halgrim city guard on our side, we'll be in much better shape." She bit her lip. "The rest of you . . . well, I think the neighboring islands should be warned about what's out here. I don't think these Kalvamen are going to sit still. Everyone needs to be prepared."

Tam stiffened. "Sorind. It's the biggest population center to the east."

He was thinking of Vorrin and the rest of the crew, just like Jendara was. Their eyes met, both unhappy.

"There's also Flintyreach. It's just as close," Sven reminded them. "I think the bulk of the group should head there."

"This is a good plan," Jendara agreed. "We break up, we warn people, we mobilize troops. We're not going to stand by and let these barbarians eat us alive."

Someone shouted agreement, and the rest of the group took it up. Sven had to lean close to Jendara to be heard. "You're a natural leader."

She shook her head. "Not me. I'm just good in an emergency."

He opened his mouth as if to argue, but another man tapped him on the shoulder and distracted him with questions about restocking supplies. Jendara closed her weary eyes for a moment. Making a plan was one thing. Following it through was another.

Gerda pushed a chunk of driftwood over and settled onto it, her dark eyes pinned on Jendara's face. Strands of her silver hair twisted out of her braids and billowed on the wind. She thrust a mug at Jendara. "Drink."

Jendara raised a hand. "I'm fine."

Gerda pushed the hot mug against her palm. "You're not. You're exhausted, you're injured, and you're upset about something you're not willing to talk about. This is just honey and ginger and willow bark."

Jendara took the mug and sipped. The willow made her screw up her face. "Could have used more honey."

Gerda ignored the jibe. "You have no interest in the spirit realm or the ties of clanship, but you should not mock all my wisdom." She crossed her arms. The blue spirals on her cheeks settled around her frown lines.

Jendara sighed. "Look, you're a fine herbalist—"

"Much of the suffering of this world happens in the spirit. Some people comfort their spirit with religion, others good works. Some turn to drink. But I can help, Jendara. We of the Wise don't just make altars and encourage people to remember the past." She reached into her belt pouch and brought out a silken bag. "We can speak to the spirits of our ancestors and ask them for assistance."

She shook out a handful of small discs of bone or ivory, a rune incised in each one's face. She tossed the rune discs into the air, catching them neatly in the berry-colored folds of her skirt as they fell.

The network of wrinkles around Gerda's mouth deepened. "You are nearly to your crossroads." She ran her fingers through the discs, thinking for a moment. "The Kalvamen are growing stronger. They stand as a wave of darkness poised to drown us all."

Jendara leaned closer to the old woman. "Can we fight them?"

"Without their leader, they are nothing. She must be destroyed."

Jendara nodded. "That's what I thought, too. The moment I saw them staring up at Kalira, ready to do whatever she told them, I knew she was the key to all of this."

"Kalira?" Gerda stared at Jendara. "Wasn't that your sister's name?"

Damn. Jendara really was tired, to let that slip so easily. Maybe she could try to play it off as a coincidence . . . but no. What was done was done. "Yes. The witch is my sister."

She prepared herself for the inevitable accusations— no doubt Gerda would think she was weak for leaving out such key information, maybe even call her a traitor. Yet the old woman said only, "How?"

"When she was taken, as a girl, she was rescued by one of the Kalvamen. Because of her powers. I can't even believe she's alive after all of this."

"But . . . if she's the leader . . ." Gerda trailed off. "Jendara, Kalira knows you. Your father raised you both. She knows how you'll think, how you'll fight. She'll use this against you."

Jendara swirled the bitter liquid in the mug. "I don't know. I'm not the same person I was when Kalira knew me."

Gerda put her hand gently on Jendara's shoulder. "Neither is she. From what you say, she lives as they live. She leads them. They wouldn't have come to our islands if she hadn't ordered them to." She looked deep into Jendara's eyes. "You know what you have to do."

Jendara put down the mug. "I know. Those people at the quarry . . . that's because of her." She covered her mouth, suddenly sickened. "Not just her. Me. This is my fault. If I hadn't gone off on my own, I would have been there to protect her."

"And died like your father," Gerda said firmly.

Jendara shook her head. "It was just me and her, growing up. After our mother died, our father's trading took him away a lot, and I had to look out for her. I would have done anything for her. Even though I never really let myself believe, part of me always hoped she'd survived. That I'd find her someday."

"And now you have."

Jendara nodded. "And I wish I hadn't."

Gerda squeezed Jendara's shoulder, the old woman's grip still iron-hard. "She's not your sister anymore, Jendara. She's not that little girl."

Jendara remembered the sweetness that had filled Kalira's face back in that tent. "I wish you were right, but a part of her is. A small part, but it's there. Trapped inside the monster she's become. I saw it."

Gerda sighed. She gathered up the rune discs and returned them to their silk bag. "Remember those men back at the quarry. The Kalvamen are evil, and Kalira has nurtured that evil and given it wings. She must be destroyed."

"I know," Jendara said. She picked up the mug and handed it back to Gerda. "That's why I'm going to Halgrim. Kalira has to be stopped, and if I'm not strong enough to do it, then I'll find someone who is."

Gerda held Jendara's gaze. "The ancestors will help you, if you wish them to."

"Will they?" Jendara got to her feet. She was too tired to do anything with the sudden flash of anger inside her belly. "Try telling that to Kalira."

Gerda didn't answer. Jendara was glad of that.

Chapter Fourteen
Guarded City

Battlewall lay a full day's sail to the south, even at the speed of Hazan's faering. Fambra's fishing boat kept up surprisingly well—too well for an ordinary fishing boat. Jendara couldn't help wondering if the boat had some modifications Fambra wasn't revealing. If so, it wouldn't be the first "fishing boat" that made a little extra money carrying interesting cargo quickly.

Jendara sank onto the wooden seat and pulled a piece of jerky from her pocket. She knew she was hungry, but her stomach showed no interest in the stuff. She bit off a hunk and tried to remember when she'd last had a solid meal. Breakfast on that heap of rocks didn't count; she'd managed a few bites of porridge, but nothing else. Now she wanted a real breakfast, with mounds of scrambled eggs, fluffy pancakes—the kind of meal Vorrin and Kran begged for on winter mornings.

She sighed. She hoped she was doing the right thing, running for help instead of heading for Sorind to protect her family. She hoped she wasn't leaving Vorrin and Kran in danger.

"You look tired."

She hadn't realized she'd closed her eyes until Hazan spoke. She worked her eyelids open. "I don't want to talk about it. You're just here because I want to keep my eye on you."

He sighed. "You're right. You have no reason to trust me. But you're the one who got me out of that boat back when I was a bloody mess. The way I see it, I owe you. And I'm going to earn back your trust."

She gave a dry laugh.

"Hey, watch me. I'll man the sails, you just sit tight and relax."

"You're in no shape—"

"And you are?" He snorted. "You ought to bind up that hand, you know."

She looked down at her hand. A scab had formed over the seared brand, but she must have bumped it at some point. Blood seeped from the scab's edges, dripping down almost to her wrist. She rubbed at it absently and cursed. "It hurts."

"Of course it hurts. It's a burn, ain't it?" He shook his head as if she were particularly dense. "There's bandaging stuff in one of those crates."

"Thanks." She reached underneath her seat and rummaged through the crates. A beautifully worked knife scabbard caught her eye, and she picked it up. Someone talented had tooled the name "Marga" down the side.

"Who's Marga?" she called back over her shoulder.

"Check the other crate," Hazan grunted. Jendara made a face at his tone, replaced the scabbard and began to dig in the other crate for first aid supplies.

"My girl," he blurted. "Got that as a present for her."

Jendara looked back at him, surprised. "That's nice," she said. "She'll like it. You going to try to see her when we get to Halgrim?"

He hesitated. "Probably not. She and Byrni were real good friends." His voice roughened. "Can't tell her what happened to him until I can tell her I killed the ones that got him."

"I'm sorry." Jendara could understand that. It had been hard enough just to tell all the islanders that the witch who'd killed their loved ones was her sister. Jendara turned away from his obvious discomfort and pulled out a white box. She didn't find any ointment inside, but there were bandages, and at the least the bandages would keep the salt spray out of her wound. That had to be the reason it hurt so much. Salt, finding its way into an open cut.

She used an end of the bandage roll to wipe the dirt and blood from her hand. It looked bad, everything swollen and off-color. The scab stood up from the jolly roger, looking less like a bird's wing and more like a thick slash through the old tattoo. Jendara studied it a moment, wondering what Besmara or her priests would say about it. It was impossible to know. Besmara wasn't the kind of goddess to stand on formality. She could be amused by the whole thing.

Jendara frowned. The wound still looked dirty. She reached for the cask of water nearby and trickled a little over the scorched flesh. The dirt didn't rinse off. She scratched at it with a fingernail, scraping off a bit of her scab. The dirt looked just as dark as ever, as if it had sunk beneath her skin.

She remembered the black sludge Brynorm had plunged her hand into. It must have been a dye that had absorbed into her wounded flesh. Her nose crinkled. She hurried to wrap the linen around her hand, covering every bit of the ugly scab and dark stain around it.

Maybe it wouldn't bother her so much if she couldn't see it. Maybe it would go away after the scab healed. Or maybe she could find something to bleach the stain out of her skin. But in the meantime, she had to get to the king.

When the sun rose again, Jendara was glad to see the gray rocks of Battlewall off the port bow, still small, but growing. Fambra's boat passed by and she followed it toward the harbor. Halgrim, the capital city, crouched on the edge of the harbor like a big, smug cat. In a few short hours, they'd be ready to appeal to the court.

At the thought, Jendara's tongue clung to the roof of her mouth. It was easier to imagine fighting a troll without weapons than to imagine entering the palace and facing the king. There would be ministers and advisers thinking over her request. There would be courtiers sneering at her, men and women in fine furs studying her every move. None of them had spent the last week traveling around in boats dealing with cannibals. None of them would be covered in bruises and scabs or stinking of a dozen unmentionable stenches.

Jendara took a minute to wash her face and brush the worst of the dirt off her pants. She tried not to meet

Hazan's eyes as she fussed over herself. No point in anyone else knowing how nervous she felt right now.

The boats stayed between the red markers that circumscribed the safe channel into Halgrim's harbor. Jendara studied the way closely. She'd spent very little time on Battlewall, the largest island of the Ironbound Archipelago. The island's stony face wasn't just a front. The rocks extended beneath the water as well. She'd heard that on a stormy night, this harbor was one of the deadliest in the world.

The sailboat eased into a slip. Jendara and Hazan tied down everything on board and gathered their things, then waited for Fambra on the dock.

Fambra hugged Sven. "I'll be back soon. Keep your mother out of trouble and stay close to the harbor. With any luck, we'll be leading a dozen ships out of this port, and we want to impress them when we leave." She kissed him long and hard, then pulled back to stroke his cheek.

Sven grinned. "Make Jorgen stop by here before we go. Man owes me a bottle of aquavit after that last poker game."

Laughing as she went, Fambra led Hazan and Jendara through the docks. Halgrim's harbor wasn't half the size of Magnimar's, but the docks were crowded with sailors and fisherfolk, wholesale agents looking for cargo, and even the occasional meandering landlubber, hoping for transport to the mainland. Jendara kept a sharp eye out for pickpockets.

Fambra wove in and out of the crowd with ease. She grinned back over her shoulder. "Hope you're keeping up okay."

Jendara stepped out of the path of a cart loaded with tuna. "I'm surprised to see you doing so well. I wouldn't have pegged you for a city girl."

"I've spent my share of time in the city. Because of Jorgen, I visit every few months."

"Just because of your cousin?" Jendara raised an eyebrow. She couldn't help remembering the surprising speed of Fambra's fishing boat.

Fambra winked. "Sometimes trade brings me here, as well."

They reached a flight of stairs connecting this part of the marina to the real city streets of Halgrim. The sounds of trade and chatter fell behind them as they climbed. At the top, a few carriages rumbled past on the cobblestone streets. The stone houses looked down on them, their gray-painted shutters like lowered eyebrows.

"Got to love the older part of town," Hazan muttered. "So inviting."

"You're familiar with Halgrim?" Jendara asked.

"Grew up here," he said. "Well, on a farm outside the city. Moved here to work in the shipyards once I looked old enough to pass as an apprentice."

Fambra gave him a glance. "Didn't stick with it, did you?"

He shrugged. "Not to my liking." He gestured up the street. "Anyway, lived here long enough to know this street ought to take us to the castle."

"I need to find my cousin," Fambra reminded them.

"We can split up," Jendara said. "You go to your cousin and explain what's going on. Hazan can take me to the palace and see if we can get an audience with the king."

"Not a bad idea," Hazan agreed.

"All right. We can meet up back at our boat, hopefully with good news for all." Fambra clapped Jendara's shoulder, then Hazan's. "May the lady of fortune smile upon you!"

Jendara waved at the red-haired woman, then turned to Hazan. "Let's go, before I realize I have to face nobility."

He laughed and they hurried onward through the narrow streets, which climbed sharply up from the harbor. Halgrim's buildings clung to the steep flanks of the hills, the streets beginning at the very front doors. Jendara missed the neat gardens of the cottages on Sorind and the comforting green of thatched roofs. She couldn't imagine living in this gray city.

Then the hills sloped downward again and Hazan led her over a stone bridge. "This is an island," he explained. "The Rustflow breaks in two to go around it."

Jendara nodded in acknowledgment. Here the houses were even more tightly packed together. She studied them a moment and gave up trying to place their age. She didn't know enough about stone and architecture to make even an educated guess. Hazan led her across a second bridge without an announcement, although the stonework looked finer and more ornate.

He pointed ahead. "We're almost there."

A city square interrupted the regularity of the street scheme, great flagstones replacing the cobbles. Jendara stopped to take the measure of the building at its head.

"The palace," he explained.

He needn't have. There were larger palaces in the world, even in the Lands of the Linnorm Kings, but White Estrid's palace stood out from Halgrim's houses like a peacock amid chickens. For one, it was easily many times bigger than the cramped gray buildings around it. For another, someone clever had added colored stonework around all the windows and doors, giving the white granite palace a hint of a town meeting hall. That hint was helped by the steeply pitched roof and the dragon jutting out from the roof projection. Though Jendara had never seen the king's dragon—or the king herself— she'd bet a galleon full of gold that the sculpture depicted Boiltongue, the linnorm White Estrid had defeated and enslaved to prove herself worthy of the throne, rather than slaying one as the other Linnorm Kings had. A subtle reminder to any visiting kings that Estrid's gender was the least of the differences between them.

Jendara grinned. She'd always admired Estrid, and while her palace might not be the humble painted timber of a village meeting hall, it struck the right tone. Over the great door, the king's white-and-blue pennant snapped in the breeze.

A guard in a white tunic with blue sash clicked his heels, catching her attention.

Jendara hurried up the stairs. "I seek an audience with White Estrid. It concerns an enemy of our people. Sir."

"All citizens are allowed entrance to this palace, but your weapons must stay with me." The guard indicated a stand already occupied by a sword belt and a lance.

Jendara undid her belt and slipped off her sword scabbard and belt knife. The guard took them and placed them gently on the stand.

Jendara took a step forward, but the guard blocked her way.

"Your axe?"

Jendara's hand fell to her axe. She had almost forgotten its presence at her side—it was a part of her. She bit her lip as she released it from her belt. She hadn't gone without knife or an axe since she was a child. She felt naked.

He gave a little cough. "It will be perfectly fine with me."

Hazan caught Jendara's eye. "I'll stay out here, too," he said. "I have a feeling someone as dirty as me doesn't belong past those doors." He gave a wry smile. "Don't worry, I won't leave the guard's sight."

She ignored his jibe and stepped inside. The door closed behind her with a solemn *whump*. Jendara stood on the threshold a moment, letting her eyes adjust. The main entrance hall had been designed to mimic the meeting halls of Estrid's people, just as the building's exterior. Dark woods swallowed the little light entering from the clerestory windows, and flames filled a long central hearth.

"You look lost, stranger."

At the far end of the fire pit, someone sat at a little desk. The soft glow of a lamp illuminated a gray beard and not much else. Jendara's hand moved to her belt to touch the reassuring bulk of her handaxe and touched nothing.

Her boots tapped on marble flooring as she approached the desk, a subtle reminder of the power of the crown: there were no marble quarries on the archipelago that she knew of. That flooring must have cost a fortune.

Jendara's shoulders straightened. "I am Jendara Eriksdottir of Clan Eirkillsing, lately of Sorind. And I wish to address the king to secure aid in a matter of grave import." Her voice sounded small in the vast hall. Very likely it was meant to.

The man turned a page on a book opened across his desk. "What sort of matter?"

Jendara was better used to the darkness now. She looked around herself a moment, seeing the great staircases flanking the hall and the massive unlit chandeliers hanging overhead. What she could make out of the desk beside the fireplace looked very fine, with ornate carvings along its legs and sides. She studied the man at the desk. He wasn't a large man, but she noted the set of his broad shoulders and the way he kept his free hand at the ready on the edge of his desk. He might hold a pen in his other, but this man was no mere secretary or clerk. She knew a warrior when she saw one.

"I come on behalf of the people of Sorind and Flintyreach. Our islands have been attacked by outsiders," she said, leaning closer. "They have a strange kind of magic that threatens all the archipelago."

The man turned back the page he'd just turned, tapping the paper with his pen. Jendara could see a grid of boxes and notes and realized she was looking at a calendar, each hour of the day parceled off into its scheduled activities. Today's page was already covered with ink.

"Jendara Eriksdottir," he mused.

"Yes." She waited for more questions. He should ask her for details, for the name of her clan chief or someone to vouch for her. He must need to know a great deal of those petitioning the crown.

"Her Highness is not on Battlewall today." He ticked off something on the paper. "But her steward is available this hour. I will arrange for a meeting."

"Steward?"

"The man in charge of the castle and state affairs while Her Highness is unavailable."

"I know what a steward is. I just . . . can he help us?"

"He is authorized to." The man smiled. A scar wrinkled the skin on his cheek, tugging up the heavy beard. "I knew your father. A good man." He reached out for the small hand bell perched beside the lamp, and gave it a sharp shake. A boy appeared at his elbow.

"Take this woman to the small meeting room and return to me," the man ordered.

The boy nodded and turned toward the left-hand staircase. Jendara had to hurry to keep up with him, and yet his feet made no noise on the great flagstones. She thought of Kran then. When he ran through the cottage, the whole house shuddered.

She reached again for her axe handle and settled for squeezing her hands into fists. While she was here studying the fine floors and luxurious fireplaces, her son was in danger.

At the top of the stairs, her footsteps turned hushed. Here fine-grade whale oil lamps lit the hall to afternoon brightness, illuminating an expanse of glossy paneling and thick carpets in Estrid's blue. The boy opened a door Jendara hadn't even noticed. She ran her fingers along its beveled edge.

"I'll have tea brought up, ma'am," the boy said. "There's schnapps on the mantel, if you'd like."

Jendara stepped inside the meeting room. "No, no, tea will be fine." She turned a slow circle, studying the space.

"The tea will be here shortly, ma'am," the boy said.

She hardly noticed his exit. The meeting room had absorbed her entirely. High above, a cunningly lit fresco—no doubt magic was involved—showed a map of the Ironbound Archipelago on a robin's-egg-blue sea, the large islands outlined in gold leaf, the small in copper. Her eyes traveled automatically to Sorind, then Crow's Nest below it, tiny copper-edged things. It seemed impossible anyone could concern themselves with such small places.

Jendara's knee knocked against the sturdy back of a leather-covered armchair. She stroked it, recognizing the fine grain and suppleness of the hide. No musty pelts like the stuff in Kalira's tents; this was the kind of work master tanners like Morul spent hours upon. A blanket lay casually across its back, its blues and greens and red reminiscent of the Dagfridrung clan flag.

Frowning, she looked around the room again. There, a soapstone carving of a wolf. There, a tapestry of a ship at sea, its figurehead a sharp-beaked eagle. There, a shield emblazoned with a crow's silhouette.

Clan totems. She sank into the armchair. So many clan totems. Her father had taught her the names and colors of dozens of clans, but she'd driven it all out of her head the day she'd smashed their own soapstone token. She wondered if White Estrid and her steward knew them all.

The door opened. Jendara jumped to her feet. A tall man entered, his face unreadable. He scanned Jendara from head to filthy boots and then studied her face a long uncomfortable moment.

"Good day, sir," she managed to say. Nerves made her throat tight. He had to be the steward. The freshness of his black doublet, with its subtle blue and white piping, suggested his importance, as did the silver work on the knife in his belt. The fact that he even carried a knife in this place was a warning of his power.

This was the man who held the fate of the islands in his well-manicured hands.

"Jendara Eriksdottir," he said in slow, measured tones.

"Yes, sir. I'm here to request your aid." She hesitated, then dove in, explaining Kalira's power, her people's sick appetites, her growing army of skinwalkers. His expression did not change as she spoke. His gray eyes stayed on her face, cold and hard as the marble floors downstairs.

Jendara pushed onward. "So I believe the best way to stop these cannibals is to organize a major force and strike hard, now. We need your help, sir."

The steward joined his hands behind his back and began to circle the room, his face thoughtful. "Cannibals. Kalvamen, coming south to invade us. Kalvamen with the power to transform into animals."

Jendara set her jaw. "They make skinwalkers, sir. Not truly animals, but men in animal form."

He shot her a tight smile. "Of course. Thank you for correcting me."

She watched him pause before the small fireplace. She had forgotten the schnapps on the mantle, but now the steward reached for the glass decanter and extended it to her. "Schnapps?"

She shook her head. He put the bottle back on the shelf and brushed an invisible bit of dust off its side.

"Serving as the steward of this land is not an easy task. There are so many requests for assistance, and there are only so many available resources. Our patrols have hundreds of miles of coastline to protect. Right now, I've sent our patrols on a mission I'm not at liberty to discuss. Unfortunately, they're combing southern waters right now and aren't available for diversion."

"Aren't available?" His words made perfect sense, but Jendara couldn't believe there was no one to help them.

"They should be back in about a week and a half," he answered, his tone utterly bland. She thought she might even see a smile tugging at the corners of his mouth.

"You don't believe me, do you?" She shook her head, stunned by the notion. "How can you think I'm making this up?"

His mouth stopped hinting at a smile and became a full-fledged smirk. "I could say it's because your story is so incredible, but that would a lie. I don't believe you, Jendara Eriksdottir, because I know who you are."

He took a step forward. "You see, my sister married a Chelish merchant. A hard man, he had developed a very successful shipping business."

Jendara folded her arms across her chest, unsure where he was going with this tale.

"For some reason, a pirate named Ikran the Bloody decided to target my brother-in-law's ships in particular. He and his vicious crew captured ship after ship, burning and pillaging every vessel until my brother-in-law went bankrupt and killed himself. And do you know what happened to my sister?"

Jendara couldn't answer.

"She sank to a life of crime. She finally made her way back to me and these islands with her virtue and her health ruined. She lives with me now and can't even leave the house. You did that."

"I'm not asking you to help *me*!" Jendara blurted. "I'm asking for the people of Sorind."

"I don't believe you." He took a deep breath. He was shaking. "You're here for your own purposes, of course. You want me to send our Iron Shields and patrols of seasoned soldiers up to your little islands to leave Halgrim undefended. Then you can bring your ship and probably the ships of half a dozen other scum-pirates and backwater raiders into this city and pillage it, just like you've pillaged so many little towns. Well, not on my watch."

"You son of a bitch. You're going to risk the lives of every islander—"

"What do you care about the islands and their people? You turned away from them." The steward shook his head. "Erik Eriksson was a great man. It's a mercy he didn't live to see what his daughter became."

Jendara's fist whipped out. A crack resounded, and the steward staggered backward, clutching his face. Hissing, Jendara shook out her hand. She'd broken something—his nose, she'd bet, by the crimson leaking out of his fingers.

"Are you all right?"

"Get out!" he bellowed. "Guards!"

The door burst open and strong hands grabbed Jendara's shoulders. She kicked and shrieked, but nothing loosened the guards' grip. They wrestled her down the servants' staircase and flung her out the back door.

She landed in a trash heap, knocking her head against a rock. She sat up, rubbing her temple. She thought about getting up, but flopped back against the mounds of rubbish. The pungent stink of night waste assaulted her nose.

"Shit."

She closed her eyes. What he'd said was all true. How many men and women had she killed as a pirate, and how many lives had she ruined? She'd stopped worshiping Besmara, she'd changed her profession, but she couldn't put her past behind her. And now it had just ruined her best chance to help her people.

"I heard a ruckus."

She opened her eyes to behold Hazan's inquisitive face. "I bring out the best in people," she explained.

He held up her sword. "I reclaimed your weapons. The guard was more than happy to be rid of them."

"You should have gone in with me. You could have had schnapps." It was a poor attempt at humor, but it restored a little of her dignity.

"I like schnapps. But from the looks of things, I was safer out here." He tapped his nose. "You've got ash on your nose. And green stuff in your hair."

She sighed and brushed off the worst of the filth. "Let's get back to the harbor. Maybe Fambra's had some luck with her cousin."

"You know, I don't set much store in kings and officials. We're islanders. We take care of ourselves," Hazan helped Jendara out of the trash heap and started toward the harbor. "We just need to muster the right kind of manpower."

Jendara looked back over her shoulder at the palace. It still looked like a village meeting hall made large. Perhaps the open minds of Sorind's villagers had spoiled her, but she had expected more from the people inside that palace. She had expected someone who saw the big picture, written in the colors of all the islands.

She remembered the map of the islands and hoped her little copper-edged one was safe.

Chapter Fifteen
Book-Learning

The smell of salt water and fresh fish raised Jendara's spirits a bit. They were the two strongest notes of a harbor's perfume, after all, and any harbor was a kind of home to her. Her chin lifted a little as she strode down the steps leading to the docks. The palace had been a bust, but there had to be other ideas out there.

"Jendara!" Fambra called.

Jendara picked up her pace. The redhead waved happily. A man stood beside her on the deck, his own hair a faded version of Fambra's. He wore simple leather armor and a pleasant smile.

"Ahoy!" Jendara called. "This must be your cousin, the guard."

Fambra grinned. "Jorgen, meet Jendara."

"Pleased to meet you. Although, I must say after Fambra and Sven's stories, I was expecting someone seven feet tall and breathing fire." He clasped her forearm in islander fashion, then clapped her on the shoulder.

"Sorry to let you down." Jendara glanced over her shoulder at Hazan, still making his way slowly down the docks. "This is Hazan, our . . . companion."

Fambra frowned. "Hazan, are you well? You look pale."

He walked up the gangplank. "Think I bumped my ribs on the stair rail. Nothing serious."

"Well, sit down. Sven will bring you something to drink. Rest yourself." Fambra turned to Jendara. "You don't look so good yourself. There's cabbage in your hair."

Jendara scowled. "I got thrown out of the palace. I should have sent you to do the talking—the steward knew my history and thought I was trying to organize some kind of pirate attack on the city."

"Then we'll just have to find some other kind of help," Fambra said. "Jorgen, you've heard our story. Do you think you could organize any volunteers from the other Iron Shields?"

"We'd all go," he said. "Every one of us would believe you and Jendara. We'd go in a heartbeat if you asked us to."

Jendara shook her head. "You can't all go. The steward's right about one thing: if we take the best warriors from Halgrim, we risk leaving the capital city defenseless. We've been worried about Sorind and Flintyreach, but we know for sure that Kalira has her eye on this island. Maybe she's hoping we'll do exactly this. Gather up all of the city's defenders and leave it open for her attack."

Sven handed Hazan a glass and joined the group. "Battlewall is the most heavily populated of the islands.

If Kalira's looking to crush the archipelago, she could start here and hope it leaves us paralyzed with fear."

Fambra looked skeptical. "I don't think she has the numbers to take on Halgrim, let alone the whole island. I think an attack this far south isn't very likely until she's taken more ground. But you have a point, I guess."

"I'm just not sure what we should do next," Jendara admitted. "I don't know how quickly Kalira's forces can move or how many fighters she has. And I don't know if there are any weapons or tools we might use against her skinwalkers. Nobody's ever faced anything like this!"

"Not anybody in recent history," Sven reminded her. "But there are stories about skinwalkers. We've all heard them. They must be based on some kind of fact."

"That's true," Jorgen agreed. "Even here in the city, we knew better than to leave a hide untreated. That kind of wisdom has to come from something."

Fambra nibbled her thumbnail, thinking. "Something historical. There might be a record of it someplace." She caught Jorgen's eye. "Are you thinking what I'm thinking?"

He raised an eyebrow. "The Basalt Library? No one enters those gates. We run a patrol out there, now and again, but there's never any sign of activity. I wouldn't be surprised if those librarians were all dead by now."

"What are you talking about?" Jendara dropped onto a cask, looking at the arguing cousins. Her head hurt, and so did her branded hand. She rubbed it irritably.

Fambra pulled a lobster trap close to Jendara. The others took it as a cue to sit down as well. Sven disappeared below and reappeared with more glasses and a second bottle of the honey-colored liquor he'd given Hazan. He poured a scant measure for each of them.

"About five years ago," Fambra said, "just a few years after White Estrid took the throne, a group of scholars and explorers asked for her permission to build a library."

Jendara sipped her liquor. The honey sweetness played over her tongue. She sipped again.

"Estrid allowed them to build their library in the northern cliffs, just outside of the city. They kept to themselves, but for two years, ship after ship brought them crates of books." Fambra lowered her voice. "Some of the ships came in the dead of night, and those who saw the crates heard strange sounds and saw strange lights."

Jorgen rolled his eyes. "Gossip and superstition. I checked many of those crates myself, working harbor patrol. Books, plain and simple. Moldy old books."

Fambra sighed. "After construction was completed, members of the order went out into the islands, collecting old manuscripts and interviewing people. One of them spent a lot of time talking to Gerda, writing down the stories she remembered. But about a year ago, they just . . . stopped."

"That's true," Jorgen said. "They closed the doors to the library, and no one has hear a peep out of them since then. They may have left the island, for all we know."

"You haven't checked?" Jendara frowned.

"They wouldn't have appreciated our meddling," he answered. "These were strange men."

"But you think their library may have records of the incidents behind the old stories," she mused. "Well, it's worth checking, anyway. Where is this library?"

"I can give you directions," Jorgen said. "I want to go talk to some of the other guards. I can probably organize a group of volunteers to leave for Sorind on tomorrow's outgoing tide."

"That's terrific. Fambra, perhaps you can talk to some of the fisherfolk. If I can't get any information out of this library, our best defense is going to be a lot of fighters. Maybe you can get us some."

"Absolutely."

"Hazan, if you bumped those ribs, maybe you should just rest here," Jendara suggested. "I need to you in good shape for any sailing tomorrow morning."

"No," he said. "I'm coming with you."

"Hazan—"

He cut her off. "I've heard plenty of stories about these librarians. I'm not going to leave you in their hands, not if they're practitioners of black sorcery and book-worship. Even if they're not, well, I can read. I want to help."

She shrugged. At least he'd be easy to keep an eye on. "All right. You can come with me."

She got to her feet. "Jorgen, I'll take those directions. And hopefully, I'll meet you all back here in very little time."

Jendara reread Jorgen's directions and noticed that the paper she held in her right hand trembled. She flexed, feeling the scab pull taut and sting. She made a face. She'd taken plenty of wounds, but never one this irritating. She rubbed the edge of her bandage. It didn't just hurt, it burned and itched and swelled. It was as if an angry wasp had drilled into her hand.

She wondered again just what was in the black liquid Brynorm had forced her hand into. Had Kalira really mentioned adding her blood? What kind of ritual or spell was she going to do to make Jendara one of her clan? Jendara was glad she'd escaped before she'd seen it.

Jendara studied the buildings around her. Here at the edge of town, the slate shingles of the old city were gone, and humble thatched roofs dominated. In a crowded city like Halgrim, fire was chief among fears. But on the outskirts, there was enough space between the run-down establishments to allow cheaper—if more flammable—materials.

She noticed a weather-beaten sign advertising ale and food. She glanced back at the directions. This was probably the closest eating establishment to the Basalt Library. If anyone knew if there were still people living in that fortress of books, it was likely these folks.

"Let's go check in with the natives," she said, pointing at the cheerless pub. "Ask a few questions about the mysterious librarians."

They pushed open the swinging doors and waited a minute in the dim light within. The unpromising smell of overcooked cabbage lay heavily over the place. Hazan took a seat at the cleanest of the tables.

Jendara shook a few coins out of her pouch. "Can you order us some ale? And whatever the lunch is? I've got to find the jakes."

She didn't wait for his nod. She picked her way through the taproom, her stomach churning at the smell of spilled beer and stale grease. Probably just a remnant of her concussion. She shoved open the back door and was glad to see a courtyard with its own well. The privy stood a sensible distance away, its door sagging on its hinges.

Jendara hurried to the well. An exploratory adjustment warned that her bandage stuck to the raw flesh beneath it. Jendara set her teeth and tugged it free. The stink of singed flesh welled up, along with blood from the cracked and ripped scab.

With her good hand, she cranked up a bucket of ice-cold water, then rinsed her hand clean and studied it closely. The bubbled, scabbed outline of the bird's wing stood out clearly. Beneath it, the jolly roger looked faint, its ink fading into her flesh. She rubbed at it, wincing at the pain. There was a grayness to her skin, a darkening around the lines of the brand. She thought she'd seen that earlier, but it had spread somehow. The veins themselves looked darker, an ugly purple running toward her fingers and wrists.

"This can't be good."

She ladled more water over the wound. She tried to remember what herbs helped with blood poisoning, but drew a blank. She needed to get back to Sorind and have a wisewoman look at this wound. If it got much worse, she could lose her hand.

She rewrapped the injury and headed back to their table. Mugs and bowls already sat in front of Hazan. She sank onto a bench. Circles of grease floated on the surface of her soup, shining up at her like eyes.

She forced down a bite. The weight of their mission settled onto her shoulders, pulling them down, choking off her throat. She sipped her ale to wash down the feeling.

"You look worried, Jendara."

"I am worried." The words tumbled out, despite her mixed feelings about the man. "I already failed once on this expedition. I don't want to fail again."

"You won't fail. I believe in you." He gave her a smile over the top of his mug.

She shook her head. "I just hope there's someone left at that library to help us. When it comes to books, I'm not much use."

He rolled his eyes. "You're a smart woman."

She speared a lump of potato out of her soup. "Not smart enough to talk to that steward. I think with my fists, not my brain."

"You organized this entire expedition. You got up on the podium in the Sorind meeting hall and inspired people—not with your fists, but with your words."

"You know what I mean. My father was always trying to teach me about diplomacy. 'That's the heart of leadership right there,' he always said. That's how I knew I wasn't meant to be a leader."

Hazan pushed aside his meal. "Jendara, you might not be your father. And you're right—your diplomacy stinks. But you're what we have right now."

The potato slid down Jendara's throat like a stone. Hazan was right. Maybe she was still more of a pirate at heart than she'd like. But no one else had looked at those dead men back at the quarry and known they meant something bigger than a single attack. No one else had looked into Kalira's eyes as she threatened to turn the entire island chain into a string of Kalvas. It was up to her.

She dropped her spoon into her bowl with a splash. She was going to stop Kalira, no matter the cost. Even if it meant killing her own sister.

"You folks need another round?"

The gravely voice interrupted Jendara's thoughts. The server wiped her fingers on her grease-stained apron and reached for Hazan's tankard.

"Another ale?" she asked, and waggled the empty mug.

"Yes, please," Jendara agreed for him. "It's a fine brew you serve here. Do you make it yourself?"

The woman gave her a disbelieving look. "Ayuh. I make it up in the basement. Course soon it'll be too cold for ale. Have to switch to lager." She spat on the floor. "Piss-tasting stuff."

The ale wasn't much better, but Jendara wasn't about to tell her that. "We're traders, out from Flintyreach. We heard there's some kind of library out here?"

"That'd be the Basalt Liberry up the road a pace. Ain't never set foot in it, but once in a long while, one of them liberrians comes down here for a drink. Reckon he gets lonely out there."

Jendara exchanged glances with Hazan. "Him? Is there just one who drinks here?"

"Ayuh. Real nice fella. Likes the fancy fruit beers from the mainland. He was right broken up when he came in last week and we din't have any."

"I see," Jendara said. "Well, thank you for the information. We'll just take that second round and go visit him ourselves."

The server waddled away, and Jendara turned excitedly to Hazan. "The Iron Shields need to spend more time talking to the neighbors. It sounds like the librarians aren't only still on the island, they're regular customers."

Thudding footsteps announced the return of the server. She dropped two dripping tankards onto the table and then fished in the pocket of her apron. She held out a corked bottle. "If you're goin' to the liberry, you might want to buy one of these to take with ya. Like I said, Master Lomont is powerful fond of these soft mainlander brews."

Jendara took the bottle of fruit beer and beamed. "I reckon I could."

The chilled glass felt like hope in her hand.

The dark basalt of the Battlewall cliffs reared up on their left. Jendara could hear the ocean beyond the ridge of stone, could even smell its brine, but the cliffs cut off the view. Overhead, a seabird shrieked, its voice high and lonely.

"This is a strange place for a library," Hazan grumbled.

"Well, it's secure. That's one thing it has going on for it."

"Lonely, if you ask me."

"Yes," she agreed. On this wind-scoured stretch of rock, without any trees or shrubs to soften the landscape, it was easy to feel cut off from the rest of the world. She knew that off to the southeast, the rest of the island supported the finest farms in all the Ironbound Archipelago. Tracts of forests grew lumber for the Halgrim shipyards. All of that existed, inland.

Here, there was only wind and stone and the sounds of the sea.

Hazan was right about this being a strange location for a library. Wasn't the point of a library to make books available to people who'd want to read them?

"That's it."

He pointed at the structure ahead, a shape carved into the cliffs themselves. Jendara couldn't believe it had only been built a few years ago. Everything about the Basalt Library, from its sharp edges to its heavy turrets, suggested it had sprung up from the earth when the stones thrust themselves above the ocean. The library looked ancient—and impregnable. Jendara half expected an army to rush out of the fortress and put her in shackles just for daring to approach it. She found herself holding her breath as she walked.

A wall surrounded the landward side of the library, a narrow gate its only access point. Jendara laid her hand beside one of the heavy iron hinges. It dwarfed her palm and fingers.

"Nothing's cutting through this hinge," she said. "Not very quickly, at least. Do you think they used magic to build this?"

"Who builds a fortress for books?" Hazan asked.

"We do."

Jendara's head snapped up. A man stood on top of the wall, his black robe obscuring his face. He held a staff in his hand, an iron knob capping it. A staff like that could split open a man's head like a muskmelon.

"What brings you to the Basalt Library?" He didn't shout, but his voice cut through the wind. Jendara could feel his gaze upon her, picking out the weapons on her belt and the knife in Hazan's boot.

"We come seeking information about the islands' history," she called. "And we have a gift for Master Lomont." She raised the beer bottle.

"I am Master Lomont," he said. "I'll be down in a moment."

For a long series of minutes, Jendara peered into the gloom and saw nothing. Then a flicker of movement announced Master Lomont. Without a sound, the gate swung open. The pair stepped forward and the gate eased shut behind them.

Jendara held out the beer. "We stopped at the local pub, and the owner suggested we bring this."

Lomont pushed back his hood and took the beer. "She knows me too well." He nodded at Jendara. "Come inside so we may speak."

The face beneath the hood surprised Jendara. She couldn't quite guess where Lomont hailed from—his tea-colored skin and black eyes could have originated from any number of nations. A few lines around his eyes suggested he was about her own age, although his shaved head gave no further clues. The full-length robe suggested monasticism; the way his cloak bulged along his hip warned he carried a sword. Curiosity pricked her.

She brushed her hand over the wall of the hallway he led them through. There had been no effort to polish or cover the raw stone. A few unlit lamps hung on the wall, and the sun's rays provided scarce illumination.

Lomont pushed open a heavy oaken door and they entered a room filled with cool brightness. The shock of the transition made Jendara blink. She immediately searched for the source of the illumination. This was not lamplight.

Lomont pointed above. "There are skylights on the roof. And mirrors on every level to redirect the light."

"Clever," Jendara said. She noted the mirrors dotting the room's perimeter. Tables and chairs clustered around the edge of the room to take advantage of the pleasant light. Four or five sat empty, although one had a thick volume sitting on it, a quill and ink resting on a metal plate at its side.

"What is this place?" Hazan couldn't stop staring. He walked into the center of the room with his head tilted back.

Jendara followed his gaze. Beyond using the clever system of skylights and mirrors, the library had been built around an open core to maximize light penetration. She could make out two floors above with careful railing around the light well, bookshelves extending away from the open space. She tried to guess how big the place must be and drew a blank. It had looked large enough from the outside, but much of its shape was indiscernible from the cliffs around it. It could be vast.

"This is the Basalt Library," Lomont announced. He spread his arms, indicating the empty tables. "And this is where we study and repair the texts we bring in."

"Who are you?" Jendara asked.

"Humble members of the Pathfinder Society. You may have heard of us—adventuring scholars who travel in search of lost knowledge. Some of us are philosophers, others historians. Some of us," he gave a crooked smile, "have rather more interesting skills."

Jendara had indeed heard of them. The Pathfinders were legendary, even out here in the islands. She'd seen their headquarters, the Grand Lodge, during her time in Absalom. She began to circle the space, noticing dust on a desk, the remarkable coolness of the space, and the lack of smells, save perhaps a hint of hide glue. "Where is everyone? It's so quiet."

He inclined his head in agreement. "At any one time, there are only a few of us inside the library. The majority of our work takes us out into the world." He swept open his heavy black robe, revealing a sheathed sword. "But protecting the collection is also an important part of our work."

Jendara raised her hands. "Relax, librarian. We're not here to hurt you or your books. I am Jendara, lately of Sorind, and this is Hazan. We're on a mission to learn about the history of these islands—to better understand a dangerous enemy."

He pulled out a chair, then flipped it around and straddled it. He waved a hand at the nearest chair. "In that case, I need to know more." He rested his arms across the chair back. "What is this enemy?"

Jendara sat down. "Have you ever heard of creatures called skinwalkers?"

"Skinwalkers?" His dark eyes glimmered. "By chance, I have. In fact, I have a particular interest in shapeshifters."

"I see," Jendara said.

"No." He slid his shirt collar back, revealing the beginnings of an ugly puckered scar. Not a brand like Jendara's, but the furrows of some terrible claws. "Now you see."

Jendara's heart raced. This place, this strange place of books, was just what she needed. She rested her elbows on her knees and began to explain Kalira's ability to turn men into monsters.

He led them into the lower stacks, a warren of bookshelves on the ground level. Jendara couldn't stop gaping. She knew nothing about the value of the books themselves or the information they contained, but every twist or turn revealed some new treasure: a series of volumes bound in dragonhide, their covers winking in the soft light; a book bound in blue burnt velvet that almost begged to be stroked; an entire shelf covered with a linen sheet that she swore chirped and tweeted as she passed by, rather like a sleeping aviary. Occasionally they passed the implements of the librarians' work, carts full of glue pots and dusters and sacks of charcoal.

Lomont noticed her curious glance toward one cart. "Moisture is ever our enemy," he explained. "Most of the bookshelves have been enchanted to repel dust and dampness, but even the best charm fails after a few years. Moreover, our feet bring in dirt and molds every time we enter the chambers. Constant vigilance is needed in the fight to preserve these books."

"I had no idea your work could be so consuming," she murmured, peering at the painting of a nymph stretching across the spines of a multivolume set. She rubbed the back of her neck. "This art is remarkably like the real thing."

"Yes," he agreed. "A magically enhanced image. I wouldn't recommend looking at it for too long.

"Nor would I recommend touching *that*!" he bellowed, catching Hazan's hand as he reached out to a glossy black volume. "That shelf is for books about magical combustion. Many of them require special handling—if you see what I mean."

Hazan nodded, his face very white. He gripped his hands behind his back and walked with his elbows close to his body.

Lomont directed them around another corner, where the labyrinth of bookshelves ended and small study nook opened up. He pointed to one of the study carrels. "Hazan, you can read, correct?"

"Yes," Hazan snapped.

"I'll bring you a few works so you can begin looking for information on the skinwalkers. In all my studies, I've only found a few references to them, so I'm not certain how much will be relevant to our search today. You are welcome to use the graphite sticks and parchment on the desk."

Lomont hurried away. Hazan pulled out the chair at the little desk and looked at Jendara. "He's a little pompous, but this place has to have the information you've been looking for."

She nodded. "I think you're right." She smiled a little. "I have to thank you, Hazan. You've been encouraging me ever since I organized that scouting party on Sorind. You lent me your boat. You helped me out of that garbage heap back at the palace. Maybe I was wrong about you."

"Thanks. I just wish Byrni were here to help." He fell silent, his gaze pensive.

"Hey, we're going to make those bastards pay for what they've done." She gave him a fierce grin and felt her fingers fold into fists. Studying books might get her the information she needed, but she was already spoiling for a fight.

Lomont reappeared, pushing a cart full of books. He offered some to Hazan, then crossed to Jendara with a full armload. "Are you all right?" he asked. "You look pained."

She realized the back of her balled fist stung. She shook out her hand, surprised by how much it hurt. "Just a little burn, that's all."

"Very well, then." He unloaded his stack of books. "You've got a lot of reading to do. You'll need to be focused."

Jendara surveyed the heap of texts. None of them had velvet covers or scantily clad women on the spines. She opened the one on top and stared at the tiny letters in dismay.

Lomont clapped her on the shoulder. "Don't worry. I brought out the magnifying glasses."

She sank into her seat. She had a hunch she'd rather be facing a rabid wolf than this heap of books.

Chapter Sixteen
Smoke and Mirrors

Hours passed. The light from the clever system of mirrors waned, and Lomont brought out some kind of charmed lantern. It glowed with a cold blue light. Every now and then it flickered, and he tapped it a few times until the glow went steady again.

He unfolded his lanky frame, a small book dangling from his hand. He stretched and then crossed to Jendara's side. "Look at this."

Jendara set aside the massive tome of Linnorm history she'd been looking at. "What am I looking at?"

He hooked a chair leg with his toe and pulled it close to Jendara's seat. "You said Kalira and Brynorm gave you some kind of brand."

Jendara flexed her hand and winced. "It hurt like hell. Kalira said it would make me part of her clan."

He shook his head. "I don't think that's why she branded you." He tapped the page. "Marks like this can be used to influence people's behavior—compelling them to do certain things or forbidding others."

"So you think my brand is some kind of . . . spell?"

"I think I want to take a look at it." He got to his feet. "Let's go out to the kitchen and examine the brand under some better light. Hazan, if you need anything, follow the leftmost aisle and take the first two left-hand turns, then the second right. You'll find yourself in the entry hall."

"I'll be fine," Hazan answered.

In the kitchen, Lomont lit whale oil lamps and beckoned for Jendara's hand. He unwound the dirty bandage covering the brand. The fabric tugged and yanked at the scab.

"Oh no," Jendara breathed.

The black stain around the now-reopened wound had spread. It ran down to the first knuckles of her fingers and up past the base of her wrist. Where it touched healthy skin, an ugly red seam showed, livid as a burn.

"It's grown?"

She nodded. "A lot."

He pushed gingerly at the flesh at the base of her thumb. "Does that hurt?"

"No."

He prodded the reddened skin of her wrist. She grunted, startled by the pain. He turned her hand over, looking at the charcoal-colored skin of her palm.

Lomont put down her hand. "The spreading stain is just like the book described. The magic of the brand is moving into your bloodstream."

"What do you think it's doing to me?"

He reached for a cake of soap and rubbed it over the seeping wound. "It sounds like some witches use similar brands to influence important people in their community. Maybe that's how Kalira was able to bring the Kalva clans together so easily."

Jendara's hand burned as he rinsed it. She tried to ignore it. "That's all the more reason to take her out of the picture right away. If she's using magic on her own people, the attack will definitely fall apart without her."

He began rewrapping her hand, binding the wound firmly. He paused. "Do you smell something?"

Jendara stiffened. "Smoke!

Lomont threw aside the roll of bandages. "Oh gods, no!"

He raced into the book maze, Jendara on his heels.

Jendara dropped to a crouch, trying to keep her head beneath the smoke level. "Lomont!" she called. He didn't answer. The man had moved faster than she could have imagined, vanishing into the cloud. She coughed and pressed onward. Cold sweat trickled down the back of her neck. She couldn't remember which turns to make.

She hesitated at the next junction. Was the smoke thicker to the left? Something clattered ahead, and she launched herself forward. She hit a book cart and fell.

"Forget this," she growled and put her shoulder to the nearest shelf. Let Lomont worry about his books: she was worried about his life. The bookshelf toppled with a crash and a volley of tiny shrieks. Gods only knew what kind of books she'd spilled. She leaped over the pile, pushing onward. There was a faint blue glow ahead. It had to be the lantern.

"Lomont? Hazan?" She coughed too hard to repeat the call.

A shadow streaked past on her left, and she spun around.

"Hazan?"

But it was already gone. She dropped onto her hands and knees, crawling forward. A dark figure lay on the floor ahead, outlined in the blue light of the lamp and the sooty glow of a smoldering desk.

Jendara checked the body first. Blood ran down Lomont's face, but she felt his chest moving, and that was all that mattered for now. She looked around herself for something to smother the fire, but there were no rugs, no tapestries, no water. She should have grabbed a bucketful on her way out of the kitchen.

A fat book on the smoking desk exploded into flames, belching out coppery smoke. These weren't ordinary books—she had to remember that.

She grabbed her belt knife and sliced at the neck of Lomont's robe, ripping it off his motionless body. It felt like good heavy wool. Jendara slapped the robe against the flames, breaking up the heaps of books and stomping on one that tumbled onto the floor. If she didn't get this under control, they'd both be dead.

A bookshelf fell over behind her.

She whirled around. Saw nothing.

She turned back to the fire, working faster now, slapping at the smoldering stuff, stomping on the coals. Someone had knocked Lomont over the head to take him out of the picture, and now this fire was destroying the books Jendara needed to stop Kalira. She yanked one out of the flames and hoped it was worth the blisters on her fingertips.

"Jendara?" Lomont groaned. "It was Hazan. He hit me over the head with a chair."

"What?" Jendara stopped moving. "What?"

It made a sick kind of sense, she realized. All Hazan's quick talking back on that island had been just that—words. She'd been right to doubt him, and he'd talked her into believing in him. She stomped on a smoldering book and watched the coals fly. Besmara take the bastard, she'd even started to like him.

A knife whizzed past her ear, plunging into the wall. "Shit!"

No time for firefighting now. She tossed the remnants of the robe over the desk and hoped it would smother the last of the flames. She whirled around, looking for her assailant. No sign of anyone. She doubled over, hacking.

"We've got to get out of here," she gasped, grabbing Lomont's shoulders. "Don't move."

She began to drag him backward, praying she wasn't hurting him worse as he jolted over the books and scrolls strewn across the floor. She paused a second to orient herself.

"Left," he gasped. "There's a door to the stairwell."

She turned, fast, colliding with something hairy and tall. She dropped Lomont and stumbled backward. If only she'd grabbed the Pathfinder's magic lamp, she could have avoided this.

The smoke eddied, warning her of her attacker's movement. Jendara struck out with her boot, hitting something soft. With a grunt, her attacker stumbled back. In the clearer air, she could see his wide form and dark hair. Whoever was in the book maze with her, he wasn't Hazan.

Jendara charged the stranger. They hit the ground rolling and ricocheted off a bookshelf. Jendara scrabbled to get her knees beneath her. She found purchase and came out on top, her forearm digging into a man's throat.

His fingers caught in her braid and yanked her head backward. She squeezed his ribs tighter with her knees, trying to keep her weight on her forearm. She couldn't let him up.

He dropped the braid and clawed at something behind him. Jendara slammed her free hand into his nose and dug her arm into his throat. If he got a knife—

But he didn't have a knife. He had something furry and he was pulling it up against his cheek. Jendara had a moment to gape as the hide touched his face, the animal skin melting into his own flesh, stretching, rippling, hair covering everything. And then he snarled. He shook himself, and Jendara's arm slipped off his greasy fur. She tumbled off the body of a bear.

It roared and the bookshelves shook.

She'd seen grizzlies before, but she'd never seen anything like this. The claws he reached toward her must have been at least four inches long.

Jendara stopped thinking.

She'd never moved so fast, twisting under the huge paws so quickly she felt a breeze against her neck. She shoved a bookshelf, bringing down a stack of books that burst open around the beast. Light burst out of one, and the grizzly snapped at it. The book fell to the floor, sending up golden beams.

The grizzly blinked in confusion and swatted its paw blindly.

Jendara grinned and reached for her sword.

The creature snapped its head toward her. The sound of steel on leather must have alerted it, but the movement only helped Jendara find her target. She thrust the sword at its face and grinned as the blade sank into the grizzly's eye. The hilt vibrated with the force of the blow.

The grizzly screamed, pawing at its face, and Jendara took a nervous step backward. It should be dead, with a foot of steel plunged into its brain. Impossibly, the bear lunged at her, its teeth clicking closed just a hairsbreadth from her cheek. She felt hot drool spatter her face.

Then it sank to the floor.

Jendara staggered away from its body, trying to clear her lungs. She'd inhaled a lot of smoke. Her head swam.

She crumpled to her knees, gasping for air. Something brown seemed to twist and swirl on the marble floor. She fell forward, her filthy hand landing on the wriggling thing. It felt soft against her palm, sleek and warm.

"Jendara? Are you all right?" Lomont croaked. He had pulled himself to her side, and now he clung to a bookshelf. A shroud of smoke clung to the ceiling, but it didn't seem to be spreading. The fire must have gone out.

She looked down and realized she was holding the last three inches of her own braid. The grizzly's claws had sheared it off. She pulled herself to her feet, laughing a little, and yanked her sword free of the dead creature. "I'm fine."

Movement drew her gaze back to the skinwalker's corpse. The magic was fading, the body becoming human. The edges of the bear skin pulled back. Jendara frowned. "The hide—it's been tanned. The old wives' tales were wrong about that."

"We've got to get some fresh air," Lomont said. "Come on." He stumbled toward her, and she took his weight on her arm, her mind spinning. She hurried the injured man across the room.

He fumbled for the key ring on his belt and passed it to her. "The big gold one," he said.

She jammed it in the keyhole and pushed open the door. Its weight reassured her. Once this was locked, even a grizzly would have a hard time getting it open. She shivered at the thought. How many of Kalira's people were down there? Were they all skinwalkers? Hazan must have let them inside the library while Lomont was looking at her brand.

She unlocked the door at the top of the stairs and held it open. A cool blue glow filled the staircase, illuminating the confusion on Lomont's face. "This whole time," Jendara growled, "he's been lying to us. He's been working with them all the time."

"Kalira's secret spy." Lomont sighed. He pointed out a bench sitting at the end of a hall lit blue with enspelled lamps. "Let's sit down. Please. My head is killing me."

She helped him to the bench. He sank down, letting his head fall back against the thick black curtain covering the wall.

"I'm sorry," Jendara said. "This is all my fault."

"Your fault?" He lifted his head to give her a sharp look. "Your fault that you trusted a man who had good reason to help you? Your fault that you asked me for help?"

"Well—"

He raised a hand for silence, listening hard. He twisted around, wrenching the curtain open.

Thin moonlight filled the hallway. A massive glass window looked out over the windswept moors on the inland side of the library. Lomont tapped on the glass. "Look at them go."

Jendara peered down. A small knot of men had emerged from the building, four or five hide-cloaked figures bunched tightly around Hazan. They ran south, toward the city.

"Fambra!" Jendara gasped, realization hitting her. "They'll scuttle her boat so we can't follow!"

"Go, then." Lomont put out his hand. "Good luck, Jendara. My duty is here, with the books, but if I could go with you to fight these beasts, I would."

She shook his offered hand. "I'll do my damnedest to make sure you never see any more of them. Thanks for all your help."

He led her out to the library's gates and paused. "I wish we'd found a way to remove that mark. But curses can be broken—trust me on that one. The knowledge is out there, somewhere."

Jendara's mind went back to the boar hunt on Sorind—had it only been a few days ago?—and Morul scorching the boar's hide. There had been skinwalkers once before. Her people remembered at least a ghost of those times. She wondered how much of the legends were true.

"I sure hope so." She glanced back into the entrance hall. It still smelled of smoke, but she couldn't see any. With any luck, she'd put out the fire.

She turned, and Lomont hurried back inside to protect his books. The smell of smoke clung to Jendara as she raced back toward the port. She wasn't going to forgive herself for endangering the library—if not all of Halgrim—by bringing a traitor inside. Not until she had Hazan's head.

Chapter Seventeen
Tripping a Trap

The stairs leading down the docks thudded under Jendara's boots as she ran. People grumbled as she pushed past them. She leaped over a pile of crates filled with ice, then skidded to a stop. A crowd blocked off the dock, most of them men and women wearing simple leather armor with plain iron shields slung onto their backs.

"Jendara? Is that you?" a ginger-haired man on the edge of the crowd asked, and she belatedly recognized Fambra's cousin.

"Jorgen." She paused to catch her breath. "Is everything all right?"

"Terrific. I talked to some people, and a bunch of them wanted to hear details from Fambra. They'd certainly like to hear from you, too."

"Is that Jendara?" Fambra called from the bow of her boat. "Let her come through." She waited for Jendara to join her on board, then frowned. "You smell like a bonfire. Are you all right?"

"I'm fine. But it turns out Hazan's been a spy for Kalira all along. He just attacked one of the librarians and left with a bunch of Kalvamen. I thought for sure he was going to come back here, but I guess all the Iron Shields kept him away."

"A spy?" Fambra's nostrils flared. "

"I should have killed him there on the beach," Jendara fumed.

"Jendara." Fambra's tone was suddenly sharp. "We need to get back to Sorind. Now."

"Agreed," Jendara said, but something in Fambra's face chilled her bones. "What is it?"

"Hazan," Fambra said. "Kalira's your sister, and from what you said, she wants to catch you. But she has no idea where you live—you were out in the fishing grounds when she caught you. But if she turned Hazan—"

Jendara stiffened. "Kran."

"We let him into our homes." Fambra spat, then cupped her hands to mouth and called for Jorgen. They conferred for a few minutes, and then Jorgen pounded her on the shoulder.

"We'll join you on Sorind as soon as we can. Maybe we can round up a few more volunteers." He hurried down the gangplank and tossed up the mooring rope.

Jendara twisted the rope in her hands. *Kran*. How could she have placed him in this danger? She stared out at the sea and for the first time wished she could use magic. She would summon all the winds to speed her journey.

The sun slid over the horizon, needling Jendara's eyelids. Unwillingly, she pulled herself awake. Sven had taken the last watch, but Jendara hadn't been able to sleep much, worrying about Kran and what might be happening on Sorind.

She scrubbed her face with her palms, watching the cold brilliance of sunrise over the sea. The wind caught her hair and tossed it in her face. She ran her fingers through the stuff. It felt strange this short.

She worked out the worst of the knots with her fingers. Fambra surely had a comb in the little sleeping cabin up front, but Jendara wasn't about to bother her with something so trivial. Fambra had been up very late, making adjustments down in the cargo hold. Her boat had moved across the water at double the speed of an ordinary fishing boat. There was magic involved somehow, but Jendara didn't want to know the details.

Jendara pulled the strands of hair tight and began rebraiding them. The breeze smelled fresh; they were sailing true and fast. A seagull spun overhead. The thieving birds often followed fishing vessels, hoping to snatch fish out of the nets when they were brought in. Jendara wrapped the tail of her braid, smiling. She had to admire that kind of cleverness. They were such pirates of birds.

The seagull lowered itself circle by lazy circle, dropping down to keep pace with the boat. It turned its head, fixing its bright eye at Jendara.

Its beak opened. "Jenny," it called. "Jenny!"

Jendara tumbled onto the deck, then leaped back onto her feet.

"Just you wait, Kalira! I'm coming for you!"

Her sword flashed, but the seagull wheeled away, rising into the clear blue sky until it was only a spot.

It cried out, the long haunting cry of a gull. Jendara stood watching it go, feeling sweat soak through her linen shirt.

Sven touched her shoulder. "What was that?"

Jendara clenched her jaw. "Wake up Fambra. We've got to go faster."

It was late afternoon when they finally reached Sorind, and not a single vessel fished in her waters. Every slip in the harbor held a boat. She glanced at the *Milady* sitting silent in her berth. Her decks looked abandoned.

"Where is everybody?" Fambra asked. She leaped over the side of the boat, landing beside a mooring cleat.

Jendara tightened her sword belt. "It's too quiet."

"I see smoke." Sven pointed up the hill, to the cottages clustered around the meeting hall. "More than one family's got a fire going."

"But no one's in the streets." Jendara moved quickly up the dock, listening and watching and smelling. No clanging from the smithy. No bitter stink from Morul's tannery. She peered down the main street. No one stood outside the tavern, waiting for friends to arrive from the docks. "I don't like it."

Then the tavern door opened and a voice bellowed: "Jendara!"

"Morul!"

She broke into a run, relieved and strengthened by that familiar voice. He hurried toward her.

"It's good to see you, Dara." He looked over her shoulder. "I was hoping to see a war party at your back.

The other scouts told me your plan to ask White Estrid for aid."

"White Estrid is away, and her steward wasn't inclined to send guards away from Halgrim. But I do have a group of volunteers—mostly Iron Shields—following behind us. They should be here in half a day."

He stoked his thick yellow beard and led her toward the tavern. "I hope that's soon enough. A lot has happened while you were gone."

He opened the door. Lamps lit the small space and every seat was taken. A few people sat on the floor. Only one or two people sipped at tankards of ale or glasses of mead—most folks were polishing weapons or cleaning some kind of armor. Tam caught sight of Jendara and jumped to his feet.

"The captain had us join the villagers here to help prepare for battle, ma'am," he explained.

"Where's Vorrin? And Kran?" Jendara hoped her voice didn't sound as strained to others as it sounded to her.

"Up at the meetinghouse, settling in some of the refugee families from the north end of the island," Morul said.

"Refugees?" Jendara asked.

"Yes. During the night, creatures attacked a farm on the coast. The family escaped, but a number of their goats were killed. Other farmholds reported wolves in the woods. Given the news your scouting teams brought, we thought it might be wise to pull those outlying homesteads in to the main village."

"And Yul? Did he come?"

Morul nodded. "He's up at the meeting hall, reinforcing the pen he and some of the other farmers built. They're worried sick about losing their livestock."

"Livestock are the least of their worries," Jendara said, absently rubbing her wrist. The skin throbbed. She needed to find a wisewoman, and soon.

Fambra had been talking with an older fisherman. She patted him on the shoulder and crossed the room. "These are your fighters?"

Morul nodded. "Everyone in this room has experience. Some have dabbled as raiders, a few have tried their luck as guards in Halgrim or on the mainland. Whatever those Kalvamen are planning, these are the men and women to face it."

"You need more gear," Fambra said. "I'm going back to my boat. I've got a few items to contribute stashed away in my hold."

Jendara's certainty that Fambra dealt in more colorful business than mere fishing was further strengthened. She couldn't help smirking at the other woman. Fambra was a fighter, a smuggler, and a damn fine mother. Jendara had no doubts that if anyone was coming out of this battle alive, it was Fambra.

"I'm going to go up to the meetinghouse and see what needs to be done. It'll make a good defensive location for our noncombatants."

"I agree," Morul said. "Leyla's been organizing a team. She'll show you what's been done." He hesitated, then leaned close. "Tell her to keep Oric inside. He's a good lad, but I don't want him on the front lines. He'll distract me."

Jendara nodded and spun on her heel, pushing open the tavern door with her forearm. She could already feel the familiar blend of tension and excitement she always felt when battle approached. It had been a long time since she'd planned to get in a fight. Usually the fights just found her.

A surprising sight met her as she made her way uphill: a crew of boys and women setting logs into the muddy ground around the meeting hall, and a stout blonde woman overseeing another group's effort to raise scaffolding against the building's sides. Jendara waved, and the woman's face spread into its usual jolly smile.

"Jendara! Come see what I've been working on."

"Leyla." Jendara squeezed her tightly. "I see you're putting in a stockade."

Leyla eyed the nearly completed wall. The logs' sharpened tips jabbed outward from the meeting hall, forming a bristling perimeter not even the most courageous or hungry wolf would want to leap. "It's something, anyway," she said. "Given the reports from the northern homesteads, I'm glad I've got this." She pulled back her long sweater, revealing a wicked-looking axe on her belt. Jendara had no doubt she could use it well.

"That bad, eh?"

Leyla pulled her aside. "My cousin's wife watched six bears and two wolves meet at the edge of the woods and start pulling down the stock fence. Big fence. Six feet tall. The bears' claws ripped through it like it was balsa wood."

Something in Leyla's voice warned Jendara that wasn't the worst. "What happened?"

"Two crows flew down and joined the creatures. Then the things herded out every last animal. They led them off someplace in the woods." Leyla folded her arms across her chest. "You ever see a cow go with a wolf? It ain't natural."

"They're organizing," Jendara mused. "Stocking supplies for their troops. Kalira's not just raiding. She's planning an invasion." Jendara rubbed her forearm. It burned, almost as if in response to Kalira's name.

Leyla's smile returned. "Anyway, looks like there's someone here pretty excited to see you."

Kran stumbled forward, throwing his arms around Jendara. Mud streaked his face and clumped his hair. He smelled earthy.

"Kran's been an excellent help building defenses. He's a right natural at construction."

Kran pulled back, smiling up at Jendara. He patted her cheek, an unusual display of affection for a boy his age out in public.

"I'll just leave you two for a moment," Leyla said. "I want to make sure these archers' scaffolds are strong enough."

Jendara met Kran's eyes, studying their dark depths. "You weren't worried about me, were you?"

He nodded solemnly, then reached for his chalk. *I knew you had to go, to protect us. But I wanted to protect people too. So I helped with the wall.*

Her heart swelled with love and pride. "I'm glad you did."

But he was still writing. He swiped the chalkboard clean, a smudge of mud following his sleeve's passage over the slate, then scribbled, *I know you don't want me to hunt. But I was really hoping you could give me that spear now. My knife isn't very big.*

Jendara stared at her boy, looking, really *looking* at him. He was tall for a ten-year-old, just a little shorter than she was, and his eyes were very serious. A little constellation of mud spotted high on his cheekbone. She'd seen him muddy before, but this dirt wasn't the ordinary grime of a boy playing outdoors. This mud had come from honest work building the defensive wall that might be the only real protection the village offered its people tonight.

Jendara's shoulders sagged. What a fool she'd been, keeping him away from that boar hunt. She'd brought him to these islands to keep him safe from pirate attacks and brigands in the harbors of the mainland trading posts her travels took her to. She'd brought him here because he was an adventuresome boy who deserved an honest place to explore. But she hadn't taught him what he needed to keep out of danger.

Traveling in rough places wasn't the danger she should have worried about. Hunting wasn't the danger.

Life was the danger.

No matter where he went, there was bound to be trouble. She could worry about that, or she could prepare him for it.

Because Kran was a lot less safe fighting monsters with just a belt knife.

She ruffled his hair. "I don't have that spear for you, but if you're going to be working with the defense team up here, a spear's not a good choice anyway. Too close of quarters to get a really good stab in."

His eyes widened. He leaned closer, like a plant turning toward the sun. By the gods, he was her boy. Jendara resisted a sudden urge to laugh with delight.

She stooped to put her mouth closer to his ear, so no one else could hear. "I think Fambra's got some extra weaponry on her boat. Why don't we go down and see her?"

A dagger. That's what the boy needed. Not a knife, but a real fighting blade to hold off anything that burst through the sharp stakes of his wall. They might not have much time until Kalira's creatures attacked, but they had enough time for Jendara to teach Kran how to use a dagger.

Jendara sat on the floor cross-legged, looking around the meeting hall's great fire pit at the faces shown by the flickering light. She didn't recognize most of them. The farmers from the northern end of the islands had come the closest to the flames, as if it could hold back the things they'd seen out there. She took a bite of her meat pie, wondering how much longer they all had to wait.

"Dara." Vorrin squeezed her shoulder.

She smiled over at him. They hadn't had a chance to talk yet. He'd been busy helping build the archery scaffolding while she'd been working with Kran and fielding questions about the Kalvamen. Everyone needed her, it seemed. Morul and his fighters had a thousand questions about the way the creatures transformed and moved and fought. She wished she'd had more information for them.

"I heard a little about your trip," Vorrin said. He picked up his meat pie and put it back down. Then lifted it again. Whatever he really wanted to say, he clearly didn't know how to proceed.

"I wished you'd been there," Jendara said. She put her hand on his knee. "In that palace, you would have known what to say. You would have convinced the steward. I missed you so much."

"Is that the only reason you missed me?" The fire danced in his eyes. In the dim light, shadows outlined the strong planes of his face. Her heart skipped a beat.

Jendara dropped her gaze to her meat pie and felt its gravy catch in her throat. She was glad for the cover of the coughing fit. These feelings were awkward. After all, Vorrin was Kran's uncle. Her dead husband's brother.

It had been close to five years since Ikran's death, and whole months passed when she didn't think of him save for Kran's resemblance to him. She no longer mourned his laugh or missed his warmth in her bed. Ikran was gone. She had come to accept it. If Vorrin had been any other man, she wouldn't have the slightest compunction about her feelings. But he wasn't. It just wouldn't be fair to Kran to have his uncle for a stepfather.

Noise at the front door was a welcome distraction. Across the room, Morul caught Jendara's eye. She got to her feet, meeting him halfway across the hall.

"The fog is coming down from the highlands," he said. "I imagine they'll attack under its cover."

She nodded. "I'll go join the outer defenses."

Morul stopped her. "They're accepting final blessings from the wisewomen. You might want to give them a moment to finish."

"Thank you." She hadn't realized he'd noted her aversion to such things. "I'll use the time to speak with my son."

The crowd of refugees was murmuring now, picking up on Morul's grim expression and possibly his hushed words. Leyla looked to her husband. At his nod, she got to her feet.

"Friends, hear me now. The battle approaches."

Everyone went still.

Leyla pointed toward the back of the meeting hall. "As most of you know, we built a cellar when we rebuilt this meeting hall. It's not a large cellar, but it connects to an escape tunnel. I want the smallest children, their mothers, and any pregnant women to go down to the cellar now."

People began gathering their things, the small bundles they'd need to make it through the long night. Jendara knew Leyla had cached diapers and dried apples in the cellar in case of a retreat. She patted her sword's pommel grimly. It had better not come to that.

"The rest of us will stay inside. I'd like anyone with arms to man the perimeter of the building. Those without weaponry, prepare yourselves to fight as well. Even a belt knife will be valuable."

"You won't be alone," Jendara called. "Our archers are already in position. Our best fighters are waiting just inside the barrier wall you worked so hard to build today. Those beasts aren't coming in here."

Someone shouted a battle cry, and others joined in, first raggedly, then louder. Kran waved his fists above his head. The sight of him made Jendara's mouth go dry. She hoped she was right.

She pressed through the crowd toward him and crushed him in her arms. He'd looked so tall and strong earlier, but now he felt thin, too fragile to risk against the tide of Kalira's monsters. "I love you, Kran," she whispered, pressing her cheek against his mop of dark hair.

"Jendara." Vorrin put his hand on her shoulder.

"I know you wish you were out there. But you're the most experienced swordsman I know. I'm not letting you leave Kran's side. He's safer with you than with me."

"That's not true. You're the toughest fighter I've ever seen."

"Yes, but—" she broke off. She hadn't had a chance to tell him about the brand or the spreading black stain. He didn't know what had happened to Hazan. "I have my reasons to worry."

He cupped her cheek in his hand. "If there's anybody who can take on these bastards, it's you."

She threw her arms around him, squeezing him hard. "Take care of my boy. And for the gods' sake, don't let yourself get hurt." She stared into his brown eyes, memorizing the gold tones in their depths, the little dark flecks around the pupil. "I'd never forgive myself if something happened to you."

A loud booming sounded outside. The warning drums from the watchtower at the edge of town, sounding the alarm. Jendara kissed Vorrin's cheek and Kran's forehead, then darted outside.

Behind her, someone slammed home the door bolt. The reinforcing timbers made a comforting thud. The meeting hall was secure.

Jendara eased her sword out of its scabbard, listening hard. Her eyebrows drew together. "Do you hear hooves?"

Morul swore. "The stolen stock."

"To the stockade, and take spears," she barked.

"My hunting spears," he grunted. "They're on the front steps."

She raced up the stairs, grabbing the bundle of weapons. Their iron points gleamed in the lamplight. She paused a moment as an idea struck her.

"Morul!" She rushed back toward him. "Get someone to light the lamps you placed. I want this place so bright it burns the eyes of any wolf or cougar in her party. Let's make her regret choosing night predators."

"I'll help."

Jendara hadn't noticed Gerda among the fighters, but the wisewoman stepped forward now. She had dressed herself in hunter's leathers, the blue tattoos on her cheeks the only hint of her status. Twenty years seemed to have slid off her, and she carried a sturdy-looking staff. "I can light lamps as well as anyone."

Jendara gave her a tight smile. "Thanks." She moved toward the gate, calling for her men: "Tam! Yul! Sven!"

She tossed them spears. "This gate's the weakest stretch of the stockade. Kalira's people are going to drive the stampede straight into it. We've only got a few spears, so make them count. I don't want anything getting past us to the meeting hall."

Morul hurried to the gate. "We're bringing reinforcing timbers around, but rebuilding isn't going to be an option once those barbarians hit."

She grinned. "I'll try to keep them busy." Her eyes flashed with sudden excitement.

"You mad woman," he muttered, but he was already hurrying away.

The open space behind Jendara had filled up with lights as Gerda and her fellow lamplighters planted torches and lit lanterns. The light should have been welcome, but Jendara cupped her hands around her eyes, hoping to keep a little of her night vision. She peered between the narrow gaps in the stockade wall, but it was impossible to see into the darkness beyond.

The ground shook beneath her boots.

A tremendous shudder shook the wall as the animals hit it. A horse screamed in pain. Hooves thudded against the wall. The Kalvamen urged the stampede forward.

The timbers in front of Jendara creaked. She dug her heels into the ground and braced her spear against the first wave.

The gate toppled down, a tide of horses and cows surging forward. A bay horse lost traction and slid sideways, slamming into Jendara's spear and knocking her backward. The horse shrieked and leaped up, wrenching the spear out of her hand. Blood ran from its side and pink foam burst from its mouth.

It reared up, flailing its hooves.

"Calm!"

The horse stumbled back to all fours. Jendara scrambled away from it. A hand on her shoulder stopped her.

"You've got to get that gate back up!" Gerda's voice was urgent. Sweat shone on her forehead, and her lips were tight. Jendara realized, with a start, that the animals around her were standing still, trembling but silent.

"You did this," she realized.

Gerda nodded. "It won't last long. Hurry!"

Jendara ran toward the gate. The opening in the stockade was jammed with fallen cows and horses and sheep, some dead, some injured, some standing calmly. Her boots skidded and squelched.

"Jendara!" Sven shoved a dead sheep aside and caught up with her. "What happened?"

"Gerda did something, calmed the animals. But I don't know how we'll fix the stockade with all this livestock in the wa—"

A clatter of lumber cut her off. With a grunt, Morul plunged a shovel into the bloody ground. "We'll build right through them if we have to. Just hope the archers keep picking 'em off."

Bowstrings sang overhead. The Kalvamen had arrived.

A howling figure sprang up on top of the mound of fallen livestock. A Kalvaman, his voice raised in the pure shriek of barbarian battle lust.

Laughter bubbled up inside Jendara. She drew her sword and charged forward. The Kalvaman raced forward to meet her. Her steel struck his coarse blade and sent it flying. With a snarl, he charged at her, barehanded. Her sword caught the side of his neck and bit down through it. Blood sprayed into the air.

The scream she heard came from beside him and she glanced aside to see another man leaping across the barricade of cow corpses. His mace gleamed in the torchlight. She yanked on her sword, but it had caught in the other man's collarbone. A hand shoved into her back. Tam's own sword flickered, skewering the mace-slinger.

"Fall back!" Tam bellowed.

She kicked the dead Kalvaman off her sword and hurried backward, her weapon at the ready. Morul shoved her aside as his team pushed the body of a heavy wagon into the space where the gate had been. Men and women scurried to plant more stockade timbers around the unwheeled wagon and pile wood and debris on top of it.

Jendara shook out her fingers and breathed deep. She couldn't tell if the roaring, screaming, and howling on the other side of the barricade came from the throats of beasts or men. The first wash of adrenaline was fading, but that sound spurred a new burst of fear-powered energy.

The first wisps of fog trickled through the stockade. Her hopes to keep the skinwalkers blinded by lamplight were going to be challenged.

The bowstrings sang out again. The archers were the village's best hope. Her fighters could do a lot of damage to a ground force, but not if Kalira's troops overran them.

"Got to bring down their numbers," she growled to herself. Above her, a man screamed.

With a horrible screech and scrape, an archer tumbled down from the scaffolding, gripped in the claws of a creature Jendara almost couldn't identify. *A cougar*, she realized, as she caught the beast's long silken tail and yanked hard.

The cougar snarled and slashed at her with its long claws. Jendara struck out with her sword, but missed. Claws screeched against metal as the cat slapped the blade out of her hand. Jendara hissed as a claw ripped open the side of her hand. The cat lunged forward. Jendara's fist struck out, slamming into the space between its golden eyes. It shook its head, stunned, but she was already striking at its ribs. She grabbed at her belt knife. The archer was still screaming. He could possibly live.

The cougar's claws slashed again. Jendara ducked just in time, rolling under the sweep of its huge paw to come up under its chest, driving her knife into its side. She felt the archer's leg snap under her boot and winced, but she didn't fall back.

The cougar wrapped both forelegs around her and squeezed her tight. It bit at her shoulder, its teeth grinding on the studs in her leather vest. A quick uppercut to its jaw snapped its head backward. It grunted.

Her knife struck the exposed throat. Blood sprayed. The big cat's mouth opened and closed, like someone straining for last words. Its body went limp against Jendara's.

She pushed it away.

The creature slid to the ground, the fur fading off the cheeks and forehead of an ordinary-looking woman. Her pale eyes glassed over.

The adrenaline washed out of Jendara's system. She sagged against the wall of the meetinghouse, her stomach churning.

"Dara?"

She blinked at the archer the cougar had brought down. She couldn't believe she hadn't recognized him earlier. "Glayn?" She shook her head, trying to make her brain work again. "I didn't know you could shoot."

"Little hobby. Picked up a lot of them over the years." The gnome struggled to smile. "By all that's holy, I hurt."

She moved to his side. Deep gashes ran down the sides of his scalp: she could see the bone beneath. "Don't move. It'll only hurt worse." She wouldn't tell him how badly injured he was.

"Man down!" she shouted. "I need help!"

"I've got him." Tam knelt beside the caulker. "Oh, Glayn, what have you done to yourself?"

"I can't believe I fell," the gnome said. "I've been sailing all these years, and I let a little kitty knock me off a perch that wasn't even moving!"

"You'll be fine," another voice said. It was Gerda, a roll of bandages already in her hands. "Tam, help me get him inside."

Tam lifted the gnome gently, cradling him against his chest. He moved toward the door, taking the steps with great care.

"He will be all right, won't he?" Jendara asked Gerda.

Gerda narrowed her eyes. "You doubting my word?"

There was something so ferocious about the old woman's expression that Jendara shook her head. Death itself would be afraid of that face. "You I believe."

Something caught Jendara's eye—the glossy wood of Glayn's bow, miraculously undamaged. She picked it up and tugged its string. The bow was small, but the draw was stout. She reached for the last bundle of arrows. Behind her, wood crackled, the ominous sounds of a large creature rushing the stockade. "Get inside now. It's going to get ugly."

Gerda nodded and raced toward the meeting hall. Jendara swallowed down sudden concern for the old woman. She didn't want to like Gerda, but the old bird was admirably tough.

Jendara turned to face the wall. A group of fighters held the barricade, but the rest of the wall sagged. Something threw its weight against the timbers and it shook. It couldn't hold much longer.

Her hand spasmed, and she nearly dropped the bow. Jendara hissed at the pain in her arm, a thousand times worse than the burning and prickling she'd felt back at the library. Heat seared up her forearm, stinging the flesh at her elbows.

Jendara breathed deep. She wasn't about to let Kalira's beasts walk in here just because this brand was hurting her hand. With a grunt, she pushed the pain to the back of her mind and charged the wall.

Gaps showed between the sharpened timbers, just large enough for Jendara to dig her toes and fingers into. She scrambled up the inside of the wall and took an awkward stance near the top. Up here, it was easy to make out the three bears just to the side of the demolished gate, throwing their weight against the wall. She nocked an arrow and let fly.

The arrow sliced through the bear's ear.

Cursing, she drew another arrow and forced herself to take her time. She let it fly. The arrow soared, outlined for a second in the powerful light of the many torches and lamps.

It struck the bear's cheek and sank up to its fletching. The bear screamed.

From behind her, another volley of arrows streaked. Jendara saw an arrow pierce a wolf's skull. She watched in glee as a shapeshifter stopped in mid-transformation and raced away from the gate, his golden cougar tail disappearing as he ran.

An owl flew at her face and she threw up an arm, nearly falling over the wall. She swatted at the bird, launching it into the spiked logs. It hung from a pinned wing a moment before falling to the ground.

Another owl circled overhead, hooting louder than any owl Jendara had ever heard. She went cold as the glowing eyes of a dozen creatures turned up at her. She was the perfect target up here. A single cougar could take her down—let alone an enemy marksman. She hadn't seen any archers in the attack, but that didn't mean there weren't any to come.

She shot several quick arrows into the huddle of bears and jumped down to the ground, giving a tight smile at the shrieks of pain outside the wall. At least one of her arrows had hit home.

"They're retreating!" someone shouted.

She cheered, and voices joined her. The men and women of the defensive line shouted with jubilation.

And then, from behind her, up in the archers' scaffolds: "Oh no."

Chapter Eighteen
Searing Flesh

They've got fire!" an archer shouted.

"Lift me up," Jendara snapped at the nearest man, and he boosted her up on his shoulders. She cursed. The archer was right. Out of the mist, a flaming brand soared and landed on the barricade blocking the gate. A woman stamped it out, but others flew down to join it.

Fambra raced up, her empty quiver bouncing on her back. "They've got shields now! And a battering ram!"

"That wall can't hold against a battering ram," Jendara said. "We need to rush the ram bearers."

"Send good people over the barricade to face those things? I don't think so."

"We don't have a choice, Morul! We're going to run out of arrows soon."

"Some of us are out already," Fambra agreed. "If we go out there, we can collect our fallen arrows while Jendara leads a team to attack those carrying the battering ram."

But at that moment, something hit the gate with a resounding thud. The whole structure rippled.

"We're too late," Jendara said.

Smoke billowed up over the top of the wall. Kalira's torchmen had reached their targets despite the archers' work. Jendara threw aside Glayn's bow and drew her sword. Her fingers spasmed around the hilt. Her gut cramped hard enough to make her double over.

Fambra caught her elbow. "Are you all right?"

"I'd better be," Jendara snapped. She managed to straighten up. "I want you to find some arrows and go into the meeting hall. Get Leyla to show you out the escape tunnel so you can cover the exit. If they have to use it—"

"I won't let those bastards get our people while they're running," Fambra said, voice grim. "Take care of yourself, Jendara. If you can't fight, you should run."

"I can fight," Jendara said. She took a deep breath and sank into a fighting crouch. "They're going to wish I couldn't."

The gate burst inward with a blast of splinters. A shard of wood caught Jendara in the cheek. She yanked it out. "To me!"

She charged forward.

The battering ram had caught in the remains of the wall, its bearers exposed. She plunged to the right side of it, her sword driving into one man's chest. She didn't bother wrenching it free. She kept running, spearing the next man. He screamed. She twisted sideways as the battering ram, no longer supported on the right side, crashed down.

With a crunch, the massive log shattered the still-screaming man's legs. Jendara's breath caught in her throat a second. That could have been her under that log. Her mind faltered, but her arm knew what to do. It was already pulling her sword free of the two skewered men.

But she wasn't ready for the shield that smashed into her face. She toppled backward, tripped over a snapped timber, and fell into the mud. Her nose throbbed with agony. She grabbed it and squeezed it back into alignment, ignoring the streaming blood. She could feel her face swelling as she pulled herself to her feet.

A Kalvaman pushed past her, knocking her aside with an elbow. The runners carried torches beneath their shields, protecting the flames with their bodies. They were headed straight for the meetinghouse.

Jendara swayed on her feet. Her head spun and she had to spit blood to keep from choking on it. Her sword fell from her aching fingers.

She lashed out with her toe and kicked up the hilt. She caught it in her left hand. Despite hours of practice using her left hand, the weapon didn't feel right. But nothing felt right. Her body resisted her every attempt to spur it forward.

"To me!" she managed to croak. "To me!"

A swordsman spun toward her. She raised her sword to protect herself.

"Jendara!" Morul's voice shook some of the strangeness out of her head, and she recognized him just before she swung.

"Morul. The meetinghouse." She managed to wave at the runners with their torches, now gathered at the corner of the building.

"You stay here. I'll stop them!" He raced forward even as Jendara slid down against the wall. Her legs wouldn't pick her up again.

Flame flared on the side of the meetinghouse, but Morul was there, his sword flashing in the firelight. Both the runners fell. Morul ripped off one of the men's fur cloaks and pounded at the flames.

Jendara's head fell back against the stockade. She was glad the whole thing hadn't fallen. It made a good place to rest her spinning head. The skin of her upper arm crawled and stung. Maybe someone would find her resting here and cut the damn thing off.

"More torches!"

The voice sounded right in Jendara's ear. She lifted her head, turning so she could peer between the logs of the wall. A fire glowered in the street beyond, its orange light filtering through the fog. A horse and rider stood in silhouette beside the fire, the rider's top half strangely elongated and misshapen.

A crow suddenly landed on the rider's shoulder, and then Jendara understood why the rider looked so odd. It was Kalira, wearing her horrible crow-winged headdress. Jendara's right hand opened and closed spasmodically. She squeezed it into a tight fist within her left hand.

"Rip them to pieces, my walkers!"

Jendara gasped. This was it. This was the moment. Kalira had rode in with the next wave of skinwalkers, and Morul was still busy putting out that fire. The stockade had broken open. There were no more arrows. Jendara pushed herself upright. She had to fight.

She stumbled forward, outside the protective wall. A few of her fighters had gathered out there, driving back Kalvamen. "You!" she shouted. "With me!"

The group pushed forward. Tam kicked a twitching wolf's corpse aside.

"We've got to get to Kalira," she said. She winced as her hand spasmed again.

Tam noticed. "You're hurt."

"Not badly. Come on!" She pushed herself into a run, skewering a woman on the edge of the advancing Kalvamen. The man behind her leaped forward, fur flickering over his face.

Animal sounds filled the air: roars, growls, snarls, shrieks. Goose bumps rose on the back on Jendara's neck. A half-man, half-coyote thing lunged at her. Tam slammed the pommel of his sword down on its head.

Jendara stepped over the unconscious coyote man and pressed forward. She had to get to Kalira.

A woman with a bear's snout and ears growled at her. Jendara headbutted her, then sliced through her throat. She pushed onward. Kalira. Had to get to Kalira.

But the big white horse with its white-robed rider was already in front of her. Kalira's face stared down at her beneath the horrible headdress. Her eyes were barely visible slits ringed in kohl.

"You can't hurt me, Jenny."

Jendara felt the weight of her sword double in her hand. She set her teeth and tried to raise it. She might as well be lifting the *Milady*.

"No!" she shouted. Her sword fell to the ground. She reached for her belt axe, but her fingers wouldn't move. Her whole body had gone stiff.

You won't hurt me, Kalira commanded. Her lips didn't move: the words simply reverberated inside Jendara's skull, rumbling through her whole body. Her legs went out from under her.

Kalira wheeled her horse. "Attack the meetinghouse!" she called.

Jendara managed to lift her head. She lay in a sea of beasts. Kalira shrieked, the high sound of an angry crow, and cougars and wolves and bears raced toward the meeting hall. A coyote with a woman's face leaped over Jendara's legs.

"No," Jendara whispered.

A small round stone fell just beside her hand. She lifted herself on elbow to look for where it came from.

"Ow!" Kalira clutched her face. Something had struck her in the mouth, splitting her lip.

The projectile landed close enough that Jendara could see its smooth polished gleam. It was no stone. It was a wooden marble. One she'd seen before. Jendara's blood went cold.

"Kran," she breathed. She sat up, her head suddenly clear. Kalira slid down from her horse, her attention focused on something on the far side of now-empty street. She walked toward the small figure with calm, purposeful steps.

Jendara snatched up her sword. The pain in her right hand had halved. Maybe it was because Kalira was distracted, or because she was moving away from Jendara. Or maybe it was simply the power of a mother protecting her son. Whatever caused it, Jendara would use it to her own advantage.

She used both hands and threw the sword as hard as she could.

It sliced through the air, catching Kalira on the side of the thigh. She stumbled and fell.

"Kran!"

Jendara leaped over her fallen sister, aches and pains forgotten. Her son, her ridiculous son, lowered his sling. She grabbed his elbow and dragged him along.

"We've got to get to the meeting hall!"

There was no time for questions, no time for remonstrations. She would tan his hide when they got out of here.

Behind them, a crow shrieked.

Beasts and men battled in the area just in front of the meeting hall, but the front steps were clear. Jendara yanked Kran up them and hammered on the door. "Help!" she bellowed.

The door flew inward. Vorrin caught her as she tripped over the threshold. He caught sight of Kran and his face darkened. "How did you—"

But Gerda cut him off. "Bar the door! Merciful Desna, look at you."

Jendara sank to the floor. "It's not as bad as it looks." She glared at Kran. "What were you doing out there?"

"That's likely my fault," Tam said. He was propped in a corner with his sword across his lap, but his left arm was bound to his chest. "I got bit pretty bad and they brought me in here. I was telling Vorrin—"

"That you went out there hurt, like some crazy woman," Vorrin interjected.

"And Kran must have snuck out when the next of the wounded came in." Gerda's mouth settled into a grim line. She took Jendara's arm and sliced open the sleeve. "This is bad."

The black stain had spread to the elbow, and gray tendrils ran up toward Jendara's shoulder. A smell rose off the flesh, like sticky tar and spoiled meat. Jendara turned her head away.

"Can you do anything?"

Gerda was already wrapping a bandage around Jendara's bicep. "We need to cut off the movement of the poison." She tucked a few sprigs of herbs into the linen. "These will stimulate your body to fight off the evil. Other than that, all I can do is pray."

Gerda began to chant, her voice low and intense. Her eyes rolled up in her head, revealing only the whites.

Jendara flexed her fingers. In the soft glow of the whale oil lamps, they looked dark, almost black. But they could move again without burning. She wasn't sure if it was the affect of being away from Kalira, or having her wound bandaged. "It feels better," she admitted.

The door shuddered. Tam caught Jendara's eye. "The battering ram. They're turning it on the door now."

"We've got to get these people out," Jendara said. "Where's Leyla?"

The ram hit again. The door's hinges shrieked.

"We don't have much time," Vorrin shouted, dragging Jendara to her feet. "Hurry!"

"Let's go! Let's go! Faster!" Leyla called from the far end of the hall. She must have opened the escape tunnel when she heard the first thud of the battering ram. "Pregnant women and little ones first," she reminded them.

People packed into the little space, making way for the younger children. Someone fell. A baby wailed.

Jendara reached out for Kran's fingers and squeezed them. He squeezed hers back.

The door burst open behind them.

Jendara swung around, her belt axe in hand. But there would be no repeat of her attack at the gate—the ram and its bearers had already pulled back. A wolf slipped in, meeting Vorrin's blade snout-first.

"Head for the escape tunnel," he commanded.

"I'm not leaving without you," Jendara growled. She kicked a second wolf in the teeth and then stabbed it fast.

"To hell with that!" he shouted. He brought down two snarling coyotes with a slash of his sword.

Kran tugged on Jendara's elbow. A faint thudding noise sounded at the southern wall, and a bit of plaster rained down. Kalira's battering ram was already hard at work.

"We've got to get out of here," Jendara shouted. Vorrin was bringing down the creatures as fast as they could squeeze through the front door, but if the southern wall fell, they'd be inundated with skinwalkers.

The huge figure of a grizzly filled the doorway. Vorrin slashed at it, but the bear slid under the attack, lashing out with its claws. And then something golden bounded over its back, leaping impossibly high over Jendara's head, its fangs flashing in the light.

"Behind you!" Tam yelled.

Jendara spun around, but the cougar was already closing its teeth on Kran's shoulder. "Kran!"

Vorrin spun toward the boy.

The grizzly slapped him aside and he flew through the air, hitting the wall with a terrible crunch.

Jendara launched her axe at the cougar, but the weapon missed by an inch. The cougar leaped back toward the door, dragging Kran behind it.

The grizzly bounded forward, putting its massive bulk between Jendara and her son. She reached for her sword, but she must have dropped it someplace. She fumbled for her belt knife. The beast swiped at her.

Tam rolled under the grizzly's limbs and jabbed upward with his sword, spearing the tender spot beneath the bear's jaw, skewering its brain. The beast twitched and fell backward.

But the cougar, and Kran, was already gone.

Jendara stood frozen a moment. Kran. That thing had Kran.

She turned to Gerda. "Don't let Vorrin die," she warned.

"I'll do my best," Gerda answered. She tossed Jendara the sword she'd dropped while Gerda tended her arm. "Go get your boy."

"I'll do *my* best," Jendara growled. Then she raced out of the broken door and into the night.

Out in the fog, she ran alone. She had expected a chaos of battle, but with the exceptions of a few knots of fighters, the night had gone quiet. No snarls echoed off the walls. No screams filled the streets. Jendara slowed a little, listening.

No, the only sounds were soft calls from down on the waterfront. Jendara almost stumbled. The waterfront. Kalira's people were headed for the docks, and that could only mean one thing: they were leaving.

She burst forward, ignoring the pain in her arms and head. Kalira might be injured, but Jendara hadn't killed her, and she knew her sister wouldn't leave without getting what she came for. There had been a reason behind this attack. Hadn't Fambra warned her, back on the boat? Hazan knew what Jendara most treasured. He must have told Kalira and Brynorm. That cougar hadn't taken Kran by accident.

Jendara skidded down the harbor ramp. Here, it wasn't quiet at all. Waves splashed as bears and wolves leaped into the water, swimming for the approaching longships. Flames crackled as a few human-shaped Kalvamen lobbed brands into the bottoms of Sorinder boats. Jendara sent a terrified look at the *Milady*, but the brig looked unharmed, sitting out on the longest pier. But flames already crawled up the masts of a half-dozen boats. None of the others would be safe.

A man pushed past her, nearly sending her into the bay. She recognized the hank of long braids streaming down his back.

"Hazan," she growled, and followed.

A longship approached the end of the dock. Jendara watched a man in its bow toss a mooring rope to a huge man standing on the dock. Brynorm.

Then she saw the woman striding down the dock, a wriggling bundle thrown over her shoulder. Jendara's eyes narrowed. The woman had wrapped her cougar skin tightly around the boy, but Kran wasn't the kind of kid to take being kidnapped meekly.

Jendara sprinted down the dock and launched herself at the woman. She hit the woman's shoulder and sent them all tumbling off the edge of the dock, falling into a dinghy.

The woman bellowed, but her hands were full of kicking boy. Jendara's fists pounded at her ears and neck. The woman's head bounced off a lead fishing weight and she went still. Jendara clawed at the pelt binding her boy.

"Get her!" someone shouted.

A kick caught her in the shoulder blades and she fell forward, narrowly missing the same weight that had knocked out the other woman. Her arms wrenched backward as a cruel hand gripped them. A man grunted as he lifted her out of the boat.

"Damn it, Jendara," he growled. She recognized Hazan's voice and kicked at him. Her shoulders screamed. They'd been abused much too recently for this kind of treatment. She felt a moment's relief when he switched to gripping her by the throat. Then her head began to spin. Her arm burned.

Kalira moved forward, leaning on a man's shoulder, her pale face ashen. She had removed the crow headdress.

"You tried to kill me," she said.

Jendara could barely speak. The arm around her throat was squeezing tight. "You would have killed my boy," she managed to grate.

"You should have stood at my left hand," Kalira said. She drew herself up tall. "You should have led my troops to victory on Battlewall."

Hope surged in Jendara's chest. Did this mean Kalira hadn't mobilized an attack on Battlewall yet? Could it mean that this was the bulk of her fighting force right here?

"But instead, I will take your son and raise him as my own." Kalira smiled. "Family should be together, don't you think?"

Jendara tried to answer, but the words only gurgled in her throat.

Kalira snapped her fingers. "Kill her, Hazan. The rest of you, get to the ships."

"Watch out!" a voice shouted. Kalira spun around as the fishing weight soared past her head.

Jendara's eyes widened. Kran hopped out of the dinghy, holding a fishing spear tight. He raised it, looking from Hazan to Kalira and then back to Jendara.

"The woman," Jendara choked. Gray spots threatened to blot out her vision of her son. "Kill . . . her . . ." Her feet slid out from under her.

Kran threw the spear.

Hazan grunted. The spear had struck Hazan's thigh mere inches from Jendara's own leg, and it had pierced the big artery in the leg. Blood seeped out, hot and damp. His arm slipped free of her. Kran's aim had been perfect—for saving his mother.

"You fool," Kalira laughed. Her sword flashed, snake-fast, the pommel hammering the top of Kran's head. His eyes rolled up and he crumpled to the wet planks.

"No!" Jendara screamed, and launched herself at Kalira.

A Kalvaman intercepted her, bringing her to the ground. She kicked and punched, trying to get out from under his weight. The man clawed at her eyes. She batted his hands away. At the end of the pier, Kalira's guard had Kran in his arms and Brynorm was helping Kalira into the longship. Jendara only had a few seconds.

The man sank his teeth into her wrist. Jendara grunted and twisted, fumbling for her belt knife. Her fingers closed on the hilt and she plunged it into his back.

She rolled free of her assailant, but it was too late. Rowers had already moved the last longship away from the dock, too far for her to jump aboard. The boats around her were burning.

Kran was gone.

She spun around. Hazan lay gasping on the deck, the color draining from his face as his blood left his body.

"You bastard." She drew back her foot and kicked him as hard as she could. He gasped. She'd hit his broken ribs.

"You treacherous vermin." She kicked the injured spot again, pleased by the twist of his face. She dropped to her knees. There was a new heat in her hands now, not the burning pain of Kalira's brand but the familiar pleasant warmth of the jolly roger tattoos. Jendara whipped out her knife.

Hazan's eyes widened.

She grabbed the front of his shirt and sliced it open, revealing his dirty bandages. She doubted they'd been changed even once. She grabbed the neatly tucked bandage tail and yanked hard, loosening the strip.

"What are you going to do?" His voice quivered.

She drew the dirty bandage around the base of his leg and yanked it tight. "I'm going to stop the bleeding from your wound," she said. She grinned wider than she'd ever grinned in her life. "And then I'm going to torture you until you tell me everything I need to know. Or die. I don't care."

She reached for the spear still stuck in his leg and wrenched it free. He bellowed with pain.

"Where are they taking him?" she snarled.

"To her new camp!"

She dug her fingers into the open wound. He screamed, his back arching. She imagined her father screaming like that when the Kalvamen impaled him.

She twisted her fingers deeper.

Tears ran down the traitor's face. "Jendara, I'm sorry," he gasped. "My story was true. They killed Byrni, and they took Marga. That witch said she wouldn't hurt Marga as long as I came back with information. And she put one of those brands on my arm. I had to do what she wanted."

She slapped his face, leaving streaks of his own blood behind.

"Look at my arm!" he cried. "You know it's true!"

She didn't want to look. The grinning thing inside her didn't want any reason to stop its work. But the rest of her knew she had to see the mark on his arm. She needed the full story if she was going to save Kran.

She ripped open his shirt at the shoulder seam. Black tendrils rose up the side of his neck and strained across the muscles of his chest. A solid black spot sat on top of his heart. The heat began to trickle out of her body. She knew those marks too well.

"Do you think I really wanted to leave you back on Battlewall? Or that I enjoyed trying to kill you? Do you know what it's like to not be in control of yourself?" He trembled. He was going into shock.

"I do know," she whispered. She scrambled away from him, horrified by the filth on his face, the blood spreading around his body. She looked at her hands, sticky with blood and gobbets of tissue. "Oh, gods, how I know it."

She leaned over the side of the dock and retched. She couldn't get the stench of blood out of her nose or escape the fainter stink of tar and rotten flesh that her arm gave off. She rinsed her mouth and hands with seawater and carried a bit back to Hazan. She rubbed his blood off his cheeks.

"You're going to be all right," she said. "You might lose your leg, but with that tourniquet, you won't lose any more blood."

He gave a dry bark of laughter. "I think you overestimate your skills as a healer."

"But I'll get Gerda. She'll help."

"I won't make it another five minutes." He swallowed. Sweat stood out on his brow. "Look, Jendara, I don't know where Kalira's headed. I don't know where the new camp is. She didn't trust me. No one did." His eyelids fluttered.

"Shh," Jendara whispered. "Save your strength."

He sucked in a stuttery breath. "You'll find Marga for me, won't you?" he gasped. "Don't let those bastards hurt her."

"Hush," she repeated. "You're going to be fine. Marga is, too." She squeezed his fingers in hers. They were very cold.

"You're a bad liar." He smiled up at her, his eyes bright. His fingers twitched in her grip and went still.

Jendara pulled her hand away and closed his eyes. Despair—for Kalira, for her own failure to save Kran, for Hazan and all the other dead—filled her throat, but she choked it down.

She could cry for her mistakes later. She had a son to save. And she couldn't do it with her arm like this.

She got to her feet. Each footstep jolted her throbbing head. She was vaguely aware that she was exhausted, that she'd been fighting hard for hours and with no downtime in days. Every muscle screamed as she made her way up to the meeting hall.

She needed fire. Good clean fire, and someone with healing talents when she was done. She pushed past a bearded man at the broken door. He nodded at her and she nodded back. She should have recognized him, but her exhausted brain could only focus on one thing at a time right now, and fire took up all the space.

The big central fire pit had been stirred up. The room felt far too hot. Jendara stumbled forward. People kept talking to her, but their voices were only distant thunder. She dropped to her knees beside the fire and saw the perfect chunk of wood. Her fingers closed on its unburnt end.

"Jendara!" Morul bellowed, and his voice echoed and reechoed as she brought the flames down on her stained right hand.

She only smelled burnt flesh a second before she passed into darkness.

Chapter Nineteen
Awakenings

Jendara pried open her eyes and lay still a moment, staring up at huge cedar rafters that didn't belong in her house or her cabin on board the *Milady*. The wonderful smells of bacon and pancakes filled the mysterious space. The events of the night tumbled through her mind. "Kran," she whispered.

"Ah, I see my stupidest patient is awake."

That sour voice could only come from Gerda. Jendara pushed herself up on her elbows and scowled at the Alstone wisewoman. "That's some beside manner, Granny."

"Sometimes the truth hurts. What did you think you were doing back there—burning the brand off your hand?" Gerda rolled her eyes. "I suppose you thought that would be a very dramatic way to take care of your problems, didn't you?"

"It made sense at the time," Jendara protested.

Gerda thrust a mug at her. "Drink this. And stop trying to think. You're no good at it. Luckily, you were too worn out to do much damage to yourself."

Jendara took a sip of the steaming brew and made a face. It tasted too bitter for a stomach to manage. "Did I . . . pass out?"

"Honestly, I think you just fell asleep. You gave yourself a minor burn, but you had no real signs of shock. I'd guess you simply overexerted yourself." Gerda's eyebrows drew together. "You're not drinking."

"It tastes horrible."

"It'll make you feel better."

Jendara took an obliging gulp and shuddered. It tasted even worse this time, almost as bitter as the feeling of loss inside Jendara's heart. "Any news of Kran? And is Vorrin all right?"

"He'll live," Gerda said. "But it will be a long while before he gets out of bed. His leg is broken in three places, he sprained a wrist, and he cracked two ribs. Still, an unluckier man would have snapped his neck."

Jendara swallowed. She'd come awfully close to losing him last night. She closed her eyes a second. "And Kran?"

"We organized a fire brigade and managed to save a handful of smaller boats, including Fambra's. She took off after the Kalvamen, but a fog came up. She got turned around in it, which stinks of some kind of magic. We sent out patrols this morning, but no one found hide nor hair of those devils."

The lump in Jendara's throat grew larger. She'd been hoping for better news. "The *Milady*?"

"Ah, she's fine. The Kalvamen never made it out to her dock—that's how Fambra's boat came through all right. They're lazy, these Kalvamen." Gerda pressed the back of her hand to Jendara's forehead. "Islanders would have done much more damage."

Jendara managed to smile.

Gerda sat back on the little stool beside Jendara's cot. "It was ugly enough," she admitted. "We've lost some good people, and there are at least a dozen missing. I'm guessing Kalira's people took them. Plus, Chana and I have our hands full of wounded. Nearly half our defenders had some kind of injury."

Jendara followed the old woman's gaze. Chana, Sorind's wisewoman, was tending another patient beside the fire pit. The meeting hall looked full to bursting with wounded folk. Jendara looked back up at the ceiling. This must be pretty close to the spot where Hazan had slept after they found him knocked out in his own ship. Had he known, lying here staring at the rafters, the kinds of trouble he'd be involved in? She caught herself staring at the bandage on the back of her hand.

"I don't know what to do," she admitted.

Gerda absently stroked the blue spiral on her cheekbone. "Things are difficult for all of us," she answered.

"I don't know where Kran's been taken. Hazan said she moved her people to a new camp, but he didn't know where. Kalira could be anywhere in these islands. Plus, if I get close to her, this brand could act up again. I couldn't even hold my own sword back there." Jendara threw back the last of the bitter brew in her mug. "I'm tired, I'm sore, and I just want my boy back." She puffed out her cheeks. "I can't think straight about all this."

"The brand is what worries me," Gerda said. She took Jendara's hand, staring at the ugly raised flesh of the mark, now half-covered by a fresh burn blister. "I think you were lucky last night. The brand's poison hadn't spread enough to completely control you. But it's going to keep growing, Jendara. And so's her hold over you."

"I can't let that happen. I'd rather lose my arm—"

Gerda cut her off with a wave of her hand. "There's something else we can try first." Her lips tightened. "It's dangerous, especially for someone like you."

"Someone like me?" Jendara's eyes narrowed. She felt an echo of the anger she'd felt when Gerda scorned her home for its lack of clan totems.

"You have no faith in the ancestors. And to do this thing, you will need their help."

"What can a bunch of spirits do for me?" Jendara snapped. "They didn't protect my father when he needed help! They didn't stop those Kalvamen from torturing my sister into absolute madness! Why should I have faith in them?"

Gerda's eyes filled with tears. She leaned forward, cupping Jendara's face in her hands. "Because they have faith in you."

Jendara shook her head, but the hands stayed, warm and gentle. "I don't understand," she whispered.

"You don't have to," Gerda said. "You're an islander. We're not like other people. We keep to ourselves and we keep to our islands. Even our dead can't bear to move on to the other planes. Why would they want to leave the fog and the wind, the stones and the sea?"

Jendara had heard this before, she realized. She could remember the words in her father's low voice as he put a loaf of fresh hot bread on the altar beside the crow totem. *Why would anyone want to leave the islands? All this fog and wind. Is there anything more beautiful than this place?*

She closed her eyes, remembering her father's face, his blue eyes dancing above his thick white beard. She remembered the lines that outlined his smile and the boom of his laugh. There was a rumble in his laugh that reminded her of the sound the sea made when it hit the shore of Sorind's bay, a sound felt more than heard, vibrating up through the ground.

She opened her eyes. Gerda was still staring at her, studying her face as if she could find the answer to a question Jendara hadn't heard her ask.

"The ancestors," Gerda said, "like these islands, can only make you more yourself."

Jendara felt the hair rise on her arms. Did she want to be any more herself? And just who was she, anyway? She looked down at the backs of her hands. On her left hand, the black tattoo of the pirate goddess stood out sharply. That wasn't her anymore, she knew that much.

On the back of her right hand, hidden for now beneath the snow-hued bandages, there was Kalira's bird-wing symbol, forcing Jendara down an ugly road she knew she would have never chosen. A road that could only break Jendara into the shape Kalira planned for her.

Jendara put her hands down on the soft woolen blankets. "I don't know how much I believe in the ancestors," she admitted. "But I'm willing to look for them. I'm willing to let them help me."

Gerda's expression remained serious. "Then you might survive your trip."

"My trip where?"

"To the place where the wisewomen of Sorind and Flintyreach quest for knowledge. The place where the great ones of our people go to be buried. To the Isle of Ancestors and the norns who live there. If anyone can help you find your boy, it's them."

Jendara sank back against the pillows. There was a reason wisewomen and shamans were rare creatures on these islands. Many had gone to the Isle of Ancestors. Few had returned.

"I'll need a map," she answered.

Jendara looked around the tiny kitchen of her cottage. The window hangings she'd made the winter before—in red and orange, Kran's favorite colors—hung askew. A mug Vorrin had bought for her sat on the table, a dead fly floating on the surface of someone's forgotten tea. Her heart twisted. The house felt empty.

She bit her lip as she made her way to her bedroom. Kran's door stood open, revealing the preternatural neatness. He liked his bed made with sharp corners, his sleeping fur folded at the foot. The only sign that he had left his room in an unusual state of mind was the ball of string sitting on his pillow—he must have tossed it out of his belt pouch to make room for more sling ammunition.

She picked it up. He was like a sailor that way, always fiddling with knots and rope. He would miss this, wherever he was.

"I told you," she said, turning the ball in his fingers. "I told you not to get so attached to using marbles. You'd have had room for this if you would have just used rocks."

She squeezed her face tight, holding in a wave of pain and tears. Her fingers dug into the string ball.

She spun on her heel and hurried to her room. She needed to get her gear and get moving. The ball went into her belt pouch. Kran would need it when she found him again.

Jendara readied herself quickly, keeping her eyes focused on her clothing and weapons. She refused to look at the curtains when she tore through the kitchen, gathering dried fruit, nuts, and a bit of hard bread. She closed the door firmly behind her and stepped out into the garden.

"Jendara!"

She turned toward the familiar voice. "Fambra."

The other woman pounded her on the shoulder. "I heard you were laid up in the meeting hall, but when I got there they said you'd left. Glad I finally found you."

"Glad to be found." On impulse, Jendara gave Fambra a hug. Today it seemed very important to show the people she cared about how very much she liked them, no matter how awkward it felt. She cleared her throat. "I'm leaving soon."

Fambra frowned. "Where are you going?"

"To the Isle of Ancestors."

"To the norns? Are you crazy?"

"They'll know where Kalira's taken Kran. They might be able to do something for this arm, too. Gerda thinks it's my best chance."

"It's half a day's sail there and back," Fambra warned. "And they say there's a sea serpent that guards the entrance to the only harbor. There's no guarantee you'll make it back out of there. And even if you do . . ." She shook her head. "Look, not everyone who goes to the Island of Ancestors comes back *right*. Most of us aren't meant to see our futures or hear our ancestors. There's a fine line between wisdom and madness."

"I know all of that." Jendara shifted her knapsack to her other shoulder. "But I have to do something, don't I? He's my son."

Fambra sighed. "I'd do the same, stupid and desperate as it might seem." She slung her arm around Jendara's shoulders. "So you're lucky I'm your friend."

Jendara gave her a confused look. "Why?"

"Because I own the fastest boat still sailing around here, that's why." She grinned. "I haven't taken her to top speed for ages. This is going to be fun."

Jendara laughed. "You're amazing, Fambra. Absolutely amazing."

"I know. I'll go ready my boat. I imagine you've got one last thing to do around here before you leave."

Jendara's smile faded. "Yes. Something important."

Morul and Yul had already brought sawhorses out to the front of the meeting hall, ready to work the wood that would go into its new doors. Boruc sat with his crutches propped against his chair, removing the valuable metal pieces from a broken chunk of one of the old doors. He waved at Jendara.

"Morning, Jendara. Glad you're up and about."

She waved back. "Yep. You look like you're having fun."

"That's what my mother always said just before she got out her paddle," Boruc answered. "Being with my brothers makes my backside nervous."

"Good thing you're stuck sitting on it," Morul grumbled. "I think you planned all of this just to make us wait on you."

Yul smiled at Jendara, his eyes kind. Morul cleared his throat, but settled on just clapping her on the arm as she walked by. They both knew her well enough to see her mind wasn't on banter. She gave the brothers a small, tight smile and pushed back the heavy canvas covering the meeting hall's entrance.

Gerda and Chana were still moving between the ranks of wounded. Jendara knew they'd probably been on their feet all night, but neither woman showed signs of flagging. Jendara hoped someone was bringing them food.

In the closest corner, someone had set up a sort of canvas tent, shrouding the bed beyond. A familiar sword belt and boots sat beside the tent, a basket next to them. She couldn't resist peeking beneath the basket's lid. Vorrin's clothes had been neatly folded at the bottom. A silver coin worn smooth and a clean handkerchief lay on top. She picked up the latter and was surprised by its weight. Curious, she lifted the linen's topmost fold and frowned at the soapstone crow inside. After a moment, she tucked it in her belt pouch and squared her shoulders.

She knew Vorrin lay behind those fabric walls—with his injuries, he'd be stuck inside for a few weeks, and the privacy would be a blessing. Right now, she wished he lay in an ordinary cot. She had no way of knowing if he was awake or asleep in there.

Hesitating a moment, she brushed at the wisps of hair that had escaped from her braid. Then she pinched her cheeks for quick color and pushed back the tent flap.

"I'm trying to sleep in here," Vorrin growled.

"I can go," she said.

"No! I thought you were Gerda or one of her minions, here to fluff my pillows and force me to drink something disgusting." He managed a wry smile. "I don't know if I can stomach another mug of bitter stuff."

"She dosed me up this morning." Jendara perched warily on the edge of the cot. One of Vorrin's arms and one of his legs had been raised up by a complicated scheme of pulleys and ropes. Plaster encased him like armor. "I do feel better."

"Were you hurt?"

"Not badly. Just a burn on my hand, general aches and pains. Nothing like you."

"It's my own stupidity." He bit his lip. "Any word on our boy?"

She shook her head, but his words resounded within her heart: *our boy*.

"I should have watched him more closely. I should have made him run for the escape hatch. I shouldn't have let that stupid bear distract me—"

She put her fingers on his lips, stifling the flow of words. "Stop it. I didn't protect him enough, either. You can't take all the blame."

"But I made a promise," he reminded her. "I told Ikran I would watch out for Kran."

She fumbled for his uninjured hand and gripped it tightly in hers. "And you have. You've done an amazing job taking care of Kran. You just haven't been doing a good job taking care of yourself."

He eyed his casted arm. "You might have a point there."

"Vorrin, when you hit that wall—" She broke off, remembering the sound his body had made when it struck the timbers. "I thought you were dead," she finished, softly.

"I'm sorry."

"Why are you apologizing? You wouldn't even have been there if it weren't for me! This attack was personal. Kalira was after me. Everyone else was just incidental." Jendara's eyebrows knit together as she realized the truth of it. The attack made little sense as a military effort—Kalira had only taken a few prisoners, and she'd lost dozens of her troops.

Vorrin twisted his fingers through Jendara's. "She loves you too much to think straight. Just like you love Kran."

"I do. I can't let her turn him into a Kalvaman." She leaned closer, lowering her voice. "I'm going to seek out the norns. I'm hoping they can help me. I need to find a way to stop this brand from changing me any more than it already has, and I need to figure out just what Kalira's plan is. We need information, and we need it now."

"You can take the *Milady* if you need to," he said.

She sat back, awed. The faith implicit in his offer shook her to the core. "I can't take her where I'm going. Her keel is too deep. But Fambra is taking me in her little boat. It's a good craft."

He sniffed. "It's no *Milady*."

"No," she agreed. "But then again, even the *Milady* isn't herself without her captain." She suddenly could take it no longer. She pressed her cheek against his. "Vorrin, I was so scared I was going to lose you!"

He stroked her shoulder. "I'm going to be fine."

She pulled back to hold his gaze. "Yes, but you almost died before I realized something important."

"And what's that?" His voice was soft.

"That we've been idiots. It doesn't matter that you're Ikran's brother or Kran's uncle, or any of that. You're not just my friend or my business partner. You're the most important person in my life besides Kran."

He blinked, hard, as if he had something in his eyes. "And you two are the most important people in mine."

She brushed back a lock of his dark hair from his cheek. "Vorrin, not everyone comes back from the place where I'm going. The Isle of Ancestors is a dangerous place. I don't want to leave without you knowing the truth." She brushed her lips against his.

"You'll come back," he said. "You damn well better come back." He pressed her to him and kissed her back with a burning fierceness.

After a long moment, she pulled away, grinning. "That's worth coming back for."

She pushed back the tent flap and hurried outside. The harbor was crowded, people trying to salvage whatever wood and gear they could from the burned boats, but Jendara picked her way through them, her eyes focused on Fambra's boat, its multicolored pennant waving in the wind. Jendara had never been so eager to head out to sea.

Chapter Twenty
The Wise

The island rose up out of the tendrils of early morning fog, and if Jendara hadn't known what to look for, she would have mistaken it for just another stack of rocks. The slopes of the island looked too sharp to promise any kind of inhabitants. But of course, no one *lived* on the Isle of Ancestors. No one could.

Fambra studied her. "You sure you want to do this?"

Jendara rubbed her arm. Hot tendrils of pain scribbled up her bicep. "I've got to."

"We could find another way to deal with Kalira."

"It's not just Kalira," Jendara admitted. "It's everything about me. This place?" She pointed at the rocks up ahead. "It's a symbol. It's the place our clans send their best and brightest to have them transformed into the embodiment of wisdom. It's the place our ancestors' spirits gather." Jendara sighed. "I've spent the last few years living life as a half-islander and falling short. It's time I return to my roots."

Fambra raised her eyebrows. "You know that's insane, right?"

Jendara shrugged. "Insane's not so bad, you know. Living with my arm like this has got to be worse than insanity."

"Okay." Fambra pointed up ahead at a narrow inlet between two arms of rocky cliff. "Things might get a little rough going through that." Waves pounded the rocks in powerful explosions of spray and foam. Anemones and sea stars peered out from the froth like suspicious orange and purple eyes.

But the gaze Jendara could feel came from nothing as innocent as sea anemones. Two large eyes blinked from beneath a chunk of rock near the base of the cliff. "The sea serpent." Jendara gripped the railing of the deck. "I can handle a sea serpent."

The eyes shot out from beneath the rocks, a dark scaly head the size of a bushel basket launching itself toward the boat. At the last second, it split open to reveal an array of spiky white teeth and a pink tongue. Jendara dropped to her knees as it dove at the last second.

"Did you see that?" she shrieked at Fambra, who was too busy cursing at her tiller to answer. The boat twisted to the left, barely missing an outcropping of rock the waves had hidden.

Jendara scrambled upright. The serpent lunged again, threatening, its black scales throwing off droplets of water. She tried to make out just how long it was, but its hide matched the rock walls too well, down to the barnacles. Only its gaping maw gave it away. Once more, it dove back beneath the water.

Then the port side of the boat lifted into the air. Jendara slid across the deck. The boat slammed back down, sending up a spray of water.

"It's going to tip us over!" she yelled.

"I have an idea!" Fambra bellowed, and then muttered something unintelligible. The sail snapped as a sudden gust of wind filled them. The boat leaped forward. The inlet narrowed, but she steered them at a nearly suicidal pace.

Jendara peered behind them, searching for the sea serpent. It had moved so fast. There was no way they were going to simply outrun it.

The thing's head broke out of the waves. Jendara could smell the brine and iron stink of it. Could see the glittering gray light in its ancient eyes. A sudden hunch made her move toward it.

She raised her palms to show they were empty. "I'm here on a mission!" she screamed at it. "To help our people!"

If it understood, it didn't show it. Its head shot forward, teeth flashing in the light. Jendara twisted aside, hissing with pain. Those wicked teeth had caught her on the forearm, slicing open her aching right arm.

The serpent lunged at her again.

"You son of a bitch!" she snapped and threw an angry punch at its snout. Her fist hit scales as hard as rock. She skidded on the deck, clutching her left fist. Flesh had scraped off the knuckles, and now they stung from the sea salt caked on its hide.

The creature cocked its head, its tongue flickering in and out of its mouth. Jendara reached for her sword, then hesitated. The serpent looked . . . confused.

"Hold out your hand," Fambra called. "The left one!"

Jendara unfurled her fist. Her fingers trembled as she stretched them toward the giant beast.

Its tongue fluttered over them.

"It's smelling me," Jendara said.

"Smelling your blood," Fambra corrected. "Look at its eyes."

The eyes, dull and gray just moments ago, had turned a luminous gold. It bowed its head.

"We can pass?" Jendara asked, confused.

"It can taste that you're one of its people," Fambra whispered. She eased the boat forward. The sea serpent slipped aside, its eyes fixed on Jendara.

Jendara gripped the deck railing tightly, uncertain of the creature. "Thank you," she murmured.

The serpent's tongue flickered again, and its eyes narrowed. Its head shot forward to snap at her right hand, resting on the railing.

She whipped the offensive limb behind her. The serpent slipped away from the wall, filling the narrow inlet with its bulk. It watched her suspiciously as she stepped away from the side of the boat.

Jendara reached into her pocket and found a handkerchief. She didn't take her eyes off the creature as she bound up the gash on her arm. With any luck, the bandage would help contain the smell of her right hand's tainted blood.

"Look up there," Fambra said. "The cove. I should be able to tie up fairly close."

Jendara turned to study the beach ahead. The half-moon of the cove was made up entirely of round gray stones, the kind of rock only formed by the hard pounding of waves.

She could understand stones like that. Hadn't her life pounded her into this shape?

Beyond the beach, there was nothing.

A blank wall of fog obscured the rest of the island, pale and heavy. Its edges furled and unfurled over the rocks, surging toward the sea and then curling away. Jendara wondered what kept it in place here on the island, what forces kept it from burning off under the sun's rays or spreading out over the sea itself. There was nothing natural about a fog like that.

"It's not a big island," Fambra reminded her, squeezing her shoulder. "Wherever the norns are, it can't be that far from here. I'll be able to hear you if you call for me."

Jendara shook her head. "I don't think it works that way." She studied the fog bank, searching for any kind of outline or shadow hidden behind the strange veil. But there was only roiling whiteness. "Don't get out of the boat. Don't touch the fog. And if it moves toward you, go back to sea."

"You mean pass by that monster again?" Fambra glanced over her shoulder at gap in the cliffs. "Oh, no. Look at that."

Jendara turned. "That's not good." Fingers of fog had slipped around the edges of the cove, shrouding the cliffs' bases and filling in the narrow channel. The cove where their boat sat was the only clear space to be seen. "Just . . . stay here. Go into the hold if you need to."

"Maybe I'll look for a lantern or two," Fambra answered in a sour voice. "I won't even be able to see my hand if that fog gets any thicker. Probably fall overboard."

"Hey." Jendara shook a finger at her. "None of that talk. I'm going in, I'm getting the information we need, and I'm coming right back. Stop worrying."

Fambra sighed. "I hope it works that well. You'd better get going."

Jendara peered over the side of the boat. The water seemed unusually clear, not a hint of mud or algae to obscure the rocks and broken bits of wood at the bottom. The worn shape of a dragon figurehead caught her eye. At least one longship had met its demise here. "No way to get the boat closer, I see. Looks like I'm swimming for it."

She bundled her sword belt, clothes, and gear into a square of oil cloth, then tied it tight with waxed cord. She hoped it would stay dry enough. She stood on the deck a moment, feeling the late summer breeze draw up goose bumps on her bare skin.

She hesitated. "Fambra?"

"What?"

"If it doesn't work—"

"It'll work. It has to, because I don't have another plan. Now go!" Fambra gave her a shove between the shoulder blades, and Jendara hopped over the side of the boat. She treaded water a moment, waiting for Fambra to pass her the package of gear.

"It's freezing." Her teeth were already chattering. The water was colder than any water she'd ever swam in before, cold as ice melt right off a mountainside. She couldn't imagine how it could possibly be this cold right now.

"Swim fast. And don't forget—this is the Isle of Ancestors. They're your people, you know. They want you to win."

Jendara bobbed her head. She lifted the package of gear over her head and managed a clumsy one-armed crawl toward the shore. It looked farther away now, as if a hand had pushed back the curve of the crescent-shaped beach while she wasn't looking. She picked out a cluster of rocks and focused on them, swimming steadily.

Her raised arm wobbled. The package grew heavier— as heavy as a child, then as heavy as a small woman. She shivered. She should feel warmer; the sun was shining right down on her. A wave splashed in her face and she blinked away water. The rocks looked no closer than before.

A wave hit the side of her head, covering her eyes and nose, and she nearly dropped the package. She spluttered on foam and resisted the urge to paw water from her eyes. She was a good swimmer. She knew better than to get worried about a little water in the eyes. She breathed deep and kept her eyes on the rocks. It wasn't really that far now.

Another wave hit, battering her off course, pushing her away from her rock cluster. She inhaled salt spray, began to cough. She was sinking! She needed to drop the package, tread water, get away! She tossed her head, trying to breathe. Her foot scraped rock. She yanked it back, gasping. What if it wasn't a rock? What if it was another serpent?

Jendara paused, taking her bearings. She could still see her cluster of rocks, now farther away than ever. It was as if she had begun paddling backward, away from shore. Her sore arm trembled, tired and achy from holding up her bundle of gear when already wounded.

The gash the serpent gave her had begun bleeding again, a small rivulet of blood running down her arm.

Jendara closed her eyes. This wasn't working. Struggling against the waves wasn't the right way to do this. All the ridiculous fears she'd felt as a child learning to swim kept bombarding her, overwhelming her brain. She couldn't swim like this.

She opened her eyes. Maybe that was it. Maybe she wasn't meant to swim to shore. Maybe this was a test.

She closed her eyes again and let herself sink. The water rose up over her head, up her stretched arm.

Her feet hit rock before the water reached her elbow. She didn't open her eyes, but simply gripped with her toes, balancing on the angled slab of basalt. It wasn't as rough as she had feared. She took a step. Then another.

Her head rose above the water level. She swiped water off her face with a mostly dry forearm and kept walking. The stones felt flatter here, not nearly as difficult to walk on. She walked a little faster.

Her cluster of stones stood directly in front of her. Jendara smiled at them, delighted to see the little pile, and stepped out of the water. Stone clanked against stone beneath her feet. It was a pleasant sound, like one of the wind chimes her father had hung up on the front porch of their house.

She knelt beside the stone cluster and patted the topmost stone. "Thank you," she said. The stone vibrated beneath her fingers. She pulled her hand away and dressed quickly. Her damp shirt bunched up in her armpits.

With one hand on her sword hilt, Jendara faced the fog. It had moved farther down the shore as if to touch her, and its leading edge swirled in eddies of tiny breezes. The water droplets moved in minute flurries and spirals. She suddenly understood the spiral tattoos wisewomen and shamans inked into their cheeks.

Her stomach clenched. Something about this fog stirred up cold currents of fear that made no sense. It was just fog, after all. Just a low-flying cloud.

She took a small step forward and let the fog surround her.

The world disappeared. There was no east or west, no sun, no shade—if it weren't for the clank of stone beneath her feet, she couldn't have told up from down. Her breath ruffled the whiteness, thinning it in front of her face for a second. Beyond the opening, the fog went on forever.

If she thought about it for too long, she could forget all sense of direction and wander this beach forever. Already, she doubted which way to turn to find the shore—there were no landmarks to guide her memory, nothing to derive a course from. Jendara closed her eyes for a moment, fighting vertigo. If she couldn't trust her senses, couldn't trust her common sense, she'd follow her instinct. Forward was forward. If she kept her eyes fixed on the path her breath carved in the fog, she would find the norns and get off this island before it got any more of its eerie fingers into her brain. She was tired of doing battle with things that fought inside her mind.

Her right arm prickled. She resisted the urge to slap it. She was done with distractions.

She strode forward. The beach climbed steeply, the surf-rounded stones turning swiftly to cut slabs of the island's bedrock. She scrambled up the rock slope. The fog seemed thinner here. She caught a glimpse of green off to her right, but she focused on moving forward, paying careful attention to the rock and scree underfoot.

The fog broke. She turned back to see she'd climbed up a tall slope, the fog huddled doglike at its feet. The water beyond was completely free of the stuff—Fambra's boat sat in the cove, untroubled by even a whitecap. Jendara scowled. First waves that she couldn't swim through, now fog that tried to get her lost. This island was full of tricks.

She looked to the green stretching ahead of her. A flat, verdant valley lay in a ribbon between two ridges of gray rock. At the end of the valley, a knot of darker green tied the ridges together. Some kind of forest, she guessed. It didn't look very far away, but she'd already learned that distance was subjective here.

Less than fifty yards away sat an ordinary cottage, its stone walls clean-scrubbed and its thatch a fresh yellow. A shaggy goat had scrambled up on the roof, enjoying a soft bed. The sun broke through the clouds strongly enough to outline the goat in gold, its large horns askew—one pointing up, one pointing down.

Jendara glared at the goat. It seemed like too cozy a touch for a place like this. But she walked toward it anyway.

She tried to remember what she knew about the norns. They could tell the future, that was the main thing. And they were canny and tough and huge. She couldn't imagine one living in a cottage no bigger than her own.

On the front door of the cottage, someone had hung a wreath of ivy and hawthorn, rowan and rue. Some kind of purple spiked flower peeked out between the larger leaves. She brushed her fingers over it and crinkled her nose. Pennyroyal. All fey herbs, if she remembered right. And the doorknob looked to be polished copper—the metal the fey favored. The hairs on her neck stood up.

She raised her hand to knock and paused in midair. After the sea serpent's attack, she wasn't trusting her right hand in this place. She rapped with her left hand instead.

The door swung open.

It was dim inside; she couldn't make out anything except a great fireplace, a cauldron squatting in the flames. The sharp scents of sage and pennyroyal stung her nostrils.

"You are invited inside. You'd best come inside before the invitation expires." The voice echoed oddly, but the command in it was obvious.

She stepped over the threshold and nearly lost her balance as the room stretched and skewed around her. The flagstone under her boot looked twice as large as an ordinary flagstone, and the bench beside her stood as tall as her hip.

"You're letting—

"—out the warm—"

"—air."

Were there three voices? Or one woman with three throats? Jendara had never heard a voice like that. She reached behind her for the doorknob and stopped when her fingers slipped over rough wood. She turned and stared at the door. She distinctly remembered the copper doorknob right there at ordinary doorknob height. But on this side of the door, she had to stretch nearly to her chin to reach the thing.

"Things here—"

"—are not always—"

"—what they seem."

There were definitely three speakers this time, the voices no longer blended together but layered one after another with just an instant's overlap. Jendara whirled around.

A figure arose from beside the fireplace.

"Weren't you expecting us?"

"Or didn't you know—"

"—what we norns are like?"

The voices had blurred together again. Jendara scanned the dim room. Something stirred in the far corners, two great dark blots. They drew themselves tall and joined the first figure in front of the fire. In another house, they would have scraped the ceiling— no, in another house, they would have cracked the ceiling. Here, it was Jendara who was out of proportion.

"You're norns?"

She watched the firelight play on their faces. They were women, but they were something else as well. There were no lines on those massive cheeks, yet also no softness. They could be any age. Every age. Their full lips bent into the same broad smile.

"We—"

"—are We. And you are—"

"—Jendara."

"How did you know that?"

Their hands waved at a massive bag sitting on the table. Beside the bag she could also see a massive pair of shears and a spindle tucked into a basket of carded wool. A stack of knitting needles lay on top of the bag, but beneath them, gold glimmered within the sack's folds.

"Is that my fate in there?"

The norns cocked their heads. Overhead, the goat bleated.

"The spirits—"

"—are—"

"—stirring."

One of the norns stooped to look into the fire. Jendara stepped forward. The flames flickered wildly. A cold breeze shot out of the fireplace, carrying a long ribbon of blue mist. The mist twisted itself around the norn's neck to brush against her ear.

"Yes, spirit!" The norns laughed, and the huge fey creature nudged the blue wisp.

"We see—"

"—your girl—"

"—is here."

"Is that an ancestor spirit?" Jendara stared at the bit of blue, no more substantial than a wisp of smoke. "It is, isn't it? You see the future and you talk to the voices of the past. Is there anything you don't know?"

"About these—"

"—islands? Not—"

"—much."

The norns stood together again, looking down at Jendara. She felt very small beside them, like a child separated from her parents and lost in another clan's land. She couldn't even read their faces. They were truly alien creatures.

But she had come to them because they were her best, her only real hope. She held out her scarred and burned right hand toward them. "Please tell me how I can be rid of this poison. I need to help the people of these islands, and I can't do that if this brand is turning me into an enemy."

"We will—"

   "—demand a price—"

      "—for this," the norns warned.

"It will—"

   "—be very—"

      "—dear."

The room felt darker. They didn't like being asked for help.

"What can I give you?" Jendara opened her belt pouch, her heart heavy. She had the horrible feeling that if she didn't offer the right payment, she wouldn't make it out of this room.

"Something—"

   "—very dear—"

      "—to *you*."

"All right." She reached inside the belt pouch, feeling for the ring she kept at the very bottom. She held it up.

"Ahh." Their breath stirred the loose bits of Jendara's hair.

"A—"

   "—wedding—"

      "—ring?"

"The last thing I have of my dead husband's. It's solid gold."

The norns scowled.

"But you—"

"—do not treasure it—"

"—any longer."

"Are you—"

"—trying—"

"—to *cheat* us?"

Their voice made the floorboard rumble beneath Jendara's boots. Jendara took a step back. "No! Of course not. I just—I'm sorry."

She reached back inside the belt pouch, cursing her stupidity. She felt the broken edges of Kalira's crow pendant and knew instinctively it too would hold little value, not now that her sister had stolen Kran. Any dearness it had once held had been driven out by that treachery.

Kran.

Her fingers stopped moving inside the pouch. Yes, there was something dear to her here. Her heart clenched a little as she pulled out Kran's string ball, the one she'd found in his room.

"Would you accept this?"

"You care for that," the norns acknowledged.

"But it is not—"

"—yours—"

"—to give."

The room grew darker, and their rage stirred up a hot wind that drove ashes into Jendara's face. The fire leaped up in the hearth, clawing at the edges of the walls. She covered her eyes against the brightness. The heat of the fire made the air ripple.

But a hint of coolness brushed her cheek and she saw a sudden flash of blue. It settled on the handle of her handaxe.

And then she knew. She *knew* what the norns would take for their payment.

"Here." She wrenched her axe from her belt. "Take this."

The norns did not move, but the axe slipped out of her grip and rose up in the air. Jendara blinked back tears. Her father had made this. She had watched him carve its fine handle and grind its edge. It had been one of the last things he touched before death claimed him, and she had kept it as close to her as she wished she had kept him. It was all she had of her father. It was all she had of the home, the clan, and the people she had cast aside after his murder.

"Yes," the norns said. "This—"

"—is what you hold—"

"—most dear."

The axe floated toward the fey creatures.

"Father," Jendara breathed. "Oh, Father . . ." The tears ran freely down her cheeks.

Sunlight returned to the room. The fire subsided. There was no sign of the axe.

"We will help. But you will not—"

"—find what you seek—"

"—inside this house."

Their voices blended into unison once more. "*Follow the goat.*"

"The goat?" Jendara pointed at the ceiling. "The goat on the roof?"

The fire crackled, and she was suddenly alone in an ordinary cottage, sunlight streaming in to show a few dusty yarn-making supplies on the table. Jendara looked around herself. Other than the fading fire, the place looked as if no one had set foot in it for years. She checked her belt. No axe. She hadn't been dreaming.

She hurried outside just in time to see the shaggy goat jump down from the roof. Gold glinted in its eyes for a second. Then it began trotting toward the forest at the far end of the valley.

"All right. I'm following the goat." She jogged after the creature.

The valley wriggled its way between the two great ridges of rock, growing narrower as it went. The rocks leaned closer to each other as the gap between them closed. They loomed over Jendara, grim and sere. She reached for the comforting heft of her axe handle and felt a pang at its absence.

The goat looked over its shoulder, bleating softly. It shook its head from side to side, showing off its mismatched horns, one curving down, one curving up. It snorted at her.

"I'm coming." She picked up her pace. It had kept its lead on her, despite showing no signs of hurrying. But then, it had four legs and she had only two.

The goat hopped over a fallen branch. Jendara hadn't realized the little forest was so close. She paused a moment, studying the trees that choked the end of the valley. The foliage stood out black against the cloudy sky.

She looked back down and saw the goat's tail disappearing between two stocky pines. "Hey, wait!"

It kept running. She chased after it, her feet thudding on the thick humus of the forest floor. Yet within a few moments, she slowed to a halt. The goat was gone. And she felt eyes on her.

She turned a slow circle, peering between the trees. No birds chirped. No wind ruffled the tree branches. The air sat heavy, like a held breath caught in a throat. She was alone.

She took a few steps forward. A shiver ran through her. It was cooler in the little forest, shut away from the sun. But that didn't explain the clamminess in the air or the breeze she could have sworn she felt against her cheek but which somehow didn't ruffle the branch beside her. No, there was something uncanny about this place.

She strode forward again, letting her eyes rove around her. She couldn't help but hope the goat would appear, nibbling leaves off a seedling or munching a fern. Her eyebrows drew together. Had she even seen any ferns? She scanned the area for undergrowth, herbs or brush or bracken, and came up blank. There were only trees, large trees, stretching to the sky. Not even a deadfall or a seedling to break up the endless field of dead leaves and pine needles.

A branch snapped under her boot. She flinched at the sound, but felt reassured. At least there were fallen branches. She stooped to pluck the branch from the ground, wondering how fresh it might be. Perhaps the area was simply kept cleared by the norns.

The branch in her hand was not wood. She turned the mossy thing over in her fingers, taking in the steep curve of it, the brittle shards where it had snapped underfoot. It had to be a rib. She dropped the bone onto the ground.

"Is it too much to hope that wasn't human?" she asked out loud. She took a careful step forward and felt the leaves shift over something hard and lumpy.

A tendril of fog crept across the dead leaves and spread across the ground, obscuring the unevenness below. But Jendara had to look. She squatted and brushed aside the thick layer of leaves and dirt.

She wasn't surprised to see the half-unburied skull staring up at her.

The fog twisted on the leaves, snaking out and wrapping around her leg. Its touch was icy even through her pants. She shook it off. But already more mist wended its way between the trees, breaking off from a heavy fog bank that already obscured the forest ahead.

Her right arm prickled. Jendara stood up, narrowing her eyes at the stuff. She was beginning to get tired of mist, especially when it refused to behave like ordinary fog.

A low moan came out of the fog bank.

"What do you want from me?" she shouted. Her voice sounded flat, muffled by the fog.

"Traitor," something whispered.

Her left hand went numb. Jendara flexed her fingers. Her arms felt strange, hot on the right, cold on the left, and tingly all over. Her eyes went wide as tiny stinging welts rose up around the edges of her jolly roger tattoos.

"You turned your back on your people," a voice groaned in her ear.

A tree branch smashed into Jendara's face.

She stumbled back. She was alone, she'd swear to it, but the voices—she couldn't fight those here with so much fog to hide them. Maybe she could draw them out.

"See if you can catch me!" she shouted. She spun and ran back toward the entrance to the forest.

Bones jutted out from the forest floor and threatened to trip her. Skulls rolled and crunched underfoot. She stumbled. What was this horrible place?

Something cackled behind her, and she risked a quick look over her shoulder to see.

The earth dropped out beneath her, and suddenly she was falling. She hit a rock and skidded down some kind of bank, landing in a clump of ferns. She lay still, glad for the soft landing.

Ferns. She looked up and saw that she'd left the forest behind. With a grin, she sat up, rubbing her side where the rock had scraped her ribs. Nothing felt broken.

The bank she'd slid down loomed over her, a good tall stretch of rock and dirt that looked as if it had recently washed out. Just beyond her clump of ferns, a small stream gurgled, hurrying along in its bed of round gray rocks. She clambered out of the ferns and drank right out of the stream. It chilled her teeth, but tasted delicious.

She got to her feet. To the left, the ground sloped upward, disappearing into the darkness of the forest. To the right, the stream ran downhill. She'd follow it. It couldn't be far to the ocean from here. Maybe she'd run into the goat again. Even a goat had sense enough to follow a stream.

It was strange how she'd lost the goat in a forest with no undergrowth. It was almost as if the creature had disappeared. A silly thought to have about a goat. She couldn't imagine a less magical creature. She'd spent her childhood herding them and milking them, chasing them all over the island of Crow's Nest. Her father's best goat, a nanny named Silver, was a wild thing, always racing off and climbing into the cormorant's nesting area—

The chatter in Jendara's mind caught up with itself there. She paused, remembering the big shaggy nanny goat from her youth. Hadn't she had one horn that tipped up and one that tipped down, just like the goat Jendara had chased into the forest?

She scrubbed goose bumps off her arms. "No wonder wisewomen act so crazy. This place drives them insane." There was no way her father's goat was prancing around this island, leading her into a forest filled with skeletons. No, all of this had to be like that moment in the waves when she forgot how to swim: a mind trick.

Jendara strode forward briskly. She would follow this stream to the ocean, circle back to the cove, and confront the norns with her sword. They owed her some answers.

A woman sprang up from the ground, appearing out of nowhere, her face entirely blue with spiral tattoos. "No one owes you anything, traitor!"

Jendara's fist shot out. Cold mist furled around her knuckles, freezing cold. Jendara gasped. She tried to shake off the stuff.

The woman laughed again, even though half of her face had turned to mist and twisted off to grip Jendara's hand. Further wisps broke away from her cheek and jaw and spun into spirals. They floated in the air like gnats.

"In the Forest of Souls, only the Wise may survive. You'll be crab food before nightfall, pirate."

The mist broke into droplets. The woman vanished.

"The Forest of Souls. I should have known." Jendara cursed herself for forgetting. This island wasn't just a testing place for shamans and wisewomen. The most powerful of them returned here to die so that their deaths might strengthen the ancestor spirits. It took great dedication to keep one's soul on this plane, bound to one's people. This was the place that made souls strong.

She lifted her chin. She might not be a ghost, but the spirit inside her was getting tougher by the minute. This place couldn't break her. She was an islander—an islander who had made her way in the most dangerous job the world offered.

"And I'm not a traitor," she growled. "I've had my doubts, but I'm starting to see things your way."

She felt a powerful prickling in her hands. She flexed her fingers. She had no axe to grip, and the things she'd seen on this island were impervious to sword and knife. If she was fighting spirits, she was truly unarmed.

But then again, maybe she didn't need weapons to win this kind of fight.

She raised her hands over her head. "Come and get me."

The wind struck her with a scream.

Ribbons of blue mist twisted around her. Faces flashed in the fog, their voices strident and cruel. She ignored the show and dropped into a fighting stance. She might not be able to punch these ghosts, but she wasn't going to be caught off balance.

"Is this the best you've got?" she bellowed.

A transparent wolf snapped blue teeth at her. She laughed.

Hooves thudded against the earth, and she turned to face the sound, a grin spreading across her face. If they were planning to run her down with some kind of ghost horse, she could handle that. She opened her mouth to toss off another jibe.

And stopped.

A huge creature broke through the mist. Its massive red body flashed in the sunlight and its horns spread wider than anything Jendara had ever seen. Its hooves sounded like thunder.

It was red. Red, when the fog and all its spirits were blue. The elk dropped its horns and charged straight at her.

She leaped into the creek.

Its hooves kicked up earth as it surged past her, and Jendara felt her heart miss a beat. A red elk. There hadn't been a red elk on the archipelago for at least a thousand years. She stared at it a moment, absorbing its long legs and powerful haunches, the heavy ruff around its neck. It whirled around and stared back at her with liquid black eyes. She could sense the great age in their depths. Its nostrils flared.

Ancient or not, it was drawing itself up for another charge. Jendara broke into a sprint. She couldn't outrun a creature like this, but she was dead if she didn't try. She leaped over a boulder in her path, splashing down into deeper water. Her ankle twisted. Jendara ignored it.

Its hooves splashed behind her. She jumped onto the next big rock, then to the next. The creek sounded louder here, its plash and gurgle turning more serious.

She jumped again, knowing the elk was right behind her now.

She landed on a slick boulder and just caught herself. The creek bed dropped here, following the steep slope of the island bedrock. Below her, the water made a dark pool before spilling out in a narrow stream. The stream glistened as it ran out to the stony beach and then cut through the thin strip of sand beside the sea. She'd found the far side of the island.

The elk snorted. There was no place to go but down.

She jumped.

She got lucky. Her mass drove her to the bottom of the pool, a deep basin, and her knees buckled on impact. She paddled toward the surface, fighting the force of falling water. An eddy dragged her back under. She flailed around herself and found a handhold, pulled away from the center of the pool.

Lungs screaming, she burst out of the water. The red elk soared over her head.

She had hoped to leave him behind, but clearly this was still his territory. She scrambled out of the pool. It was no place to fight.

The elk pawed the ground. Jendara raced past him. Maybe, just maybe, he was only defending his stretch of the forest. She could leave his territory, find safety, get back to the norns. She put a burst of speed into her legs. The stones clattered beneath her feet. She hit open sand, the ocean just ahead.

The elk bugled behind her. It exploded onto the beach. Jendara could feel the sand vibrating under the force of its hooves. She spun around, drawing her sword.

At top speed, the elk raced past her, hooking her sword in the tine of one great antler. The blade flew from her hand and landed point-down in sea foam. The elk twisted around, putting its body between her and her weapon.

Jendara's mouth went dry. There was no cover. Nothing to distract it. And all she had was her belt knife.

The wind tugged strands of hair into her ears. She shook her head. She needed to think. The wind gusted again, whipping up currents of sand.

That was it. Maybe she could blind it with sand and get to her sword. She dropped into a squat, digging her fingers into the grit. The elk whuffed at her.

Something heavy and smooth pressed against her fingers, buried in the sand. A shaft of some kind. She tugged at it, eyes widening as a six-foot length of pale wood came free and the wind swept the surface clean. She brought up the spear and immediately couched it in the sand. Tendrils of fog twisted around the elk's hooves.

Once again, it dropped its antlers and charged.

Jendara gripped the spear with both hands, staggering as the tip punched into the elk's ribcage and sliced through its heart. She felt a moment's pang. It was a magnificent creature, beautiful and ancient. It flailed its antlers in its death agony. She twisted away from the wicked tines and tumbled into the sand.

The elk cried out, its voice nearly human, and its antlers burst into twists of blue and gold mist. Light streamed from the hole in its chest. Jendara shielded her eyes, but there was no escaping the brightness. The light surrounded the creature, surrounded

Jendara, filled her and flooded her entire being. Heat pulsed within her every muscle. Her eyes tingled. She cried out as her right arm seethed and twitched, burning inside.

Then she was just herself again, alone on a beach. The spear lay on the sand, perfectly clean.

She got to her feet, her legs like jelly, and looked herself over. She was dry, and nothing hurt. She touched her face, feeling for the bruises from the battle on Sorind. She pulled back her sleeve. No gray stain, no wriggling black lines beneath the skin. And the right hand itself—

Her jaw dropped. Her hand was suntanned and square, just as it always looked, but the back of the hand was nearly smooth, the burns and brand gone, the jolly roger missing. A black dot sat on the skin, a thin circle of silver scar tissue surrounding it like a moat.

She brought up the left hand for comparison. The knuckles looked fine, the scrapes gone. The skull and crossbones remained, the ink gone blue like the tattoos of a very old sailor.

Jendara plopped onto the sand, stunned. Something had happened. That elk—or was it an elk? Where had it gone? And what about the spear? Where had it come from? Why hadn't it disappeared when the elk vanished? And what about that light?

"The bit with the sand was my idea."

Jendara's mouth fell open. She jumped to her feet, searching around herself for the source of that voice—a voice a she had never hoped to hear again.

"Father?"

The wind blew past her cheek like a caress. "I'm here, Jendara."

She shook her head. "I can't see you. Where are you?"

The wind rustled in her ear and she heard his familiar laugh, but with it, interwoven, the sounds of other voices, some chuckling, some scolding, some chattering idly. She screwed up her eyes, trying to focus on the voices. Their voices remained distant, like a conversation heard echoing across a long distance.

"You'll hear—"

    "—them some—"

        "—times."

She turned to face the norns. "Who are they?"

"Your ancestors." The norns dipped their heads, smiles twitching at the corners of their lips. Here on the beach, they looked even less human than they had in the confines of their strange home. Their height was more pronounced, their thick skin more hide-like. Their heavy cloaks obscured the details of their bodies, and Jendara couldn't help wondering what they must really look like. They were not creatures of this world.

Jendara frowned. "But I heard my father just now."

"He's an ancestor, isn't he?"

"I . . . guess so." Jendara pointed at the spear still waiting on the sand. "Did you do that? Send that elk and the spear? Was that what my offering paid for?"

They each raised an eyebrow.

"Did it—"

    "—solve—"

        "—your problem?"

Jendara raised her hand. "There's still a black spot. What does that mean?"

"Your sister is—"

"—powerful. Your ties to your people are—"

"—strong as well, but—"

"—they are fighting each other."

"You will be in danger—"

"—as long as she lives."

The norns turned to face the sea. Their shoulders rose and fell as they breathed in a unison so exact Jendara had to look away. She bent to recover her sword, and a glint of gold caught her eye. She realized one of the norns held a sack in her hands. A golden light rose up from the bag.

"What's that light?" she asked.

"Your fate, Jendara."

"Today its threads—"

"—touch your ancestors'."

"I have to stop Kalira, but I don't know how to fight her magic. What do I do?"

The wind gusted against Jendara's back. She glanced over her shoulder, unsurprised by the wall of fog that had formed on the beach behind her. Voices sounded within the fog, growing louder, then louder again.

"Fight!" her father's voice called out in her ear, and the voices in the fog cheered.

"But how?" she asked. "I don't even know where she is."

The norns tipped their heads to the sky. "Not yet," they agreed. They watched something overhead intently.

Jendara followed their gaze. Her hand fell to her belt for her handaxe and closed on nothing. She grabbed her belt knife instead. A bird flew above, its black shape outlined against the clouds.

She relaxed her grip. "Just a cormorant, not a crow." Her eyes widened. "Crow's Nest. Of course that's where she'd set up camp next." That's where all of this had begun for Kalira: the nightmare of her torture, the destruction of her clan. What better symbol for her success than rebuilding her new people on the ashes of her old?

Fog began to curl around Jendara's feet and gather itself above the spear in a thick mass of white swirls. The fog's edges pulsed for a few moments and then it sank onto the weapon, soaking into the wooden shaft. A pattern of blue spirals appeared along it.

Jendara stooped and lifted it. The wood was warm in her hands. Her stomach felt suddenly heavy. This was no ordinary spear, not any longer. This was a gift of the ancestors. To get this spear, she had lost one of Besmara's marks—the last and strongest memory of her pirate's life she still had. To get this spear, she had given up her father's handaxe. But if it kept the islands free, it was worth it. If it helped Kran, it was worth anything. Maybe that was what ancestor magic was all about: giving up the past to serve the future.

"Trust your gut," her father's voice said. The steel spear tip gleamed blue for an instant. The wind stopped.

Jendara gave the spear an experimental twirl and then planted it in the sand. Her eyes narrowed. "Kran," she murmured, "I'm coming for you."

Chapter Twenty-One
Inside the Crow's Nest

Jendara was unsurprised by the dock leading out into the cove, even though it hadn't existed earlier. Change seemed to be the nature of this island. She glanced over her shoulder at the steep and rocky grade leading into the valley. There might have been a small gray cottage hunkered down at the edge. But then again, it might have been a very large boulder. Shaking her head, she made her way down to Fambra's boat in soft midday sun. Fambra leaned over the side of the boat, watching the water with fierce concentration. She stood up and stared at Jendara.

"What are you doing? You just jumped into the bay a minute ago. And where did that dock come from? Why are you dry? What's that spear?" She blinked a few times. "Where did all the fog go?"

"Would you believe me if I told you the fog's in the spear? Or that I spent all afternoon chasing goats and elk to get it?"

"No. Maybe?" Fambra pointed at Jendara's formerly branded hand. "What happened to your hand?"

"It was healed. We don't have time to talk. We've got to get a war party to Crow's Nest as fast as we can, before Kalira can regroup."

Fambra cast off from the previously nonexistent dock. She looked down uncertainly at the rope in her hands, one that hadn't been there moments ago, then shrugged and began coiling it. "Crow's Nest? Are you sure?"

Jendara reached for an oar and pushed them out into the open channel. "It's familiar ground and easily defensible. It's where I'd go."

Fambra eased the boat into the inlet cutting through the cliffs. She eyed the rocks for signs of the sea serpent that had attacked them earlier, but Jendara didn't spare them a glance, gut-sure that the creature wouldn't show itself. She'd passed her tests back there on the island. She was welcome here, now.

The fishing boat slipped into the open sea. "But why didn't she set up on that island first? And what were they doing at Alstone Quarry?"

"She's been scouting things out for a while," Jendara said, more to herself than Fambra. "She's been probing our weak spots."

"So killing my clan was just a test?" Fambra slapped the tiller with the flat of her hand. "What kind of monsters are these?"

Jendara's lips tightened. "That's just what they do on Kalva. They get strength from savaging whatever they can. And," she paused to glance at the spear the ancestor spirits had given her, "Kalira's chosen to be a Kalvaman."

A lump formed in her throat. She had known it was true, but it hurt more to say it out loud. Kalira had chosen her path.

She brought her two fists together and studied the marks on the backs of them, the faded jolly roger and the silver circle containing the last of Kalira's poison. There were three paths there: the way of the islands, the way of a pirate husband, and Kalira's way.

"I choose a path," she murmured. "Mine."

She adjusted the rigging and sat down with her sword and whetstone. It was a long trip. She would use her time wisely.

Jendara emerged from the tiny sleeping cabin with mugs of tea and a pocket full of hardtack. She gave Fambra a mug.

Fambra gave her an abstracted nod in thanks. "Do you see anything off to starboard?"

Jendara frowned. Specks broke up the horizon line, small enough to be indiscernible. "Maybe. You have a spyglass?"

Fambra jerked her head toward the sleeping cabin. "In its box, lashed to the wall."

Jendara hurried to get the glass. As a pirate, she would have kept her spyglass in her belt pouch to check the horizon at routine intervals. But then again, as a pirate, she was usually searching out a particular moving target, a vessel she'd researched for its particular cargo. Honest folk saw spyglasses as an expensive luxury, not a necessity.

She put the glass to her eye and trained it on the specks. "Ships. Three good-sized ones and a smaller vessel trailing behind a bit. Hard to make out the details, but I'd guess they sailed out of Halgrim. They've got those triangular sails the newer ships are using."

"I'm going to approach them, then," Fambra said, adjusting the tiller. "They might have news." She flashed a grin. "Normally I'd avoid any ships coming out of the capital. I like to do my Halgrim business quietly, usually under the cover of darkness. Funny how the taxman hates the dark, isn't it?"

It was as obvious an admission that she was a smuggler as Jendara was likely to get. She wondered how much of Fambra's lawbreaking came from a genuine desire to avoid tariffs, and how much was just pure orneriness.

She braced her elbows on the railing, waiting for the gap to close between their boat and the approaching ships. "It's funny, you and I working together like this. Neither one of us has too honest a background."

"Why do you think I didn't go with you to the palace?" Fambra laughed, and the wind suddenly filled their sail with a snap. The boat flew toward the other vessels.

Jendara brought up the spyglass again. "We're in luck! That looks like the Iron Shields' flag!"

"Jorgen came through for us."

Jendara put the spyglass back in its case. "He did. I'm so glad you asked him to help. But now I need you to do something else for me. For all of us."

Fambra raised an eyebrow. "Whatever it is, I can handle it."

Jendara eyed the horizon. There was still no sign of the islands ahead, and the afternoon was fading fast. It was going to be a long night. She hoped whatever magic sped Fambra's ship along was in full working order.

"The question is," she said, "can your boat handle it?"

Starlight danced on the wind-stirred surface of the sea. Jendara wished she could just stand at the bow and admire it, but the same wind drove Jorgen's ship—now carrying Jendara as well—toward the little island at a breakneck pace. With luck, it helped Fambra on her journey to Sorind, too.

Sunset had long passed and the moon was not yet up, giving them the perfect opportunity to sneak into Crow's Nest's harbor unobserved. She had the unnerving feeling they had already been seen by some kind of animal spy. The island looked too quiet for a place hosting an invasion force. No smoke plumes rose over the rocky bluff, no boats stood watch. It could have been abandoned.

Or a trap.

Jendara gripped the spear tighter. Every instinct told her Kalira was ready and waiting for her on this island. She tried not to think about what her sister might have done with Kran. Thinking about him was a sure way to lose this battle.

The crew dropped anchor and began the lengthy task of lowering the boats. The volunteers broke up into small groups, the first teams to head toward land. Jorgen led Jendara and two men bristling with armaments toward the nearest dinghy. No one spoke as they lowered gear into the boat, took their places, and began rowing for shore. Jendara winced. The splash of their oars sounded very loud.

Jorgen tapped her shoulder. "Look," he whispered, pointing off the port bow. A sharp triangle broke the water's surface, racing away from the boat.

"A shark," one of the volunteers whispered. Jendara watched it sink beneath the water.

Jorgen frowned. "But it's not acting like one. I saw fish jumping on the other side of our ship just a minute ago. What shark would swim away from its dinner?"

"I don't like that." Jendara narrowed her eyes and reached for the spyglass case lashed to her belt. She was glad Fambra had made her take it. It was too dark to see detail, but she could just make out a figure racing down the beach toward the pilings at the end of the harbor. She lowered the spyglass.

"Someone's seen us," she announced. "Let's ready the archers."

Jorgen snatched the glass from her hand and scanned the shore. "It's just one man. He's wading into the water, wearing some kind of robe."

Jendara squinted at the shore, wishing for more light. The man waded farther out, paused when he hit waist-deep water, and then went rigid. Jendara reached for the spyglass, but Jorgen didn't notice. He gasped.

"He's changing into a shark!"

Jendara didn't need the spyglass to see the silver shape leap forward through the air, hitting the water with hardly a splash. For a second after, all that showed were ripples, and then a sharp triangle appeared in the water, streaking straight toward their boat.

"A skinwalker . . ."

"Skinswimmer," Jorgen said, his voice grim, and handed back the spyglass. "That other shark is probably one, too. And we're in a dinghy."

"Row!" Jendara shouted.

The boat rocked as the shark slammed into the side. The stout oaken wales held. Jendara gripped her spear between her feet and put her back into rowing. That thing would circle back in a moment or two.

"The other one's coming," one of the Iron Shields said.

Jendara eyed the shore. It looked impossibly far. "We can make it," she said, not sure if she believed it herself.

"They're going to try to crush us between the two of them," Jorgen warned. "We can't risk that."

"If they try, I'll kill them," Jendara said. "I didn't come here to be eaten by sharks." She loosened her sword in its scabbard. If it came to a fight in the water, she didn't dare lose the spear of the ancestors.

"Cut starboard!" Jorgen snapped.

The boat banked right and a gray fin streaked past them. But the second shark followed, closing in fast. It pushed itself out of the water, its teeth snapping on an oar.

Jendara yanked on her own oar and slapped the shark's side. It twisted away. The boat rocked wildly.

"Row!" Jorgen ordered.

The shark snapped its teeth again, but the boat shot past it. Jendara felt the muscles in her shoulders burn with the effort. The shore looked much closer now.

The boat's bow bounced up in the air. Jorgen lost his seat and slid backward, losing his grip on his oar. The first shark had turned back and rammed them. It slapped the side of the boat with its heavy tail. Jorgen rolled sideways over the boat's side.

"Jorgen!"

Jendara dropped her own oars and caught him by the shirt collar. He flailed to catch hold of the boat, twisting aside to just miss the shark's bite. The thing tossed its head and lunged, but Jorgen lashed out with his heel, pounding its sensitive snout. Jendara dragged him back into the boat.

She caught a sudden darkness in the water ahead and remembered the constant danger of underwater rocks. "Hard a-port!" she shouted, but she was too slow.

The dinghy ground along the boulder with a horrible crunching. Jendara jammed her oar against the rock and they came loose, but water already seeped between the crushed planks. Jendara bent her back into her rowing. They slid onto the shore with half a foot of water in the bottom of the boat.

Jorgen leaped out of the dinghy first. "Are they following?" He stared wide-eyed at the water.

Jendara looked over her shoulder. "I don't think so. They don't swim well this close to land." She grabbed the spear and climbed out to help one of the men drag the boat up onto the sand. "But now I worry about the other teams."

She peered out at the sea. The second and third ships were just arriving and readying their utility boats. She hoped the sharks caused them no trouble. If she was right about Kalira's plan, they were going to need every warrior they could muster for this fight.

"Let's go," Jorgen said. "Our job is to find your boy while the next teams get into place. They're going to depend on the information we bring back."

Jendara nodded. That was his job. Her job was to kill her sister.

Stakes flanked the entrance of the path into the wood, each stake capped with a shriveled head. The pits of their long-gone eyeballs stared out at Jendara accusingly. Jorgen paused to examine one.

"These people are sick."

"Yes." Jendara picked up her pace.

The spruce forest thickened as the path wound along. The heavy branches cut out the thin starlight, and Jendara wondered how long they had to wait until moonrise. It couldn't be long now. When it came, they'd have to move twice as fast and hit twice as hard. And Kalira's people would be watching for them.

"Do you hear that?" one of the volunteers whispered.

She cocked her head. Something creaked overhead. Any other night, she would have assumed it just a loose tree branch moving in the wind. But not tonight. She peered up into the branches.

Eyes blinked down at her.

"Crows," she hissed. "Lots of them. Keep moving and don't run. They're probably just spies. They won't hurt us unless she tells them to."

They moved forward slowly, Jorgen's companions keeping their bows low and arrows ready. Jendara wished she'd had the foresight to bring her own bow. Maybe Morul and his men—should Fambra succeed in bringing them tonight—would bring an extra. Jorgen reached the next switchback in the trail and beckoned. A twig snapped under his foot.

A crow hurtled at his head.

The crows fell like black rain, and the rustling of their feathers covered the sounds of sea and wind. One's beak scored Jendara's scalp. Another closed its claws around her wrist. The man in front of her shrieked as a beak jabbed through his cheek.

Jendara brought up the spirits' spear and spun it around her. The spirals on its shaft gleamed a pale blue. A crow flew into the spinning wood and ricocheted off with a cracking sound.

Shrieking, the crows flew away from Jendara. One group settled on the man in front of her, pecking and slashing. He screamed. She dropped the spear and ran to him. Tiny bones crushed as she beat at the mass of birds. He fell to his knees.

"Get away from him," she snarled. She ripped a crow off his head and flung it against a tree. One settled on her spear and she kicked it away, then snatched the spear closer.

Blood streamed down the man's face, but he still had eyes. She used her sleeve to wipe the worst of it off his face. "Are you okay?"

He nodded. "Ain't never seen crows act like that. Not natural."

Jendara suddenly remembered watching crows mob a hawk that threatened their nest, or other times watching them harass a family of robins until the parents were too distracted to notice another crow sneaking into the nest to steal their babies. She rubbed the scratch on her scalp. Maybe this behavior wasn't so unusual, after all.

Maybe it was why Kalira had picked crows.

Jendara's hand slipped into her belt pouch. Her fingers closed on the broken soapstone pendant. The crows had always felt like a tiny connection between her and Kalira. Not anymore.

She flung the pendant aside and heard it bounce down the path. Good. Maybe someone's boot would grind it into dust.

"Keep moving," she said.

They pressed into the darkness of the spruce grove and were glad not to hear any suspicious sounds. Jorgen urged them forward, pausing now and again to check the ground for tracks. He stopped again and knelt beside a tree to study its bark.

"What do you see?" Jendara asked.

"Claw marks. Probably a cougar, marking territory." He shook his head. "This island is barely big enough to support one cougar, but this is the second set of cougar markings I've seen."

"It's from a skinwalker," Jendara said. "Kalira likes cougars."

"I was afraid you'd say that." He stood up.

Something reddish gold flew out of the tree and smashed into his chest. Man and cougar somersaulted down the trail.

"Jorgen!"

Jendara turned toward him, but just then an arrow plunged into the cat's chest. It snarled with pain. Behind Jendara, the archer who hadn't been injured by crows took out another arrow, but the cougar went still. Jorgan pulled himself to his feet, his dagger dripping blood. Jendara sagged with relief.

The archer toppled against Jendara, a knife buried in his eye.

"Run!" Jendara shouted. She grabbed Jorgen by the elbow and urged him up the hill. The remaining archer swore as he ran.

Roars filled the air behind them as they raced up the path. Down on the beach, someone screamed. The crows must have alerted Kalira's troops, and now Jorgen's volunteers were being cut down on the beach and the trail. Jendara had to get out of this bottleneck before she wound up like that archer. She pushed past her friend.

"Where are you going?" Jorgen shouted, but she didn't slow down to answer.

A boar plunged out of the brush ahead and stared at her. Jendara hesitated, unsure whether to rush it or run away. She didn't dare risk breaking the spear—she would need its power when she faced Kalira.

The boar bellowed and charged her.

Without thinking, Jendara dropped to her knees and whipped out her dagger. The creature's eyes widened and it veered at the last second, but too late.

Blood burst from its throat as her dagger slid in, hot enough to steam in the cool night air. The boar toppled onto its side. Jendara stared at it. It had died so easily. Now that she got a better look at it, she could see that it was much smaller than the boar she'd hunted on Sorind. Its eyes blinked up at her, large and dark. The tough hide melted back, revealing tender skin and a gasping mouth, surprise showing in every desperate attempt to speak.

Jendara pressed her fingers over her lips. He was just a boy, not much older than Kran or Rowri.

His milky eyes went wide. His body twitched, once. Then he went still.

"Oh, gods," Jendara whispered.

Jorgen had caught up to her again. "Are you all right?"

She nodded, unable to find her voice. Those dark eyes, so much like her boy's. Was that what Kalira would do to Kran once she had marked him and turned him to her kind?

"Who sends children to war?" she whispered.

"A monster," he answered. "One we're going to stop."

He offered her his hand and pulled her to her feet. She wiped her bloody palms off on her pants. After this was all over, she was going to have to burn these clothes.

"We're almost there," she said, and took a better hold of the spear. "Let's get this over with."

They darted toward the end of the spruce grove. In the east, the moon had risen, full and bright. Jendara hadn't even noticed it in the cover of the trees. Despite her original wish for the cover of darkness, now that she'd been discovered, the moon would aid her people more than Kalira's night predators. Its glow filled her with hope.

Kran, she thought, *I'm coming.*

Chapter Twenty-Two
Skinwalker

Jendara smelled smoke and roasted meat before they entered the goat meadow. Her nose crinkled with disgust. Down on the beach, Kalira's people were fighting and dying. Up here, her sister was enjoying a feast.

But as her little group crept closer, she realized just how wrong she was. A bonfire burned in the center of the ruined town of Crow's Nest, and five or six dancers circled it. Their bodies twisted and writhed in the ruddy light. Jendara caught only an occasional glimpse of the fire itself, but that was enough to make out the big cauldron squatting in the coals and the boy lashed to a post beside it.

"Kran," she growled.

Jorgen took a preemptive hold on her arm. "We don't know what's happening up there yet. Just watch a few seconds."

"I see enough to know she's brewing up something evil," she snapped. "And she's got my son handy for testing it."

"You don't know that," he growled. "Now I'm going to circle around the other side to get a better look. You stay here."

Jendara nodded, but she didn't watch him go. Her eyes were fixed on Kran. Maybe it was just his bindings, but his back was ramrod straight and chin high. His posture showed no fear.

She felt a hot wave of pride for her boy.

She crept forward a few feet, pressing her belly to the dirt. Jorgen had vanished into the surrounding forest. He was good at this kind of thing, she realized. She'd been lucky Fambra had gotten his help.

Fambra. Had she reached Sorind all right? Were there enough usable boats to get any fighters to the island? Jendara bit her lip. From the fighting she'd heard back there in the woods, Kalira's force was larger than Jendara had hoped. Even though Jorgen's volunteers were all blooded warriors, she knew things would get desperate if there weren't reinforcements coming from Sorind.

She inched closer and felt the cold touch of iron on the side of her hand. She whipped back her arm, but something metallic shot up in the air with a horrible clang and then crashed down again, striking her shoulder, hard.

A bear trap. Damn, but that had been close.

A man broke out of the circle, sprinting toward her as she leaped to her feet. She kicked him in the chest and he flew backward, tripping a second bear trap. It snapped shut on his torso with a sickening crunch.

Jendara spun around. Ferns and berry bushes covered every inch of ground, hiding any other traps. A single wrong step could mangle her.

Crows flew out of the clearing, battering her head and neck and cutting off her vision. Beaks snipped at her ears. Talons closed on her shoulder, and then hands grabbed her arms and dragged her forward.

She kicked and bucked, but eyes closed tight against the crows' questing beaks made it hard to tell where her attackers were coming from, or even how many there were. She twisted away from the hands, but another set grabbed her ankles, pinning them. With a grunt, she managed to bend her knees and headbutt the man holding her legs. The man gave a satisfying groan.

"Stop struggling, Jendara." Kalira's voice rang out over the cacophony.

Jendara's hand stung as the remnant of Kalira's brand pulsed with sudden fire. Jendara went still. The spear! She'd dropped the spear! She hoped whatever magic the spirits had worked on her hand would hold out without the spear's comforting presence.

"Such a touching reunion, don't you think, Brynorm? Mother, son, and favorite auntie." Kalira chuckled. The crow fluttered off Jendara's shoulder, slipping inside the horrible headdress perched on Kalira's head. She had swapped her white gown for fighting leathers and a cloak of inky black feathers.

"It's hard to believe she's your sister," the big Kalvaman answered. He stepped closer to Kalira's side. Jendara narrowed her eyes at him. With his thick dark beard and great height, he looked suddenly very like a dark version of her father.

Her stomach clenched at the realization. He was why Kalira had gone over to the Kalvamen. He had saved her from torture and inevitable death. He had given her a place to belong. And under it all, he looked like their father, *led* like their father. How could Kalira have resisted that when she was lost and lonely in that terrible place?

This was all his fault. Jendara bared her teeth. As soon as she was free, she was going to make him pay.

"Defiant. You two have that in common, at least." He stepped away, nostrils flaring. "We need to join our warriors. The battle grows fierce."

"In a moment," Kalira snapped. She moved closer to Jendara. "Give me her hand." She dug her long filthy nails into Jendara's hand, staring at the tiny mark the spirits had made of Kalira's brand. "How did you do this?" she snapped.

Jendara laughed. "Wouldn't you like to know?"

Kalira slapped her. Jendara flexed her jaw muscle and the joint protested. "You hit like a child," she lied.

"I can still change you," Kalira growled. "Although I doubt it would be worth the effort. You've broken every promise you ever made me."

"What?"

Kalira grabbed Jendara's throat. "You never came back. You left me behind, and you never came back!"

The Kalvaman gripping Jendara's left side crumpled to the ground, an arrow sticking out of his gut.

Jorgen shoved Kalira aside. "Come on!" he shouted. "Get the boy and get moving!"

He slashed out with his dagger, blinding Jendara's other captor. Brynorm launched himself at Jendara, but Jendara twisted aside. She ran to Kran. With her belt knife, she sliced his wrist ties.

A fist drove into the back of her head. Jendara slid onto her knees, her head spinning. The knife slipped from suddenly nerveless fingers. She pawed at the base of Kran's post to steady herself, but a boot drove itself into her ribs. She fell sideways.

"You're not taking him!" Kalira screamed. "He's the last of my family!"

Jendara pushed herself onto her elbow. The knife. It was here somewhere.

But Kalira had Kran by the arm now, and her fingers looked strange. They were growing, their tips turning black and lengthening. Jendara's eyes widened as the feathers of Kalira's headdress crawled across the surface of her forehead and down her cheeks. The black cloak roiled across her back and quills sprang up from her shoulders.

Jendara's fingers closed on the hilt of her belt knife. She staggered to her feet, her head spinning. "I'll kill you for touching my boy," she growled. As Kalira's face stretched into a sharp black beak, Jendara lashed out at Kalira's feathered arm.

But Kalira's hand closed on the blade, squeezing it tightly. Kalira's eyes gleamed for a moment. A burning cold spread up Jendara's arm. She began to shiver and tremble so hard the knife fell from her freezing hand.

Kalira snapped her beak shut around Kran's arm even as her fingers stretched into long pinions. She flapped her huge wings, once, twice, the wind of their motion churning up dust. Jendara shielded her eyes and charged forward. A powerful gust pushed her backward as Kalira took to the air.

"Kran!" Jendara screamed. She grabbed for his legs, but he was already out of reach. She whirled on her companions. "Shoot the witch!"

A bowstring twanged, but the arrow fell short. Jendara looked frantically around her. There was only one way on or off this island, and Kalira couldn't fly forever. She would take him to the beach. It was the obvious next step.

A fist caught Jendara in the gut and she fell backward. Brynorm laughed, a hard, ugly sound.

"You're not going to stop her," he declared. "She is the savior of my people." He drew back his foot to kick Jendara in the head.

It was just what she needed. She caught his ankle and twisted, pulling him off balance. He fell, hard, and she leaped on top of him. She drove her knife at his eye, but a quick wrench of his head spun the blow harmlessly down the side of his cheek. Blood welled up, but it was not a killing blow.

He punched at her throat, connecting with her temple instead. She saw stars for an instant but didn't lose her seat. She whipped back her knife and stabbed it into his shoulder.

He roared with pain, and she brought the heel of her fist down onto his nose. It crunched beneath the blow. He grabbed her neck and squeezed hard.

She bared her teeth at him again, anger replacing the fear she felt for Kran. The Kalvaman looked nothing like her father now, covered in blood. "Where's your savior now?" she croaked.

She drove the knife down one more time, right through his throat. His hands clenched horribly tight and then fell.

Jendara jumped free, rubbing her throat. The space around the fire was empty of Kalvamen, the barbarians having followed Kalira or fallen to Jorgen's archers.

She looked down at Brynorm, with his tattooed forearms and the ugly brand on his neck. He had saved her sister, in his fashion. Taken care of her. Believed in her. Jendara shook her head. In any other situation, Jendara would have thought such a man a good one. But he was a Kalvaman. She freed her knife from his flesh.

"You all right?"

She nodded at Jorgen and spun once more in a slow circle, searching for the fallen spear. Even shrunken, the marking on her hand had burned when she'd faced Kalira back there. She needed the ancestors' spear if she was going to win their next fight.

Beside the fading fire, a flicker of blue winked at her. Jendara snatched up the fallen spear. "We've got to get back to the beach."

Jendara raced down the spruce grove trail in a blur. Arrows whizzed past her, men and women darted by, beasts snarled and wrestled with fighters. She thought she saw Morul's bronze helm as she skirted a knot of skirmishers, and she might have seen Fambra's red hair flash in the moonlight on the edge of the beach. But mostly, she just ran, ignoring any interruption.

When she hit the sand, she slowed, awed by the activity on the shore. Kalira's people had been busy. She wondered where they had hidden all their ships, because there were now half a dozen longships on the beach, with more in the water, and Kalira's creatures were protecting them with their lives. Sharks circled in

the water, driving back invading vessels that might cut
off the Kalvamen's escape. Kalira's fighters might make
good raiders, but this time they were the ones caught
unprepared. Their best hope was to run away from this
attack force.

An ungainly figure stood beside a group of beached
canoes. It took Jendara a second to realize it was Kalira,
human again and wearing her horrible headdress, Kran
slung over her shoulder. The boy didn't move.

Jendara's blood boiled. She vaulted over a fallen man
in an Iron Shield uniform and raced toward the boat.
A crow threw itself at her, but she batted it aside with
the spear without breaking stride. A Kalvaman stepped
forward and swung out with his sword, but she parried
and shoved him out of her way. Nothing could stand
between her and Kran any longer. Not even her sister.

"Kalira!" she roared.

Kalira tossed aside Kran's body and spread her arms.
A piercing note rose out of her throat, so high and shrill
Jendara wanted to cover her ears. The back of Jendara's
hand stung.

In the forest behind them, someone screamed.

"Come, my friend!" Kalira shouted. "Get vengeance
for your child!"

A man in scale armor flew over Jendara's head.
Jendara spun around.

The massive troll chuckled with a sound like rocks
grinding together. Kalira's black wing brands dotted its
torso and its saggy dugs. A female, this creature stood
a good two and half feet taller than the weakened troll
Jendara had dispatched. An arrow sank into its forearm,
but the troll simply yanked it out and kept walking.

"Shit," Jendara breathed. Kalira laughed.

The troll's arm swung out and launched Jendara across the beach. She landed on her side, head bouncing off the sand. She fought to get air back in her lungs. Coughing, she struggled to her feet.

The troll lowered its head and charged. Jendara switched the spear to her left hand and unsheathed her sword. That thing was between her and her son.

"Get out of my way!" Jendara ran forward to meet the creature.

The troll's claws sliced down at her. At the last second, Jendara twisted away, her sword scoring a mark in the giant's thick hide. The troll growled.

Jendara pivoted to face the creature, her sword chopping into the meat of the troll's thigh. Blood gushed from the wound and the troll slapped at Jendara. Jendara flung herself backward, barely dodging the blow. The creature was faster than it looked.

The troll limped closer, its upper lip curling back from its pointed teeth. Its tusks winked in the moonlight.

A battle axe smashed into the side of its ribs, chopping out a chunk of green flesh. With a shriek, the troll whirled around to face Morul.

"I've got this covered, Dara! Stop that witch!"

A knot of warriors ran to join Morul, their voices raised in island battle cries. Fambra's red hair stood out in the crowd.

Jendara spun to face the water. Kran still lay on the sand, motionless, while Kalira pushed a canoe down to the waves. Jendara raced to Kran's side and dropped to her knees. Her sword and the ancestors' spear fell to the sand beside her.

"Kran? Wake up." She shook his shoulder. His head flopped in the sand. She grabbed his hand. A blood-soaked hunk of fur bound it tightly. She clawed it off, reeling at the stink of tar and spoiled meat. An ugly gash ran across the back of his hand, and black tendrils already wound out from around the wound.

"Get away from him!" Kalira shrieked.

Jendara shook Kran again, but the boy didn't move. "What've you done to him?"

"He's my son now. He'll be powerful and strong!" Kalira grabbed Jendara's shoulders to yank her away from the boy.

The spear beside Jendara's knee surged with sudden warmth. She snatched it up and jumped to her feet. "This isn't your home," she snapped. "You turned on it."

"I'm here to make it better," Kalira said. "The Kalvamen taught me something, Jendara. They taught me that the world is cruel and ugly and you can only trust your own strength. Well, I'm strong! And I can make this place strong, too. As strong as my skinwalkers!"

A Kalvaman dove into Jendara's shoulder, sending her staggering away from Kran's side. His hunting knife slashed down at her eyes, skittering off her forehead. She slammed the shaft of her spear sideways into his throat. His corpse-white eyes bulged as he slid to the ground. Jendara swiped blood out of her eyes and plunged forward.

Kalira had bent over Kran to hoist him up. Her face twisted as she saw Jendara charge her. She leaped to her feet, sword in hand.

The spearhead drove into her gut, punching through and out the other side. Kalira went stiff. The crow in her headdress shrieked, a thin, piercing cry.

The shaft of the spear burst into white light.

Jendara dropped to the ground, covering her face. This light was brighter than the brilliance that had surrounded the dying red elk, brighter than the sun and the moon and the stars all combined. A hundred voices sang out in triumph.

The crow screamed and screamed.

Jendara raised her head, arm still shielding her eyes. The light was fading—no, it wasn't fading: it was soaking into Kalira, rising up inside her body, lighting her up from the inside. Her face began to glow softly. The black brand of a crow's wings across her collarbone began to smoke.

"By the isles," Jendara breathed. Kalira's hair rippled as tendrils of pale mist ran out from her scalp and twisted around her head and throat. The black smoke rose up from her collarbone and struck at the mist.

Faintly, Jendara heard snarls and growls, and couldn't have guessed if they came from the battle around her or from the strange stuff boiling out of Kalira's body. Her hand dropped to her side. She couldn't tear her eyes away.

Kalira's headdress crumbled into bits and the crow flopped free, its body motionless. It fell onto the sand. With one final puff, the last of the crow wings disappeared from Kalira's collarbone. A cloud of blue mist twisted out of her scalp, absorbing the wisps of black steam. There was a sudden flare of light, and then

Kalira fell to the sand. Ordinary moonlight illuminated her limp body.

Someone tapped Jendara's leg. She whipped out her belt knife, then fell to her knees. Kran stared up at her. He held up his hand. A raw cut ran across the top of it, the flesh around it an ordinary pink. Kalira's magic was gone.

Jendara hugged Kran to her chest, staring at her sister. There was no sign of the spear, just a bloodstained gash in her leathers. Kran pushed himself free of the hug, his eyes huge.

Jendara didn't trust her legs. Some part of herself had gone into that fight, as if she had lent the spirits her own strength. She crawled to her sister's side.

"Kalira?"

Kalira's eyes flickered open. "Jenny?" Her voice was small, the soft sweet tones of the young girl Jendara remembered.

Jendara stroked her cheek. "It's me. I'm here. I came back." A faint breeze stirred Kalira's hair, sweeping the white tendrils back from her forehead.

"Something terrible happened, didn't it?"

"Yes. But it's going to be all right." Jendara's shoulders shook. She saw the pool of blood spreading out from beneath Kalira, staining the sand in a widening circle.

"Don't cry, Jenny. I've got Father to take care of me now. And we'll both be here, watching over you."

Jendara pulled her closer and bent to kiss her sister's forehead. "I love you, Kallie. I love you so much."

Kalira's hand squeezed Jendara's. Jendara pressed her cheek to Kalira's and watched the sky grow light in the east. Somewhere overhead, a cormorant called. Its voice resounded, thin and tired. It was on its way home.

Chapter Twenty-Three
Family

Jendara sat on the beach beside the canoe, watching the peaceful gray waves. Kran tapped her shoulder and held out a mug of tea. Jendara smiled at the boy. "Thank you."

He squeezed her shoulder and kissed her cheek.

Jendara rubbed her eyes. She felt weak, her head foggy. The ancestors had given her back Kalira, if only for a few seconds. All these years she'd cursed them for abandoning her family, and they did this for her. She wasn't sure she understood it all.

"Your trip to the Wise went well, didn't it?"

Gerda had appeared beside Kran. The boy looked worried, but Gerda had a smile stretched across her face.

Jendara hated to see her so smug. She put down the mug. "What was it like when you went to them?"

"Terrifying," Gerda said. "But hearing the ancestors was more than worth it." She cocked her head. "You can't hear them right now?"

Jendara shook her head. "I think all of that went into the spear. Now that it's gone, I'm just ordinary." She shrugged. "I never wanted to be a wisewoman, anyway."

Gerda glanced over her shoulder, where a group of Kalvamen stood, their wrists bound. "Morul and Jorgen have rounded up the last of the Kalvamen," she explained. "They want you to decide what should happen to them."

Jendara studied the survivors. They looked so thin and poor and sad, in their shabby hide cloaks and their mismatched clothes. Kalva was a hard place. It wore out its people fast. She sighed. "I'm sick of seeing dead people."

Gerda waited.

"We should send them home. Take their weapons and any hides so they're not a threat, then give them enough water and supplies to make sure they get back to their island. And warn them they'd better never show their faces here again." Jendara squeezed her mug. She hoped she was doing the right thing. She knew she couldn't change Kalva, but at least her people could show the Kalvamen what mercy meant.

Gerda looked carefully at Jendara. "You're sure?"

Jendara nodded.

"A fine choice." Gerda smiled. "It's the kind of thing your father would have done."

She turned to go meet with Morul, and Jendara folded her arms across her knees. The wind rustled in her ear. It felt warmer than the breeze against her face, like the soft breath of a whisper.

Maybe she hadn't lost all of her abilities to hear the spirits, after all.

Kran caught her eye and grabbed a stick. *Breakfast?* he wrote in the sand.

Her stomach grumbled. An hour ago, she couldn't have imagined eating. But things felt different now. "I'd love some."

She watched him run across the beach to a makeshift camp. He skidded to a halt beside a thin woman she didn't recognize, sitting beside Fambra. Fambra patted the woman on the arm, then got up from the fireside, stopping first to kiss Sven. She jogged toward Jendara.

"I started some porridge," she said, "but there'll be sausage in a few minutes. Not much—we found a handful of prisoners when we flushed out the Kalvamen's camp, and those people were hungry." She sank down in the sand beside Jendara. "You doing okay?"

Jendara watched Kran hunkering down to write a message to the thin woman. "Was that woman one of them?"

"Her name's Marga. She's one of the healthiest—she wanted to help me cook for the others. Kran seems to have taken a liking to her."

Marga. Hazan's girl. Jendara's heart lurched: there was one promise she'd managed to keep, or at least her fighters had. She watched Kran for another moment.

"I don't understand," she said, turning toward Fambra. "How do you work as a smuggler with a son? Aren't you terrified you'll be arrested and leave him alone?"

"It helps to have an in with the city guard." Fambra shrugged. "Besides, if something happened to me, Rowri wouldn't be alone. He has Sven and Gerda and an entire clan to take care of him."

"What's that like?" Jendara wondered.

"Don't be silly," Fambra said. "You know full well that the people of Sorind think you're family, and you've got the *Milady* out there with a captain *and* crew that would anything for your boy." She grinned. "Plus, you're probably an honorary member of the Dagfridrung clan after all you've done for us."

"Don't let them talk you into joining," Jorgen said, dropping down beside his cousin. "When the Dagfridrungs throw a party, everyone gets drunk and tells embarrassing stories about each other. I don't think I want you hearing about my youth." He cocked his head. "Have you ever considered life as an Iron Shield?"

"What?"

"Seriously," he said. "You impressed me out there, and Vorrin's not going to be able to make a trip to Varisia this winter. You've got what it takes to be a great guard."

"A guard." Jendara reached up with her right hand to tuck a stray hair back into place, then stopped. A black mark still showed within the silver circle of scar tissue. She rubbed it, feeling a faint buzzing. "The stain didn't go away when Kalira died. That means that poison is still in me."

"Not much," Fambra scoffed.

"Yeah, but some. The only thing keeping it from spreading is that circle the ancestor spirits made."

She looked from Fambra to Jorgen. "Do you think their magic still works on the mainland?"

"Why risk it?" Fambra said. She slung her arm around Jendara. "You know, it might be nice for me to have another connection down in Halgrim."

Jendara grinned and looked back at the fire where Kran was busily telling stories in the sand. He had nearly died last night, and yet now he looked so happy. Maybe he belonged on these islands as much as she did.

She glanced back at Jorgen. The shield-shaped brooch pinned to his collar gleamed. Just a few short years ago, she would have been on the run from a guard like him. Now they were friends. She absently rubbed the faded jolly roger on her left hand. Crime was behind her—but she still knew it. Wasn't that the perfect background for a guardswoman?

"I'll think about it," she said. She threw back her head and laughed. "I can't believe I just said that! I used to be a pirate!" She caught her breath. "But first I have some business to take care of."

Fambra sobered. "Kalira. We should do something with her body." She reached into her pocket. "I found this. It was hers, wasn't it?" She held out the broken soapstone pendant.

Jendara took it. The fire opals winked like tiny flames. "Yes. But I don't think I could burn it with her. I think . . . I'll leave it on our clan shrine at the top of the hill." Her throat felt suddenly tight.

Shouting from the water distracted her. Jendara looked up. A small boat moved toward shore, and aboard it, Glayn waved at her. He bellowed again.

He looked impatient, and Tam was rowing hard. She waved back. She hoped they were coming to take her to the *Milady*—and that Vorrin was on board. After all this, she was ready to hold him tight.

"After you take care of your sister," Fambra asked, "then what?"

Jendara grinned. "Then I need to teach my son to hunt."

About the Author

Wendy N. Wagner writes sad poetry about dinosaurs and funny stories about evil druids. Her short fiction has appeared in anthologies like *Armored* and *The Way of the Wizard*, and in many online magazines. This is her first novel. Jendara, Vorrin, and several other characters from this novel first appeared in the Pathfinder Tales web fiction story "Mother Bears," available for free at **paizo.com/pathfindertales**.

Wendy lives with her family in Portland, Oregon, where she also teaches writing for youth. An avid gardener and board gamer, she can be found online at **winniewoohoo.com**.

Acknowledgments

First, I'd like to thank the great team over at Paizo for giving me a chance to play in their universe. My terrific editor, James Sutter, did an amazing job helping me understand Golarion and develop Jendara's story—I honestly don't think I can ever thank him enough. I'd also like to thank Florian Stitz, who drew the artwork for "Mother Bears." Florian's vision of Jendara was really inspirational while I was writing this book.

I can't explain how much I owe to my wonderful husband John and daughter Fiona, who not only put up with my flaky writerly ways and endless talk about cannibals and Viking ships, but even played Pathfinder with me so I could really understand the system. A big shout-out goes to my brother Jak, the best GM anyone could ask for.

Writing a book is hard, but I'm lucky to have the support of amazing friends. Thank you to all the Inkpunks, but especially to Galen Dara—who inspired Jendara, in more than just name—and Christie Yant, who has been my biggest cheerleader. I owe Minerva Zimmerman chocolate cake and drinks for her help with nautical research. Anything that makes sense when I talk about boats is because of her; the errors are all mine. Most of all, I have to thank Jeffrey Petersen, who read this book in its early phase and caught jillions of stupid mistakes.

But the biggest thank you goes out to the Pathfinder Tales web fiction readers who read "Mother Bears" and asked for a Jendara novel—you made my dreams come true. This book is for you.

Glossary

All Pathfinder Tales novels are set in the rich and vibrant world of the Pathfinder campaign setting. Below are explanations of several key terms used in this book. For more information on the world of Golarion and the strange monsters, people, and deities that make it their home, see *The Inner Sea World Guide*, or dive into the game and begin playing your own adventures with the *Pathfinder Roleplaying Game Core Rulebook* or the *Pathfinder Roleplaying Game Beginner Box*, all available at **paizo.com**. Those readers particularly interested in the Lands of the Linnorm Kings should check out *Pathfinder Campaign Setting: Lands of the Linnorm Kings* and *Pathfinder Player Companion: People of the North*.

Absalom: Largest city in the Inner Sea region, located on an island far to the south of the Ironbound Archipelago.

Alstone: Small village on Flintyreach, devoted to fishing, farming, and mining a local quarry.

Averaka: Town on Flintyreach populated primarily by half-orcs.

Battlewall: Most heavily populated island in the Ironbound Archipelago, and the seat of power for those archipelago islands controlled by the Linnorm Kings.

Besmara: Goddess of piracy, strife, and sea monsters.

Cheliax: A powerful devil-worshiping nation located on the mainland south of the Lands of the Linnorm Kings.

Chelish: Of or relating to the nation of Cheliax.

Crow's Nest: Small island in the Ironbound Archipelago.

Desna: Good-natured goddess of dreams, stars, travelers, and luck.

Dragon's Rib: Large, uninhabited island in the Ironbound Archipelago.

Erastil: Stag-headed god of farming, hunting, trade, and family; also known as Old Deadeye.

Fey: Magical creatures deeply tied to the natural world, such as dryads or pixies.

Flintyreach: Large island in the Ironbound Archipelago; populated but still infested with trolls and other dangerous creatures.

Garund: Tropical continent far to the south of the Lands of the Linnorm Kings.

Giants: Race of brawny humanoids many times larger than humans.

Gnomes: Small humanoids with strange mind-sets, originally from the First World.

Half-Orcs: Born from unions between humans and orcs, members of this race have green or gray skin, brutish appearances, and notoriously short tempers, and are mistrusted by many societies.

Halgrim: Capital city of the portion of the Ironbound Archipelago controlled by the Linnorm Kings. Seat of power for White Estrid.

Iron Shields: The Halgrim city guard.

Ironbound Archipelago: Network of cold islands off the coast of Varisia and the Lands of the Linnorm Kings. The largest population center in the Steaming Sea, though the residents are rarely more organized than local villages. Partially independent, with the northern islands controlled by the Linnorm Kings.

Inner Sea Region: The central focus of the Pathfinder campaign setting, named for the large sea that fosters trade between the continents of Avistan and Garund. The Lands of the Linnorm Kings represent the northernmost edge of the region.

Isle of Ancestors: Island where heroes from certain islands in the Ironbound Archipelago go to commune with their ancestors and become wisewomen and shamans.

Kalva: Cold and forbidding island north of the Ironbound Archipelago, notorious for its barbaric cannibal tribes.

Kalvamen: Residents of Kalva, legendary for their savagery and cannibalism.

Katapesh: Mighty trade nation on the eastern coast of Garund.

Kintargo: Port city in Cheliax.

Lands of the Linnorm Kings: Nation ruled by an alliance of the various Linnorm Kings

Linnorm Kings: Warrior-chieftains who dominate the larger settlements of the Lands of the Linnorm

Kings and together rule the nation, each of whom must defeat a linnorm to claim a throne.

Magnimar: Port city in southwestern Varisia, best known for its many monuments, including the enormous bridge called the Irespan.

Norn: Fey creature concerned with fate and gifted with the power to see the future.

Orcmoot: Town on Flintyreach founded by half-orcs.

Pathfinder Society: Organization of traveling scholars and adventurers who seek to document the world's wonders. Based out of Absalom and run by a mysterious and masked group called the Decemvirate.

Skinwalkers: Shape-changing humanoids who can magically take on the forms or aspects of particular animals.

Sorind: Small island in the Ironbound Archipelago, devoted mainly to farming and fishing.

Trolls: Large, stooped humanoids with sharp claws and amazing regenerative powers that are overcome only by fire.

Ulfen: Race of pale, viking-like humans from the cold nations of the north, primarily the Lands of the Linnorm Kings.

Varisia: Frontier region at the northwestern edge of the Inner Sea region, just south of the Lands of the Linnorm Kings.

Werebear: Lycanthropes with the power to turn into bears. Unlike skinwalkers, werebears are generally reputed to be highly ethical guardians of nature and the innocent.

White Estrid: The only female Linnorm King, who gained her status not by killing a linnorm but by enslaving it. Rules a portion of the Ironbound Archipelago from her fortress in Halgrim.

Wise: Local term used by wisewomen and shamans in the Ironbound Archipelago to refer to the collected wisdom, magic, and practices of their ancestral traditions.

When murdered sinners fail to show up in Hell, it's up to Salim Ghadafar, an atheist soldier conscripted by the goddess of death, to track down the missing souls. In order to do so, Salim will need to descend into the anarchic city of Kaer Maga, following a trail that ranges from Hell's iron cities to the gleaming gates of Heaven itself. Along the way, he'll be aided by a menagerie of otherworldly creatures, a streetwise teenager, and two warriors of the mysterious Iridian Fold. But when the missing souls are the scum of the earth, and the victims devils themselves, can anyone really be trusted?

From James L. Sutter, author of the critically acclaimed novel *Death's Heretic*, comes a new adventure of magic, monsters, and morality, set in the award-winning world of the Pathfinder Roleplaying Game.

The Redemption Engine print edition: $9.99
ISBN: 978-1-60125-618-8

The Redemption Engine ebook edition:
ISBN: 978-1-60125-619-5

The
Redemption
Engine

JAMES L. SUTTER

Gideon Gull leads a double life: one as a talented young bard at the Rhapsodic College, the other as a student of the Shadow School, where Taldor's infamous Lion Blades are trained to be master spies and assassins. When a magical fog starts turning ordinary people into murderous mobs along the border between Taldor and Gideon's home nation of Andoran, it's up to him and a crew of daring performers to solve the mystery before both nations fall to madness and slaughter. But how do you fight an enemy that turns innocent people into weapons?

From fantasy author Chris Willrich comes a new adventure of intrigue, espionage, and arcane mystery, set in the award-winning world of the Pathfinder Roleplaying Game.

The Dagger of Trust print edition: $9.99
ISBN: 978-1-60125-614-0

The Dagger of Trust ebook edition:
ISBN: 978-1-60125-615-7

The Dagger
of Trust

CHRIS WILLRICH

When a mysterious monster carves a path of destruction across the southern River Kingdoms, desperate townsfolk look to the famed elven ranger Elyana and her half-orc companion Drelm for salvation. For Drelm, however, the mission is about more than simple justice, as without a great victory proving his worth, a prejudiced populace will never allow him to marry the human woman he loves. Together with a fresh band of allies, including the mysterious gunslinger Lisette, the heroes must set off into the wilderness, hunting a terrifying beast that will test their abilities—and their friendships—to the breaking point and beyond.

From acclaimed author Howard Andrew Jones comes a new adventure of love, death, and unnatural creatures, set in the award-winning world of the Pathfinder Roleplaying Game.

Stalking the Beast print edition: $9.99
ISBN: 978-1-60125-572-3

Stalking the Beast ebook edition:
ISBN: 978-1-60125-573-0

Stalking the Beast

Howard Andrew Jones

After a century of imprisonment, demons have broken free of the wardstones surrounding the Worldwound. As fiends flood south into civilized lands, Count Varian Jeggare and his hellspawn bodyguard Radovan must search through the ruins of a fallen nation for the blasphemous text that opened the gate to the Abyss in the first place—and that might hold the key to closing it. In order to succeed, however, the heroes will need to join forces with pious crusaders, barbaric local warriors, and even one of the legendary god callers. It's a race against time as the companions fight their way across a broken land, facing off against fiends, monsters, and a vampire intent on becoming the god of blood—but will unearthing the dangerous book save the world, or destroy it completely?

From best-selling author Dave Gross comes a new adventure set against the backdrop of the Wrath of the Righteous Adventure Path in the award-winning world of the Pathfinder Roleplaying Game.

King of Chaos print edition: $9.99
ISBN: 978-1-60125-558-7

King of Chaos ebook edition:
ISBN: 978-1-60125-559-4

KING OF CHAOS

CHAOS

Dave Gross

In the war-torn lands of Molthune and Nirmathas,
where rebels fight an endless war of secession
against an oppressive military government, the constant
fighting can make for strange alliances. Such is the case
for the man known only as the Masked—the victim of
a magical curse that forces him to hide his face—and
an escaped halfling slave named Tantaerra. Thrown
together by chance, the two fugitives find themselves
conscripted by both sides of the conflict and forced to
search for a magical artifact that could help shift the
balance of power and end the bloodshed for good. But
in order to survive, the thieves will first need to learn the
one thing none of their adventures have taught them:
how to trust each other.

From *New York Times* best-selling author and legendary
game designer Ed Greenwood comes an adventure of
magic, monsters, and unlikely friendships, set in the
award-winning world of the Pathfinder Roleplaying Game.

The Wizard's Mask print edition: $9.99
ISBN: 978-1-60125-530-3

The Wizard's Mask ebook edition:
ISBN: 978-1-60125-531-0

The Wizard's Mask

Ed Greenwood

A pirate captain of the Inner Sea, Torius Vin makes a living raiding wealthy merchant ships with his crew of loyal buccaneers. Few things matter more to Captain Torius than ill-gotten gold—but one of those is Celeste, his beautiful snake-bodied navigator. When a crafty courtesan offers the pirate crew a chance at the heist of a lifetime, it's time for both man and naga to hoist the black flag and lead the *Stargazer*'s crew to fame and fortune. But will stealing the legendary Star of Thumen chart the corsairs a course to untold riches—or send them all to a watery grave?

From award-winning author Chris A. Jackson comes a fantastical new adventure of high-seas combat and romance set in the award-winning world of the Pathfinder Roleplaying Game.

Pirate's Honor print edition: $9.99
ISBN: 978-1-60125-523-5

Pirate's Honor ebook edition:
ISBN: 978-1-60125-524-2

PIRATE'S
HONOR

CHRIS A. JACKSON

PATHFINDER
CAMPAIGN SETTING

THE INNER SEA WORLD GUIDE

You've delved into the Pathfinder campaign setting with Pathfinder Tales novels—now take your adventures even further! *The Inner Sea World Guide* is a full-color, 320-page hardcover guide featuring everything you need to know about the exciting world of Pathfinder: overviews of every major nation, religion, race, and adventure location around the Inner Sea, plus a giant poster map! Read it as a travelogue, or use it to flesh out your roleplaying game—it's your world now!